PRAISE FOR I

Redemption

"*Redemption*, by Deborah J. Ledford, gets under your skin. Fresh and ferocious Native American deputy Eva 'Lightning Dance' Duran never lets up in her quest woven through the Taos Pueblo land. Atmospheric and awash with color, customs, and ancient ways. I loved this."

—Cara Black, *New York Times* bestselling author

"Deborah J. Ledford has artfully woven the voices of multiple characters connected to the Taos Pueblo to create a pattern of stories that illuminate the challenges as well as the enduring power of Native American women. The rhythm of daily life is evident in Ledford's lovely, intimate prose. I eagerly await the new adventures of Eva Duran, who will, no doubt, unearth more mysteries in the buried layers of New Mexico."

—Naomi Hirahara, the Mary Higgins Clark
Award–winning author of *Clark and Division*

"*Redemption* is a page-turner! I loved reading about sheriff's deputy Eva Duran and her battle against dark forces on the reservation. Sharp characters, a great setting, and a plot that keeps you guessing. A riveting thriller that hits hard and keeps you hooked."

—David Heska Wanbli Weiden, Anthony and
Thriller Award–winning author of *Winter Counts*

"A riveting tale of murder and intrigue on a Native American reservation from an immensely talented voice in crime fiction. Deborah J. Ledford has created a page-turner featuring an unforgettable hero in Eva 'Lightning Dance' Duran."

—Isabella Maldonado, *Wall Street Journal* bestselling author

Snare

"White-knuckle suspense at an electrifying pulse."
—*Suspense Magazine*

"*Snare* is a gripping read that won't be easy to put down."
—*Midwest Book Review*

"Ledford, who is part Eastern Band Cherokee, shows enormous empathy and insight. Despite many obstacles, Katina battles her demons and reclaims her spirit power in time to confront her tormentors in a harrowing finale. *Snare* is a well-deserved nominee for the Hillerman Sky Award."
—Steve Schwartz, Poisoned Pen Bookstore review

Crescendo

"Inola Walela becomes the avenging angel of death, leaving no stone unturned in order to bring justice for one small boy in this knife-edge drama. Walela's search brings her closer to the truth in a cataclysmic chaos of events. Following in the footsteps of J. A. Jance, the police procedural genre has birthed a new author to follow. In *Crescendo*, Deborah J Ledford raises suspense to a higher level as she intertwines her Cherokee heritage with her writing, exposing all of us to her award-winning style."
—*Suspense Magazine*

"Since I read the first book in the series, *Staccato*, I've loved the character Inola, a Native American cop who's constantly having to prove herself to her police department colleagues in the relatively backwoods town of Bryson City, North Carolina. In spite of her stubborn nature, her inability to communicate with those she truly loves (Steven and her grandmother Elisi), and her insistence on going out on her own despite obvious dangers that threaten—you can't help but love her. Tough, focused, and smart, she's everything you'd want in a heroine."

—*Midwest Book Review*

Causing Chaos

"Standing round of applause for this dynamic blast of a thriller."

—*Suspense Magazine*

REDEMPTION

ALSO BY DEBORAH J LEDFORD

Smoky Mountain Inquest Series

Staccato

Snare

Crescendo

Causing Chaos

REDEMPTION

DEBORAH J LEDFORD

THOMAS & MERCER

Text copyright © 2023 by Deborah J Ledford
All rights reserved.

Published by Thomas & Mercer, Seattle

www.apub.com

Amazon, the Amazon logo, and Thomas & Mercer are trademarks of Amazon.com, Inc., or its affiliates.

ISBN-13: 9781662510472 (paperback)
ISBN-13: 9781662510465 (digital)

Cover design by Laywan Kwan
Cover image: © Sean Pavone / Getty Images

Printed in the United States of America

To John
my compass, my light, my everything

PROLOGUE

Ten days ago

She needed to start her plan of action, and where better to find a drug dealer or two than at the local high school. Her Winnebago had barely come to a stop when a young man in the back parking lot, straddling a bright-green Kawasaki dirt bike, coasted to her.

A helmet hid his face until he raised the visor and asked, "Drugs or guns?"

A bit shocked by his boldness, she reared back. "Drugs," she said, already owning all the guns she needed.

"How much?"

This she wasn't sure about. "How much do you have?"

A smile split the young man's face, revealing a mouthful of ruined teeth. "Follow me."

She held her breath during every curve along the Taos, New Mexico, back roads as she clutched the steering wheel, unsure whether her wide vehicle would be able to fit along the tight two-lane track of a residential area, tree limbs so low that branches screeched atop the roof of the motorhome.

She waited a full two minutes for traffic to clear enough to turn onto Paseo del Pueblo Sur, the main drag through the heart of town. Even on this Saturday afternoon, three weeks before the summer season began, tourists lined the streets carrying shopping bags stamped with the insignias of the local shops. The trek so slow, she was able to enjoy stunning oil-painted and photographic captures of the area displayed in art gallery windows—gold and rust profusions of leaves on trees shared with pueblo structures, and realistic open mesas dotted by shrubs and iconic billows of thunderclouds above the Sangre de Cristo Mountains.

A few minutes later the motorbike curved to less dense traffic on US Highway 64 and headed north. She breathed easier, taking in the clean air and open landscape—a profusion of eye-popping yellow flowers on both sides of the highway that split the endless desert fields, devoid of structures.

The rider motioned her to turn after they passed a sign that stated TAOS PUEBLO 1 MILE, and that road soon evolved into a rutted dirt track. She swayed and sometimes bounced in the seat as she traveled the path at a crawl, the Kawasaki having to stop a few times until the lumbering hulk of a vehicle could catch up.

Thankfully she encountered no other cars, and she began to relax. The scent of woodsmoke and a hint of skunk wafted through her open window. Dogs barked and growled and burst through overgrowth and charged the RV as she passed the occasional home.

At this point, she figured they were fully onto reservation land. Excitement tapped her chest now that she had reached the most awe-inspiring place she had ever encountered. Atmosphere ethereal, she could all but feel the ghosts of ancient passed Native Americans that must surely haunt the area.

Another turn and the motorbike rider motioned her to a modest adobe-style house. She parked beside three other motorbikes and waited as the man dashed into the house, then a minute later ducked out of the doorway and motioned her to him.

She patted her scrubs pockets, folds of cash in each, then gazed at the removable bench, where her guns hid, and contemplated taking at least the handgun. But she felt confident, and stood a good amount taller and wider and surely stronger than the scrawny man, and so decided she would be fine without the firepower. She went to the RV's side door and descended the steps, leaving the door open in case she needed to sprint to safety.

Smells assailed her nasal cavities the moment she stepped in the front room. Unmistakable stink of cooked meth, cigarette smoke, unwashed clothes and bodies. The rider stood beside the front door, eyes on another man who sat on a couch in front of a television the width of the wall showing the still frame of a paused video game, feet propped on a coffee table, legs splayed wide, asserting his manhood.

Next to him sat an adult female. Although clearly drug addled, the Native woman's bearing oozed poise. She held back a gasp, recognizing her right away. White Dove. The most amazing hoop dancer she had ever seen perform over the years at Indian festivals she had traveled across four states to watch. For a moment she wondered how such an iconic figure wound up here, then remembered her purpose and couldn't believe her luck.

The other woman looked through her, then turned her head to two other Native women sitting on the floor, legs crossed, heads nodding on their necks.

"What'll it be?" the seated man asked.

"What have you got?" she asked.

"Whatever you want."

Her eyes traveled the bare arms of the seated women, injection sites evident. She said, "Heroin."

"Yeah, I can do that." He pulled out a wad of miniature zippered plastic bags stuffed with beige powder and shook them at her. "How much you need?"

Unsure of the price or what would be demanded, she reached into one pocket and withdrew those bills, took a step closer, and tossed the cash to the table. He leaned forward, counted out the money, slid three of the baggies her way. She snatched them up and stuffed them in her pocket.

Another Native American woman came in the room, head down, shame evident in her posture and reddened cheeks, a man close behind her, tucking his shirttail in his pants. The three women followed her with their eyes but said nothing.

"She's got a big rig," the motorbike rider said. "Plenty of room to get them outa here. They got no more money, so what good are they?"

The leader of the men seemed to ponder the statement.

She hid her hands behind her back to hide her crossed fingers and said, "I could take them."

He shrugged. "Whatever. It'll cost you though."

"Do you want help?" she asked the famous dancer.

White Dove raised her head and they locked eyes. "Yes. I want to stop."

Both men laughed and the dealer said, "Yeah, right. Like that's gonna happen."

She ignored him, gaze unwavering on the Jewel of the Pueblo. She reached into the other pocket, tossed that wad of cash on the table.

"Come with me. I can cure you. I know I can."

White Dove said nothing more as she rose and stepped to the door, a limp hindering her gait.

She led the way, followed by the most famous hoop dancer in all of Taos Pueblo history, the other three women trailing close behind.

CHAPTER ONE
EVA

Now

Showered and dressed in a uniform of a sand-colored shirt and dark tactical pants, Eva Duran moved closer to the mirror hanging on the back of the bedroom door, wound her long hair into a tight bun, then pinned on a gold-and-silver star-shaped badge. Above her right breast pocket she fastened a nameplate stenciled with the letters DEPUTY E. DURAN.

Next she put on the thick black strap she had yet to become comfortable wearing around her waist, fastened the keepers of the duty belt lined with leather sheaths to her personal belt, and snugged it tight. The equipment consisted of handcuffs, a collapsible steel baton, spare magazines stuffed with ammunition, pepper spray, a pouch for her cell phone, and a small tactical flashlight—gear she relied on to stay safe and enforce the law in her county. Most important, for well-being and to complete her routine, she withdrew her firearm from its holster, ejected the magazine to make sure it was fully loaded, slapped the magazine back in place, then checked the chambered round of the Glock 22 semi-automatic. Satisfied, she reholstered the weapon on her right hip and removed two extra ammunition clips from their sheaths and made sure they were each stacked with fifteen Smith and Wesson 9mm rounds.

A bead of sweat trailed down her temple as she sat on the bed and laced up the composite-toe boots she had shined to a gleam the night before. She stood and adjusted the Kevlar vest under her uniform shirt and tried to convince herself the material consisted of ice-soaked cotton as she left the bedroom.

In the kitchen she poured fresh coffee in a travel mug, finished off a protein bar, took up her keys and police radio, locked up and stood on the porch to enjoy a moment of the late-afternoon peace before her shift started. The magpie that had laid claim to her since the first day she'd moved to the rental within the Taos city limits landed on a fence post at the edge of her driveway, let out a squawk, flicked its back tail feathers, strutted on the column of wood.

"Hello to you too. Keep an eye on the place, all right?" she told the creature she had come to know as her personal spirit animal.

The bird screeched and waved its impressive white-and-iridescent-black wings as she made her way to the Taos County Sheriff's Department pickup truck. The moment she slid behind the steering wheel, the dash-mounted radio crackled to life. "Sierra-Ten-Twelve, do you copy?"

Eva took up the handset and plunged the side button. "S-Ten-Twelve here."

"Disturbance complaint at Arroyo Seco. Location, Sabroso Restaurant. Can you cover?"

"On my way."

Head on a swivel the entire drive, as she had for the past nine days and sometimes late into the night, she searched for the best friend who had been banned from the reservation after betraying her people so many times. All but a few believed Paloma Arrio still walked the physical plane. The troubled woman had disappeared before. Gone for days, once for a full week. But this time felt different to Eva. She sensed a darkness more perilous than the drug-induced pit Paloma had fallen into.

She shook off thoughts that often spiraled to the worst-possible scenarios. She had seen too much despair and pain and violence during her time on patrol. She pivoted to her training and tuned out any potentially devastating thoughts. Focused on the road ahead, she blasted past the sign that announced the entrance to her Taos Pueblo reservation.

It took Eva ten more minutes to reach the unincorporated community, on the same State Road 150 that led to Taos Ski Valley, which boasted over a hundred ski runs. Eva had never raced down any of them, but she had responded to numerous disturbances in the main parking lot. Most involved enthusiasts who had been overserved at one of the restaurant bars or arguments that had turned bloody for the "perfect" parking spot.

She turned into the dirt lot and parked under the canopy of trees that shaded the entire fine-dining restaurant structure. The scent of a smoker and roasting meat wafted in the cab as she opened the truck's windows. She watched two Native men, hands clamped in fists at their sides, mere feet from each other, shouts and accusations overlapping, spittle flying from their mouths.

Eva took up the handset. "Dispatch, Sierra-Ten-Twelve. Arrived at location."

"Copy. Do you need backup?"

"No need. I've got this."

She reached for the portable radio, got out of the pickup, clipped the handheld to her belt, then started toward the males, who didn't seem to realize she had arrived.

Eva pinched her thumb and index finger to her tongue and blew. The high-pitched whistle halted the argument. They turned to her, took her in—four eyes resting on her badge. The men, twice Eva's size and weight, stepped back from each other, put on contrite expressions, lowered their heads.

She loved this part of being a law enforcement officer, even out of uniform. The ability to convey complete control of any situation was a learned behavior, and counterintuitive to her traditional Taos Pueblo upbringing. *Be invisible,* her mother had warned time after time when Eva prepared to venture off the reservation—even for a short trip to Taos. It took Eva her entire stint at the academy to feel she deserved to assert the knack. Now she wore the skill proudly.

She stalked to the two, her gun hand behind her holstered weapon for full view, stopped ten feet away in case she needed to pull the Glock. She wouldn't, though. She had known the identical twin brothers for decades.

"Navi. Paco. Why am I back here again?"

Both men pointed at each other and said in unison, "He started it."

It took all of her composure not to laugh. "Five times in as many months. You're making our people look bad." She hitched a thumb to the patio, where diners looked to be enjoying the show. "This is a nice place. You're fortunate to work here."

"Bison brisket tonight," Navi said.

"Truffle fries are even better," Paco offered.

They both turned to each other, grinned, rubbed their stomachs. This time Eva did chuckle.

A voice crackled from the radio. "Sierra-Ten-Twelve, do you copy?"

She unclipped the unit and responded, "Go ahead, Dispatch."

"Request for you at the Gorge Bridge, ASAP."

"Me specifically? Current call is still in process."

An uncomfortably long silence followed before the voice said, "Comes from the top. ASAP."

"Copy that. On my way." She reseated the mic and turned her attention back to the two men. "Do you two *gentlemen* hear that? I'm needed elsewhere." She reached behind her back, unsnapped one of the leather cases on her belt, withdrew the handcuffs, tapped the circles of steel in her palm. "Or do we need to *discuss* this further? Somewhere without brisket and fries."

Four hands reached for the sky. "We appreciate you, Deputy Duran," Paco said. Navi gave an emphatic nod of agreement.

"Okay, good. Get back to work. And give them an extra hour, no pay."

"No pay?" both brothers whined.

"Do it."

They nodded, kicked the dirt, turned around, walked shoulder to shoulder as they approached the back exit that led to the kitchen, and disappeared behind the door.

Claps from a few diners made their way to Eva. She glanced to the patio, where the bartender who knew she loved their special mezcal margaritas gave her a thumbs-up.

A ball of dread settled in Eva's stomach as she returned to the pickup. The directive for her explicitly to appear on scene could mean only one thing: someone from her tribe would be in trouble. Or distress. Hopefully not dead.

She sighed. The 4x4 needed gas, she needed a decent meal and to hydrate, but all comforts would have to wait until she responded to the dispatch call. Now her bleakest imagination spun with the prospect of what she would face ahead. Prayed the call would not be connected to Paloma Arrio.

Near panic drew Eva closer to the destination she hoped wouldn't crush her soul. She accelerated the Ram to race along US Highway 64. Open mesa devoid of a single house or structure, dotted with sage bushes and a proliferation of goldweed topped by bright-yellow blooms, whizzed past as she chased the sunset.

Impressive mushroom clouds building by the minute threatened a downpour and Eva's worry about her friend stretched her already-taut nerves. The cop in her worried about having to halt her personal search because of weather, and of possible destroyed evidence if she found a crime scene. She willed that troubling thought from her mind. Her fears would vanish if she could figure out where the once-famous hoop dancer could possibly be.

She focused on the task at hand and spotted the scene from the moment she reached the final half mile to the Rio Grande Gorge Bridge. In the distance, a cluster of motorcycles was parked on the south-side shoulder of the two-lane, 1,200-foot-long span bordered by sidewalks on both sides. She counted half a dozen law enforcement cruisers and SUVs, lights flashing, that blocked the westbound lane. One state trooper waved on the few vehicles that crept past the fascination.

"Oh no," she muttered, the sight confirming the initial call. Keying her radio mic, she said, "Dispatch, Sierra-Ten-Twelve. Approaching location, midpoint Gorge Bridge."

"Copy, S-Ten-Twelve."

Eva knew the dispatcher inwardly advised her to proceed with caution and stay safe but would never state the obvious over the intercom. There had been three successful suicides from the same location in the past eight months. Too many.

She traveled to the middle of the span to a lookout where the railing extended out, which would allow pedestrians to safely pass as others took in the view. She slowed to a crawl and parked with the official cruisers that diverted other nonemergency vehicles. Easing out a breath, she turned to whoever had chosen this otherwise calm evening to end it all. One state trooper paced back and forth, blocking her full view.

A wail, deafening even beyond Eva's closed window, tore her attention to the people standing near the motorcycles. A barrel-chested man held a distraught woman's arm while she bent low, tears streaming down her red cheeks. The commotion urged Eva from her vehicle.

She assessed the scene for a moment. An oversize hoodie hid their identity, and yet something about the figure seemed familiar to Eva. Riveted to the incident, none of the officers from various agencies greeted her. The most familiar to her—one a Taos city cop, the other a tribal policeman—glanced at each other and turned their concerned expressions to Eva. Confused, she didn't approach either of the men who had competed for her affections the past year.

Instead, she tucked an errant lock of hair behind her ear, then adjusted the gun belt loaded with all the items she could ever need to enforce the law. When she reached the group of onlookers, she said, "Ma'am, I'm Officer Eva Duran. Is there something I can do to help you?"

The lone woman pleaded, "Don't let them—please . . . make it stop."

Eva stepped in front of the woman to block the sight that elicited so much pain. "We'll do all we can, ma'am." She scanned the others. They all appeared tormented and looked anywhere but at the individual on the railing. "Maybe you should all head on out."

"She won't go," the man holding up his companion said. His auburn-gray beard nearly touched his belt buckle. Dark wraparound sunglasses hid his expression, but sorrow radiated from his bear-size body. He leaned closer and said in a low voice, "Her son. Last year."

Eva reared back. "Here?"

"No, Indiana. We're on a road trip, hoping to heal."

Eva nodded, knowing the loss all too well. "Do what you can to convince her." She hitched a thumb to the person who had triggered the emotions. "I'll do the same for . . ."

"Please, please, please," the woman whispered as Eva broke away.

She stopped at one of the uniformed officers from her same unit. "Compton. What's going on? Why isn't anyone talking to them?"

Troy Compton, two years younger than Eva, flicked his eyes to her for a moment, then back to the person sitting on the thin balustrade. "No one wants to approach. We don't want to say anything wrong, because he's . . ."

"What? You're freakin' me out, Troy. What do you know?"

"Pretty sure he's one of your people. We need your help, Eva, like you've always done before. Everyone's afraid they'll say the wrong thing." He ran a hand across his crew cut. "He's gonna do it, I can feel it."

She let out a relieved breath, now knowing this troubled person couldn't be her best friend. For the first time, Eva focused her complete attention on the person she hoped would not be yet another casualty in her county. Closer now, she made out the form of a teenage male, shoulders hunched, back bowed so low his head nearly reached his lap. His body language screamed distraught. Despondent. Jean-clad legs and high-tops entwined in the steel rail where he sat. A precarious balance.

Eva peeked out at the endless horizon, cut in half by the gorge, and then to the perilous drop of over six hundred feet to the Rio Grande.

Two hundred and fifty suicides in twenty years had occurred from the most spectacular view of the region. If this person was from her tribe, it would be too much to bear if she couldn't succeed in talking him down. She cautioned herself to stay in the moment, before thoughts could turn to those who would miss him for every dawn to come.

Hands held outward, fingers splayed, palms up, she approached the boy as she would a skittish colt. "Hee-yah-ho," she chanced, greeting him in the Tiwa language of her people. He didn't respond, and she thought maybe he wasn't from the local rez after all. "I'm Eva Duran. Lightning Dance. Have you heard of me?" No reply or movement came.

She gave it a moment, then took cautious steps closer. A breeze kicked up and she tensed. Knuckles on the hand she could see turned even whiter as he grasped the rail tighter. She caught a hint of burned sage and musty clothing coming off his body.

Another minute passed. Sunset waned. Thunder rumbled. A single fat raindrop tapped Eva's shoulder. Patience wouldn't work with a storm this near, so Eva stepped even closer. She pinched the point of the sweatshirt's hood, eased the covering downward to expose long hair dark as her own, and leaned far enough to clearly see his face.

Eva's heartbeat roared in her ears. Heat rose from her collar. Every muscle tensed. Unable to look away, terrified to reach out, wanting nothing more than to turn the clock back to yesterday, she took in the sight of the young man she still considered a little boy.

Kai Arrio.

The one she thought of as her own.

The son of Paloma Arrio. Her missing best friend.

CHAPTER TWO
PALOMA

Paloma Arrio scratched at invisible bugs crawling under her skin. Scared. No . . . unhinged. She needed escape. Now. The one thing keeping her sane was the thought of relief in a syringe. For three years demons and pain had pursued her, until too exhausted to run any longer, she had started her disappearance. First with booze, then meth, now needles filled with poison she could not do without, no matter how much her son loved her or how desperately she had once been cherished by others. No longer White Dove, a shining jewel of the Taos Pueblo.

She feared only her boy would be missing her, and maybe not even him. She looked at the wall above her pillow, where she had scored single lines for each day of her rescue from the drug house. Eleven slashes now. In a moment of clarity she remembered today's date. Her son's birthday. She was pretty sure his eighteenth but couldn't quite work out the math. She wondered if he would be expecting the plum pie she always tried to remember to make him.

The single realization that provided a hint of solace was that her best friend always found her and would surely be out looking. Again Eva would get her clean, remind her that goodness still lived in her and that their people and the spirits would eventually forgive her, and welcome her back to the embrace of the tribal community. The hopeful thought brought stinging tears to her eyes.

The evening her world took the terrifying turn, she recalled the mistakes that had spun her life into her current whirlwind. So many. No one to blame but herself, she had finally realized after the years of abusing her body and everyone in her orbit. She'd sworn this would be her last fix. Live the life she saw in her mind. Make her son proud. At that moment, the door had opened, and the woman entered the house where she, Kishi, Dora, and her favorite cousin were blissed out on heroin.

The stranger said only a few words, and Paloma still felt confused by what was being offered, but she hadn't been lying when she'd said she wanted to quit the drugs. Paloma, always the leader, merely waved her hand for the other women to follow her to the RV parked out front of the drug house. Steps later, they all got in and started on their newest path of unknowns.

She had nodded off and had no idea if they traveled hours or minutes by the time the vehicle turned, then bumped over a rough road. The motorhome stopped, and the woman chattered again in her annoying childlike voice. They were then ushered inside a run-down house Paloma thought she recognized but wouldn't have visited in many years.

They were led to separate bedrooms, two single beds in each room draped in clean sheets, a Jack and Jill bathroom between the sleeping areas. Paloma puzzled over the plywood screwed over the one window high up on the wall, which allowed only a couple inches of moonlight to peek through. Her cousin Tonita plopped onto one of the mattresses and fell asleep right away, but Paloma thrashed in the bed with worry until the next time the woman came back.

Her thoughts turned to when she had once been a champion. Traveled throughout New Mexico, Texas, Arizona, and Oklahoma, where she would dance at Indian festivals and competitions, making real money and spreading the pride of the Taos Pueblo people. Then a drunk driver slammed into their team's van as they returned from winning a competition in Texas, killing two of her hoop dance friends and her husband, the Navajo driver everyone on the Pueblo had learned to adore. She alone survived. The healing took months, aided by as much oxycodone as she could stomach.

Because her husband and the deceased companions' spirits haunted her nonstop, and the legitimate meds were no longer allowed by her doctors for fear of addiction, she turned to cheap vodka, then meth, and now heroin. She never danced again. Never heard the pound of a drum urging her feet to rise and strike hallowed red clay. Never visited the ancient *Hlauuma*, North House, and *Hlaukwima*, South House, reservation dwellings, where her lineage had thrived for over a thousand years. She had often danced there in private and public ceremonies, draped in a supple leather hand-beaded dress, long tassels whipping as she spun and spun and spun.

Her back flat on the mattress that had melded to her body, unable to even turn over, she wondered how she had allowed this to become her life. Not even actual living. Mere existence. Paloma had soon realized she and her Pueblo sisters were now entirely trapped. Only the stranger visited, right on time, to make them all well. A hamster-wheel life of high and waiting to get high.

She hadn't heard a single word coming from the other bedroom all day and could only hope her other two friends weren't any worse off than her and Tonita. She turned to where the window hid, daylight fading through the slender gap, hoping someone had remembered her boy's birthday. She closed her eyes to concentrate and summoned the one person she had yet to drive away. "Where are you, Lightning Dance? Please come for us," she whispered.

"She's not coming," Tonita slurred from the other bed across the room. "No one is coming."

The door opened wide and banged against the wall, startling Paloma.

"Time for your medicine, my princesses," the woman chirped, carrying a silver tray topped with their salvation.

Relief battled defeat as Paloma released a sob, tears trailing to pool in the ears once adorned with shining handcrafted baubles.

CHAPTER THREE
EVA

Eva resisted the urge to wrap the boy in a body hug and drag him to safety. She shuddered, knowing she could misjudge and push him forward by accident. Or he could anticipate the action and lunge out to oblivion. Instead she searched for words to convince Kai that all was not lost.

"Single Star, why are you here?" She used his Native name, hoping to make a shared connection.

Ignoring the direct question, he said, "She's gone. I know it. I felt her yesterday but not today." His chin quivered as he fought not to cry.

Eva did her best to hide her own consternation. She hadn't felt her best friend's essence for days. "Don't give up, Kai."

The boy continued to hold the railing with one hand, reached into the front pocket of his hoodie and took out a leather pouch, fringe along the bottom. Eva recognized the palm-size medicine bag. She had helped Paloma choose the perfect items to hide inside for protection and comfort—smooth stones from the shore of the water below, twigs of sagebrush and rosemary from his grandmother's house, his father Ahiga's treasured silver ring taken from his finger after the fatal car accident that had shifted so many lives forever.

Her heart raced when he adjusted his position on the hard metal rail. Fearing the worst, she took in a deep breath, pivoted her torso, swung one leg over, and straddled the barrier. Mumbles and curses erupted from the other law enforcers, but they stayed put. Vertigo slammed her entire body when she glanced out. She swayed, both hands gripping the guardrail in front of her, the edges biting her palms and fingers as she tore her gaze away to focus directly on Kai's face.

"What are you doing?" Kai shouted, eyes wide.

"If you start to go, I'll grab you. Don't think I won't," she warned. "Then we both go down."

Kai gaped at her, shaking his head.

"The spirits will not be happy," she said.

"Or kind," they said in unison. Slight smiles lifted their lips as they completed his mother's favorite reprimand.

The light moment vanished as he returned his attention to the perilous view. "Today's my birthday. Eighteen years old."

"I know. I remember. You came out all red face scrunched and fists raised. Then you opened one eye and caught sight of your mom and giggled."

"Haven't done that in a long time."

"Yeah . . . me neither."

"You miss her too?" he asked.

"Of course. She's more sister than friend. Always will be."

"Then why haven't you found her? You're not even trying."

His disappointment in her crushed Eva. Shame and embarrassment nearly overwhelmed her. "That's not true, Kai. I haven't stopped searching from the minute you told me she was missing. I *will* find her—"

"Yeah, right."

"I will. And then everything—"

He snapped his head to her and snarled, "Don't!"

She caught movement in her peripheral vision as two or more of her colleagues took aggressive steps forward. She released one of her hands and motioned for them to stop. Pumped twice, indicating to wait, she's got this.

"Don't say 'Everything will be all right.' 'Cause it won't," he snapped, then dropped his eyes to the pouch and whispered, "It won't."

Both hands back on the cold steel, she said, "I wouldn't lie to you, Kai. Never have."

"What's gonna happen to me, Auntie?"

The twilight made it difficult to read Kai's expression, but she sensed that the crisis had passed. She pivoted her body, swung her leg over the railing, and stood on safe ground. "You're coming home with me. Then we'll figure out what's next."

"What's next is getting my mom. I'll only promise not to jump if you promise I can look for her with you."

A bolt of lightning momentarily brightened his face. Determined. Defiant. Genuine Taos Pueblo Warrior. Deafening thunder cracked, as if to verify the young man would not stand down.

Eva lowered her head, knowing she would never overtly agree to such an ask. Authorities from any local jurisdiction would never allow a nonprofessional, let alone the relative of a missing person, to be directly involved in an ongoing investigation. But she needed to get him to safety now, and later figure out how to get his mind off the request. She let out an exasperated sigh, knowing an official inquiry hadn't even been launched because the woman had disappeared and reappeared more times than Eva could count. No one else had been, or would be, looking for Paloma "White Dove" Arrio. Their people had given up on the addict and the three others most likely with her. And the city and county cops probably didn't even know who they were.

Eva needed help, and Kai probably knew a lot more than he was letting on. Still, this would be an unusual and possibly risky undertaking. She could lose her job. And who knew the danger they could encounter. If anything happened to Kai under her care, it wouldn't only be the spirits who would not be kind.

"Promise me," he pleaded, leaning forward, perilously close to the edge of the steel he sat on.

She focused her gaze on his tear-filled eyes and, protocol for the moment be damned, said, "I promise."

CHAPTER FOUR
ALICE

Alice Jones fired up her silver Zippo and held the flame under the bent spoon, melting the ragged chunk of heroin until it bubbled and turned to liquid. Then she took up a clean syringe, dipped the needle to the spoon's bowl, and drew back the plunger with her thumbnail. The cylinder filled with the magic potion that kept her patients compliant and comfortable.

Satisfied, she prepared another dose and thought of the first time she'd met one of the patients who now awaited the special treatment. On a whim, she had attended the Austin Powwow and American Indian Heritage Festival. Rainbow colors of every hue decorated the elaborate costumes, headdresses ringed with long feathers fascinated her, and bells tied to moccasin laces tinkled everywhere she turned. The mouthwatering scent of fry bread sizzling and cinnamon roasted nuts enticed her. Everything about the experience was so unlike anything she had ever encountered.

One hoop dancer captivated her the most. The young woman had been introduced as representing a tribe located in northern New Mexico. Too shy to approach after the stunning performer won the first-place trophy, Alice discovered more about the dancer secondhand from a gleeful couple who seemed to know everything about the young woman and her Taos Pueblo. The couple traveled every year to that reservation and had followed the dancer's career since she started performing at six years old. They told Alice about an upcoming public festival at the Pueblo. That next month Alice gazed upon the most spectacular sight she had ever witnessed.

Fascinated by the Taos Pueblo people and their traditions, for five summers, as well as every ceremony day open to tourists, she would return to the Pueblo and delight in the celebration of hoop dancers draped in the most beautiful costumes, purchase the pottery and baskets made by the actual tribespeople selling their wares, and marvel over the jewelry crafted from stones and minerals gathered nearby. And the music. Drums that beat in her heart weeks after the songs ceased. Most of all she went to watch the mesmerizing performer dance and dance and dance.

Her own European heritage didn't interest her. Both of her parents' families had resided in Texas for generations, and Alice had never lived anywhere but the small town of Dalhart, a few hours from Amarillo. Knowing more about her lineage didn't appeal to her. Electricians and carpenters for the men, homemakers and bookkeepers for the women. Alice had been the first in the family to complete college and had shocked her parents when she'd announced she would be going to medical school. All of her relations laughed, and after they beat down her resolve, convincing her she wasn't good enough to become an actual doctor, in order to appease her family and end their berating, Alice became a nurse. But not merely an RN, she decided—the next best thing to a doctor, a nurse practitioner who could treat patients privately, prescribe medication, heal them completely without the heavy hand every doctor she had ever met wielded.

Three years ago she had returned, only to find the Pueblo shuttered, assuring no outsiders could endanger the tribe. Although she'd been assigned to working fourteen-hour shifts caring for COVID-infected patients in her own community, the memories of the dancer and her majestic Taos Pueblo rarely left her mind.

One night the idea to offer a mobile medical clinic woke her from sleep. A jolt of inspiration so bright and insistent she knew the message had come directly from the Native American spirits she had read about, and only for her. She shot out of bed and made a plan. First she would need to prove legitimacy beyond her nurse practitioner certification. She remembered seeing an RV parked in the far lot of the Walmart up the street, a For Sale sign on the windshield. Already fully licensed and certified by the state of Texas as a primary care provider, and as a travel nurse authorized to also cover New Mexico and Arizona, she could practice independently. The Winnebago would be perfect to bestow the healing at even the most remote areas of the 110,000-acre reservation.

Securing an appointment with the Taos Pueblo Tribal Council for permission had been relatively easy. She followed their instructions, and, fingers flying on her keyboard, she noted her every thought about the care she would provide to the tribe, then compiled a PowerPoint presentation featuring colorful pie charts and projections of success rates of treatment versus nontreatment, focusing on diabetes and heart health issues that had plagued the tribe for decades.

She envisioned the upcoming meeting the entire four-hour drive to the reservation. In her mind she regaled men dressed in traditional garb of tassel-edged leather jackets and beaded moccasins. Instead, she sat at the end of a conference table surrounded by seven men dressed in button-down shirts, jeans and cowboy boots.

She trembled under the harsh questioning and stone-faced stares of the nearly mute men who made every relevant decision pertinent to the people and their reservation. Alice spoke for a full hour, doing her best to spark a hint of excitement. None of them even appeared to be listening. When Alice had run out of words, one of the men cleared his throat. His companions turned their full attention to him. She assumed he must be the leader of the group, so she sat taller in the uncomfortable cane-back chair and smiled. The man asked if she treated drug addicts, and if so, how could she cure them?

That very moment the idea of curing rather than merely treating patients came to her. She remained on point and vamped about therapies that had been successful but warned that the biggest "cure" would be up to the abusers. She assured them she could and would try to provide the service the councilmen seemed to want most, but the decision should be the addicts' to change their lives. At that, all the men lowered their heads and stared at their folded hands atop the gleaming walnut table. Figuring this was not the answer they wanted to hear, she assured them she would do all she could to provide the best care possible, no matter the ailment.

After a moment the leader rose from his chair, and the others followed him out of the meeting room, without even a *thank you for the presentation*. The woman who had introduced herself as the council's liaison rushed into the room and, kind but insistent, ushered Alice from the building. Dejected and confused, she returned home and did her best to not be disappointed.

She waited months to hear back. Each week she called the friendly and respectful liaison with the voice of a singer, but no one in actual charge would provide updates. Then one morning, when she had all but abandoned her dream, the same elder who had asked her about drug-abuse treatment called to ask how soon she could get started. No specific duties were mentioned, but Alice knew the man had an agenda in mind, and after endless anticipation she devised a plan.

Excited beyond measure, two days later, Alice arrived on the reservation, rig fully stocked with bandages, salves, syringes, and basic medications. Days one through thirty, no one knocked on the door. No one called to make an appointment. No one was curious enough to even drive by. Then a teenage boy appeared and refired Alice's determination. He said he was looking for his mother. She and three others had been gone for a couple of days. Had they been there looking for drugs?

Now she had four of the tribe's most acclaimed members in her care. Making them well. Whole again. Able to create new memories. A daunting responsibility, but one she alone could achieve. Failure wasn't an option. She set down the syringe and picked up another, preparing for the next injection. The Taos Pueblo people needed their stars back. And Alice craved to shine in the glory and appreciation as fiercely as her four patients craved their drugs.

She stowed the remaining illicit medicines in a strongbox under the bench that converted to a bed. As had become her ritual, she ran a gentle hand over the Ruger eight-shot .22 caliber revolver beside the drug kit. She made certain the QuickStrips prestaged with rounds of ammunition were also there, ready for rapid reloading of the concealed carry handgun. She cast a gaze across the tight aisle, imagining the model 870 Remington shotgun and four boxes of shells beneath the foldout bed, then made sure nothing worth stealing was visible.

Satisfied, she restored the hiding place to the bench seat position, then balanced the tray with one hand, went down the Winnebago's springy steps, locked the RV, then entered the shuttered house. Assured the two patients in their beds could wait, Alice unlocked the first bedroom, then she passed through the Jack and Jill bathroom, unlocked the adjoining bedroom door, and stepped inside.

"Time for your medicine, my princesses," she sang out.

Alice first approached the woman closest to the door. Arm extended, hurt in her eyes, the patient pleaded for Alice to hurry.

"Why are you doing this?" the famous hoop dancer, who had captivated her so many times, said from the five steps that separated the beds.

"Shhh. Don't you worry, now," she said, administering the medicine in the IV port secured on top of the woman's hand. "I'm saving us. All of us."

"I need to see my son. Please," she begged, attempting to sit up.

Alice crossed the tight space and laid a tender yet firm hold on the dancer's razor-sharp shoulder and eased her back against the mattress. She took up another loaded syringe and dispensed that shot as well.

"I'm your biggest fan," she said, a little embarrassed at the reverence in her voice.

Her first patient didn't even stir.

Moments later, neither did Paloma "White Dove" Arrio.

CHAPTER FIVE
EVA

Convincing the other officers to let Eva take Kai to her house proved to be easier than she expected. New Mexico Department of Public Safety and city law enforcement agencies already had a tenuous relationship with the Taos Pueblo Tribal Police Department, so she figured they didn't want to alert them about yet another Indian kid ready to off himself. Eva no longer lived on the reservation, so what would be the point?

Kai buckled beside her, she drove the tight two-lane turns on back-streets to avoid the city-traffic congestion. Although she missed the wide-open spaces of the rez, no visible neighbors in houses on the plots of eight- to sixteen-acre lots, she appreciated the proliferation of trees that bordered the neighborhood streets and the green landscapes of bright flower blossoms that dotted the rows of houses.

She turned and parked in the short driveway beside the house she had been fortunate to rent from a local who refused to let outsiders snap it up. Just in time, she remembered not to graze the pine tree that shaded the entire house. Getting out of the truck, she reminded herself to pull up the bright-yellow-blossomed goldweed that had taken over any hint of grass . . . if she ever found the time.

A bird that resembled a small crow, with a white belly and wingtips, its blue-green iridescent tail and top feathers shining like oil on water, lit on a wooden fence post near the Beast, her workhorse 2000 Land Rover Discovery. The bird had first visited Eva the day she moved her meager belongings into the house and had welcomed her every morning and evening since.

Kai waved at the winged creature and said, "That's a black-billed magpie. Indigenous to the area, like us. Most people don't like them, but they're smart and clever and curious." The bird let out a high-pitched, chattering *wock, wock wock-a-wock, wock*. "And loud when they want you to pay attention. I've studied them since I was a little kid. They're like people. Never witnessed the exact same behavior from one to the other."

The winged creature became even more treasured to her after Kai's accounts.

"You should name it," he said.

The bird squawked again, preened, bounced from one foot to the other atop the post, as if agreeing with the boy. "True. What should I call it?"

Kai thought only a moment before he replied, "Rio. You know, like the river."

His statement caused her to wonder if his perch high above the water continued to weigh heavy on his mind before she said, "Nice. Rio it is."

When they entered Eva's modest two-bedroom, one-bath home, Kai breathed out a dejected sigh. She let one out, too, along with a prayer to help her put the boy at ease. And for counsel from the spirits because she had no idea what to say or even how to be around a teenager for more than a few hours at a time.

"Are you hungry?" she asked, unsure if a single edible item could be found in her house.

Kai shook his head. He stood in the front room making a slow revolution, the leather pouch cradled in one hand, his eyes taking in everything. Not much, actually. She had simple tastes and needs. One side table next a well-worn leather chair, bookcase stuffed with crime novels and police procedural manuals, television atop a rickety cedar chest, and a comfortable couch arranged under the picture window. A beehive fireplace hugged one corner, the reason she absolutely had to have the house—the one element that felt like her grandfather's house on the rez. There had been nights when only a raging fire kept the bad spirits at bay.

"I've never been here," he said.

"No, I moved off the rez last year."

"To join your white man's job and white man's life."

"That's your mother talking."

"Is she right?"

He had yet to give her his eyes, so she placed herself in front of him. "I go where I'm needed. And wanted."

Finally he looked at her. "Our people turned on you too?"

Eva crossed the room to hide her wince. "We should call your uncle," she said, ignoring his painful question.

Kai whirled to her, wide eyed. "No. I'm not going there."

"Well . . . you have to go somewhere. You can sleep on the couch tonight, but the second bedroom is crammed full of my grandfather's and parents' stuff. A bed doesn't even fit in there. Santiago is your closest blood relative. He'll want you with him."

He gave an adamant shake of his head. "I'm an adult now, remember? And I've been taking care of myself *and* my mom for three years. Anyway, nobody's seen Tonita. I bet she's getting high with my mom somewhere. You can't ask any of the others. No one will take me." Red faced and ramped up, he glared at Eva. "Mom killed any chance for anyone caring about me. Stole from every house she ever walked into the past couple years. Yours, too, probably."

Eva tried to mask her embarrassment, suddenly recalling the silver and gold jewelry that had gone missing the last time Paloma dropped by.

"Kai, that's not—"

Full-on in tears, he shouted, "Nobody wants me, so just shut up. Don't you get it?" He swiped his nose on the cuff of his ragged sweatshirt. "I stole too. For her."

Eva turned from the boy's shame, inwardly cursing her friend, not for the first time. She hoped Kai didn't expect her to reply because she didn't have a clue how to put the boy at ease. Avoidance often her go-to, she changed the subject completely. "Well, I haven't eaten since this morning. I've got eggs . . . maybe," she said, crossing the room designed ideally for one person to the kitchen.

A thought came to her, and she spun back to Kai. "Wait. What was I thinking—we should go to your house and pick up some of your things."

Voice thick with exhaustion, he said, "Power's out again. It'll be too dark to find anything."

"What? When did that happen?"

He shrugged and dropped to the couch. His eyes began to droop as he scrunched deeper into the hoodie.

"Kai, why didn't you let me know?"

"Does it matter? We've gone without before. Probably will again."

Muttering curses, she went to the kitchen and opened the fridge. Apprehension confirmed, she found only half a carton of long-expired eggs, a full shelf of energy drinks, and condiments she couldn't remember ever using stowed inside.

She scrambled up the questionable eggs, added extra hot sauce to kill any unpleasantness, then took the plates to the front room.

"Just pretend to like them if . . ." She stopped and watched Kai on the couch, one foot on the floor. Soft snores puffed from his lips.

Eva's attitude softened. He looked so much like the little boy unwilling to leave the comfort of the two people most important to him. She remembered the times he would curl up on the same couch, sleeping between her and Paloma, while they laughed and shared tall tales until dawn.

She put the plates on the chest, eased his leg to the couch, tugged off his shoes, covered him with a blanket. His heartbeat thumped a calming rhythm under her palm. It had been a long day for the teenager, and he reeked of unwashed clothes and skin, but a sweetness emitted from his hair when she kissed his forehead. His unique scent of cinnamon and sage. The fragrance he shared with his mother.

The young man's warrior spirit didn't fool her. Yes, he acted tough, but a little boy still hid inside. She had been shocked when he told her he'd been taking care of himself alone for so long. She'd assumed his direct family would step up for their Single Star. But depending on others was not the rebel creed. Knowing better than most, she would need to figure out ways to provide for and assist him without him realizing. Even better, turn the tables on him, as if her brilliant ideas were actually his alone, like his mom would do from the time Kai could reason with her.

The kid forgot nothing. Even as a little boy, he'd tested Eva the times she would watch him when Paloma and Ahiga traveled to performances out of state. She would promise candy if he finished his elk stew, ice cream if he tried buffalo, a new pair of kicks if he sank a three-pointer. Always up for a challenge, and even better, to show up a grown-up, the boy would shock her with his exuberance to triumph. And both were winners, actually. Kai expanded his knowledge, and Eva learned how to care for someone other than herself. Now Eva realized his adventurous spirit would aid him throughout adulthood. It also made him fearless and more than a little careless. She couldn't even imagine what Paloma had endured to keep the boy safe and alive. He scaled two-story roofs, skateboarded and bicycled over any obstacle, sprinted across water-starved mesas even knowing rattlesnakes could be under every rock.

A warning pinged in Eva to remain vigilant. The kid was capable of anything. Good and bad. Two years ago he had been caught trying to steal a loaf of bread and lunch meat at the Allsup's Convenience Store at the south entrance to the reservation. The next day he picked up trash around the property, regret evident as she watched him from her vehicle parked in the lot. Eva didn't know Kai and Paloma needed the food and had no way to pay for it. From then on she had dropped off a box of essentials every week, even if he refused, eyes bugging out at the supplies and treats. Beyond proud, he had never asked for her help. Until now.

Tears blurred Eva's vision and she stifled a sob.

"Everything will be all right," she whispered over and over. A mantra of hope.

Words she could only wish the spirits would allow.

CHAPTER SIX
PALOMA

Another dawn. Paloma mourned the day to come, knowing the hours would be exactly the same as so many before. Most of all, she grieved for her son. She hadn't felt Kai's presence for the second day now. She prayed to every spirit that had ever appeared to her—most of all to her precious Ahiga, and to her mother, who had perished from cancer ten years earlier—and still her Single Star did not shine.

"He's all right," she told herself, an unconvincing comfort.

She turned to Tonita, who hadn't stirred since their shots the night before. She worried for her too. Neither of them had eaten much in days and had choked down the peanut butter toast and protein drinks offered when the nurse threatened to stick tubes down their throats and force-feed them if they didn't finish everything. The first few days, Alice, the nurse, offered all kinds of different foods Paloma would have loved three years ago. Burgers, fried chicken, fry bread and beans . . . *Anything, just eat,* Alice would beg. But all Paloma and Tonita wanted was to be free from the odd woman and their even weirder situation.

She turned to get a better look at her cousin and winced. The intravenous needle the nurse had inserted on day one of their captivity pinched the tender skin on top of her right hand. The nurse had become frustrated, unable at first to find a vein well enough to accept even the smallest butterfly needle. Four pokes later the saline that promised to keep her hydrated flowed.

Her full bladder forced her from the bed. Dragging the IV pole with her, she first checked the door she assumed led to a hallway. As before, she found the door locked from the outside. Then she checked to make sure Tonita was still with her and had not become one of the spirits who refused to comfort her.

Hand to Tonita's nose and mouth, Paloma detected a steady breath. Not quite convinced, she placed the palm to her cousin's chest. Relieved, she detected steady, faint, very slow thumps. She stroked the crown of her cousin's once-prized hair a moment, then shuffled to the bathroom.

Relieved there was no mirror to confirm what Paloma assumed would be a death mask reflection, she splashed cold water on her face and matted hair, then took the two steps to the toilet.

She shot upright, nearly falling off the commode. Shaking her head, she realized she must have dropped off to sleep. She shivered, stamped her cold feet, then stood, legs cramping. Unsure how long she had been in the same place, amazed she hadn't fallen to the floor, she almost missed the sound from behind the closed door that led to the adjoining bedroom.

As with every time Paloma had tried before, she risked knocking on the door. "Kishi? Dora? Are you all right?" No answer came. She didn't feel her friends' presence in there either.

Sensing total abandonment, she shuffled back to bed and prayed, this time for the nurse to hurry up and deliver the magic that would again release her, from absolutely everything.

CHAPTER SEVEN
EVA

Dawn the following morning, Eva decided her next steps would require her to fly under the radar—off duty and out of uniform. She left a message for her sheriff and hoped he wouldn't follow up. She had earned the personal day and knew her supervisor would understand the need to be with Kai after his disturbing incident, but only twenty-six fellow deputies patrolled the county, and the thought of letting anyone down left her feeling more than a little guilty.

Dressed in faded jeans, her favorite flannel shirt, and well-worn cowboy boots, she entered her front room to see Kai already awake, shoes on and tapping the floor, as if he had been waiting hours for her to appear.

"Guess I don't need to be quiet," she said. "Coffee?"

"No, I don't like coffee."

"Good. I don't have any anyway." She took the key ring from the cedar chest, motioned for him to follow, then locked up. Kai approached the sheriff's department four-door Ram pickup.

"We're taking the Beast today," she said, clicking the fob to unlock the doors of her Land Rover.

Kai sat low in the passenger seat, eyes on his folded hands, yet to speak a word until she took the sharp turn to the parking lot of her favorite breakfast joint in all of Taos.

"Pancakes?" Kai asked, excitement in his tone for the first time since Eva could remember.

"Hell, yeah," she said. "I think we've earned it."

"Hell, yeah."

"Language."

He shrugged a silent *whatever* as he slid out of the vehicle.

They entered Michael's Kitchen Restaurant and Bakery, skirted the crowd at the entrance waiting for tables, and made a beeline for two empty seats at the counter. Mouthwatering scents of bacon, fresh pastries, and every other heavenly first-meal foods met Eva as they sat on the stools. She scanned the menu and tried not to moan in anticipation.

Wasting no time, she raised a single finger and the waitress hustled over, pen in hand. "The usual, Eva?"

"Perfect. Kai?"

"Same as her, I guess."

The patient waitress held her pose and stared at the young man. Eva suppressed a smile and winked at her favorite server.

Kai finally grasped the silent admonishment and tried again. "I would like what Eva ordered, please."

"Could you add a short stack, too, Carol?"

"You bet. Have it to you in fifteen."

Always the cop, Eva scanned the patrons, on alert for anyone she should keep an eye on. She noticed only friendly faces of tourists and a few locals she recognized, all enjoying their food, chatting, or ogling the pastry case.

Confident she wouldn't need to be on point, she said, "Guess I should have checked to make sure you did your homework last night. I'm not very good at looking after people."

"Don't worry about it. I take care of myself. Like I told you yesterday, I'm not a baby," he said in what sounded to Eva like a completely childish tone of voice.

They sat in silence until the food came, then Kai obliterated three scrambled eggs, a pile of hash browns, half a dozen slices of crisp bacon, and most of the pancakes. Eva matched his every bite.

She tossed the napkin to her empty plate. "I'm taking the day off. Anything you need to do this morning?"

He gaped at her like she had dropped from the sky. "School. I need to get to class in an hour."

"Oh. Well, I . . . didn't think you'd want to do that."

"It's Wednesday," he said, as if that was all the explanation necessary.

"True. Okay, let's roll." He didn't follow when she slid off her stool. "What? You need more food?" She chuckled, then worried maybe he hadn't been fed enough.

"I need to go home and get my books. The assignment is in my backpack."

"Okay, let's do that."

She paid the check at the register and then dodged the crowd awaiting tables as they made their way through the door. A breeze kicked up when they reached the Rover, and she detected a hint of rain in the air. Her mind rewound to the night before. She had expected a deluge after she convinced Kai to go home with her. Instead, the thunder and rain had ceased the moment he had secured his seat belt. Then, and now, she couldn't help but think the Spirit Guides sensed the urgency and had helped move things along.

"I probably should pack some clothes anyway," Kai said, snapping her back to the present. "And my pillow. Yours suck."

She frowned, unsure how the conversation had taken such an unexpected turn.

He froze, hand on the door pull. "I'm staying with you until we find my mom, right? You promised."

"Yeah, you're right," she said, warning herself to beware—there might be another loaded bomb she hadn't remembered promising the young man, who, she realized, never forgot a single word she had spoken to him.

CHAPTER EIGHT
ALICE

Alice tried her best not to be too disappointed about not figuring out the proper blend of medications to bring comfort to her first test patient. For twelve days now she had tried different dosages on the drum maker to no significant difference. Every combination she had tried the previous days resulted in the same pattern of withdrawals. Still, rather than daunted, she remained focused. She would figure this out.

Being patient proved to be the biggest challenge. Knowing she needed to be careful not to administer too much foreign substance to an already-compromised system, Alice had to wait an entire day before she could try different drugs and dosages.

Again, inspiration woke her in the middle of the night. She jotted down her thoughts and soon fell back to a dreamless sleep. Excited and confident that she had broken the conundrum, she awoke before dawn and prepared the reworked test dose. This time she chose to add a trace of Dilaudid to the heroin.

She smiled as she prepared the cocktail. "Perfect," she whispered to the filled syringe.

Careful not to mix up the medications, she took up a red Sharpie and drew a smiley face on the barrel of the prized blend's hypodermic.

Alice put her tools of the trade away, took up the silver tray topped with four loaded hypodermics, and locked up the RV after her.

As with every time Alice entered the first bedroom, the two women shirked away, bodies tucking small as they hugged their legs and wedged themselves in opposing corners of the tight room. Only the temptation of the syringes containing what they craved most allayed their trepidation.

To assuage the fear, Alice continued to give a slightly higher dose of heroin to the drum maker's companion in the other bed, then waited patiently for her to drift off. Back to her first patient, needle ready. Then a thought occurred to her, so intense she halted the needle midway to her mark. Yesterday's batch, heroin laced with fentanyl, had been a near miss. So close, in fact, Alice had needed to administer a dose of naloxone rescue meds, saving the woman just in time.

The younger woman whimpered, anticipation dashed, so close to relief.

"What's your name, dear?"

"Kishi Reyna."

"What a lovely name." Alice leaned in and whispered, "If you had a wish, where would you spend your last moments?"

The addict reared back, confused, on the edge of panic. No answer came from her trembling lips.

"It's not a trick question," Alice said. "I really want to know." She issued a smile she hoped didn't look too fake.

"Where I find the sacred animals for my drums," she said in a low voice.

"You make drums?"

The woman nodded her head, the first spark of enthusiasm Alice had witnessed from the girls. Intrigued by anyone with the gift of creativity, she asked, "How do you go about that?"

"First I hunt the animal, then prepare the hide. Takes a while to cure the leather. Then drape and lash it to wood frames. Takes months to make one. My happiest times are in the forest, at the hunting grounds, on the way to the ski slopes."

"Fascinating." She hitched a thumb at the drum maker's companion. "What about her? Does she have a special place?"

"Dora Pando makes jewelry from the stones she finds in the gorge. Probably there."

Alice had marveled at the massive ravine about fifteen minutes north of Taos when she had arrived the first time in the area. Had even walked midpoint and looked out at the endless crevasse carved eons ago by the Rio Grande.

"And the other one—"

The woman reached out her hand. "Please. I can't wait any longer."

Alice raised the hypodermic, taunting her patient. "The one with White Dove. Is she special too?"

"Baskets. Tonita weaves baskets. From the willow tree in her grandfather's old yard. Biggest in all of Taos."

"I thought only White Dove was extraordinary." Alice couldn't help but keep the excitement out of her voice. "You're *all* jewels of the Pueblo."

The drum maker lowered her gaze. "Not anymore."

"Well, I'm doing my very best to heal you. Are you ready?"

Kishi nodded and scootched closer to the edge of the mattress.

Alice administered the red-marked concoction to the drum maker, then patted her knee. "There you go. Better?"

The Pueblo woman sighed and nodded. Ten seconds later, her head canted back, veins on her neck straining. Her eyes rolled up until Alice saw nothing but whites. The drum maker began to convulse and it took all of the nurse's strength to ease her off the bed to the linoleum floor and then position the shuddering woman on her side so she wouldn't choke on the vomit spewing from her mouth.

"No, no, no," Alice pleaded. She reached into her scrubs pocket, extracted a dosage of Narcan, plunged the receptacle into the woman's nose, shoved the stopper.

The woman called Kishi bucked and bucked. Her bladder emptied, adverse reactions continuing, as if the rescue medicine had no effect at all. An eerie moan emanated through her clenched teeth, then no movement or sounds came. For one full minute.

Three minutes.

Five.

Until she stirred no more.

CHAPTER NINE
EVA

Eva crossed the city, then county boundaries, and entered sovereign land of the Taos Pueblo reservation. Her heartbeat ratcheted up, nervous and unsure about what the reception would be if she encountered any of her people. Whenever Cruz Romero wanted to go somewhere, she always met him in Taos, one mile from the ancient Pueblo village. Kai looked nervous, too, and that brought on more anxiety. She had no idea what she would find up ahead.

The "Indian security system" of rez dogs off leash charged her Rover or bounded to wire fences surrounding the houses, barking and growling at the intrusion. After a few more minutes of bouncing on their seats as the Beast dipped in and out of deep craters of the dirt road, she pulled into the unpaved drive that led to Paloma and Kai's house, owned by the tribe. She spotted the distinctive *horno* Eva had helped Paloma's husband build—the outside oven used primarily to bake bread. No houses anywhere in sight, the next dwelling half a mile away, this part of the reservation felt lost in time. Cottonwoods swirled in the breeze as birds hidden in their leaves sang cheerful tunes.

Rage fired in her when she parked in the dirt drive and spotted a fluorescent orange sign plastered to the front door.

Kai slammed the car door and charged to the porch. He raised a middle finger to the Immediate Notice of Eviction sticker and unlocked the door. Shocked, Eva scanned the demand. The warning hadn't been there yesterday, when she had driven by for the tenth time to see if Paloma had sobered up enough to come to her senses. Someone from the tribal police must have posted the notice overnight. She scowled and added a blistering call to tribal cop Romero to her already-full list of things to do today. No more dates for him if he was the jerk making her charge's life even more difficult.

Unpleasant aromas of spoiled food, dirty laundry, and an amalgam of other unidentifiable smells hit Eva the moment she walked in. Kai made a beeline to the short hallway as Eva took in the ruins of the front room.

She remembered when Paloma and Kai had moved in, so proud of the little house. Although the tribe owned the deed, she'd considered it her own. *Small, but all Ahiga and Kai and I need,* her friend had told Eva when she gave the tour fifteen years ago that had taken all of two minutes. The money to continue paying the lease had come from the life insurance policy her husband had, unknown to Paloma, secured. Paloma had painted and decorated the space in cheery reds and blues, throw pillows on the used leather couch, traditional pottery for a few houseplants. What Eva now saw looked worn, uninviting and unkempt. Abandonment everywhere she turned.

The sound of a shower turning on wrenched Eva from her reverie. She made her way to the kitchen, where the unpleasant smells became stronger. She didn't dare to open the fridge, imagining the remains inside. She took out her phone, clicked a photo of Kai's Taos High School class schedule and class times taped to the refrigerator.

Unlike what she had encountered in the front room, this area was spotless. No dirty dishes in the sink, the window above the basin sparkled, countertops scrubbed. Even the usually overfilled ashtray on the kitchen table had been emptied and polished. Kai would have cleaned up in his mother's favorite room for her return. Grief pierced Eva.

Paloma's bedroom broke Eva's heart further. Unwashed sheets in a tangle, cigarette burn scars on the bedside table. She whipped open the curtain and almost choked on dust from the disturbed cloth. Waving her hand in front of her face, she looked in the closet to find mostly empty hangers, and she wondered, like so many, if the former hoop dancer had merely run off, abandoning her son.

The only items remaining in the closet were sashes, one for each hoop-dancing competition Paloma had won over the years. Eva sorted through a few of at least fifty and found the one she remembered most vividly. Her friend's first win. The one draped over her by the governor of the tribe—the highest honor for a dancer. Later that day, the two had traveled to Santa Fe to celebrate the achievement at a tattoo parlor. When the two stood side by side, the designs made a perfect match of an angel's wings. Eva placed her hand on her bicep, where her left sleeve hid ink that paired Paloma's. An impulse that Eva never once regretted.

Less than a year later Paloma had dropped out of school and went on tour with a group of other champion dancers. In Arizona she met the Navajo man who stole her heart and her innocence. They soon married, and Kai arrived far away from home and her people.

"Ready," Kai said.

She whirled to the boy, who watched her from the doorway. Pillow tucked under his arm, he clutched a bulging duffel bag to his chest, and a loaded backpack bowed his posture. He wore fresh jeans and a different hoodie. "Gonna be late. The bus already left. Can you take me?"

Distracted, Eva didn't grasp the question. Instead, she said, "Kai, there's less food here than at my place. What have you been eating?"

"A lot of bread." He hitched his head to the front room window. "Been using the horno. Grandma taught me before . . ."

His words trailed off. Nothing further needed to be said. Eva thought of Paloma's sweet mother, who always doted over her only grandson, as Kai crossed the room to the front door.

"You sure you want to go to school today? I can call—"

"No. Let's go," he said, no further explanation forthcoming.

She followed him out of the house and watched him lock up. He gave the notice pasted to the door the finger again. This time Eva didn't hide her chuckle.

CHAPTER TEN
PALOMA

Paloma heard the door beyond the bathroom open and recognized the now-familiar steps of the nurse approach. She let out a relieved breath when the woman entered their bedroom carrying the silver tray.

Never knowing what mood or persona the caregiver would wear each time she appeared, Paloma studied her and frowned. Eyes red, nose running, the nurse kept averting her eyes. She wondered if normally meek Dora, or sometimes volatile Kishi, had caused some sort of trouble that had upset the one person keeping all of them alive.

"Are you *trying* to kill us?" Tonita snapped, teeth chattering. "It's not right you keeping us here if you're not going to care for us right."

The woman Paloma now considered their kidnapper whirled on Tonita and scowled. Eyes blazing, she said, "Are you implying I'm not a good nurse?"

"Uh . . . yeah," Tonita said, a little milder this time.

Alice thinned her eyes and pursed her lips. "You have no idea how difficult it's been to keep you girls safe and thriving." She set down the tray, pulled a tissue from beneath her buttoned sleeve, blew her nose, dabbed her eyes. "I'm doing the best I can. Far more than anyone else has ever tried, I'm quite sure."

"You've been wonderful." Paloma gave her cousin a warning shake of the head. "We're grateful. We really are."

The woman turned to her. "It's nice to see *someone* appreciates me. Thank you, White Dove."

The nurse took up one of the syringes and approached Tonita, who held out the top of her hand for easy access to the IV port. Not so gently, the woman repositioned the basket weaver's arm to expose the tender underside skin of her arm and proceeded to insert the needle in the crook of her elbow. Tonita yelped but didn't pull away. She glowered at the older woman, then fell back against the mattress. Moments later, lost in bliss, Paloma's cousin dropped off to oblivion.

The woman picked up the tray, crossed the tight space. Paloma wondered why one of the empty syringes had a smiley face drawn on it, then puzzled over when she had given the woman her Native name. Only her own people called her that . . . and how she was introduced when she performed at competitions.

Recognition hit Paloma. She realized where she had seen the woman before. Actually many times over the years. "Alice?" she asked.

The woman startled. The movement nearly drove the loaded hypodermic from her fingers. "How do you . . . ? Did I tell—?"

"I remember you from when I danced. Competitions in Arizona. No, wait . . ." Paloma thinned her eyes, pinpointing the location in her mind. "Texas. You came up to me after the contests. Always told me how much you enjoyed my dancing."

"You remember me?" the nurse gushed.

Years of addiction had taught Paloma how to deceive. Now the consummate liar, sensing an opening to connect with the woman, she mirrored the excitement. "Of course! I always looked for you, wherever we traveled, hoping you would be there."

Tears filled the fan's eyes. "You always made me so happy. You will again, I promise."

Paloma held the other woman's gaze and hoped she didn't look too desperate as she said, "Alice, would it be okay for me to see Kishi and Dora?"

A faraway look clouded over Alice's expression. She paused, as if unsure how to answer. Afraid her question risked her missing out on her injection, Paloma opened her arm so the nurse could give her the shot in the same location as her cousin.

After an endless minute Alice took the steps to Paloma and gently turned her hand. "No, I won't mark you, White Dove. I've almost healed the tracks between your toes. Soon you'll be perfect again."

Paloma grasped the thin sleeve of her blouse that hid the tattoo that matched her best friend's. She hoped the bookended wing would find its match soon.

She closed her eyes and envisioned Eva flying to her rescue.

CHAPTER ELEVEN
EVA

After dropping off Kai at the high school, Eva considered what she should do about the boy. She needed to be free to investigate without involving Kai directly. He would never forgive her for reneging on the deal they had made on the bridge, but she couldn't risk losing her job.

The only option she could think of came to her. The young man would not be happy. And the mere thought of how she would approach the most imposing member of the tribal council made a chill run down her arms. Both conversations would take finesse.

A speech playing in the back of her mind, she turned into the Taos Police Department visitors' parking lot and approached the main entrance. Always the professional, on and off duty, she hoped the unannounced visit wouldn't seem too suspicious.

She entered the main lobby, took the badge cover from her back pocket and flashed her credentials to the officer manning the front desk. He buzzed her through, and she strode to where she assumed Andrew Kotz would be filling out the endless piles of paperwork he often complained about. An outsider, she put on the "invisible cloak" reserved for times she would be the only Native in the room. None of the officers confronted her or even turned her way.

She hurried the final steps when she spotted the man who had more than a little crush on her. "Time for a late breakfast?" she asked, still full from her meal with Kai.

Kotz reared back, appearing confused to see her. His puzzlement lasted only a moment. He didn't look around to see if anyone watched them or seemed embarrassed by what could be overheard. Instead, he gave her the smile that always preceded an ask for a date.

"Naw, can't. Shift just started. But I'm happy you stopped by."

She scanned the open room to see only a few officers, tapping on keyboards or busy on the phone. She had applied for a patrol officer position but felt the sheriff's department suited her better. Glancing around the area, devoid of women, she felt confident about her decision. Although she hadn't yet become close friends with the three other female deputies, she knew they had her back and were as tough emotionally and physically as Eva.

"That was pretty wild on the bridge yesterday," Kotz said.

"I was surprised to see you there."

"Heard chatter on the radio. I was already driving on patrol. Thought maybe I could lend a hand. Is the kid okay?"

"Okay as he can be for now. He slept pretty good. Just got back from dropping him off at school. I assume he'll stay there."

"He's probably scared enough of you to stay out of trouble now."

"Scared?"

He blushed and stammered, "I—I mean . . . you're pretty tough. And he respects you, right? Knows that you're worried about him without his mom around . . . you know, all that stuff."

"Keep digging. You'll get out of that hole eventually."

Kotz chuckled, red faced, his embarrassment evident. "What can I do for you, Deputy Duran?"

"Oh, we're being official now." She grinned and his face reddened an even deeper shade.

"No, I . . . I—"

She joined him and said in Tiwa-spoken acknowledgment, "Ah-mah, Cruz."

Oozing smooth confidence, the rez cop was one of ten officers who served to protect the three thousand residents of the reservation. He leaned against the grille of his official vehicle, a handheld radar gun on the hood next to him. He raised a half-eaten Klondike Bar in greeting.

"Ice cream for breakfast? My kinda guy."

He scanned her head to toe. "Taking a day off, middle of the week? My kinda gal."

They shared chuckles.

She nodded to the radar unit. "Catch anyone yet?"

"Just got here. Waiting."

"You'll get one."

"Always do," he said, licking a trail of vanilla ice cream from his hand, then finishing the treat. "Unfortunately."

A car's engine reverberated up the road. Cruz crumpled the ice cream wrapper and tucked it in a pocket of his sharp-creased slacks. He reached for the radar gun, took an imposing stance, lifted the unit, and pointed it at the oncoming vehicle. The lowrider sedan slid to a halt, then crawled toward them. Neither the driver nor his four passengers looked their direction as they rolled by.

They both laughed when the Chevy continued its snaillike pace. "Haven't seen you on the rez for a while."

"Second time here today, actually."

"Impressive. Getting to be a habit."

"Not likely. I won't keep you, just wanted to know if anyone's offered anything on Paloma. Kai needs to know."

"No, *you* need to know."

"Yeah, so what? Why aren't you more worried? The three of us learned how to walk together, Cruz. Lifelong friends. Doesn't that mean anything to you?"

"I do care. But she's taken off before. Left her boy to look after himself more times than we can count. And I've got other heavy shit to handle right now than someone who may or may not be missing."

"Someone? Paloma was like a sister to you growing up. You used to follow her around like a puppy. Wanted to be her first boyfriend."

"Long time ago. She's not the same person. Neither am I."

Eva couldn't remember when the three of them had last spent any time together, other than special occasions. Even during festivals, Cruz went out of his way to avoid her and Paloma. He never mentioned her during their infrequent dates.

"You can't even say her name."

"Names have power. She has enough. Been manipulating our people for years. Most are finished with White Dove."

"Did you put up the notice-to-vacate order? To make sure she'll never have a home on the rez?" No answer came from Cruz. "Not helpful, by the way. It's Kai's home too. He'll have nowhere to go."

"Eviction is the responsibility of the Pueblo sheriff's deputies. Us cops never know what they're doing for the tribal leadership. And I check on Kai every day." His eyes blazed when he said, "Do you?"

Shame burned her cheeks because she hadn't.

"I'm done with this conversation." He pushed off the cruiser, took up the radar gun and stepped away.

"Wait, what's so important?" she asked.

Confusion creased his brow when he turned back to her. "Say again?"

"You said you've got some heavy shit to handle. Shit's not heavy, by the way."

"Well, this is." He waited, as if pondering whether he should tell her more. He folded his arms tight against his chest and said, "Rumors, for now. But you know what they say about rumors on the rez . . ."

"They always come true," they said in unison.

"Word is somebody is making ghost guns. Teacher at the high school found a 3D printed handgun frame in the workshop, and frames to a dozen more. School board's panties are in a wad."

"They think a rez kid did it?"

"Don't they always?"

Eva thought about the potentially dire prospect. "Untraceable, unregistered firearms. That is bad."

"Someone's gonna get killed. Hopefully not one of us."

Eva wondered if *us* meant cops or someone from the tribe. Either option would be devastating to the community. "Be safe," she told him, never able to stay mad at him for long, then headed to her vehicle.

"Might BOLO a Winnebago," Cruz said.

Grateful for his reevaluation, she struggled to tamp down any possible excitement. "I'm listening."

"Someone's using an RV as a mobile medical unit. Maybe Paloma went there for treatment, or the caretaker has seen her around. Won't be easy to find. Tribal council gave the person running it full clearance to treat the people on the rez. Could be anywhere."

Eva knew *anywhere* meant more than 110,000 acres. "More rumors?" she asked.

He shook his head as he opened the driver's-side door of his SUV. "Nope. Kai found it himself. Told me about it, couple days ago."

She fought hard not to let her mouth drop open, exasperated by yet another secret held by the boy.

CHAPTER THIRTEEN
PALOMA

Through her haze, Paloma heard the distinctive cough of the RV's engine starting up. She turned to the covered window, then willed herself to get up and try to look out the crack that allowed the midmorning light to slant a path across the wall. By the time she found the strength to sit upright, the vehicle had already driven away.

Another sound ratcheted her senses up a bit more as she turned to the bathroom. Maybe moaning from her other friends' room?

"Tonita, did you hear that?"

Her companion grunted, nothing more.

"The nurse left, and I think something's going on in the other room."

Another grunt, fainter this time.

Unable to quash the worry, Paloma struggled to stand upright, then used the rolling IV pole for balance. Her bad leg screamed in protest, the pain nearly doubling her over. Far too much time off her feet would cost her. She gritted her teeth and managed to accomplish a slow limp to the bathroom.

Panting from the exertion, sweat trailing from her hairline, she leaned against the closed door that led to the other bedroom. Hand on the knob, as every other time before, she found it to be locked. She placed her ear to the thin covering and listened. Paloma thought she detected whimpering but couldn't be certain.

"Dora? Are you and Kishi still in there? Are you okay? Please, tell me what's happening." She jiggled the doorknob. "Can you let me in?"

Fear pinged throughout Paloma as she imagined the worst scenarios playing out mere feet away. A full-body shudder rippled through her. Teeth chattering, feet cold on the floor, she fought down the bile that stung her throat. For a moment she thought the nurse might have laced her dose with something different by accident. But nothing had been accidental from the first moment she and her trio of sidekicks had been under the older woman's care.

She dropped to the toilet and squeezed her eyes closed, pushing her mind to a more pleasant time in her life. She imagined the sun, warm on her face and through the supple leather of her performance dress, spinning atop hard-packed dirt, drums keeping time for her, cheers from the non-Natives, chant-singing from her own kind. Lost in the meditation, her muscles relaxed, breaths became longer and deeper.

She slowly opened her eyes, as if seeing the room for the first time. Hand to her mouth, she looked down at the tiles under her feet, a few of them cracked, grout missing in the most well-worn areas.

"Can't be," she muttered, realization coming to her.

She had been here before. Countless times growing up. Eva's grandfather's house.

More focused now, she reached out to the door beside her and knocked. And knocked. And knocked.

CHAPTER FOURTEEN
EVA

Thankful she'd had the foresight to take a picture of Kai's school schedule, with Wednesday circled in red, Eva noted that he finished school a few minutes past eleven o'clock. She wondered why he would even bother going to classes for only a couple of hours after all he'd been through the day before. Eva parked near the entrance and kept an eye out for the boy. She reminded herself not to blow up at him for holding back the information he had found while searching for his mother. But knowing more about who ran the mobile medical practice, for instance, could hold a hint to finding Paloma. How could he not realize every detail might be important?

She strangled the steering wheel and reminded herself to keep the anger she wanted to hurl in check. He might have merely forgotten to mention the clue that could lead to his elusive mother. But it had been ten days now since Kai had asked for her help. Cruz said Kai had mentioned the Winnebago two days ago. And Santiago had known about it since the first request to set up on the rez. Angry heat rose out of her collar. She figured the boy had withheld the crucial detail on purpose. Kai's uncle had some answering to do too.

Secrets caused damage. And sometimes they got people killed. Not that she didn't have her own that would never be told to anyone, not even Paloma. She kept her own counsel for the most personal details of her life. And chose not to ramble incessantly as so many of her generation did. Instead she listened and watched. SBD, "Silent but Deadly," had been her nickname at the academy, and she continued to wear the moniker well. Her stealthiness kept people guessing where she would appear next, and her bull's-eye accuracy at every range gained respect from the fiercest cops.

She smiled, remembering the first time her grandfather positioned what he called the squirrel-killing rifle, nearly as long as her, to her shoulder. Her first shot pierced the paper target, then the next and every try after. Her elder did a jig around her, whooping and pumping his arms. So proud.

Tears caused her sight to waver as she looked through the windshield and watched Hispanic, white, and Pueblo teens mingle and mess around. Some wore Taos Tigers sweatshirts and letterman jackets. Others shivered in their short sleeves. She wondered if their experiences were much like those she and Paloma had shared at the same age. She hoped not—because they'd been hell-raisers, along with Cruz, at that age.

He seemed to always be alone, and she wondered if his solitude was how Kai had managed to be awarded a full-ride biology scholarship to the University of New Mexico–Taos. Because of needing to care for Paloma, he had dropped out of high school before his senior year to help his mother during her dark days and darker nights. He studied the entire time he was officially out of school, even checked out books from the library and borrowed study materials from his classmates.

Single Star could usually be found looking down at the ground, gazing at what most thought were his feet. Eva and Paloma knew otherwise. The boy was always searching. First for the plants, then as he grew older, for the knowledge that would help him better understand the concept of life and living. The boy, undoubtedly brilliant, could be impossible to manage or even read. Most often the only thing offered would be stone-faced silence.

Fauna of every kind had fascinated Kai since childhood. The flora and herbs in relation to healing held his particular interest, and Eva always wondered if it was because during his grandmother's final days, riddled with cancer, she had cursed the "white man's poison," as she'd called it. Kai rarely left her bed in the family home for weeks at a time before his grandmother finally passed. A painful death, for her and all of those who adored her, including Eva.

The entire tribe had been proud when Kai announced his intent for college was to learn more about how to treat and cure disease and ailments using plants found on reservation lands all over the nation. Then a few years later Paloma fell into her pit of despair, and Kai's future became as questionable as his mother's. Now that he was back at school full time, and with no one else to keep him on track, Eva vowed he would be able to keep his scholarship and attend UNMT that fall.

Still a no-show. She checked the schedule photo again, then her watch, thinking maybe she got the end of class time wrong. When she looked back up, she spotted Kai. Head down, hoodie up, he walked with no one. Eva felt sad for the boy. She couldn't have imagined growing up without her friends. Then she remembered that she really didn't have anyone close in her life at the moment either. Certainly not like when she was Kai's age.

Paloma had always been her sidekick. Every day, Eva missed what they'd had a mere three years ago. What they were supposed to have now. Nothing about this was fair. First Ahiga's death, along with the three dancers from Paloma's group. Mourning the loss of her husband nearly put Paloma in the grave beside him. Then her friend's painful physical recovery. Her left leg had nearly been shorn off below the knee, and therapy had been halted when the new widow refused to leave her bed. Finally after a full week, Eva burst through the door and literally carried her friend's birdlike frame to the clinic.

The only words that got Paloma moving again was the warning she would never dance again if she didn't start working the now-atrophied muscles. Then the drugs took over, and the once-famous hoop dancer didn't even care about performing in front of adoring fans or making her people proud of her accomplishments.

Eva whirred down the passenger window, rolled ahead, and blocked Kai's path. So unaware he almost walked into the Rover.

"What are you doing here?"

"Picking you up. Let's go."

"Where?"

"Get in, I need to talk to your uncle about something."

"No. I told you I'm not going there."

"I need to ask him if he knows something that might help us find Paloma," she said, certain he would be intrigued.

Bait taken, Kai opened the door and tossed his backpack to the rear seat before sitting down. She pulled out of the pick-up lane and prepared to berate him for withholding information, then he said something that blasted all rational thought from her mind.

"I want to change my name," he said. "How do I do that?"

"What?" She turned to him, stunned, nearly bumping into the car jockeying for position beside her. "What's happened?"

"Kai's a pussy name."

"Your father insisted you be given a Navajo name. It honors him. Do you know what Kai means?"

"Willow tree. Lame."

"Doesn't have to be. The Pueblo people named you Single Star so you could shine bright. Light a path beyond even the darkest night. See farther than anyone's lessening words. Your father's first name, Ahiga, means 'fight.' And his last name—"

"Warlike," Kai cut in, spitting the word. "Uncle Santiago says I'm too much like my dad. 'Stupid Navajo isn't worth my spit. Lazy and ignorant.' I heard him tell my mom that a bunch of times."

"But he wasn't. Your dad was a good man. Gentle and kind. And you're more than the name he intended for you, too. Willow Tree is actually the perfect name, even though it's Navajo." She risked an amused smile he didn't return. "Willow trees on the Pueblo bend with the wind, provide protection from the elements, gift us with the ability to make beautiful baskets people all over the world have seen. Please, Kai. Don't be ashamed of your name. None of them. They all make you who you are. It's up to you to decide what path you will take for others to follow."

Kai looked at her for the first time. "No pressure, right?"

"Ha!" Eva said, now only a few minutes from the reservation. "We're Taos Pueblo. Everything we are is pressure." She pointed to the storm clouds that roiled in the north sky, gradient shades from white to the deepest gray. "Like those. The only release is rain, but it doesn't always reach the ground. Sometimes we only get the mad male energy of crazy wind. We Pueblos learn to live with the energy, whether there's a storm or just a pissing of moisture. We adapt. But the old ways go away hard. Your uncle doesn't think you're stupid. He's proud of you. Santi just doesn't know how to tell you."

"Because he's full of furious power and is batshit crazy."

A puff of surprised air burst from Eva's lips. "That's not exactly what I meant."

"Fits though."

It took her only a moment of thought before she said, "Yeah, you're right."

CHAPTER FIFTEEN
ALICE

Alice shifted the Winnebago to park, then sat there, surveying what she had claimed. It had taken her a week of driving the most remote areas of the reservation to finally discover the perfect location. When she had first found the ramshackle little place, she worried that someone would find her, and the tribal council would evict her for trespassing and ban her from the reservation. But night after night she became more confident when no one arrived to question her being there.

The two-bedroom, one Jack and Jill bathroom had become the perfect hideout. The only road that led to the property assured Alice that she would have plenty of time to lock up and hurry to the RV, as if awaiting a clinic visitor. She couldn't risk anyone questioning the property's upkeep and often had to remind herself to resist the urge to pull up the tall weeds from in front of the house and replace the most rotted boards on the porch. Although she would need to be careful where she stepped, Alice had always wanted a porch, and now she had one. The inside had fared better and only needed plywood to cover the bedroom windows and hasps and padlocks to secure the doors to keep the girls safe.

And the house had a little fireplace in the corner of the front room. She loved that detail, even though she hadn't dared to light a fire for fear someone would see smoke and become nosy.

The kitchen had been stripped of appliances, and no furniture remained in the front room. Over two weeks, careful about being identified, she purchased four single beds and frames and building materials from a town thirty minutes away. Toting the supplies had been a breeze with the RV, and no one seemed interested at all in the inconspicuous white woman who always paid in cash.

It looked like electricity hadn't been hooked up for years, so she purchased two portable generators for minimal power needs and to pump water to the house, grateful for the skills necessary to do so after helping her handyman father throughout her time living at home. Fortunately the late spring's mild weather didn't necessitate heat or cooling for now. She slept and made their meager meals at the cramped kitchen area in the motorhome, but if her experiments took longer than she expected, she would need to rethink the housing situation. No. She would not think about that. Because she would *not* fail next time.

Sitting there, she thought of the young woman named Kishi. She had been so frail that Alice hadn't even become winded while transporting the listless form to the RV. But first she dressed the woman in one of the ceremonial dresses she had found hanging in a Santa Fe shop. A magical find. The saleswoman said the supple leather frock had not actually been created by a Taos Pueblo seamstress, but every detail had been a perfect replica, down to the tips of real antlers that decorated the bodice. Alice marveled over the beautiful costumes every time she opened the closet to gaze at them on their hangers.

She had hoped the dresses would be for their celebration unveilings as she returned the healed, no longer drug-addicted women back to their people. Instead, the least favorite covering had been selected to hide the failure.

Finding out where Kishi's favorite place was located took less effort than she thought—merely a couple of packs of American Spirit cigarettes offered to an ancient Indian, skin weathered and lined so deep she had no idea how old he could be. The old man went on and on about the area where generations of Taos Pueblo's finest hunters discovered game that would feed their families and the tribe.

Alice's anger and frustration heightened the more she thought about how the drum maker's body had betrayed her. One could never know how someone would react to potent medications when even more illicit drugs were already in their system, right? And maybe the junkie's death was her own fault. Probably not even a reaction to what had been injected. She only wanted to help. To heal. And then the girl went and died on her. Fully enraged, when Alice had reached her destination, she had grabbed the woman by the hair and dragged her lifeless form deep into the trees.

As she sat behind the wheel, a switch flipped in Alice. Sorrow replaced her anger. Wet streaks ran down her cheeks. She sobbed, hiccupping gasps of air until she thought she might pass out. After a few minutes she managed to calm herself by imagining White Dove dressed in the very best of the ceremonial dresses, fringe dancing as she twirled.

"No more tears. You have to be strong for her," she scolded herself, balling her hands into fists so tight her fingernails jabbed her palms. She locked up the RV and walked to the house, feeling much older than her forty-eight years. After the third try she finally got the small key inside the front door's padlock.

As Alice entered the closest bedroom, she reminded herself to stay professional and focused. The jewelry maker didn't say a word. The younger woman had tucked herself in a tight fetal position. Thumb stuck in her mouth, she hummed the same scale of five notes over and over. Alice knew that shock had taken over the woman and that probably no amount of heroin would erase what the girl had witnessed by Alice's hand. She was supposed to find a cure. Instead, she had brought harm. Not even a mercy killing. But after seeing so many people die throughout and beyond the pandemic, even after the finest care she administered, Alice found it second nature to shut off the valve to caring.

She took in a deep cleansing breath and ripped the bedclothes off the now-vacant bed, stormed out of the room, and began to mentally prepare for round ten of the healing.

The jewelry maker's five-note tones continued. A mocking tone that continued long after Alice secured the door.

CHAPTER SIXTEEN
EVA

Butterflies launched in Eva's chest the moment she wheeled the Rover onto the rutted road that led to Paloma's original family home. Kai held a death clutch on the door handle, and she guessed he must be nervous too. She had no idea how long it could have been since the boy had visited his elder, but Paloma had been forbidden to cross the threshold of the generational dwelling for over two years.

Santiago had probably spotted the cloud of dust swirled by her silver Beast as Eva drove the half mile up his personal drive, because when they got close enough, she spotted him standing on his front porch. Stance open, one boot holding the screen door open, arms folded tight against his chest. A familiar pose that screamed, *I will take zero shit from you*. One she and Paloma had met more than a few times visiting Paloma's older brother growing up. Usually to get away from their strict parents, who had shooed them away for misbehaving. Santiago ruled with an iron fist wrapped in a feather. If pushed too far or feeling disrespected, he might raise a hand but would never once strike out. Silence and turning of his back was how he meted his punishment. Worse than a slap to Eva and Paloma, even Cruz. No one wanted to disappoint one of the most respected men of their people. Word had it even the tribe's war chief and governor sought wise counsel from Santiago "Hawk Soars" Mirabal.

"He looks mad," Kai said, zipping his hoodie up to his neck. "Did you tell him why we're coming?"

"Well . . . I didn't actually call."

"Maaan," he said, drawing out the word. "Not good."

"Stealth is always best when dealing with your uncle."

"At least he doesn't have his deer rifle aimed at us."

"True," she said, having witnessed that pose too.

She rolled to a stop in front of the sprawling ranch-style home. Both waited, buckled in, watching for some sign that it was okay to exit the vehicle.

"How long do we wait?" Kai asked.

"Long as it takes. Opening the door takes a while when it's been slammed shut."

"That was pretty good, O wise one," Kai mocked.

"I kinda liked it myself."

Eva kept her eyes trained on Paloma's brother, and after two full minutes, she detected the slightest of nods. "Okay, standoff is over," she said, releasing her seat belt. "You ready?"

"Not really."

Ignoring his hesitation, she exited the vehicle and headed up the porch steps. She looked back, miffed that Kai stayed near the vehicle. She gave him a stern look of silent urging, but still he didn't approach. His voice quavered a little when he said, "Uncle."

"Single Star." Santiago gestured to a smaller-scale replica of his house a few yards away. "New litter of pups are in the chicken shed."

The young man issued a boyish smile. "Really?"

"Their mother will let you play with them if you talk real sweet to her first."

No further encouragement needed, Kai headed for the little dwelling. Chickens protested and flapped their wings as he burst through the gathering of a dozen unsettled Rhode Island Reds and Lohmann Browns.

They both chuckled at the childlike manner, and Eva wondered if Santiago was transported back to when the boy would chase chicks and puppies as a toddler at that very spot.

He opened the screen door, gestured for Eva to enter the house, then followed her inside. The first thing she looked for was the work of art a renowned Pueblo artist had painted of Paloma at the height of her fame. Light-colored leather dress, fringe stopped midair, one moccasin-covered foot raised and ready to meet the other on the ground, hoops gathered in each hand. Full Warrior Woman pose, blessing and being blessed by and for their people. The piece had been featured in every Southwest magazine in print and online, even featured in the *Art in America* and *ARTnews* publications.

She did a full turn around the room, her heart sinking when she didn't see her friend captured in time long passed. And then, there it was. She spotted the edge of the frame and a third of the image, now hanging in the hallway that led to the bedrooms rather than above the fireplace. Relieved he had only moved it, rather than pitched it entirely, she let out a breath and got to the reason for the visit.

"What do you know about a mobile medical clinic?" she asked. "Supposed to be one here on the rez. Cruz told me Kai went there looking for Paloma."

Santiago pursed his lips. "Something not right about her."

"Paloma?"

"Of course. But I mean the woman who runs the clinic."

"A woman?" Eva frowned. She had expected him to say the clinician was a man. "What can you tell me about her?"

"Alice Jones. White. Late forties. Out of Texas. She presented a treatment plan to the council a couple months ago. Said she wouldn't charge us anything. Just wanted to help our people. We voted in favor. Figured why not give her a try. But hell, turns out even Tico won't see her about his gout."

Eva laughed. She knew all about Tico, the resident ninety-two-year-old hypochondriac, who regularly consulted everyone from healers to legit doctors all over the state for his various illnesses, and probably didn't even have gout.

"Why do you think something's not right about her? Did you run a background check?"

"Of course. No red flags. Nurse practitioner, licensed in a few states. She's legit."

"Did you get a bad feeling because she's a white woman trying to help us?"

He shrugged. "Seemed too eager. Can't miss that eyesore of a motorhome she's working out of. I know she got here—met with her the first day. Haven't seen her since the first week. Don't know if she's still on the rez or where she's parked the RV. Anyway, probably moved on. Good she's gone."

"What bothers you about her?" Santiago fell silent, a cue Eva knew not to push. But she needed answers, and even a hint of a revelation could lead her closer to Paloma—if she could get him to talk. "What aren't you saying, Santi?" she chanced in a low voice.

"A darkness follows her."

Before she could check herself, she said, "Darker than Paloma?"

Santiago turned to her, stone faced. "White Dove still flies in my heart. But she's not welcome in my home." He nodded to an elaborate hunting bow that now hung over the fireplace. "That belonged to the governor of the Pueblo in 1920. Porfirio Mirabal. Handed down to the firstborn males in my family for generations. Now under my care and responsibility to keep safe. Paloma stole it last year."

Eva resisted the urge to roll her eyes. She had heard the boastful provenance about the bow since she and Paloma were kids.

"Sold off to some collector in Santa Fe. Cost me a fortune to get it back."

Now Eva resisted the urge not to drop her jaw. She did not know this information. She dodged the uncomfortable revelation. "I know you miss the person Paloma used to be."

"You know nothing."

"You're probably right. But why punish Kai? He said he hasn't been invited here since his dad died."

"He's the boy of that Navajo who killed Rufina, Juliani, and Crucita. If Paloma had never met that man—" His words ceased, as if he thought finishing the sentence would take more power away from him.

"Everyone else loved Ahiga. He was a gentle giant . . . Like you in so many ways."

At that comment, Santiago snorted his disgust.

"Santi, the crash wasn't his fault."

"Maybe not."

Eva puffed out an exasperated breath. "I can't talk to you anymore." She stomped away, then changing her mind, strode back to him, hands clenched into fists. She warned herself to wait a beat before she said, "She's your sister. Kai's your direct blood. How is it so easy to turn your back? What you're doing is shameful. Everyone on the rez follows your example. You're a spokesman for the council . . . Maybe you're the one to blame."

He folded his arms tight across his chest, studied his boots, belligerence in his bearing.

Eva hoped she had embarrassed him. That maybe he realized this too.

"She broke my heart, Lightning Dance. Over and over."

Eva barely heard the words. Soft, tinged with agony.

She sensed the path they currently traveled would lead to a standoff. Stubborn was his go-to, and there would be no changing him. Even though they weren't actually related, Eva had spent nearly as much time with the man as Paloma had. She wanted his spiteful mask to drop so he could remember they were once close as uncle and niece. Nerves dried her tongue, and she had to clear her throat before she chanced the request she had been working up to.

"I want to ask a favor, brother." She softened her tone but didn't dare stroke his arm, as she wanted to. "Someone needs to keep an eye on Kai. A man, not me. A proper Pueblo he respects. Too many of our young men leave the rez. Set an example. Do the right thing. Take him in. He needs you."

No words. No expression. No alteration to his foreboding posture. "He's a man now."

"Yes. With no one to teach him to be one."

Eva heard Kai giggle beyond the screen door, then Kai charged out of the coop and nine pups bounded after their new leader. The boy dropped to the ground, and the excited balls of fur pounced and tumbled on him. They licked with abandon, and Eva chuckled at the sight. She glanced at Santiago's ever-so-slight grin, pleased to see the lead council member's attitude about his nephew shifting. Her taut muscles relaxed a bit.

"Word is the council will appoint a woman as the next police chief," he said.

A riff of surprise and excitement coursed through Eva. "No way."

"Way. You might have a chance on her force." He turned his full attention to Eva. "If you release Paloma."

Her excitement deflated the moment he issued the ultimatum. She gritted her teeth and warned herself not to spew the angry curses she wanted to hurl at him. He had every member of the tribe on his side, including whoever would take over for the outgoing police chief. For all she knew, the incoming top cop could be one of his long line of family members.

Before she could reply, Kai burst through the screen door, leaving the pups to whimper at the bottom step.

"Did you pick one?" Santiago asked.

Kai whirled to his uncle, surprise and hope on his face shining with puppy slobber. Eva, every bit as shocked, knew there was usually a two-year waiting list for Santiago's prized Belgian shepherd pups, valued for their innate abilities. Taos Pueblo PD even used the pups' sire to track people who wandered off trails or became lost in the woods, and a few times her own department had requisitioned the champion tracker to help recover two skiers buried under an avalanche on Kachina Peak at the nearby Taos Ski Valley.

"I can? I mean, you would give me one . . . sir?"

"You can help care for them while you're here. We'll see how one of them takes to you."

Kai's eyes widened, his jaw fell open, he slid his eyes to Eva.

"If that's what you want," she said. "You can always come back and stay with me . . . if you need to."

"Yeah—ummm—I mean, yes . . . Uncle—thank you—sir," he stammered.

"Settled then. You will take Paloma's old room."

"You mean like . . . now?"

"Got a big appointment or something?" Santiago asked.

"No, I just—"

"Check on Pearl. Those pups have been wearing her out."

"You got it," Kai said, rejoining the group anxiously waiting for him outside.

Eva asked when Kai ran out of earshot, "You'll make sure he stays put? He can be slippery."

"Advising me on how to raise a boy? I've got three of my own. Or did you forget." A statement, not a question. Throughout Eva's high school years, Santiago and his late wife had urged her to claim one of their strapping sons, who now rode the rodeo circuit nationwide. More brothers than romantic prospects, so she'd never given the possibility a single thought.

She stepped to the porch and turned back to see that Santiago had resumed his initial pose. "No, no," she said. "But this particular boy is determined to find his mother, and—"

"I'll keep him busy."

"Yeah, but don't make him rebuild your barn or drain the septic tank or—"

"You're wasting time. She needs you." He proceeded to shut the front door, no explanation for his ominous words. He had given her an ultimatum moments earlier. Now he wanted her to do whatever it took to find his sister?

Puzzled not for the first time by the conundrum of a man, Eva approached her vehicle, waved goodbye to the boy who didn't even look her way, then focused her attention to the what's next.

CHAPTER SEVENTEEN
KAI

Kai couldn't believe his luck. A sidekick. Something of his own. He ran his hands along the fluff of one pup, then another, until he had assessed every one's structure and muscle mass. The mother kept watch, ready to intervene if necessary. Nine possibilities. Seeing the mother dog in action, he couldn't help thinking about how long his own mom had been gone. He pushed the sad thought from his mind and turned to another regret.

He should have told Eva about the guns by now. Knew she would want to know. But he wasn't familiar with who was involved, and he hadn't actually seen them make anything. Also, he wasn't a snitch, even though those kids weren't his friends. No one was his friend. Not even the few rez kids he used to hang around with in middle school.

Everyone had their own drama, him most of all, and hanging out with a junkie's kid? Nope. Not gonna happen. And forget dating. Any girl he'd approached since sophomore year had gawked at him or ignored him altogether.

He was the weird kid who couldn't be relied on. Not as a teammate, or a lab partner, or even for a lunch companion. Kai had lived grown-up responsibilities for three years now. He couldn't even imagine any other kid at his school dealing with the heaping pile of steaming shit called his life.

Actually, he didn't know if anyone knew about his mother's addiction. But sometimes people would stare and whisper to each other when he walked past, so yeah, the whole school had probably figured it out. Rumors were another sport at the high school, and smack talk turned out to be true most of the time. Sometimes worse than reality, although not in Kai's case.

Visions of his mother on the couch, half-clothed, nodding off, needle forgotten in one hand, rubber tubing still wrapped around her arm. Middle of the day, higher than high. No food in a pot or even in the fridge. Kai had relied on neighbors to feed him the first year or so after his mom completely lost her mind and soul. Desperate for his recently dead father and nonexistent mother, he had dug his own hole and covered himself up. The second year of near abandonment, he reached out to no one, asked for nothing, relied on his wits to survive.

He reminded himself of the rez dogs that whizzed around the traditional village. No one owned them, but they always found a way to survive. Scrounging what they could, they ran from affection. Cowered when someone got too close, fearing no one could be trusted.

To Kai, it felt like Eva and Cruz were the only ones who hadn't given up on him or his mom. She would show up with boxes of food. Cereal and milk and his favorite ramen soup and Oreos. Somehow the power stayed on, and he figured Eva would be the one to thank for that. But he never had.

He felt stupid about what happened on the bridge yesterday. And ashamed that Eva had been the one to find him there. Even thinking about it made him break out in sweats and made his hands shake. So lost in missing his mom—and useless about not being able to find her, and believing deep down she was dead—he didn't even know how he'd made it there. And then there was the only person in the world who loved his mother as much as he did, saving him. And now she was in the thick of it. He'd made sure of that. Eva made a promise and had never let him down before.

The worrisome thought about the 3D printed guns returned, and he chastised himself again. The only reason he could think of not telling Eva was because he didn't want her to lose interest in finding his mom. He wanted the cop, above everything else, to bring her back to him. Not knowing if she was unsafe, or lost, or lonely, or worse tore at him day and night.

This must be what it's like to have a kid, he had thought so many times before. The once-confident woman all eyes followed when she'd entered a room had now been abandoned by almost everyone. He missed her. Phantom hands squeezed his heart until he thought he would pass out.

Needing the comfort, he took up the one curious pup that hadn't left his side, cradled the chubby body to his chest, and inhaled the sweetness at its neck. The scent of a field of clover after a spring rain captivated him. He closed his eyes and imagined his mother there with him. She would love this little guy. So he would, too, he decided right then.

"I'm naming you Shadow. You're mine now, okay?"

The little creature raised its head, licked Kai on the nose, then settled back against his new friend. He giggled, and the other pups trundled over to weave around his legs.

He issued a silent thank-you to the spirits that had softened his uncle's heart. He really did want to stay at the family home. Had always loved going there as a kid. He lifted his gaze to the house to see Santiago watching him from behind the screen door. Stance and demeanor now relaxed, he looked like the fun guy who would take him fishing and taught him how to shoot a rifle.

Kai turned back to Shadow, heart calm for the first time since he could remember. No longer alone.

CHAPTER EIGHTEEN
EVA

Relieved that Santiago would make sure Kai wouldn't go off again to hunt for his mother on his own, Eva's mind whirled with possibilities of how she should proceed. Having nothing definitive, and no real evidence to follow, forced her to alter her thought process. The pivot had worked before—to consider possibilities in a different manner rather than focus on what looked to be evident. In her experience as a cop, obvious clues rarely turned out to be conclusive. The mobile clinic could hold a key, and she would keep an eye open, but the chances of spotting the RV were miniscule with so many rez acres to cover.

Instead, she followed Cruz's advice and called her dispatcher to implement a BOLO for the Winnebago in question. The request wouldn't be official and therefore probably wouldn't even be heeded. Still, she felt better releasing the crumb of possibility to the universe.

Unwilling to pause for a meal, she munched a stale granola bar she dug out of the glove box. No particular destination came to mind, but driving helped her think. Her brain spun at tornado speed as the high desert plateau whizzed by. Still no clear ideas came to her. She decided to pull off the main road and try her search for clarity on reservation land.

She swayed in the seat as she dodged divots in a one-lane unpaved track so rough that a few times she needed to shift to four-wheel drive for the most treacherous areas of the washed-out road. Twenty unnerving minutes later, she pulled under a grove of trees at the base of the Sangre de Cristo Mountains and parked. Leaves danced, and she felt calm for the first time in ten days.

She forced a few cleansing breaths in and out, then took on an objective mental state. Four women. Paloma, always a leader. Three followers. All addicts, known to party together often. She recalled how their lives had been before the downfall, when drugs became their only ambition. Once all talented. Skills beyond the norm. Successful moneymakers for themselves and the tribe. Paloma alone had raised tens of thousands of dollars during her career as a hoop dancer, winning more awards and prize money than any female in history.

Dora created the most exquisite jewelry Eva had ever seen at any of the village's shops on the reservation, or in Taos, or even Santa Fe.

And Tonita, Paloma's cousin, wove elaborate baskets. Some followed the traditional patterns, but, much to the elders' tongue clucking, she had made each design her own.

The third woman was Eva's favorite musician and instrument maker. Kishi Rayna created traditional drums, from hand size for children to ceremonial drums three feet tall. A proficient hunter, Kishi followed the customs Pueblo drum makers had adhered to for generations: fell the deer or elk by bow and arrow, skin and treat the hides, then stretch the leather over willow branch frames and paint symbols passed down by the people on the sides. Every element found and crafted on the reservation.

The hunting grounds were on sovereign land, deep in the mountains beyond the village and most of the remote homes on the rez, on the way to the Taos Ski Valley slopes. Not far from where she'd parked.

She had zero authority to execute a formal investigation on any of the land. She considered calling Cruz Romero, knowing she probably should contact someone in authority to accompany her if she actually found anything that could help find the women. But she was 100 percent full-blooded Taos Pueblo, and this land was as much hers as even the most elite members of the tribal council and leadership. Just like what Paloma had encountered, it seemed everywhere Eva went on the rez, men and women alike would avoid her eyes, or openly stare and glare, or ignore her altogether. She had heard rumors thirdhand about untruths and hurtful comments no one bothered to temper. Some figured she was also a drug addict, or because she was a sheriff's deputy, *she* provided the drugs to Paloma from seizures that had never even happened. It had been her decision alone not to stay on the rez and to find work that didn't always follow customary beliefs. She had turned her back because they had shunned the only living person she had left. Paloma. Still, in Eva's heart and being, the land of her people was home. Always would be.

A magpie screeched, and she turned to the bird that had lit on a nearby fence post, reminding her of her own Spirit Guide. She studied the black-and-white winged creature a moment, then lifted her vision to the mountain range through the windshield. A sense of foreboding swept over her as she imagined the area. A sensation that had kept her alive on more than a few occasions. One she never ignored. And she knew exactly where she needed to go. She thanked the magpie for keeping her on point, fired up the Rover, and headed north.

She passed the turnoff that led to the main village and took a right at an unmarked road. She lost track of time while she drove until, fully on the mountain, she arrived at an area open enough to turn a large vehicle around alongside a stand of piñons. She got out of her Beast and began to walk. The place was a well-known hunting spot, and she wondered if back in the day, her grandfather had successfully stalked deer and elk to help feed the tribe right where she stood. Years ago she had visited the same area with Santiago to hunt wild pheasant and turkeys for a feast day. A lifetime ago. She recognized nothing.

Frustration mounted. The past two days had been more hectic than the past two months. A few times she had considered taking notes to keep herself focused, then something else that needed to be urgently addressed would come up before she could jot down a single thing.

A niggling that wouldn't go away pursued her as she walked and paged through her memory, starting when she woke up that morning. Then it came to her. The guns. She had forgotten to ask Kai about the 3D printed gun frame found at the school. She slapped her leg and wondered what else she had forgotten to pay attention to. Little to no sleep over the past ten days had been brutal, and she hadn't taken care of herself. She sent another round of appreciative thoughts to Santiago for making sure Kai would be seen after, rather than under her pathetic care.

Still unsure of what had called her to this particular place, she shirked off her annoyance and strode deeper into the trees. Pine cones crunched under her boots. The area felt otherworldly. No birds chirped here. A shiver traveled the length of her left arm.

Something colorful halted her steps. She crouched down and frowned at the small, round bright-yellow item, took out her phone, and clicked off a few photos, then stuck a six-inch-long piece of tree branch in the ground to locate the item later if necessary. A step farther, she spotted a round red item, then green and another yellow. Beads, she realized.

Distracted, she almost tripped on a fallen limb. Hands out to break the fall, she looked down and puzzled over side-by-side trenches that had disturbed the forest detritus. Another cautious step ahead and she spotted a deeper parallel track.

Something ahead didn't look right. An object lay atop the dead pine needles. At first Eva thought a discarded doe or fawn. Trepidation tapped an uneasy rhythm in her chest. Training ingrained in her, on or off duty, she looked down to make sure she didn't tread on anything out of place as she moved forward.

Ten yards away now. Breaths caught in Eva's throat. A buzz in her ears cranked up in volume. Her heartbeat stuttered. Chills traveled her entire body. She wanted—needed—to run, but she couldn't process how to even move.

As she eased closer, her worst fears became reality. A woman. Face up, long filthy hair covered her face, hiding her identity. A traditional ceremonial outfit permitted on the reservation only for special occasions covered her emaciated body.

This was neither special, nor an occasion.

CHAPTER NINETEEN
EVA

Eva eased her eyes closed and whispered, "Please, spirits. Be kind. Don't let this be Paloma. Please, please, please." She opened her eyes and took one cautious step after the other. She subconsciously placed her hand on her left bicep, to the tattoo that would be a mirror opposite to Paloma's. Heart pounding, she took careful footfalls, eyes on the ground in search of potential evidence as she approached the lifeless form.

Nothing stood out as inconsistent to the area. No litter or cigarette butts that could be considered evidence. She made a wide circuit around the area, then returned to where she began. She sent a blessing up to the universe and asked permission to approach her fallen sister. She waited a full minute, then proceeded, ears attuned for any ominous warnings to move along.

She reached the body and lowered to a crouch. Using her knuckle, she swept a hank of tangled hair free from the face, to reveal a grotesque mask of swollen and torn flesh. The woman would need more definitive verification, but Eva was certain who the body belonged to. Not Paloma. She released a grateful sob and placed the hair back in the same position.

Somehow she managed to get back to her Rover. She took up her portable radio from the cup holder and keyed the handset. "Dispatch, Sierra-Ten-Twelve."

"Copy, S-Ten-Twelve, go ahead."

"I've got a body. Foothills of the mountain, not far from the ski slopes."

"Copy. Reservation land?"

"Uncertain. Request you notify TPPD to verify?"

"Copy. Can you text me your coordinates?"

Not an odd request, given Eva and the dispatcher were among only five women on the force. They had often sent messages of support and solidarity. "Will do. Please specify Cruz Romero to assist?"

"Copy," the dispatcher said, voice low and full of concern.

"Sierra-Ten-Twelve, out," Eva said, then clipped the radio to the waistband at the back of her jeans and switched to autopilot.

She took out her evidence kit and digital camera from the cargo area, opened one of the compartments, and managed to struggle on one latex glove, hand shaking so hard she nearly ripped the opposite covering.

By rote, she began to catalog whatever seemed out of place or incongruous that could possibly be introduced in court, if necessary. Focused on her tasks, camera clicking, she barely registered a car's approach.

She raised her head to the Taos Pueblo Police Department SUV making its way to her at a perilous clip. She checked her watch, stunned to see that nearly an hour had passed. Relieved to see Cruz behind the wheel, she made a wide berth from the body to where he parked, next to her Rover.

"You caught a body call too?" Cruz asked. He held back at his vehicle when he got out, as if hoping the heads-up had been bogus.

"I called it in." She dropped her head, still ashamed about the relief when she'd discovered the woman wasn't their friend. "She's Pueblo, Cruz."

He winced. "Paloma?"

She shook her head. The name she needed to speak would be familiar to him—the woman known to their people as Fox Whisperer. A fitting name. Kishi had been coy and a rebel since childhood. She had learned the art of drum making from her father, who had learned the craft passed down by no one quite knew how many generations of men.

She waited for him to prepare. "Kishi Reyna."

"Noooo," he whispered. He cast a glare to the sky, then took a few steps toward Eva. "Elisio's girl?"

She nodded. Elisio, one of the best-known elders of the tribe, still lived in one of the original homes of the village.

"Overdose?"

Eva shrugged, but she knew. This was no accident. "Suspicious, I don't think she got here by herself. I hate like hell to have you here."

"She's one of us. Tribal's got to be involved."

Police procedure could get tricky given that three arms of law enforcement covered the area. And the FBI may even need to be called in. Eva chose to ignore any mention of the feds stepping on rez land. No one would want that. Instead, she told him what she had thought the moment she'd moved close enough to take in the entire scene. "Do you see anything strange about what she's wearing?"

He looked to where Eva pointed. "Traditional ceremonial dress," Cruz said. "Am I missing something?"

"It's a knockoff."

"How can you tell?"

"The stitches are too perfect. Not sewn by hand. Moccasins are too fancy." She leaned in and pointed to the material on the back of the outfit. "And look, the beads are stuck on with Super Glue. The Pueblos who make these gowns use elk or deer hooves to make the glue. It's amber in color. Really sticky. Have to know what you're doing to make the design look right. These are too uniform."

"I've heard of fake keepsakes being sold in Santa Fe," Cruz said. "And a lot of the crap comes from China. Disgraceful."

"Anyway, Kishi wouldn't be caught dead in a dress. Only pants for her. Even as a kid. Remember when elders threatened to cancel her appearance at a festival because she wouldn't wear traditional clothes?"

Cruz let out a light chuckle. "She said she would take back every drum she ever made and burn them in the buffalo field."

Eva made a full turn and frowned. "To make things more complicated, I'm not sure if this is rez land, or beyond the county boundary. Do you know?"

He assessed the area, north and then south. "I think she's on both."

"What?"

"Pretty sure the county line runs right through where she is." He pointed to remnants of fence posts linked by barbed wire. "That's the county line. Hunters cut this fence as soon as we repair it. Shortcut to and from the road and a straight shot to grazing land. Good killing grounds here." He winced, obviously regretting his choice of words.

So as not to embarrass him further, she didn't dwell on his faux pas. Instead, she said, "I hadn't noticed that. Good catch."

"I was right here last season," he muttered. "There's a blind beyond the trail over there. Think she was trying to reach it? Maybe high and disoriented, looking for shelter from the weather?"

"I don't think she walked here. Didn't notice any footprints or tire tracks." She hitched a thumb toward where she had parked her Rover. "Looks like drag marks start at the open area." She turned her full attention to Cruz so she could read his expression when she said, "This whole thing has been staged. I'm sure of it."

"You think she was forced here," he said, a statement rather than a question.

She shrugged but nodded to the gruesome bloody bald area the circumference of the palm of her hand. "Look at the side of her head. Possibly a fatal injury, and body placement doesn't look accidental."

"I agree."

"Could you make sure I didn't miss anything to take photos of?"

Cruz complied, crouching low and crab-walking a few feet away, eyes on the ground. He hummed a low non-song as he concentrated, a habit that had amused her since childhood. This time, the chant-like notes soothed Eva.

"What about that?"

Careful where she walked, she stood behind Cruz and checked over his shoulder. She raised the camera draped around her neck and snapped a few shots of the tip of an antler. "Got it. Probably from detail work on the front of the dress."

They returned to the corpse. He knelt down, outstretched his hand. "Don't touch her," Eva warned. "We need to wait for the forensics team."

"My land, my call." He looked at her over his shoulder, eyes glistening. "I need to personally verify who it is."

She felt his pain. This was their girl. No one but them should touch her. But this was how offenders escaped punishment, and she would not risk that for this woman. She reached out and took hold of his shirt. "Cruz. Stop."

He stood, frustration clear on his face. "All right. Fine. You're right."

"Do you think she got here on her own?"

Cruz shrugged. "Do you?"

"I say no, but the cop in me says we need to stay objective. Let the evidence do the deciding."

Eva relaxed her combative stance and detected the sounds of a woodpecker that tapped at a tree and doves that shared mournful coos.

Disengaged now, Eva set her vision to laser mode. She started at the feet, covered in filthy knee-length moccasin boots, scanned over the dirt-encrusted kneecaps and scuffed front of the dress, verified that a few antler tips were ripped from the bodice. She avoided studying the face and focused back on the hands. "Puncture wounds, top of the right hand."

"Could be the only viable veins to shoot the heroin," he said.

"Maybe. Lots of bruising around the site though."

"Probably took more than one stick. Don't read anything into it. Addicts try whatever access point that's worked before."

Knowing how fast news spread by moccasin telegraph on the rez, she asked him, "Can you give me an hour before you transmit the identity? I don't want Kai or Santi to hear about this from anyone but me."

Cruz glanced at the Swiss Army watch Eva had gifted him for his twentieth birthday, now scratched and scuffed. She couldn't remember ever not seeing the moon-phase timepiece strapped to his wrist. "One hour. That's all I can guarantee."

"Thanks, Cruz."

"I don't envy you. The kid's gonna freak."

"And the big man is gonna be pissed."

"Might wanna stay on the porch. He won't want the darkness in his house."

Darkness. The same word Santiago had spoken earlier that day. Hours ago felt like a week to Eva.

"What time will you notify Kishi's family?" she asked.

"Let's give Elisio the rest of the day. Need to make sure someone will be there for him."

"I'll join you—"

"No need. I can take care of it. He's still got a sister at the village."

"I want to be there, Cruz."

The cop hesitated and looked away. "Yeah, but they may not want you there."

Taken aback, she asked, "Why would you say that?"

"They already blame Paloma for leading Kishi off her path."

"And because I'm Paloma's friend, you think they'll turn on me?"

"I think now isn't the time to find out," Cruz said. "I'm certified on death notification. I'll be the one to talk to the family."

Although perturbed, Eva sighed her agreement and let the subject pass. She knew Cruz was right, and they had more pressing matters to figure out. She ran a list of what would need to happen next, and yet her mind kept going back to how she would break the news to Kai and Santiago.

"Since she could be on county *and* rez land, both of our agencies have jurisdiction," Eva said. "But my department has more resources. I'll call in my unit for forensics, and the medical examiner in Albuquerque. He's a friend. Hopefully he'll come here so Kishi won't be far from home."

Cruz let out a relieved breath.

"Let me know when they get here. I'll try to hurry back from Santiago's."

She touched her fingertips to Cruz's and returned to her Rover. From behind the steering wheel she watched her friend snap off a twig from the limb of a young ponderosa pine beside him. He spoke silent words to the cutting, then waved the cluster of needles in a circular motion, careful not to touch the body.

She sent up her own blessing as she turned the Beast around and went back down the mountain. There would be no comfort this evening, for anyone Eva knew or had ever met on the reservation. The death of a female Pueblo in her prime always hit the tribe particularly hard. She would bear no children. Stories and memories only she knew would be lost forever. No more drums would be made by her hands. And although the people had all but washed their hands free of the junkie's harsh treatment and lies and deceit, their daughter would no longer whisper with the foxes.

Time had at first decelerated to slow motion when she'd found the body, but now, before she realized it, she was off the mountain and turning on to the main road toward town.

Questions buzzed Eva's mind. The biggest one: Why would anyone kill the woman? In her experience, that answer was hardly ever adequately revealed. And so she turned her thoughts to the overall part of the puzzle that needed to be solved: *Who* did this?

"I will find out," she promised Kishi "Fox Whisperer" Reyna. "And they will pay."

CHAPTER TWENTY
DORA

As usual—Dora had lost count of the number of days—she woke up disoriented. When she wriggled to a more comfortable position, she puzzled over the crinkling noise that came from under the fitted sheet. Plastic, she realized, then peeked over the edge of the mattress. A thick piece of it surrounded her bed too.

The stink of bleach stung her nostrils. She winced and swiped the cuff of a nightgown she didn't recognize across her nose. Confused again, she realized the nurse must have changed her clothes and cleaned up in here. When that had happened, she had no idea.

She sat up, and the room spun. Hand to the bedside table to brace herself, she almost swept a fresh sandwich on a paper plate and a container of chocolate meal supplement to the floor. Dora hoped to never see or smell peanut butter ever again. Resigned that this would be the only food offered, she forced down the first bite and chased it with a gulp of Ensure. Old people's drink, she had called it when her grandma had turned eighty and didn't have a single tooth in her mouth. The drink had kept her elder alive for years, now it kept Dora going. Her head spun as she chewed, and she felt eighty too.

"Did you eat?" she asked Kishi. When no answer came, she squinted her eyes to see across the room. Her friend's bed was made, sheets and quilt pulled taut. The pillow even looked plumped and ready for the drum maker to come back.

She ate as much as she could stomach and polished off the drink, then the urge to urinate became too urgent to ignore.

"Are you in the bathroom? I need to go." Still no reply.

Dora stood and her vision whirled so fast she had to bend her knees to keep from toppling forward. Hand on the rolling IV pole, she shuffled the short distance that felt like a mile to the bathroom. The last time she had flipped the light switch and the bright bulb above the sink had nearly blinded her, so she didn't risk that shock again. Anyway, even though there wasn't a mirror in there, she didn't want to imagine what she looked like.

Hand outstretched, she swept the air until she reached the commode. No Kishi. She finished and washed up and returned to her mattress, where plastic crinkled under her feet again. For a brief moment she wondered what her little sister would be doing right now. And if her mother had ever found the iron skillet she'd been searching for. More illogical thoughts buzzed around and around, as fast as Paloma's hoop dance moves. Before everything good and real disappeared.

But the drugs had been primo here, so that wasn't so bad. She smiled, anticipating another round of relief. Then a craving slammed her so hard she drew her legs up to her chest and clenched her teeth. Early on, Paloma had taught her a trick that worked every time as they waited for the dealer to provide their rescue.

She squeezed her eyes shut and imagined standing on the bank of the Rio Grande, the Gorge Bridge hundreds of feet above her. A mini tornado of wind blew her long hair. She plunged her hands in the water and sifted small stones under the surface. The feel of the volcanic rocks, smooth from ages of being tumbled in the current that rumbled in her ears. Minnow-size fish darting at her bare feet as she walked through shallow pockets of water that glistened in the sun.

Then she imagined the jewelry design she would create. Her mind sorted out red- and green-tinted stones first, followed by a dozen shades of tan and gray. Excitement tapped her breastbone, a flutter of creativity she hadn't felt so clearly in two years or more. Ever since . . . "No. Don't go to the past. What's done is done. This is a blip." The voice, faint in her ears, sounded familiar but issued from an ancient person's mouth.

She looked around and saw no one in the room but her.

CHAPTER
TWENTY-ONE
EVA

After picking up Kai's belongings from her house, still stinging from Cruz's words about her not accompanying him for the death notification and not relishing the task ahead, Eva wished she had time to stop by her grandfather's house. She needed a little escape right now, but the last time had made her sad for days after. Knee-high weeds had blocked the path to the rickety front porch, where her only remaining relative would tell her stories about when he was a child growing up in the main village, and how every year he helped the families who lived in the North and South Houses spread mud over the structures to keep the interiors warm in the winter and cool during the summer months. In the back of her mind, she always thought—no, hoped—that she would one day fix up the place and claim it as her own.

The scent of pine logs popping in the beehive fireplace and the squeak of the seven boards she would tiptoe to avoid in search of midnight snacks or hidden birthday presents flooded her memory. She hadn't even minded the tiny Jack and Jill bathroom between the two bedrooms. Except when she had to relieve herself in the middle of the night, afraid she would bump into her grandfather with the same need.

Eva and her elder's decision to live together had come without warning, when her parents couldn't find work locally and decided the time had come for them to move off the reservation. They'd packed up the pottery wheels and boxes of clay in their beat-up pickup, returned their house keys to the tribal council office, dropped twelve-year-old Eva off at her mother's father's tiny adobe dwelling at the foothills of the mountain, then headed to Santa Fe, where they remained to this day.

She had been eighteen when her grandfather passed. Same age as Kai now. She knew what he faced if she wasn't able to fulfill her promise.

She thought back to him sitting on the Gorge Bridge. His position precarious. Unaware of his surroundings and maybe even of what was going on inside his own mind and body.

The words she would speak needed to be confident. Assure the boy nothing had changed, that she would find his mother. No doubt behind her tone. She rounded the final bend and caught sight of the boy in the distance, excited puppies weaving figure eights around his legs. She hit the brakes, skidding up a cloud of dust.

Doubt and fear captured her. All of her momentary confidence swirled away, trapped in the dusty cyclone the Beast had kicked up.

CHAPTER TWENTY-TWO
KAI

Kai dodged the pups that wove around his feet in the open area of the chicken coop. He couldn't remember the last time he'd been this carefree. Happy, even. There were entire blocks of time, when he played with Shadow and his littermates, where worry about his mother evaporated. He had begun to warm up to the idea of staying at his uncle's house. He would have a comfortable bed, fridge and cabinets stocked with snacks and treats, an actual hot meal in the evening. Best of all, Shadow, who had captured his heart completely.

He spotted the dust from his uncle's private road before he could make out the type of vehicle that caused the disturbance. It stayed there for more than a minute before the driver again proceeded closer. He froze. Eva's Rover, he realized. They hadn't expected her to return before dark. She needed to be out there looking for his mom. He cursed under his breath, angry that he hadn't insisted she take him with her. At first he had been relieved to hand the responsibility to someone else. Thought Eva would stay focused—that she wanted to find his mom as much as he did. But no, here she came after only a few hours.

The faint screech of the screen door alerted Kai that his uncle was also aware that Eva had arrived. It took Eva a few minutes to get out of her vehicle, and then she didn't say anything, just stood there by the Beast and stared at him, making him nervous. The late-afternoon sunlight reflected off a tear that slid down her cheek. He had never seen Eva cry, and that made him worry even more.

He looked down. Shadow sat on one of his feet, looking up at him, head cocked. Kai picked up the shepherd, cradled him, stroked his ear. The puppy let out a faint whimper, or maybe *he* actually made the pitiful sound. He wasn't sure. About anything anymore, because his mother's best friend's face couldn't mask the sorrow he detected without her uttering a single word.

He wanted to run. Tuck the puppy under his arm like a football and go. Anywhere but here. He lowered to a sprinter's stance and caught sight of his uncle standing on the porch. The elder wore the same expression as Eva.

Nowhere to go but forward, Kai took one step, then another, until he reached what he knew would now be his future.

CHAPTER TWENTY-THREE
EVA

Eva broke Kai's gaze and swiped away a tear she hoped he hadn't noticed. She went to the back of her Rover and took out the duffel that contained his belongings she had repacked. Santiago bounded down the steps and took the bag from her. He didn't ask, but his eyes pleaded to know the news she had come to deliver. Kai approached, one of the pups in his arms.

"Is it true?" Santiago asked.

She drilled the older man with a glare. When she didn't answer, Kai asked, "Is what true?"

"Kishi. Is she the dead Pueblo woman?"

Eva whirled on him, shocked that he would be so blunt without warning, especially in front of Kai. "Who told you—"

"There are no secrets around here. Have you been gone so long you don't remember? Or don't you consider yourself Taos Pueblo anymore?"

"How can you say that?" Eva shouted, stung to her core. "I'm as much Pueblo as you. Just because I don't live on the rez right now doesn't mean I don't deserve your respect."

"Wait," Kai said, sounding confused. "Wait! Do you mean the drum maker? Mom's friend? She's . . . dead?"

Both adults glared at each other, then she turned to the younger man. "I'm sorry, Kai. I didn't want you to find out like this."

"Don't coddle him," Santiago snapped.

"He's not one of your puppies, Santi."

Santiago hurled another glare her way, turned on his heel, and stormed toward the house. His boots thumped on the floorboards, then he slammed the front door shut. The puppy whimpered at the commotion. Kai sat on one of the porch steps and huddled over the anxious dog in his arms. He clucked his tongue and spoke a few calming words.

"Did you name him yet?" she asked.

"Shadow."

"I like that."

"Think he'll let me keep him?"

"Sounded like it."

"He changes his mind sometimes."

"We'll make sure he doesn't this time."

The words seemed to reassure the boy, and she felt comfortable enough to ask the questions that had been burdening her. She mentally prepared herself for what would be an uncomfortable conversation for them both, if he would cooperate at all.

"Why did you do it?" Eva finally had the courage to ask. He furrowed his brow, looking confused. "The bridge," she reminded him.

Kai sucked in a breath of air. Eyes wide, he seemed to have forgotten his death-defying perch above the river until she mentioned it. He turned his head and buried his face in the pup's neck.

She reminded herself to give him a chance to explain. She had never been so terrified as when she'd realized the kid on the railing was this boy next to her. She hoped he was ashamed enough not to try that terrifying nonsense again. Giving up was not an option, even when everything seemed to be lost. Which, she supposed, he probably thought to be the case.

"You sat on the north side of the bridge. If you chose the south side, toward the reservation, spirits could have paid attention to your vibrations. You have family buried in the rez graveyard whose crosses have fallen. They would have helped. I don't believe you would intentionally want to betray them."

Kai remained mute as Eva recalled the first time her grandfather had told her about the crosses against the graveyard ruins of the original church tower. *Why are those crosses stacked against the wall?* she had asked during a visit to the site when she was twelve.

The crosses are never taken from the gravesite, her grandfather replied. *When a cross falls, it means the spirit is released and no longer in the cemetery.*

Where does it go?

Wherever it wants, Lightning Dance. That's the blessing. They're always watching.

At first the explanation had worried her, that every fallen cross represented someone who could see her whenever they wanted. She thought of her grandmother and looked to where her grandfather had pointed. Where her cross once stood, now stacked somewhere in the pile with other souls released from the area. But then she felt comforted, knowing she now had an explanation of why she sometimes felt an unexplained presence join her.

When no words came from Kai, she pushed a little harder. "Because it was a choice, right? Were you hiding from the spirits? Or have you given up on our people completely?"

"I was embarrassed," he said, his voice so low she had to lean closer to him. "I didn't even know where I was going. It's like I blacked out and just found myself there. And then my butt started to hurt from sitting on the railing." A faint shudder rippled his hoodie. "I threw my bike over the edge. Wanted to see how big my splash would be. Stupid."

Another thing of the boy's gone. By his own hands this time. Fear pinged again. His choices screamed he had nothing to lose. "Stop that. Last thing you are is stupid."

"Yeah, but what I did was. All of it. I'm sorry, Auntie."

"Well, I'm sorry I didn't see how much you were going through. I got all wrapped in my own worries and let you down."

"Feels bad, doesn't it? Not to be understood," he continued. "To assume someone knows everything about you when they don't really know a damned thing."

His harsh tone surprised her. She had hoped they were past the hard feelings and rounding the bend to healing. But no, his frustration still burned, and she wasn't sure if words would tame or stoke the fire.

Eva had no idea how to respond to what she often thought herself. After a moment she nodded. The silent response seemed to appease him. His shoulders relaxed, and he set the puppy down beside them. She stroked the soft fur and smiled when it rolled on its back for her to scratch his belly.

She wanted to stay like this, sweet animal to pet, a light breeze swaying the leaves in the massive tree that shaded the chicken house and kicked up the scent of rosemary from the planter beside them, enjoy Kai's silent company. Instead, he broke the pleasurable moment, crushing her all over again.

"Kishi went missing the same time as Mom. They were together." The color drained from his face as realization hit him. "Do you think she's dead too?"

The last thing Eva wanted was for the boy's mind to spin in the same direction hers whirled. She pondered what to say. Her grandfather's spirit whispered a single word in her ear. *Truth.* And so she followed her elder's instruction. She could only pray the young Pueblo would not be broken by it.

"I won't lie, but I also won't go into gruesome details about Kishi, so please don't ask me." She pushed away the vision of the woman's mistreated body as it flashed in her mind. "Kishi was last seen with Paloma, so she could be next. The clock is ticking. Your mom and the others have been gone twelve days, and I'm still in the dark. I need all the help I can get."

"What can I do?"

She took hold of his arm, tight enough for him to realize she meant business when she said, "You can tell me why you've been holding out on me."

He turned to her, puzzled.

"Don't give me that innocent look. I'm not messing around here. Tell me."

"Tell you what?" he asked.

"Everything you haven't told me."

He pulled his arm away and avoided her gaze. "I don't know what you're talking about."

"The mobile medical clinic. You told Officer Romero about it. And your uncle is aware of it, too. Why didn't you tell me about this?"

"I honestly didn't think to. Didn't think it mattered. I thought Mom would have tried to get drugs there. Maybe even steal them. But the woman said she'd never seen her."

"And you didn't think I would want to know this? Kai, my every waking minute, for days, has been about finding your mother. I need to know everything you've found or figured out on your own. We're a team, remember? You insisted."

"Yeah, like you're telling me everything you know? Doubt it."

"That's different. Some of what I've found, or will find, could be evidence for court if—" She stopped her words in time before she caused any more harm.

They both kept silent a full few minutes, before Kai asked, "Did you tell Uncle? About me on the bridge?"

"No. But you know he knows by now."

"Guess I should keep my bag packed. He won't want a loser in his house."

"I really need you to stop belittling yourself. Yes, your life right now blows massive chunks, and you're in pain and worried and a bazillion other things are going through your mind and body right now. But you do have something to look forward to. And I don't mean welcoming your mother back when we find her."

"What, then?"

"College, baby!" She nudged his shoulder, an attempt to lighten him up. "UNM Taos will change your life. Alter you in ways you can't even fathom."

"We'll see."

"Oh, we'll do more than *see*, young man. You are going. Your scholarship is secured, and nothing will keep you from attending your first classes in the fall. This is huge, Kai. Even your uncle Santiago didn't go to college, and look at him. Big man, even without a degree. Imagine how important you'll be once you graduate. What you'll achieve will change the lives of your people and other tribes everywhere. There's no stopping now."

After a moment a slow smile turned up his lips. "It is a pretty big deal."

"Yes, it is. No more regrets, okay? Clean slate, starting now." She held an open hand out to him. "Deal?"

He met her hand, and Shadow licked their interlocked fingers, sealing their pact.

CHAPTER TWENTY-FOUR

ALICE

Alice pulled back the curtain over the little window of the RV. Atmosphere dark and still, a half moon's light bathed the area between the motorhome and the house. She felt too apprehensive about falling asleep so early, worried the drum maker would appear in her dreams. She fired up the Winnebago's stove and put the camping-size percolator on the burner to warm up the remaining coffee she had brewed hours ago.

Still stinging from the failure of losing a patient, she took out the list of concoction possibilities. Chemistry, art as much as science in her estimation, required an agile mind, and she found her own lacking lately.

The only thought that brought her comfort was the knowledge that she still had two patients to test her theories on. She would not, however, endanger White Dove. Not for the first time, she warned herself to merely keep the dancer comfortable, as she tamped down the thought that surely someone would be looking for the women. And for her too.

She hadn't even checked in with her supervisor in three days. One more day away from her work duties would be all she could get away with if she wanted to keep her job. Then she reminded herself that this work was the most important of her life. If—no, *when*—she figured out the cure for heroin addiction, she would be celebrated, not only by the Taos Pueblo tribe but by her own colleagues and other medical professionals.

Excited by the accolades that would surely come, she poured a cup of the thick brew and settled at the cramped table and foldout seating area. Letting out a weary sigh, she took a sip of the bitter brew, opened the latest volume of *Nursing Drug Handbook*, flipped to the section on Schedule II drugs listed in her preferred research guide. Most of the pages had been marked by various color highlighters. Some of the drug names and descriptions corresponded to her handwritten list.

Caffeine kicking in, finger tapping her lips, she refocused and scanned the list. Nine drug combinations had been crossed out. Nine failures. She vowed, the last.

"Which will be next?" she asked no one. She ran a finger, nail ragged from her last moments with the drum maker, along one page of the textbook, then another.

She kept circling back to Suboxone, the current alternative to methadone. Classified as the lesser traditional treatment, she figured Suboxone to be a safe choice. The drug was a combination of buprenorphine and naloxone, and all shared similar treatable side effects, including dizziness, nausea, and stomach cramping. Then brilliance came to her. How would one of the two, rather than the combination, react in the system?

Decision made, she stood up and removed the cushion she had been sitting on. The strongbox wedged in the storage space took some exertion to pull free, and for a moment she thought the inferior handle would snap off. After a few more tugs, the strongbox came free.

Lid open, she let out a satisfied breath and picked up various amber prescription bottles. Labels announced hydromorphone, Suboxone, Demerol, oxycodone, Percocet, fentanyl. But where was the buprenorphine? Her heart raced.

"No, no, no," she muttered, unable to find the proper medication. She dumped the containers out on the cushion and sorted through them again. She wasn't even sure she had stocked those meds before she left for the reservation, and that made her even more angry with herself.

Still no luck, so she shoved the containers back in the box, slammed the lid shut, and cradled it to her chest. Her father's chastising voice rang in her ears. *Get it together, young lady. Failure is not an option.*

She considered making a trip at first light to a Santa Fe pharmacy to fill the necessary specialized prescriptions. No. That would take time, and she didn't want to leave the girls alone the four hours it would take to make the trip both ways in the massive vehicle. She had Suboxone in stock. She reopened the box, found the correct bottle, and smiled at the nearly full container.

This would do, she decided. Mix more of the Suboxone than heroin. It would probably take a day or two for the results to be evident. But if she had tried two differing drugs, it would take even longer. She smiled. The universe had come to her rescue, again. Purpose reignited, she placed the lockbox in its hiding place and went to the other necessary stockpile.

The heroin hadn't been difficult to find and was even cheaper than she'd expected. Singing an upbeat tune that always put her in a better mood, she removed the purple Crown Royal bag hidden in a pullout compartment of her treatment case. She dug out the flame-scorched spoon and cotton balls and dented silver Zippo discarded by her father a decade ago. Satisfied with the paraphernalia, she rummaged for the compact resealable bags at the bottom. One after another, until she counted out five, were empty. Only white residue remained. She growled, low and guttural. Frustrated to the highest degree, she emptied everything out of the bag and shook it. Nothing else fell out. No heroin at all remained.

"How could you be so stupid, Alice?" she screamed, pulling her hair as she raged in the tight space.

Her girls needed the heroin more than anything else. They would suffer unbearable pain and discomfort in less than twelve hours. She had been so enthralled with her experiment that she had forgotten about the most important ingredient.

She glanced at her watch. Three hours until midnight. She would have to wait at least that long to make sure no one saw her. The RV stood out like no other vehicle on the road, and when she had made the first buy, she was certain cops would arrive the minute the dope was handed over.

And what if, when she got to the place, the dealer and his lackies had moved on to a different location than where they had been twelve days ago?

Panic threatened to overwhelm her. "Take it easy. Everything will be all right," she said over and over until she had almost convinced herself.

CHAPTER TWENTY-FIVE
EVA

Eva finally arrived home after she put in a few hours at her department doing paperwork so she wouldn't be buried in administrative work for days to come. Too tired to even kick off her boots, she went to her freezer and pulled out the bottle of cheap vodka wedged behind ice trays and a forgotten pint of rocky road ice cream. She had liberated the booze from Paloma's car, thankfully before the seemingly always-drunk-at-the-time woman had driven off in the vehicle.

"Two wins!" she said, pulling out both.

Going for a spoon and glass next, she wondered if Cruz had made it home from the Pueblo by now. If the entire village had fallen into mourning for their lost soul, after hearing of the death notification. It would have taken mere minutes for the news to spread through the entire community. Shops would be closed. Visitors and tourists would be ushered away. The cooking would begin.

A feast and memorial celebration would be arranged, to take place at the traditional village, where Kishi's father lived as their people had for over one thousand years. Every drum she had ever made that remained anywhere on the reservation would be gathered so the most heralded drummers and elders could stroke the leathers with willow sticks covered in soft leather.

She imagined the crowd that would assemble. All members of the community and their family members dressed in ceremonial attire, dancing in the open area between the two main mud-covered structures, honoring a life gone too soon. She would be forgiven and, due to her former standing, put to rest in the ancient graveyard, where someday her cross, too, would fall.

Then Eva's thoughts turned to whether she would attend the celebration of life. Or if she would even be invited. Probably not, if Cruz's apprehension turned out to be cause for concern. She wouldn't want to create any problems or make anyone uncomfortable, but a death brought the people together, and she missed the community of those she'd once shared every festivity with.

A knock at the door startled her and she almost dropped both deliveries of comfort. No one ever stopped by without calling or texting first. A stringent rule she enforced by never opening the door, even if she knew the guest. She thought about the Glock stuffed in its holster in her bedroom. At first she wondered why she thought danger might be visiting, then chuckled knowing a threatening intruder would most likely not bother to knock.

With no reason to be too concerned, she looked at both containers, put the ice cream on the counter, and, just in case, grasped the neck of the vodka bottle. She went to the front room, hand on the doorknob, bottle raised, and flicked on the porch light, swung the door open. Cruz stood there, squinting, arm raised to shield himself from the bright glow.

"What the . . ." Her words trailed off when he edged past her and stood in the entryway. He looked around, puzzled, as if he'd never been there before or wasn't sure why he'd come.

She stopped his confusion with a kiss. Long and deep, until he stepped back, a sob escaping from him that broke her already-broken heart.

CHAPTER TWENTY-SIX
ALICE

Too anxious to wait any longer, Alice turned the key to the Winnebago and made the wide turnaround in the dirt-packed area in front of the house. More nervous than she had been the first time, she made her way toward the dealer's base of operations.

Head on a swivel, she kept an eye out for beams of headlights. When she didn't encounter a single vehicle, she finally began to relax. A few minutes later, she turned onto the dirt road that led to an even more neglected house than where she housed the girls.

Four beat-up cars that hadn't been there during her first visit, two on cinder blocks and missing tires, were parked along the narrow lane, and she had to be careful not to clip one of them and shear off a mirror, or worse. Four bright-green motorbikes were parked in a row, massive helmets hanging from the handlebars. She held in a breath until she'd crept close enough to see lights on in the windows. All of them. Shadows of a few people moved behind closed curtains in two of the rooms.

"See?" she told herself. "No need to have worried."

She parked and got out of the RV, careful to make sure all entries were locked before she bounced toward the house. She knocked and heard people shuffling around and even something break behind the front door that barely held on to the hinges.

Someone said, "It's okay. Just that weird old lady came by about a week ago." Someone else said, "Told ya we shoulda moved before now." Another replied, "Shut up, her money's good. How much should we overcharge her this time?" A round of laughs followed that.

People had ridiculed her throughout childhood, no one more than her father. She knew how to take care of bullies. She thought about the Ruger locked in the RV and considered going back for it. Point the handgun at the leader and blow his face off. That would stop their disrespect.

But no, she couldn't do that. She needed what they had to offer and probably couldn't kill all of them in time to get away. So she waited a moment and knocked again on the door, which rattled with each assertive blow. The doorknob jiggled and she extended her full five-foot-ten height, squared her shoulders, and put on her most menacing scowl—the *Don't mess with me bear* pose, as her oldest brother called it.

The door swung open, and when she walked inside the reek of spilled beer and cigarette smoke caught in her lungs. She tried not to gag as she assessed the group in the room, more of them than last time. Most were Caucasian and one probably Hispanic. Three sat on a couch, legs in an annoying manspread, smirks on their faces. One had acne scars so deep he had most likely never been allowed to get close enough to kiss a girl or boy. Another had black teeth, so no one had probably even looked at him without running away. The third might have been handsome a few years ago, but a constant head twitch and jiggling leg and body odor she detected from ten feet away would scare off the dead.

Her eyes locked on three handguns, lined up in a row on the coffee table in front of the couch. She decided she actually should have gone back for the Ruger. Then she noticed the men's droopy eyes and slow hand movements and figured she could take all three of the wasted younger men without the need for firepower.

The leader, however, was a different sort of character. His menacing quality hadn't altered from when she had met him twelve days ago. Long and lean, and when he stood up from an off-kilter recliner covered in a filthy sheet, he towered over her as he scanned her head to toe and back again. As before, he did not appear to be wasted. Either he had a high tolerance, or he didn't partake in his moneymaking efforts. And that, she knew, made him the most dangerous threat in the room.

The boy who had opened the door, the only Native American in the room, couldn't have been more than seven years old. Alice wondered if the kid had found the house the others used as a hangout. If this acted as initiation to their sick association. He backed away from her until he hit a wall, then slid down the wallpaper to sit cross-legged and proceeded to fiddle with a rip in the knee of his jeans.

The dealer tossed a pack of cigarettes to the boy and said, "Go out and keep lookout, Pinkie." The kid complied, and Alice wished she had checked to make double sure she had locked up the RV.

She reached into her scrubs pocket and handed him a fold of cash, and he made a point of counting out every bill. "You're short."

"That's what you charged me last time."

"Things change. I'm the only guy with product right now." He held the money out to her. "Guess you'll have to try your luck in Vadito or Santa Fe."

Alice considered storming out of the house and doing that very thing. But that would mean starting over. She knew of no other possibilities, so she dug into the other pocket, withdrew more money, gave him another twenty-dollar bill. He shook his hand and snapped his fingers. She peeled off another twenty. "That's it. If you want more money, you'll have to sell me less."

"Or nothing at all." He bent down and tugged a plastic baggie, from his sock this time, and waved it, taunting her. "I could do that."

She fixed the sternest look on her face as she dared and took a step closer to the belligerent punk. "But you won't."

"All right, all right." He tossed her the receptacle of brownish powder.

Alice made sure not to turn her back on the young men as she went to the door.

"Come on back." He winked and leered at her. "I know you will."

She screwed her lips tight and vowed to put this smug jerk in his place if she ever saw him again.

Door closed behind her, safely outside, she let out a ragged breath and noticed the boy sitting on the ground a few feet away, inexpertly smoking a cigarette. "Why are you doing that? Put it out," she snapped.

He flinched and ground out the smoke. "Yes, ma'am."

He reminded her of the kid who had come looking for his mother. White Dove had birthed a beautiful boy . . . No. She wouldn't think about that right now.

"What's your name?"

"Nathan."

"Why does that man call you Pinkie?"

He raised a fist and unfurled his little finger. "Says 'cause I'm that big. Don't really know what he means." The low register of the boy's voice surprised her.

"It's late. Shouldn't you be in bed?" He didn't answer this question. Maybe didn't know the answer, so she tried another tack. "Do you live here?" He nodded and wiped his nose on his dirty sleeve. "Where are your parents?" He pointed to the house. "Are one of those men your dad or uncle?" He looked disgusted and shook his head this time.

So the parents were probably in one of the bedrooms, high and unaware the kid wasn't being cared for properly. She knew she should go to the tribal police. Have them arrive and, guns raised, arrest the offenders and kick them off the reservation. But how would she do that? Doing so would involve paperwork and follow-up and interviews and time away from her mission and the girls. No, she couldn't open herself up to scrutiny. Instead, she decided an anonymous phone call would have to do.

"What's the address here, young man?"

"Not supposed to say."

Unsure how to proceed, she looked at the RV and back at the boy. "Are you hungry?" He sat up taller and his eyes lit up. "I could make you a sandwich." She took the first steps toward the Winnebago and looked back when she didn't hear his footsteps. "Come on. I'm no more dangerous than that bunch in there."

The boy looked back at the front door and then sprinted after her. He settled down a bit when she closed the RV's door and pointed for him to sit on the foldout. "I don't have jelly or milk, but I make a mean peanut butter sandwich."

She proceeded to prepare his sandwich, rambling on about nothing to put him more at ease. As soon as she handed over the food, he snatched it from her hand and took a huge bite. "I only have this to drink, but it tastes like chocolate milk." He reached for the container of meal supplement and took a few chugs. He put his hand behind his back and shuffled in the seat.

"What do you have there?" she asked.

He reached back, pulled out a gun, held it out. Horrified, she snatched the gun from his hand. The light weight surprised her.

"It's not real," he said.

"Looks real."

"Supposed to."

"Where did you get this?" He avoided her gaze and clamped his lips tight. "You shouldn't have this," she said. "People will think it's an actual gun, and you could get hurt."

"It's just for show. They prob'ly won't let me keep it." He held out his hand. "Gimme it back or I'll be in trouble."

Anxious to get going, she still didn't want to leave the boy. More than that, she didn't want to relinquish what looked to be an actual firearm. Still, she handed over the replica and said, "There's nothing here for you. Why do you stay?"

He tucked the gun back in his waistband and then licked his fingers. "Got nowhere else to go."

"You don't have other family?" He shrugged and she tried again. "I could contact someone for you. What's your last name?"

"Not supposed to say."

"I'm trying to help you."

He took on an indignant pose, arms crossed tight to his chest. "Don't need no help."

"It's okay to ask for help. I'm a nurse. I get people of your tribe well." She leaned forward and said in a low voice, "Okay, maybe you need to trust me a little bit. I'm from a little town in Texas. I travel around four whole states to treat people." She stopped to make sure he listened, then said, "Your turn."

"My dad said his people are from Santa Fe. My mom and me were born here on the rez."

Thinking for a moment, she supposed she could take the boy with her. Make room in the RV or maybe even the house. He could help with the girls. That idea lasted a split second. Her motorhome alone was enough to draw suspicion, and if she was spotted anywhere with a Native kid, she would have a lot of explaining to do.

Before she could think of next steps, the RV door flung open, the leader bolted up the steps. "What the fuck! Why are you still here? Pinkie, get in the house."

The boy shot to his feet and whizzed out the open door.

"I'm warnin' you, lady, stay away from the kid."

"He shouldn't be here."

"We're lookin' after him. He's fine."

"He was starving. I gave him a sandwich—"

"We feed him all the time!"

She was certain his words weren't true and that he might not ever think about asking if the kid was hungry or needed anything.

She tensed when he ran his hands across the high cabinets along the wall.

"Whatcha got hidden? Better drugs than I got?"

"No. I don't keep anything worthwhile in here."

"A mobile clinic and no drugs? I don't believe that."

"How did you know—?"

"Oh, I know everything that involves anyone enjoying my product. Take great pride in it," he said, his voice singsong and spellbinding.

Alice's heartbeat skittered. She did all she could not to look at where her Ruger and shotgun were hidden. "It's time I left now." She eased by him, careful to make no contact in the tight space, and opened the side door.

"Yeah, time you moved on." He jumped the height to the ground and landed effortlessly. "Remember now, stay away from the kid."

"You won't see me again. And I'm very careful who I talk to."

He tapped his temple, then made a gun motion with his hand. "Good, that's good."

She slammed the door shut, launched herself to the captain's chair, cranked the engine to life. Hitting the gas, she looked out the sideview mirror. Dust spewing out from the tires billowed over the dealer until his form disappeared in the taillights.

CHAPTER TWENTY-SEVEN
EVA

Eva stroked Cruz's bare shoulder, surprised as always by how soft his skin felt under her fingertips. She had been on alert the minute the tribal cop had crossed her threshold, thinking Kai would come barging through the door, done with Santiago and his rules. Instead, the man she had fallen in and out of love with more than a dozen times took cautious steps toward her. She opened her arms and waited for him to fall into them.

The lovemaking had gratefully taken her out of everything. No thoughts of Paloma. No worries about Kai. No dead Native woman discarded for the coyotes and turkey vultures to find. Now, sheets damp, body glistening from the sweat that hadn't yet dried, she fell into Cruz's rhythm of breaths and could think of nothing else.

The afterglow lasted less than five minutes. A gruesome slideshow started up. A constant flicker that wouldn't stop. She unconsciously flicked her foot and tapped one finger against the bedsheet, a nervous habit she didn't realize would be annoying until Cruz said, "Can't sleep?"

She turned her head to see him looking at her, as wide awake as she felt. "Didn't mean to wake you."

"You're brain's ticking pretty loud."

"That nurse. Why do I keep thinking about her? Why hasn't anyone seen her lately? She's legit, and our people are always looking for free care because so many need it, so why don't we know of anyone who sought her out? Do you really think she's left the area?"

"Okay, which question do you really want answered."

"Well, all of them."

He let out a deep sigh and nuzzled closer to her. "She's a travel nurse. Most likely moved on. If no one turns up, why would she stay?"

"I don't know. She keeps popping into my mind. Gotta be a reason for that."

"It'll come to you. Think of something else." He stroked her neck. "Refocusing helps me sometimes."

"Okay . . ." She supposed this was as good a time as any to ask him what she'd been curious about. "What have you heard about a female being appointed chief of the tribal police?"

Cruz's amorous movements stopped. Eyes wide, he asked, "Who told you that?"

"So it's true."

"Dammit. Santiago, right? He can't keep a secret to save his life."

"There are no secrets on the rez," Eva said, her register low and gravelly, imitating Santiago's voice.

They both chuckled, lightening the mood.

"Probably never happen," Cruz said. "Rumors for now." Then he rose up and leaned against the headboard. "Wait. You don't think it'll be you, do you?"

"What? Me? The new chief? No—"

He cracked up, his laughter bouncing off the walls. She smacked him in the chest. "Asshole." She got up and draped her naked body with a robe that had tumbled to the floor. "Want some tea?"

"Naw. I'd better go." He yawned, rolled out of bed, and started pulling on clothes he had discarded earlier that night. When he caught her watching him, he made a show of inching on each piece of clothing, making sure to ripple his muscles just the right way, striptease in reverse, until *she* burst out laughing this time before she left the room.

Thoughts swirled as she took her official notepad from next to her keys and handheld radio on the cedar chest, clicked on the pen and made her way to the kitchen. She gathered her thoughts as she waited for the water to boil, and by the time she sat down, steaming mug of tea beside her, she wondered how much she should put on the record.

Often she wouldn't write in the palm-size book—especially if an NA had been the driver she'd pulled over for a minor transgression or warned to put out their campfire—but she was almost certain that tomorrow the sheriff would assign her officially to the investigation, so she needed to start documenting. At least the elements she wanted to remember in case details would need to be introduced in court. A dead local woman made the case official, and she, as the only Native person assigned to the county agency, needed to be beyond professional. She sighed, not loving that part. Following rules and regulations had been the most difficult part of the job so far.

Cruz had warned her from the first time she mentioned wanting to become a cop. He had been on the tribal force for three years at the time, her words so unexpected he looked at her like she'd just dropped from the sky. *Sure you want to do that?* he had said. *There are rules, you know. A bazillion of them. You don't like rules.*

She had taken offense at the time, but she now knew what he was actually telling her: you can't go rogue. A warning she had to remind herself of more often than she would ever admit to.

Lost in her work, searching her memory for anything she could be forgetting, something brushed the top of her head. She jumped from the chair, hand reflexively going to her hip.

Cruz put up both hands in surrender. "Just me. Kudos on the concentration, Deputy." He took up her mug and took a sip. "Riding together in the morning, right? Pick me up at seven thirty, okay?"

"I remember," she said, not actually remembering that detail they'd nailed down a couple of hours ago.

He pulled her into a kiss and tight embrace until she wriggled free. "Stand down, Officer."

"Try to get some sleep."

"Uh-huh," she muttered, concentration back on her notes.

The front door shut, and she absently sipped the lukewarm chamomile, took up the pen again, flipped to a clean page on the pad, and jotted down the most logical of the choices that could have been involved in Kishi's murder:

OUTSIDE INFLUENCES. IE: VISITING NURSE PRACTI-TIONER?

LOCAL TOWNIE?

Then she listed the choice she hoped could not be possible:

PUEBLO OR OTHER TRIBE OFFENDER?

To purge her mind from the last note, she wrote line after line of off-the-cuff ideas, figuring she could brainstorm with Cruz or Andrew or her sheriff about them later. After she filled three pages of small tight printing until her hand cramped, she read through the comments and made marks as she progressed. Frustrated, she tossed the pen to the confusion of notes, all of the possibilities now crossed out.

She didn't have a next step in mind, and certainly not a plan.

CHAPTER TWENTY-EIGHT

PALOMA

Not a hint of light from the gap around the window, only the soft purr of Tonita's snoring to keep Paloma company, she squinted in the dim moonlight at the scores of lines on the wall above her head that noted how many days she had been locked in the cramped space that had now become home. Not much different than the meager existence she'd lived before the day she and her friends had been taken captive. But at least that life was her own decision, and now all her thoughts meandered back to whether the nightmare would ever end.

She missed her son and wondered if Kai had been taking care of himself alone or if he had reached out to anyone. Eva, she hoped. She knew her boy to be the proudest person she had ever met, aside from her brother, Santiago. Actually asking for assistance wouldn't even occur to either of them.

After taking small bites and sips, she had finished her peanut butter on grain bread, banana, and half an orange, and as always, the old folk's protein drink an hour ago. She almost felt lucid and considered whether the nurse had given her something in conjunction with heroin for the last injection. The feeling in her feet had even come back. She reached down and ran her thumbs in the grooves between both big toes and could barely feel where countless needles had poked their way to her delivery.

She turned to her cousin, who didn't seem to be altered in any way. Still slept all the time, or mumbled incoherently when semiawake. Lost in a heroin cloud and nothing on her mind at all. At least that was what Paloma thought, because Tonita hadn't actually said anything meaningful all day.

Boredom would set in soon. She prepared for what would then follow. Regrets would replay in her mind. Her husband and the other three spirits would come to aggravate her. And here she was, not even slightly high enough to forget them, hours away from her next fix. But the bad memories didn't come, and neither did her beloved Ahiga.

Could the nurse actually be helping me? she wondered. "I don't feel high, but I don't feel bad either. I'm not jonesing at all—are you?" Her cousin didn't stir. "Tonita!" she yelled, trying to get her attention. The other woman rolled over, her back now to Paloma.

"Fine. Ignore me. Just like when we were kids. We're not kids anymore. We need to get our shit together and come up with a plan, or we may never get out of here."

"Enjoy the ride, cuz. There's nothing outside these walls for us. It's all gone. All gone . . ." Soft snores ended the statement.

Paloma let out a sigh and, performing a task that had become a ritual, reached up and scratched a twelfth slash on the captivity wall.

CHAPTER
TWENTY-NINE
ALICE

Alice awoke to birds creating such a commotion in the tree that provided shade for the RV she whipped the curtain aside to see what could be causing the unaccustomed stir. She found nothing but early-morning light and patted over her racing heart to settle herself.

Rejuvenated and feeling more optimistic than she had in a week, she whisked the sheet and blanket aside, then folded the bed back to the couch position. For a moment the near altercation last night came to her. The movie in her mind played as she watched herself pull out her Ruger and plug a hole through the dealer's forehead, right there at the doorway of the RV. He fell backward and slammed to the dirt. She hurried behind the steering wheel and maneuvered the Winnebago until it lined up with the man as he began to get up. Then she ran him over. Backed up over his now-motionless body. Then drove over him again. She jiggled upward in the foldout seat, imagining the motorhome go over each body speed bump time and time again.

One loud cackle of a laugh before she purged the thoughts, then told herself, "Focus. Time to heal."

She splashed water over her face and washed up, careful to conserve the resources until she could fill up the tank again at the RV park north of town and empty the waste at their dump station. The site had been an excellent resource, and she had become accustomed to the moldy showers and smelly bathrooms. Best find of all had been the washer and dryer units fed by quarters she had an abundance of. Keeping the girls' sleepwear and sheets clean had been a challenge but crucial to making them feel more comfortable. She had yet to encounter the same campers or RV enthusiasts and took it as a good sign that no one would remember ever seeing her. And the Winnebago looked identical to a dozen others she had spotted over the days since the area had become home base.

Next she turned to preparing the first-meal sandwiches. She dug out eight slices of whole grain bread, then remembered. Her good mood plummeted as she realized she now only needed six pieces. She crammed the extras back into the plastic bag and muttered a flow of unaccustomed curses, surprising herself when they ramped up in intensity.

Next, she put on her freshest set of scrubs and then prepared two of the standard remedies in hypodermics. Satisfied, she turned her attention to the special dose for the jewelry maker. She caught herself humming, and that made her happy again.

Almost giddy now, she exited the motorhome, full tray balanced in one hand, set of keys in the other. After she unlocked the padlock, she entered the front room and noticed the scuffed built-in sideboard near the front door. She frowned at the dusty surface and ran a finger along the wooden top, then made a mental note to pick up cleaning products the next time she went to the store. The house had been good to her and her girls. She vowed to take better care of the dwelling.

An assortment of supplies caught her attention as she neared the kitchen. Rolls of toilet paper, cylinders of sanitation wipes, pump bottles filled with antiseptic gel, jumbo-size peanut butter jars, bag of oranges, loaf of bread, cases of Ensure and bottled water. She had taken to eating the equivalent diet so everyone could be on the same schedule, so no special food needed to be considered.

Satisfied that her inventory wouldn't need to be replenished right away, she made her way down the hall, stopped at the first bedroom and knocked on the door.

Birdlike wings of excitement fluttered in her chest. She stood tall, confident that a new beginning started today.

CHAPTER THIRTY
DORA

Dora startled when the door opened and the nurse rushed in, red faced and enthusiastic, hypodermics rattling on the tray, alongside their morning meals. She glanced at the window, where dim sunlight peeked through the gap, much earlier than the nurse had ever arrived before.

She frowned and looked to Kishi's bed, still empty. Every time she woke to find her friend gone, Dora became more confused. Something awful must have happened to her. Her mind raced with questions. Where could she be? Would her friend have abandoned her without a word of goodbye? No, Kishi would never just leave, she decided. Her friend knew Dora couldn't bear to be alone. Never could. The youngest of five girls, she was everyone's plaything. The favored child.

"Where is Kishi?" she croaked, voice unrecognizable as her own after days of issuing so few words. She and Kishi had all but quit speaking the past few days of their captivity. They had been lifelong friends, practically sisters, and often communicated by a look or gesture. This time was different though. Dora felt more scared than she ever remembered, even the time she'd gotten lost in the woods and Paloma's brother had to get his dog to find her.

Focus, she warned herself, snapping back to the present.

"Don't you worry," the nurse said. "Let's take care of you, now. I figured it out! You're going to be so pleased." The woman bent over the bed and administered the shot. Then she patted Dora's shoulder and stood up, proud and satisfied as she watched—eyes flicking back and forth from Dora's left eye to the right one.

Dora frowned. She didn't feel any different than before. Before she could ask if there was medication of any kind in the shot, the woman tapped her mouth with one finger and said, "If you had a wish, where would you want to spend your last moments?" The question baffled Dora. Then terrified her. She had heard the nurse ask the same question to Kishi before the shot yesterday had taken effect. The woman didn't need to whisper the question this time.

Too frightened of the implications if she answered, Dora opened and closed her mouth several times. No coherent words escaped.

"It's okay, dear. I already know. Rest now. Next time you wake up, you'll feel like a new person."

The empty words didn't sound very reassuring to Dora. And her skin began to tingle. Then a burn from deep within crept upward, from the IV port to her arm and chest and neck, and then the trajectory shifted, and the sensation began to flow toward her other extremities.

She tried to tell the nurse. Warn her that something was wrong . . . And then as fast as the alarming reactions began, the discomfort left.

She felt wonderful.

And beautiful, inside and out.

Renewed.

Dora's vision wavered, tears blurring the nurse's proud face.

"See? I told you everything would be all right." She stroked Dora's arm and drew the covers to her chin. "You sleep now. I'll be back later to check on you."

Dora tried to thank her healer. But she couldn't open her mouth this time. *Why can't I move?* A thought, because words failed her. Couldn't even turn her head, so she tracked the nurse's movements with her eyes. The woman in the sky-blue scrubs moved beyond the door to the bathroom and approached the other bedroom, which, Dora assumed, still held two of her friends. Questions buzzed—were they okay? Sick?

She glanced back to the empty bed.

Alive?

Her legs began to twitch and then her arms flailed. She bucked on the bed until she thought her neck would snap. She heard a crash from very far away. The sensation of floating lifted her from her body. Then she felt hands on her biceps. Cold, pinching, squeezing. The nurse's face whizzed by each time Dora convulsed. Teeth bared—spittle flew as incomprehensible words were shouted at her.

Earsplitting noises and screams filled Dora's ears. A slap across the face. Then another. Her lip split and she tasted copper. A fist pummeled her stomach. She wanted to stop her movements but couldn't remember how. Punishment rained down on her, a flurry of unhinged brutality. A crack verified at least one rib had snapped. Then another.

And then, mercifully, everything stopped. She felt nothing more. Song-chants filled the room until the walls reverberated. She smiled, closed her eyes, and waited for the spirits to engulf her in their glorious rescue.

CHAPTER THIRTY-ONE
EVA

Eva took her time getting ready. Top on her agenda for the day would be one of the most difficult challenges she had faced since pinning on a badge. Autopsies were hard enough when they involved people she had never met, and although Kishi had not been a close friend, Eva knew her and was awed by the drum maker's talents.

First, coffee, she decided, certain she wouldn't be able to stomach anything more substantial than that. And some dry toast would be a good idea to soak up the bile she was pretty sure would rise the moment formaldehyde hit her sinus cavities.

After she transferred a load of clothes to the dryer, she took up the radio and keys to the official vehicle and locked up. Her magpie screeched at her from its customary perch on the post, and she smiled, thinking of Kai's explanation about the bird's behavior. "Happy hunting today, Rio."

Before she fired up the truck, she texted Cruz that she would pick him up at his house in fifteen minutes. As the police chief's second in command, Cruz would be the one to represent the tribe during any investigation outside the reservation, and she was glad they had arranged to go to the morgue together. Suffer and mourn as one, without subjecting anyone else to the pain. They could be objective and yet also make sure Kishi's body and conclusions about her outcome would be handled with compassion and discretion.

It helped that Eva got along with the well-respected medical examiner, Tavis Mondragon, a former medical doctor whose lacking bedside manner deemed him to be better suited to nonliving patients.

Again, Eva turned off the main highway and crossed over to reservation land. During the short drive, she had wondered why Cruz hadn't elaborated on what Santiago told her the day before—that a female police chief would be stepping in for Cruz's boss. Wondered if Cruz had even known before she mentioned it. Then she worried that his job might be in jeopardy. As usual, her mind then went to the possibility Santiago had been playing with her and that his disclosure might not even be real.

The crisp morning air revitalized her after a night of fitful sleep that had driven her from bed half a dozen times. She spotted a bus headed in her direction—always a highlight when she encountered one of the transportation vehicles. She flipped on the light bar and whooped the siren. The driver, so intent on the safety of her passengers, kept her hands on the oversize steering wheel. Rows of kids' gleeful faces turned her way, they waved and smiled and jumped in their seats as she passed.

Kai popped into her mind, and she wondered if he had made it in time for his own bus. The thought surprised her. She had never been concerned about this in the past, even from day one knowing Paloma had disappeared. Fear and worry must feel never ending for parents, and Eva was not equipped for that roller coaster ride. The white-knuckle time she had spent with Kai the past two days had proven she'd rather face a gun wielding offender than a teenager hell bent on doing exactly what he pleased. Consequences be damned.

Unlike Kai, living in the moment had been an issue for Eva since childhood. Always looking ahead, she considered every angle or misstep, whether it be a spelling test or how to reply to light banter. Not necessarily good traits when assessing a domestic violence call or traffic stop that could go sideways any moment. The trait had somewhat been drilled out of her by her supervisors, training officers, and more seasoned colleagues. But the wait time, when she allowed it to play out, made her an outstanding investigator. Rather than think outside the box, Eva stood on it.

She noticed the clouds had started to rise, billow and creep over the mountains as she made the turn that led to the house Cruz had purchased from the community a decade earlier. The youngest of any of their crowd stable enough to call themselves a homeowner, he took pride in the three-bedroom, two-bath, stark white structure, featuring an enviable wraparound porch he and his brothers had constructed on the eight-acre parcel of land.

Although he came to her house most of the time, she knew the rooms inside his place would be as pristine and orderly as the dust-free porch and neatly trimmed bushes that dotted the property. Tall lavender stalks topped with blossoms waved in the light breeze, and she caught a hint of sage when she parked and rolled down the windows.

Less than a minute later, in full uniform, Cruz was standing there, representing the Taos Pueblo people with pride. The silver badge pinned to his dark-blue uniform shirt flashed in the sun. Even his gun belt buckle and the silver caps on the tips of his boots shone. As he strode to her vehicle, he slid on a pair of wraparound mirror sunglasses, a bit of false camouflage that couldn't hide his nervous energy.

"Did you eat this morning?" she asked when he belted himself in the seat.

"Yep. Eggs and oatmeal. All set." He raised his sealed aluminum to-go cup. "Don't even need to stop for coffee. We can go right there."

"That's not actually why I asked," she muttered.

"What do you mean?"

"Never mind. How many autopsies have you been to?"

"Counting this one?" She nodded, and he tapped his chin, thinking. "One."

"Uh, boy," she whispered. "Well, at least we don't need to drive to Albuquerque for the autopsy."

"How'd you manage that?"

"Medical examiner's a friend."

Cruz waggled his full eyebrows. "Friend, huh?"

She reached across and smacked him on the shoulder. "Not that kind. I took a few classes from him at UNM. Known him for years. I was his only NA pupil, and he had just bought a place up here. Wanted to know about my favorite restaurants in the area and what to order. Introduced him to some of our artists so he could spread his wealth. Literally." A thought came to her. "Oh, god." She glanced at Cruz for a moment. "I introduced him to Kishi a while back. He might have one of her drums."

Cruz slid lower in his seat. "She was so talented. Her drums will be worth a fortune when word gets out. Knockoffs are probably already being made."

She hadn't even thought of that possibility. "How do we stop that from happening?"

He shrugged and offered nothing else.

A few minutes later, Eva wheeled the pickup behind the main structure of Holy Cross Hospital and parked near the ambulance bay.

He hesitated as he grasped the door handle, looking not quite ready to exit the vehicle, eyes on the door that would lead to a law enforcer's potential nightmare—if not that night, weeks or years in the future. "Any advice?" he asked.

"Breathe through your mouth." She slid out of the pickup before he could ask why.

CHAPTER THIRTY-TWO
PALOMA

Paloma wrenched awake and froze, unsure of what she had heard. Then a scream, followed by the wail of someone suffering unimaginable grief or pain, shook her fully awake. Something crashed in the room beyond the bathroom. And then nothing but silence.

She tucked into a tight ball and looked at Tonita. "What do you think is going on over there?"

A shrug was the only reply from her cousin across the room, who looked as scared as Paloma felt.

"Do you think she's coming back?"

"Maybe we don't want her to," Tonita said, her first rational statement since Paloma could recall.

Ears attuned for more noises, she focused on the sounds other than what she had heard a moment ago. A thump became the faint pound of a drum. Glass breaking turned to bells on moccasins as they touched the earth in dance. Someone keening turned to a flurry of song Paloma recognized from burial ceremonies. The songs of their people for those lost. Sung for the final time.

"I'm not ready," she muttered, an attempt to ward off what might be coming for her. "I need to see Kai. Tell him I'm sorry. I tried to be a good mother."

"He'll understand," Tonita said, her voice childlike.

Paloma didn't realize she had said the words loud enough for her companion to hear. Grateful for the kindness, she said, "I'm sorry, cousin. I didn't mean this life for you. I was scared and couldn't be alone after Ahiga. And the pain . . ." As if on cue, agony seared through her leg, vibrating the screws and rods that held her shin bone in place. She gritted her teeth and kneaded the muscles and scars until the pain subsided. "Inviting you into my world was selfish. You and Dora and Kishi have been the best friends—"

"No, Eva is your best friend. Always has been." Tonita's tone stunned Paloma. She had no idea her cousin could be jealous of anyone.

A familiar scent wafted to the room. Sage smoke. Paloma sniffed over and over, trying to determine if fire danger lurked somewhere in the house. "Do you smell that?"

"Sage," Tonita said.

"Yeah, but not from bushes around here."

"No. Cheap stuff. Probably gift shop crap."

Paloma knew all too well about the nonsanctioned shops statewide that sold goods packaged to look authentic. Some were even made in other countries. Hardly anything crafted by experienced artisans on the Pueblo who relied on the sales of legitimate items to survive.

They were silent for a while as Paloma anxiously waited for Alice to come with their food. That surprised her. Only the drugs were what she needed, craved, wanted before. But now her stomach rumbled with need. To take her mind off the discomfort, she asked Tonita, "Do you miss your family?"

"No. They don't want me, I don't want them."

"What happened? I mean, was it because of the drugs?"

"Some. But mostly that became an excuse. They didn't want me to make the baskets anymore."

The declaration surprised Paloma. She leaned in to see her companion better in the early-morning light. The females in Tonita's family, for generations, had been renowned for weaving baskets. Designs handed down for as long as anyone knew, even sketched from hieroglyphics etched in caves deep in the mountains.

"Yours are the most glorious. You always sell out at festivals."

"And theirs don't. Collectors started asking for my work. They got jealous. Even my mom."

Before the sadness turned to despair, Paloma changed the subject. "How do you feel?"

Tonita didn't answer for a while, and Paloma thought she had drifted off to sleep, then her friend sat on the edge of the bed and wriggled her toes. "You know what? I feel better. Good, actually. How can that be?"

"Maybe she's healing us?"

"Maybe. I'm hungry. Kinda love the taste of peanut butter now. Ha! Who knew?" Tonita smiled. She actually smiled! An expression Paloma hadn't been sure she would ever see again. "We had fun, didn't we . . . ? At first."

"Yeah, we did," Paloma said. "You'll make treasures again."

"Right. And you'll dance again."

"Right." Paloma was pretty sure neither believed the other. She couldn't even stand for longer than twenty minutes at a time. Limped every step. She still danced in her dreams, though. For Ahiga and Kai.

"Did you hear the singers?" Paloma asked, her voice quiet so she wouldn't draw unwanted attention from the forces she didn't understand.

"And the dancer and the drum," Tonita said.

"What does it mean?" she asked the most spiritual Pueblo she knew.

"They've come. Someone is gone."

The saddest words Paloma had ever heard uttered. From anyone.

CHAPTER THIRTY-THREE
EVA

Eva led Cruz down a long corridor that buzzed an annoying racket from the fluorescent lights from above and was frigid enough to warrant a jacket. She stopped at the end, where two double doors marked MORGUE halted their progress. "You ready?" she asked, then waited for Cruz to give her one quick upward tick of his head.

She went through one door, Cruz the other, and emerged into a wide-open space that held the faint smell of bowels and a slight tinge like something meaty decomposing in a refrigerator and featured a gurney in the middle of the room. A bright-white sheet covered the outline of a motionless form.

"Kishi," Cruz whispered. He took a step back, and Paloma nudged her boot against his, halting him.

"Breathe," she cooed. "Breathe." His nostrils flared a moment, then his mouth parted as he followed her direction.

As soon as he looked a little less green, she tugged free two surgical masks from a dispenser at the nearby counter, handed one to Cruz, put the other one on.

It had been five years, but Eva immediately recognized the tall Hispanic man, hair dark except for the salt and pepper in his sideburns and trimmed beard, who entered the area. He snapped on latex gloves like the expert Eva knew him to be and gave her a big smile. Her anxiety melted. She wanted to run to his arms, feel his barrel chest against her own. But she couldn't do that. And her former professor wouldn't have allowed it anyway.

Eva and Cruz stood side by side, legs and arms placed in parade rest as they waited for the medical examiner to prepare his instruments and work area. As she anticipated, the air held a tinge of decomposition, other unpleasant smells too. She cast a look to the four closed stainless-steel doors to her right and wondered if the burn victim that had perished in a suspicious house fire outside Taos city limits last night could be in one of the drawers. Then she looked around the room, temperature lower than comfortable, counted the gleaming medical instruments that rivaled Cruz's polishing. Attention going anywhere but to the table that held the body draped in pristine white in front of her.

Queasy, as she had anticipated, she was grateful for only the dry piece of toast and few hits of coffee in her gut. Cruz's Adam's apple kept a constant bob up and down. Eva figured he probably regretted eating those eggs right about now.

"Thank you for traveling here, Dr. Mondragon," she said.

"Not at all. My week to be here in Taos. And this is a privilege and an honor to look after your young lady. I appreciate you reaching out to me. I have one of this gifted woman's drums. Very special to me. I keep it locked in my study so the grandkids don't wreck it."

"Nothing would please Kishi more than to have her drum whaled on by your little ones."

The ME chuckled. "Okay. Maybe I'll do that." He took a pair of protective glasses from the breast pocket of his white lab coat and put them on. "Shall we begin?"

Eva looked at Cruz, who hesitated, then gave a slight nod.

The medical examiner reached above his head, adjusted the round light fixture studded with six separate bulbs, then flipped the switch on a microphone that hung from a cord at the ceiling. He stated the date, time, and location, followed by his name, and then had Eva and Cruz state their names, law enforcement departments, and badge numbers.

Then Dr. Mondragon reverently folded back the sheet to the top of her breasts to reveal a once-lovely force of nature. The shadow of that person now. Eva thought she looked like a wax replica of a woman she barely recognized. To her relief, the Y incision had not yet been performed, and she silently thanked the doctor for not subjecting them to that visual agony. Cruz tensed beside her. She hooked her pinkie finger to his, and the connection held him in place.

"Decedent is Kishi Reyna," the doctor said. "Native American female. Thirty-two years of age. She's in remarkable shape, given her level of addiction. More than two years, as I understand?"

He looked to Eva for verification, but Cruz issued the terse nod of confirmation. "Has Kishi been violated?" Cruz asked, surprising Eva.

She didn't realize this possibility had also been on his mind. But how could it not? Abuse of Native American women had happened on and off reservations since the beginning of statistic taking. No one knew the actual number of women, children, and even men who had been violated, even for current years. In her experience more than half the women she had advised refused to press charges against their offenders or even to notify their closest family members. Shame and a feeling of uselessness were often the reason. And on more than a few occasions, the victims knew their husband, father, or brother would, without doubt, kill their rapist. And so silence reigned. And nothing changed.

"I've only just begun my evaluation for obvious trauma. However, it appears there are no signs of sexual abuse," Mondragon said.

Eva and Cruz exchanged relieved looks.

"It seems the victim—"

"Kishi," Eva and Cruz said together, annoyance in both of their voices. Although she knew the ME meant no harm, was merely being professional and detached in relaying information, any hint of disrespect would not be tolerated.

"Excuse me. Correct. Kishi. Ms. Reyna was undernourished and yet well hydrated at the time of death. And very recently, bathed and hair shampooed, which—for the recording—I noted at time of arrival yesterday afternoon. There is residue that appears to be a bloody mix of foam and mucus in her nose and mouth. Nails on the hands and feet are clipped, no nail polish. When I catalogued her clothes after removing them, I noticed the garments were dirty, I presume from her potentially being dragged through dust and forest debris. They appear pristine and look to never have been worn previously. Also indicating she either decided to alter her behavior to the extreme during her final days, or she had help doing so."

"What do you think about the wounds on the top of her left hand?" Eva asked. "Did she shoot up there?"

"I found that curious as well. Could be injection sites. Perhaps several attempts to find a vein. If she was dehydrated at the time of the first attempt, a viable venule can be difficult to access. Also, intravenous drug use often causes collapsed veins. The bruising could be from that."

"Cause of death?" Cruz asked.

The doctor frowned. "Far too early to offer you that, Officer. I've only begun, and any number of reasons could be the final determination."

"What else are you comfortable telling us?" Eva asked.

"Bile in her throat and mouth. I'll need to dissect her lungs to verify any indication that she aspirated vomit."

"Overdose?" Cruz tried again.

"Like I said—"

"Hypothetically?" Eva tried, her voice smooth and inoffensive. "Between the three of us. Overdose or foul play?"

Mondragon took up the edges of the sheet and carefully covered Kishi from view. He seemed to be gathering his words as he took the time to smooth out wrinkles alongside her head before he said, "Deputy Duran, it would be a disservice to Ms. Reyna, and to you and Officer

Romero, for me to guess. I assure you I will copy you on my report after I've assessed all of the organs and a tox screen is evaluated. This case is my top priority. However, final conclusions will most likely take days." He took off his protective glasses, flicked the switch on the hanging microphone to the off position, then looked pointedly at Eva. "I will, however, pay particular attention to Kishi's heart."

Acute pulmonary edema, is what Eva figured he meant. The most common cause of death related to a fatal overdose. That could be the actual cause of death, but why then had Kishi's body been dumped? And the hair ripped from her head? That alone was a violation, even if not specifically connected to her potential murder.

She thanked the doctor and gestured for Cruz to follow her from the room, dozens of questions and zero answers whirling in her mind.

CHAPTER
THIRTY-FOUR
KAI

Kai found it impossible to focus on what his AP Biology instructor droned on and on about. He looked at where the man's lips should be, hidden by a bushy beard and mustache everyone but Kai laughed at behind the man's back, and didn't comprehend a single string of Tomás Salas's very long sentences. He needed to ace the class, and so far he had, but he wasn't sure how he would do on the test coming up Monday morning. Finding the mind space to study had been a challenge. All he ever thought, it seemed, related to finding his mother. Eva held those keys, and he wanted to drive.

A bout of anger flashed, and he turned to the window so the teacher wouldn't think he was reacting to him. Huge puffy clouds had started to rise above the mountain range. No lightning yet, but he was sure his ride after school on the motorbike his uncle had let him use would be a wet one.

The shuffle of chairs and voices brought him back to the here and now. He hadn't realized the class had ended, and by the time he stuffed his notepad and textbook in his backpack, he was the last student left in the lab area.

"Kai, do you have some time before your next class?"

He sighed, expecting a reprimand for zoning out.

His favorite teacher pulled two of the biggest muffins Kai had ever seen and two bottles of water from his bag and handed one of each over. They sat across from each other at one of the lab benches and settled on the tall stools.

"Are you on track for the test?" Salas asked.

"Hope so," Kai said around a mouthful of the dark-brown pastry. He frowned, expecting a sweet taste like from the prepackaged cheap stuff from the convenience store.

"Bran. My wife says I don't get enough fiber." The teacher chuckled and nudged his glasses higher on his nose. "Probably more than you want to know."

"Really good," he lied. The more he chewed, the bigger the bite grew in his mouth. He took a gulp of water to force the glob down his throat. "Did your wife make these?"

"Oh, god, no. She burns water. I keep her out of the kitchen. She comes up with a mean takeout order though."

They sat munching on the doughy snack, comfortable in the shared silence for a while. As he had a dozen times before, Kai thought about the only stable relationship he'd had with a man—someone he would probably never see outside the school grounds. Salas had been supportive and enthusiastic about his pupil's choice to make biology his professional future, and Kai didn't want to disappoint his mentor.

"Anything you want to talk about?"

Kai shrugged. The casual visit snuffed out in an instant, hesitant if the teacher was being nosy or concerned. He wasn't sure what to say so he changed the subject. "Think my grades are still good enough to keep my scholarship?"

"No need to worry about that. Listen, I get that you probably don't want to get into this with me, but I need you to know I'm here for you. No judgment, no hidden agenda. You're the best student I've ever had the privilege to teach. And that's not bullshit to get you to like me." He smiled and wiped the crumbs from his beard.

"I already like you, Mr. Salas. You've always been good to me. And I've learned a ton from you. Everything, really, about biology. Other stuff too. You made me see it's possible to actually make a living by helping people."

"And you will. I'm sure of it. Just hold on. I'm not going to say everything will work out. Life does and doesn't. You never know what fastball is gonna hit you." Salas pointed to his crooked, somewhat smashed nose. "I mean, look at mine! Too many sliders to the face."

They both laughed and then went back to their silent companionship for a few minutes before Kai blurted out, "My mom's still missing. I'm getting scared for her." He surprised himself. Didn't realize he would share his feelings until right then.

Salas didn't appear taken aback at all, and that relieved Kai. He was hardly ever honest with anyone but his mom, so his nerves jangled as he anticipated mockery or worse from the adult.

"I get that. My sister went missing for a whole month when I was fifteen. Thought I would lose my mind. Couldn't do a thing but worry about her."

When he didn't elaborate, Kai risked the question he wasn't sure he wanted an answer to. "Did you get her back . . . alive?"

"Oh, yes. Sorry. I didn't mean that to sound so ominous. She had run off with a boyfriend my parents didn't approve of. No adults would tell me a thing. Made me feel like a little kid when they would shut up whenever I walked into a room. Avoided me most of the time. That's why I thought I'd let you know there are people who care. And who won't lie. Do you have someone like that in your life?"

"I do. My mom's best friend. Getting better at letting her know what's going on inside my twisted little brain." He smiled. Salas did not.

"I realize this self-deprecating persona is your defense mechanism, but I need you to knock it off. Starting today. Right now. You will change lives. You will thrive. You are an exceptional human being."

The second person to smack him with words about being kinder to himself. Kai figured he'd better start paying attention and start altering his behavior. "Yes, sir. I'll do better about that. Thank you," he said and meant every word. "I appreciate you being honest with me. Most teachers don't care at all what happens to us."

"Mine is a sticky occupation. In every way, really. Kids don't listen, parents blame teachers for everything from not instructing the right things in class to being too tough, administration advises us to be unapproachable and hands-off so the school doesn't risk getting sued."

"Nobody wins."

"You win. So do I. Only takes one student to make a career. I could retire a happy man, because of you."

His teacher wavered in front of him and Kai realized tears blurred his vision. Exhaustion, anxiety, worry over so many days had kidnapped his emotions. He swiped his face with the cuff of his sleeve and gave Salas an embarrassed grin. "Sorry. I didn't expect that."

"Never apologize for being real. Too many people wear false masks over their faces to cover their true feelings."

A couple of students, followed by more, entered the classroom. "Better get back to it," Salas said, rising from his stool.

"Thanks, Mr. Salas. I won't let you down."

"That's not my concern. Shouldn't be yours either. You know what to do."

Kai shouldered his bag and left, feeling lighter. Confident even. Determined to focus, not only on his mother's outcome, but his own.

CHAPTER
THIRTY-FIVE
EVA

When Eva returned Cruz to his house, he still looked unnerved and made no plans to be with her after their tours were over. She figured he would be like her, preferring to be alone to nurse the wounds of what they had just witnessed. She hoped it wouldn't take more than a six-pack of La Cumbre beer for him to purge the visions of Kishi on the medical examiner's table. He squeezed her hand and offered no words before he slid out of her car and took defeated strides to his front door.

As she headed back toward town, her phone rang. She took the mobile from the pouch on her duty belt and fastened it to the charger in the cup holder. "Duran."

"Hey, Eva," Andrew Kotz said.

Not who she wanted to talk to at the moment. She needed to stay focused and already had enough distractions. She gave him a pleasant but clipped hello, and he seemed a little put off when he said, "I'm really not trying to bother you."

"No, Andrew, you're not bothering me. I've just got a tight schedule today."

"Just figured I'd offer my services."

"I don't really know what I'd have you doing."

"Come on, Eva. Let me help. Put my mad computer skills to work."

He did have abilities Eva couldn't even pretend to boast about. If information could be gleaned anywhere on the internet, restricted law enforcement sites, or even clandestine websites, Officer Kotz would find it.

"Okay," Eva said. "I appreciate that. Let me tick a few things off my list, and I'll head to you after lunch."

"We could catch a bite—"

"Naw, I really need to stay on the move today. See you later today."

"All right," he said, sounding dejected. A recent attitude Eva didn't have the patience for.

She ended the connection and thought back to the one time she had relented and spent the night with the eager younger cop. She and Cruz weren't exclusive, never had been, so it hadn't felt to her like cheating. It had, however, turned out to be a mistake she had yet to disentangle herself from.

Distant thunder rumbled for an uncomfortable length of time. She glanced at the Hiroshima-type clouds that filled the sky, now tinged black at the bottom. Bolts of lightning danced and flashed as they clashed, and when she rolled down the window, she wished she had thought to toss her department-issued slicker in the truck.

She cursed any potential precipitation, hoping that would drive it away. If there was any potential evidence hiding out there somewhere, it would be impossible to find in severe weather and destroyed or washed away completely if water actually fell to the ground. Frequently, possible storms roiled and threatened in the late afternoon, but the heat often dried up precipitation before it blessed the parched mesa. Although they needed the rain desperately before the crops all dried up, she couldn't help but be selfish about what the loss could mean to her investigation.

Sighing, she knew being in the field might not even be an option at this stage. Paperwork tended to surpass boots-on-the-ground until hard facts, rather than conjecture, came to light. For now she needed to tend to her job and figure out next steps.

Still, images of Kishi's waxen face and translucent skin haunted her. The stench of the autopsy room coated her nasal cavities, and she was pretty sure her skin and clothes even smelled like Dr. Mondragon's workplace. Nothing she could do about any of that. And so, for now, she bid farewell to worries of Kishi's death and Paloma's potential danger.

She covered the last miles to the county department while she mentally prepared to update her sheriff. And knew she had no positive news at all to offer him.

CHAPTER
THIRTY-SIX
ALICE

The words *no luck at all* played an endless loop in Alice's mind. Unfathomable failure weighed on her. Visceral, a hot bright light that pierced her eyes, a vise that clamped her temples. Every muscle ached. Knuckles swollen and scuffed—she couldn't make a tight fist. Flashbacks of beating the jewelry maker left her confused as she watched the movie in her mind from way above the sickening act of violence she'd never imagined she could invoke. *Wrath*, her mother would have called it. *Carnal pleasure* would be her father's words, delivered with a wicked grin. Her brothers would be amazed. Certainly stunned. Maybe a little scared.

And White Dove? What would she think of her rescuer if she were to ever find out she had been instrumental in her friend's death? That can't happen, she decided right then. Dosages would be raised to keep the other two compliant. No questions could be asked if they couldn't think of or speak a coherent idea. She simply could not handle any more drama today. And she had a lot to do before nightfall. So she readied two new shots, because the ones she had prepared earlier that morning had been destroyed when she'd stomped on them during her absolute meltdown.

Once she had tamped down her frustration, she unlocked and entered the back bedroom, tray of fresh sandwiches and the medicine in hand, then stopped inside the doorway. She could tell right away that she'd waited too long. Both women's faces shone from oily perspiration, and their hair stuck to their foreheads. Their eyes, wide and expecting, followed her every move.

"What happened earlier this morning?" White Dove asked. "We heard a lot of noise in the other room. Is everything okay?"

Alice avoided the dancer's intense gaze.

"Answer her," the other woman demanded as she repeatedly scratched the underside of her inflamed forearm.

Alice gritted her teeth and banged the tray on the table beside the rude one. Taking time to calm herself, she lowered her head and studied her white sneakers, pristine except for a dime-size spot near the right shoelace. She wasn't even sure if she cared whether one of the women noticed the blood or would wonder where it came from.

"Are Kishi and Dora all right?" White Dove asked. Alice continued to ignore them, and the dancer raised her voice. "Take us to them. Now."

Taken aback, Alice felt her knees almost buckle. The treasured one had never been aggressive before. Had always been the perfect patient. The betrayal twisted in Alice's gut. A knife she couldn't pull out.

When she could speak again, she held her tone low. A warning not to be ignored. "Be very careful with your mouth, young lady. I have zero tolerance right now."

And yet the woman kept prodding. "I don't know what your plan is exactly, but you're breaking the law," White Dove said. "This is considered kidnapping. And a whole lot more. My friend is a cop—"

"Her best friend," the other woman interjected.

"That's right, my best friend, and she's looking for me right now."

The nurse snorted a laugh. "Must be a truly inept police officer. Wouldn't your friend have found you by now if she really wanted to?"

That shut White Dove up. She seemed to have no comeback. Alice smirked and pulled the cap off of one hypodermic. She raised the needle and grabbed the mean one's wrist. The woman slapped her hand and tried to pull away.

"Let go. Let us see Kishi and Dora!"

Alice released her hand, pulled back her arm, and slapped the woman across the face. A yelp from across the room broke her heart a little. She didn't want to taint White Dove's opinion of her, but she absolutely would not stand for bad behavior. Her knuckles stung, and a spot of blood from her hand, wounded from lashing out at the jewelry maker, stippled the quilt. She pointed a single finger, a silent warning.

The woman settled, and Alice completed the injection, set the empty hypodermic on the tray, crossed her arms, and counted to one hundred as she watched the drugs kick in.

Then she took up the other syringe, put her thumb on the plunger, raised it for the dancer to see. "Are you going to be good?"

White Dove let out a long sigh that prompted Alice to do the same. She held out her arm, top of the hand up. In smooth, practiced movements Alice removed the Luer lock cap, tapped the barrel, inserted the needle in the port, dispensed the diamorphine, withdrew the hypodermic. Confident the dosage would make her patient compliant in a matter of seconds, she settled on the bed. White Dove shirked away, and Alice realized she had a lot of ground to make up. She needed—no, craved—respect from this person the most, the one who had brought her so much joy over the years. And the replays of the dancer's performances had kept her mind occupied and surely saved her from the crushing defeat of treating patients during the most dire times. She had even told many stories about White Dove and the other dancers—how the fringe on their costumes swayed with every movement, bells on their moccasins tinkled every time their feet hit the ground, the amazing way she tossed the hoops so high and caught them without even looking—certain her fascination would bring comfort to her ICU patients. It was now her turn to comfort White Dove.

"Your friends are fine. I couldn't help them, so they're home now."

"I don't know what that means." The last words slurred to a mumble.

"There's nothing to worry about. Let's just think about getting you well. Positive thoughts promote healing." She beamed a smile and chirped, "So go to sleep, and have happy dreams."

Alice got up from the bed and drew the sheet and quilt over White Dove. She smiled at her subject, who looked like a perfect princess falling into a deep slumber. Alice watched for a long time.

And then she got busy.

CHAPTER THIRTY-SEVEN
EVA

Eva arrived at her department, still dazed and reeling from sensory overload, and didn't lift her head long enough to acknowledge anyone as she made a beeline for the desk she shared with a nightshift deputy.

"Duran, a word, please," a voice said.

She turned to see the Taos County sheriff Clark Bowen filling up the entire doorway of his office, then crossed the open-concept bullpen and stood outside the open door to her superior's office and waited for permission to enter.

"No need for the formality, Deputy. Have a seat."

Suspicious, wary, expecting the worst before he spoke a single word, she sat on the edge of one of the two chairs opposite his desk, ready to bolt in case things went sideways. An irrational thought, but she still wasn't familiar with this man, and he surprised her every time they spoke privately.

She had no idea what to expect. For sure it wasn't what came out of his mouth when he said, "I appreciate you helping us with this, Duran. For keeping us . . ."

"Compliant?" she offered.

He frowned, confused. "No. Respectful."

Embarrassed heat rose from her Kevlar. "Thank you," she managed to say, eyes on her lap.

As usual she had jumped to the racist position. Went with the assumption that every light-skinned person would be a bigot even with no valid reason to believe so. Bowen wasn't being disrespectful, but actually *re*spectful. Everyone seemed to be learning faster than her, even the kind new commander from Oklahoma.

From day one the top cop had deployed his mission: respect the people of all colors. No excuses. No one would get a second chance to do right under his authority. Several deputies had rejoiced when the big man had been elected sheriff two years earlier, assuming a redneck ally would be sitting behind the boss's desk. They were the first to go.

Five years on the county force Eva had waited to be assigned a position. She'd graduated the academy second of all trainees, held top marksmanship honors year after year, even taught workshops on weaponry to baby cops from her department and Taos city academy recruits. And yet still she waited and did her best to be patient, rotating duties as a dispatcher and 911 operator, until a patrol slot opened up.

Newly elected Sheriff Bowen's speech at his badge-pinning ceremony gave her the first glimmer of hope. He spoke of his intent to hire more female deputies and looked right at her when he said the words.

Now she drove her own rig, emblazoned with the Taos County Sheriff's Department logo on the doors. She would be forever grateful. All over the region, locals respected Bowen, and that respect had trickled down, even to her. Fights would split up as soon as her pickup came to a halt in bar parking lots, where altercations occurred all too frequently. Local drivers would pull over right away when she bleeped her siren. When offenders realized a Native woman wore the badge, they would back down, reluctant at first, but they all knew if someone messed with her, the wrath of the sheriff would rain down on them.

Their first face-to-face came to her mind. *I'd really like you to be the county's bridge to your people,* Bowen had told her during the closed-door meeting in his office. *This is important to me. I've got some Cherokee blood and won't stand for any of our officers being unkind and unfair to anyone of color.*

Eva had bit her tongue after that tidbit. Yeah, right. Ninety-nine percent of the country claimed to have Cherokee blood, she had thought, but said, *Was she a princess?* Also what most of the nation claimed to believe.

I thought so, he said, reverence in his voice. *Kindest person I ever met, to this day.* He pulled out his wallet, tugged out a well-worn sepia-toned photograph, and handed it to her. A white man dressed in a suit stood next to an obviously Native woman holding a baby. The modestly dressed, dark-skinned woman didn't look at the camera, and neither did the man—instead, he beamed at the woman beside him, one arm draped across her shoulders, the other under their baby.

Is that you?

Maybe. No one remembers. He smiled at her and held out his hand. *I like to think so, though.*

She handed over the photo and wished she had a similar one she could show off. Her grandparents were the most important people in her life, and she didn't have a single picture of the three of them together. Another regret she'd put in the opportunities-lost drawer and slammed it shut.

The memory vanished when Bowen said, "Are you with me, Duran?"

Eva blinked a few times and sat up taller. "Yes, sir. Absolutely."

"Tourism is picking up again, and folks are relocating from all around. No one really knows who lives in the area and who's passin' through. Point is, spending is up, and that means more taxes going to the state, and that makes my bosses very happy. I don't much care about what they think or want, but that's between you and me."

The declaration hadn't occurred to Eva. She'd thought he was the boss, but of course he would have superiors too. The governor of New Mexico, for sure. Maybe even senators in Washington, DC. Tucked away in a somewhat calm county, the region they protected wasn't immune to crime, and property theft complaints had surged since Eva started patrolling on the force. Many of the crimes were drug-abuse related. Same as big-city problems.

"Point is, outsiders can cause trouble to happen," he continued. "Sometimes they're the ones making trouble. Bring their bad habits to our area. We don't want that."

"Excuse me for saying so, but I hope that's the case with whatever happened to Kishi Reyna. Because if a local did this, it would set us back years of peacekeeping and relationships between the county and city and the tribe."

He hesitated before he said, "What if it's someone from your tribe?"

She didn't hesitate. "I don't believe so, sir." And then she modified her statement. "I hope not, sir."

"You and me both. That would be a true nightmare."

They both sat in silence, lost in their own thoughts, then Bowen said, "What did the ME tell you? Are we talking possible homicide or standard overdose?"

"Dr. Mondragon is unwilling to commit to anything this early."

"Come on, Duran. Give me something. Is your woman's death suspicious?"

"To me, yes. The ME needs more time, but if it turns out she suffered an overdose, there was no paraphernalia found at the scene. Kishi's body was definitely dumped, and that's suspicious as hell. Even if this isn't deemed a homicide or turns out to be an accidental death, we've got to be looking for whoever got her to that area."

"Hunting grounds, you mentioned on the phone yesterday. Who else would know about that place?"

"Well, pretty much every Taos Pueblo who hunts or has a family member that does. That zone on the rez is popular to us but not to non-Natives."

"Point taken. What do you see for next steps?"

"I'd like to stay on this, Sheriff. If that's all right with you."

"Yes, absolutely. You're the only deputy qualified. Let me know if you need anything formal from me for the TPPD. And Taos PD might be helpful too. Just be mindful of who you divulge info to. Me first and foremost. Need-to-know basis only for everyone else."

"Copy that, sir. I completely understand and agree."

And she believed her own words, except for what she would tell Cruz. She needed him. He would be in the loop, for sure. And Kai, she remembered. He would nag her until all answers satisfied his curiosity. She could make stuff up, but he had seen through her smokescreens before. "Need to know" didn't exactly pertain to the young man. Anyway, he could be helpful.

And that's what she needed first and foremost. Help. Because the weight and responsibility of not only finding Paloma, but also bringing Kishi's offender to justice, suddenly felt overwhelming.

CHAPTER THIRTY-EIGHT
TONITA

Tonita kept waking up from nightmares. The last one so bad she'd pinched herself to keep from falling back asleep. Withdrawal bugs crawled under her skin. Hunger made her stomach rumble. More tired than she'd ever been, she could barely find the energy to keep her eyes open. Surely not ambitious enough to get up and try to break into Dora and Kishi's room to make sure they were all right. That late morning's drug dosage had hit her as hard as the first days of their captivity. Back to square one, after having felt so good the day before.

She placed a shaking hand to her cheek that still burned from the nurse's slap. She had never been struck before. Ever. The humiliation burned as much as the skin she hoped wouldn't turn to a bruise. Most of all she was ashamed for Paloma to have seen the brutality. Tonita had been told to protect her younger cousin, to look out for her no matter what, ever since the tiny dancer could walk on her own.

Maybe that's why she'd started doing the drugs. So she wouldn't be left out, be with Paloma twenty-four seven. It had broken Tonita's heart when Ahiga died—she had loved him too. Although Tonita would never have told either of them, hers would be an unrequited love, an unspoken secret she shared with no one.

Paloma and Tonita needed each other during those worst of days. The physical therapy had been the trickiest part of the healing, once she and Eva were able to coax Paloma from her mourning bed. She felt the pain every step, leg lift and squat, as if the agony were her own—a type of phantom pain neither cousin ever doubted.

Sharing the legit meds hadn't been an issue at first. Then the doctors wouldn't fill any more prescriptions, not even Percocet or Vicodin, for sure no more OxyContin. They had to get creative—almost an impossibility on the reservation. Even three years ago a zero-drug tolerance had been enforced by the tribal council and police. And so necessary trips to Albuquerque and sometimes Santa Fe became more frequent and expensive after the dealers had hooked the enthusiastic consumers, led by the once-famous hoop dancer. Somehow Paloma always found a way to provide for their new hobby.

Then the money train dried up, and they had no choice but to settle for less-expensive highs. That's when Kishi and Dora came on board. Kishi, a literal rock star, had access to endless supplies of mood- and pain-altering options. Cheaper, for sure, but also deadly when the good stuff started to show up as being laced with fentanyl. Cautious and ever vigilant, Tonita always carried Narcan overdose rescue nasal spray with her and had saved fine-boned and delicate Dora's life three separate times. Tonita was pretty proud about that . . . if she didn't think about it too much.

Again the money became an issue, and the past year or so the four friends had done anything they could think of to find the cash necessary to get them well. Tonita didn't like to think about that either. She'd had so little, even before the drugs. Only her ability and talent as a basket maker kept her going. A person of simple needs, she constantly reminded herself she needed only a place to sleep, a little to eat, and the ability to make her baskets.

The designs had often come to her in the middle of the night, so insistent she had to sketch out the snapshot in her brain before she could lie back down. But the craftsperson in her started to fade from the time she snorted her first line of cocaine. And had died once the needle slid in her arm, followed by the most glorious sensation she had ever felt. Even better than the two times in her life her grandmother had told Tonita the baskets she had crafted were as good as any the elder had ever made.

When her baskets started disappearing, she figured it was kids messing around and never would have guessed her own family had been so jealous of her up-and-coming success that they took her creations, may have even destroyed them. Not adhering to traditional concepts was all but forbidden by the women of her line, who had made vessels from designs many believed had originated at the time the village had been built, over one thousand years earlier.

With nothing to sell, no access to the favorite willow tree on her grandfather's property she had roamed from childhood, she didn't feel welcome and sometimes not even safe. The need to care for Paloma came at the perfect time. They had saved each other. But the lesser cousin needed to kick in so as not to be a burden. She had only her body. And so she used that. Over and over, shame be damned. She wasn't sure if Paloma knew, maybe not even Dora, but Kishi did. The drum maker's eyes always brimmed with tears when Tonita would hand over the crumpled bills before they found a ride to the bigger cities.

"Don't think about it."

Tonita hadn't realized she'd said the words out loud until a voice across the way said, "Think about what?"

She turned her head to Paloma, who stared at the ceiling, eyes wide open.

"Cake," she replied, so as not to bring her cousin down.

Paloma looked over, a frown creasing her still-stunning face. Then a single laugh burst from her mouth. Full throttle, wall shaking. "Now I want cake."

Tonita let out a giggle. "I'd almost kill for some right now."

"Chocolate for you and Kishi, carrot for me and Dora. Damn, that sounds good."

A sugar craving swept over Tonita. Grateful for the diversion, she said, "And ice cream?"

"Well, of course."

"If we ever get out of here—"

"Oh, we're getting out," Paloma said. No questions or ifs in her tone.

"How?"

Paloma returned her gaze to the water stains above their heads. "I'm working on it."

"What can I do?"

"Play along. No matter what I do or say. Even if it's shocking. Or ridiculous."

Tonita tucked her knees to her chest and made herself small like when they would tell each other ghost stories at midnight. "Can you give me a clue?"

"If I had one." A beat of silence, and then another raucous burst of air shot from Paloma.

But Tonita didn't worry. Her cousin was brilliant. And clever. And motivated. She must miss her son so much. Her thoughts turned to Eva Duran. The one person who might be able to find them. Many times the four had been lucky to have the cop sniffing around like Paloma's brother's prized search and rescue dogs. She couldn't recall if she'd ever thanked her for that. It was her job, but actually more than that. The woman wasn't blood related to any of them, and often Tonita wondered why Eva would endanger her heart time after time. Even risk her job. Disenrollment had been a worry, too, not only for the foursome, but also Eva for being their champion. The devotion to Paloma "White Dove" Arrio was another drug. One few could quit.

"What you said you'd do for cake?"

"Yeah."

"Be ready if it turns out we have to do that."

Although Tonita wasn't quite sure what that meant, she began to mentally prepare. She didn't want to kill anyone. But she would.

For Paloma, she would do anything.

CHAPTER THIRTY-NINE
EVA

Eva finished up the most basic paperwork she could get away with, hurried back to the official vehicle, and pointed it toward the city police department building. It took more concentration than she could spare to turn her attention away from worrying about Paloma until she almost sideswiped a BMW driven by a white-haired driver. He shocked her when he blew her a kiss rather than lifting a middle finger. For a moment she marveled that people could still pleasantly surprise her every now and then.

Concentration back to the road, she thought about what she would tell Andrew Kotz to get him to cooperate. *Don't flirt* was first on the list. That got her nowhere but where *he* wanted. She needed to find Alice Jones, the nurse who ran the mobile medical clinic, and she hoped the computer genius could help enlighten her. If someone from her own force had the skills, this would be so much easier. She had felt bad in the past leading on the younger cop when she'd needed his help. Had even been a little harsh whenever he became too obvious about wanting to start a legitimate relationship. That would never happen, she'd known from the beginning.

And yet, here she was, needing him again. She longed for a day she wouldn't need anyone, then almost laughed out loud because who didn't require at least one person. Especially in law enforcement. There had been times when an entire department couldn't get a crucial element involving a case cleared.

When she arrived, as before, she badged the officer at the front desk for him to buzz her through. Eyes ahead, back straight, in full cop mode, she strode to Kotz's desk. Guest chair pulled out, a place on the desk cleared off, he had been waiting for her to arrive.

"You're here," he said, wiping mustard from the corner of his mouth.

"So are you."

Andrew sniffed the air and wrinkled his nose. "Where have you been?"

"Morgue."

"Ah. Explains the perfume." He sat back down and held out the other half of his sandwich. "Ham and cheese. Yours if you want it."

Still unable to think about what food would do to her stomach, she held up a halting hand. "I'm good."

"Okay, what can I do for you?" he asked.

She ignored his suggestive attitude and said, "Can you run a computer search? Put your mad skills to use? Sheriff cleared it with your captain."

"Yep, got the good-to-go."

He wrapped up the rest of his sandwich, meticulously wiped every finger, and to Eva's relief, turned into a completely different person. Ramrod straight at the edge of his chair, eyes squinted to the monitor, tone professional, he asked, "Name?"

"Alice Jones. She's from Texas. Certified nurse practitioner there, New Mexico, and Arizona, for sure. Maybe other places. No one has seen her recently. She may not even still be on the rez."

"And?"

"And what?"

"What you've given me is pretty vague. I mean, Jones? Really?"

"All I got. Do your magic."

Kotz wriggled his fingers and poised them to hover over his keyboard for a moment. He motioned with his head for her to join him. She didn't want to miss anything and could maybe even give him some direction, so she reluctantly moved the chair to his side of the desk, suddenly aware of how unpleasant being this close to her would be smell-wise.

Seeming unaffected, he opened a classified site, signed in, typed a list of keywords so fast she couldn't keep up reading, before he opened another field and clacked some more.

"The tribal leadership approved her to treat Natives on the reservation," Eva offered. "Think she would need to get approval for that from someone? Board of Nursing in New Mexico or Texas, or maybe there's a union she could belong to?"

"Good ideas." He opened another site and started a search on that one. "Dead person found on the reservation. Shouldn't the FBI be involved by now? They've got all the super-secret access."

The mere thought of the feds getting involved rankled Eva. Liaison or not, she would be out of the loop the moment outsiders stepped boots on reservation ground. She couldn't have that. And she couldn't risk losing her badge either. Kotz held the key to advancing a single step forward in her private investigation. She decided to appease him best she could. "The boundary is unclear where we found our girl," she said. "Might have been county land."

"O-kaaay," he said, drawing the word out.

He didn't believe her. Why would he? She wasn't sure she believed her own explanation. Only she and Cruz had verified where Kishi's last steps had ended. If the Pueblo woman had actually *walked* there at all. The crime scene techs had taken all of the required photos, but for their official report, they relied on the Taos Pueblo officer's account of the location. They took note of the belief the victim's body had straddled county and reservation boundaries. The statement would not satisfy everyone, especially if the feds got involved.

"Like I thought," Kotz said. "Lots of options. Do you have a description?"

"Football player big, from what I'm told. Almost six feet tall. Wide and well built. Late forties."

Kotz typed some more. Then he started whistling, low and slow as he concentrated. She looked around to see if he bothered anyone with the nonsensical trill of notes. No one seemed to take notice, and she figured this must be a habit those around him had either become used to or ignored. She, however, became more and more nervous from the frenetic jazz-style improvisation.

Just as she was ready to snap a "quit that racket" at him, he stopped the noise, turned to her, and beamed his most charming smile. The one that caused her to say yes that one time.

"Might have something. Four pinged as possible matches."

"Really? Only four?"

Kotz polished his fingernails above the badge pinned to his uniform shirt. "Like you said, 'mad skills.'"

Eva took out her notepad and raised her phone to the monitor. She tapped the photo option to capture the four individuals, then jotted down some notes to remind her which sites Kotz had located the information from. "Weird. They all look similar. Think they're the same person? Maybe duplicate info loaded?"

"Not that I could tell on my end. You'd be surprised how many doppelgängers I've stumbled on when doing searches."

Again she had miscalculated the man. She barely knew the sort of "twin out there somewhere" reference. Different hair and eye color looked to be the primary distinctions between two of the four. Each listed more than a few primary addresses, and only one stated Texas as their current residence.

"Can you print those out for me?"

"Done."

As if on cue, a female officer dressed in a tight-fitting uniform, no older than Kotz, stopped by his desk just long enough to drop off the printouts. Eva issued a thank you, but the woman had already darted out of eyeshot. "Busy around here."

"Tourists are coming back. More every day. Always something going on."

He nudged her shoulder. "Don't you think so?"

Too busy collating the driver's licenses and nursing IDs, she hadn't caught what else he had said. "Sure," she replied to be polite.

"Okay, it's a date then." Kotz puffed out his chest.

She scooted her seat back, the wheels launching her a yard away. "What?"

"Ha. Gotcha. I'm kidding. Remember what that is?"

"Right." She let out a relieved breath, stood, and took her time pushing the chair back to its original place. Unable to come up with an adequate comeback, she thanked him, waved the papers, and hurried away.

Feeling awkward and embarrassed, relieved to reach the exit, she almost collided against the female officer who had delivered the paperwork.

Unlit cigarette and lighter clutched in each hand, the woman chuckled. "Caught me."

"Quitting's a bitch." Eva didn't actually know this, had never smoked more than a dozen cigarettes in her life, figured one less potential habit in her life would be a good thing. Still, she didn't want the cop to be uncomfortable.

"You're tellin' me. Seven years on and off."

"Must've started when you were a little kid."

"Yeah. Older brothers. What can you do? Either follow their lead or be crushed by body odor and Indian burns—" The cigarette flew from her hand as she covered her mouth, eyes as wide as any Eva had ever witnessed, light skin flushing a deep crimson. "I'm so sorry. I didn't mean any disrespect. It's what my grandfather called it—"

Eva had heard the term before. Many times, actually. Wasn't offended by the slur. The need to put the person at ease took precedence over any indignation. She glanced at the nameplate pinned to the uniform. "It's all right. Don't worry about it." She leaned over, picked up the cigarette, and handed it to her. "How long have you been on the force, Tallow?"

It took three tries for the lighter to fire up before she breathed in and out a massive lungful of smoke. "Ten months now. You're a sheriff's deputy, right?" Eva nodded, and the other cop said, "Does it get easier?"

"Sometimes," Eva said as she headed toward her vehicle.

"Any advice?"

"Keep your head down," she said over her shoulder. Eva wanted to add *and wear a bigger uniform* but figured that advice might be taken the wrong way.

CHAPTER FORTY
ALICE

Alice wrinkled her nose at the smell of smoke that continued to permeate the room, even the freshly washed quilt atop where the drum maker had once lain. She had bought the sticks from the same place as the ceremonial dresses in Santa Fe. The clerk promised the dried leaves wrapped in string were from reservation lands, but they smelled more like oregano than anything that would come from the desert. The smoke gagged her the moment she had lit the end of the stalk, and the harder she blew trying to get out the fire, the bigger the white puffs plumed. She'd had to extinguish the smoldering mess in the bathroom toilet.

As best she could, she kept her back to the woman, her face a bloody mess. She had checked vitals a few minutes ago, shocked to discover a faint pulse. "Not long now," she said to the motionless form. "You'll be all right soon."

At the closet, she opened the accordion door and ran a loving hand down the sleeves of the three remaining ceremonial dresses. This time she selected the simple deep-brown dress, adorned with a double row of antler tips, and matching knee-high fringed boots. Her heartbeat ramped up as she gazed at the outfit and imagined herself wearing it, the soft leather sliding down her body. She wanted one of her own, to match her girls', but they didn't have her size, as was often the case. Some cruel people called her *sir* because of her height and size. Strong as a man, she didn't let the insults get to her. Strength could be the biggest asset to a nurse. And this had proved to be the case over the past thirteen days, rotating, bathing, and clothing the women to keep them comfortable and free of bedsores.

A moment of sadness swept over her when her thoughts turned to how she would now need to take care of the jeweler for the final time. Full night couldn't come soon enough. For now she needed to begin the final preparation of the Indian woman.

She filled up a bucket of warm water from the shower, put on a double layer of latex gloves, then returned to kneel at the bedside of her patient. First she removed the IV port from the top of the hand and cleaned the area. Then took off and folded the nightgown. She squeezed out the warm soap and bleach water from the washcloth and carefully stroked each arm and leg of the dainty young woman.

It took a while to remove all of the dried blood trapped in every crevice, even behind the ears. Careful not to cut the skin, she ran a dulled scalpel under each fingernail. Alice didn't mind taking so long. She had hours and hours before she could risk taking her patient to the final resting place. White Dove might eventually find out what had happened to her friend. She didn't want to upset the dancer, she reminded herself. Alice couldn't risk any disrespect.

The driving route she would take and every movement getting there had replayed in her mind until she was certain no surprises would derail her overall plan. But she worried about rigor mortis. The onset would begin in a couple of hours, so she had to hurry.

Constant words fell from her mouth, anything that kept her mind off her task. From her failure. She told the lifeless woman about the weather, how the clouds looked so dramatic at the end of the day. And that rain had finally fallen, even though only for a short amount of time. She imagined the Pueblo people would be very happy about that.

"Maybe the corn will survive," she muttered, not knowing if corn even grew on the reservation. The research she had lost herself in pertained mostly to White Dove's hoop-dancing fame and where and when she had performed over the years.

"I'm sorry about the smell. The saleslady told me the sage was from around here, but I think she lied to me." She smoothed the hair from the other woman's face and placed a tender finger on one split lip, then the other. "I'm glad you can't feel that." Then she touched each welt and abrasion. Each time she said, "And that, and that, and that."

Alice rubbed her knuckles, sore from making the wounds on the jeweler's face. She scanned the naked torso and counted at least a dozen more injuries that would never turn to full-on bruises. And yet they seemed to be deeper in color, and the welts looked more raised than an hour earlier.

"I wish you hadn't made me do this to you. I get frustrated sometimes. I tried to help. I really did." She pulled a tissue from her scrubs pocket and dabbed her wet eyes.

Scanning the torso, then limbs, she convinced herself they seemed to be stiffening as each minute passed. Satisfied the cleaning had been properly achieved, Alice took up the dress she had selected. Less-elaborate bone work and no hand beading adorned this outfit.

"I think this one suits you."

A moan, deep and low, alerted Alice to spin around. The woman remained in the same position, back flat on the mattress, toes pointing outward.

A groan came from lips closed tight.

Alice gasped. Fringe slipped from her fingers. She crossed the few feet to the bed and took hold of a birdlike wrist. A pulse, stronger than before, fluttered under the tips of her fingers. "Can't be."

She dropped the hand as she stood. Breaths shallow, unable to speak, she urged her brain to think. "Are you in pain?" she managed to say.

The younger woman issued a faint nod and winced.

"I can help with that!"

And she could. Alice raced from the house to the RV, took out her magic chest, and tumbled the prescription bottles to the table. Oxycontin, Percocet, Vicodin. Which one would be best . . . All three? "No. Think, think, think. She can't swallow these."

She reached for the heroin works and prepared three syringes. None of them potent enough to kill, but doses strong enough to bring relief for the hours before darkness could provide cover for the final steps. Actually, this would be better. She wasn't sure if she would have been able to handle a body in full rigor. Yes. This would work out just right. She prepared another dose and added that to the third syringe. Just in case.

Hypodermics in hand, Alice returned to the house, a revived spring in her stride.

CHAPTER FORTY-ONE
EVA

Eva pulled up to her house, still reeking of formaldehyde. Real or imagined, she wasn't sure, but if she didn't change out of her uniform and shower soon, she was certain the stench would permeate her inside and out.

A neon-green motocross dirt bike parked near the front of the house caught her attention. She didn't recognize the bike and hadn't been expecting anyone. No one seemed to be around as she got out of the vehicle and scanned the horizon. Clouds continued to bump up against each other as they had all day so far, but still no drops had hit the ground.

She raised her head to the sky, opened her arms wide, and yelled, "You've made us wait this long, dammit. Don't you dare rain."

As if in answer, a single fat drop splatted on her forehead.

"Now you've done it." She snapped her attention to the voice. Kai stood up from behind the motorbike and planted accusing hands on his waist. "Cursing the rain. Never good," he said.

She ran her hand over the Kawasaki writing on the side. "Nice ride."

"Santiago's making up for birthday presents he missed giving me."

"Generous."

"He's got, like, ten of 'em. All the same color. Don't know how he tells them apart. He said take it."

"Still . . ."

"No, I appreciate being able to use it. It's fun."

"Not sure your mom would approve."

"Not an issue right now, is it?"

Eva unlocked the front door and left the door open for him to follow. "Don't you ever go to class?"

"I'm a senior. Only biology lab and math on Thursdays." He sniffed the air and wrinkled his nose as he passed her. "What is that smell?"

Last thing she wanted was to tell Kai how she'd acquired the scent. His mood seemed in a good place, and she didn't dare risk him going down the rabbit hole imagining what she had encountered in the morgue. So she ignored his direct question and said, "Wasn't expecting you. I need to shower and change."

"No really, what is that smell?"

"Kai, it's already been a really long day. Let me get cleaned up, then we'll go get something to eat. Think about where you want to go."

He kept a wide berth and skimmed the walls as he backed his way into the kitchen. She unbuckled her gun belt and emptied her pant pockets, tumbling the items on the cedar chest near the front door, along with her handheld police radio.

She heard him open one cabinet after another, then the fridge. "Yeah, 'cause you've got nothing here," he said. "Not even chips?"

"Nope. Finished those off last night." She thought about Cruz lying back, naked in her bed, as he'd tipped the final crumbs from the bag to his mouth around midnight. A flush of pleasure made her anxious to see him again.

After a quick shower and change to comfortable street clothes, she felt more refreshed than when she'd woken up that morning. As she laced up her scuffed hiking boots, she visualized the checklist of items she intended to get to the rest of the day. But with Kai in the mix, who knew how that would actually turn out, and she gave up the attempt at a plan.

Although in plain clothes, she'd remain on duty, so she took the Glock from her duty belt and stuffed it in a more compact holster, then considered what else she should have on hand. Opting for the pair of handcuffs and cell phone case, she stripped those coverings from the belt and clipped the three items to the leather belt secured to her jeans. Lastly, she took her duplicate deputy's badge from the bedside table and clipped that, in full view, beside her handgun.

She found Kai waiting for her at the door. "Jeez, that took forever," he said.

"Dude, don't start." She slid on her favorite distressed leather jacket and scooped up the keys to the Beast. "What did you decide on?"

"Tamales?"

"Ohhh, yes. Leonel's. Let's roll."

The rain had kept up a steady pace, and she didn't want Kai to be out in it. After she locked up, before she could tell him to ride with her, Kai kicked the motorbike to life and shouted, "Meet you there."

He put on a helmet that hid his identity completely and spun the throttle three times, the deafening *ree-ree-ree* making her wince, fingers in her ears to baffle the high-pitched racket. She waved her hands over her head and stood in front of his path.

He flipped the visor up and said, "What?"

"I don't want you riding in the rain."

"I'll be fine."

"Nope." She hitched her head toward the Beast. "Come on. My sweet ride awaits your little butt."

He got off the bike, removed the helmet, and glanced behind him. "I don't have a little butt."

"I've seen that butt all your life. It's always been little."

"I don't think this is appropriate talk."

She chuckled. "Get in."

CHAPTER FORTY-TWO
NATHAN

Although Nathan "Little Bear" Trujillo stood the shortest in his second-grade class, he was the fiercest. And he was fast. Could run faster than boys and girls three and four years older. Once he got started, nobody could catch him.

Hair to his waist, straight out when he sprinted, he loved his really long hair and wouldn't cut it because he'd heard about a story where the hero lost all his strength when the bad guys made him chop off his hair. He wanted to be strong, so he kept it long, even when the kids called him a little girl. Everybody said he was pretty. His hair, great big brown eyes, skin like hot chocolate. Some people didn't like to look him in the eyes because he really looked back at you. Like he could see through them, see who they really were, see how they really wanted to be. And that scared some people. He considered it his superpower.

Most of all he wanted to be invisible. Especially now. He liked to watch people and figure out what they would do next. But he couldn't figure out the big man, and so he stayed as far away as he could, in case he needed a head start to get his much shorter legs going fast enough to escape. The guy had never hit him, but he knew there's always a first time, right?

He couldn't believe it when he saw that cop car, a lady behind the wheel, drive by his bus that morning. A lady cop. He'd never seen one before. He wanted to jump up from his seat, wave his arms, ask the bus driver to stop so he could tell her about the men who were in his house and doing bad stuff to his parents and there wasn't enough food. And that this had been the first time he'd been to school in two whole weeks and he was afraid his teachers would be mad at him.

The only way he could get the man to let him go to school was when he told him they would come looking for him if he didn't show up in class. He'd missed too many days. They wouldn't though. Nobody really cared. One kid hadn't showed up for a whole month before anybody talked about him. Didn't even know his family had moved away. Just gone. Left the house and almost everything still in it.

He had heard that happened a lot on the rez, and he was just a little guy, but he knew four kids from school whose families left because there was nothing else they could do. Nothing here. The future was too scary. Not enough jobs, not enough opportunities. If you didn't make anything pretty the tourists wanted and do it the right way, you were out. No other options but to move somewhere else.

He had to swear he wouldn't tell anyone anything going on because the big man said he would hurt his parents. He'd already hurt his dog. Killed him. His favorite thing in the world. Shot Bonkers because he tried to bite him, just that one time.

Nathan didn't know what to do. The man wouldn't let him see his parents, so they couldn't tell him. Bonkers couldn't even make him feel better like he always did when he leaned against him and licked his face.

He tried not to cry but had to wipe off his wet cheeks. He'd never felt so alone as right then, under the only tree in the yard, sitting on the ground, his hand on the mound of dirt that covered his best friend.

It would be dark before too long and the people not from around here would start coming. Money and drugs would change hands, and he was in charge of letting them inside the house one by one. He didn't know why they listened to him. Scared they wouldn't get their dope, he guessed.

Nathan took the gun from its hiding place, tucked through his belt at the back of his jeans. It made him feel powerful when he pointed the barrel at the strangers if they got pushy or mean. He pointed the gun at the house now, spotted the boss through the front window, pretended to fire it at him. Imagined the bully dropping dead, blood pouring out of his chest.

Then he felt terrible. His parents had taught him not to be mean to anyone. And if his grandfather knew what he had been doing, he would give him his back and maybe never talk to him again. Silence was the most awful punishment. He loved his elder's stories and never got any if he had been bad.

Nathan thought about his favorite tale—of his grandfather racing the mesa on the back of his spotted pony. The horse knew exactly how to avoid a rock or snake without even a bridle to guide him. Bareback, like he had seen in an old movie one time.

He had a knockoff BMX bike he raced all over the reservation, even at the open area in the village, where they would watch hoop dancers when his parents visited their pottery friends during festivals. He would imagine his steel ride was a steed as he raced beside his grandpa on his own horse. But one of the bigger guys messed around on it and bent the frame, so it didn't balance right anymore.

Another thing gone. Nathan didn't have much more. Anything really. One of his grandfather's stories came to him. About when he was young, way back when they didn't even allow propane to light the stoves in the main houses. All of the work would have to be done by dark and start when the sun came up. The tribe gathered and hunted and planted together as one. All but his grandpa, who'd had a bum foot ever since a horse stomped on it. He had to live on the first floor, all alone, while his parents and sister and three brothers slept in the upper floor of their part of the *Hlauuma*. Even his cries of pain, fear, worry didn't reach the higher levels. No one came down to wipe his tears for a whole year of lonely nights.

Nathan felt like that little boy now. And then he remembered how strong his grandfather had been. How everyone loved the man he had become. Respected him. Never even limped. And he should have. Nathan had seen the old man's foot. Toes twisted and top of the foot smashed. A proud man. No one would have known the whimpers that sounded like a hurt puppy when his grandpa took off his cowboy boots at the very end of the day. But Nathan did. And the little boy felt no shame when he knelt to rub the gnarled toes until the muscles relaxed and the old man bathed the top of his head with grateful tears.

The memory so raw his own tears fell now. A rumble of thunder split the air—thicker since he'd sat down. Light rain patted the dirt around him, exploding little tufts of dust.

The last thing Nathan wanted to do was go back inside the house that used to smell like fresh bread and now stank of cigarettes and beer and dudes that never wanted to take a shower.

"Guess I better go now, Bonkers." He stood up and brushed off the back of his pants. "See you later."

Nathan took his time taking the steps to the house that was no longer his. His left foot had fallen asleep and he imagined how his grandfather must have had to walk during his days of healing. He gritted his teeth and put more weight on the tingling foot, another step forward, again and again, until he felt no pain at all.

Back straight, head up, he turned the doorknob, his grandfather's spirit at his left shoulder.

CHAPTER
FORTY-THREE
EVA

By the time Eva and Kai finished their lunch, the storm had passed. She rolled down the window and breathed in the scent of rain-kissed juniper, sagebrush, and soil. Nothing settled her mind more than after a good downpour. She chose to alter her initial displeasure about the disruption hindering her investigation, see the sign from nature as a fresh start.

"Can we go to the pet store this weekend? I want to get Shadow a collar and tag so Santiago doesn't forget which one is mine."

As often happened, she had been so lost inside her own skin she had forgotten she wasn't alone. She glanced at the boy as if he'd just appeared. "Umm . . . sure. We could do that."

Kai rolled down his own window and took in a loud sniff. "Smells goooood."

They rode in pleasant silence for a mile, until his next words surprised her. "Tell me something about my mom I don't know."

She didn't feel comfortable sharing confidences and wasn't sure what exactly he knew about her friend. To her relief he clarified. "Nothing bad or crazy or anything that will scar me for life."

She smiled and searched her memory. "Well, she can sing like no one I've ever heard."

"I know—she's known as a dancer but can sing like an angel. That's old news. Heard it a ton of times."

"Okay . . . She can spot the perfect stone from thirty feet away. Dora used to make her go with her when she wasn't having any luck. She'd tell your mom what color and shape she needed to finish a piece of jewelry and to go on the hunt, and then *boom*, no time at all later, she'd walk back and hand over half a dozen perfect rocks to consider."

"Dora told me that. What else?"

"She could run faster than any of the boys growing up."

"Next."

"She could put together jigsaw puzzles like nobody's business."

Kai rolled his hand in the air, heard it before.

"When she was a freshman in high school, she beat up five seniors who were picking on a girl. You should have seen her! Arms flailing, legs jumping and kicking out, howling like a coyote after a fresh kill. It was awesome. Kids called her 'Flying Fists' for years after that."

She turned to him. His mouth hung open in awe. "I did *not* know that."

"Surprised you, huh?"

He smiled and bobbed his head.

"No one ever messed with me again. And sure as hell not Paloma."

"The kid was you?"

Eva nodded. "Your mom looked out for me, even as kids. And Tonita, even though Paloma was younger."

A proud smile swept up his lips. "Nice."

"If you were in White Dove's orbit, you were safe. She even lashed anyone with her tongue if they bashed any of her friends. An old-timer one time, when he yelled at Cruz for kicking up too much dust while he pulled up weeds on the old guy's property. Told him Cruz was trying to make his place look nicer. That he should thank the kid instead of making him feel bad about helping his elder."

She looked to make sure Kai was paying attention, then turned back to face the windshield. "I don't know if it's because she knows she can get away with being bold due to her standing in the community, but your mom has always been the voice for those who are too shy or feel unworthy."

Eva thought of a dozen more things Paloma could and did do that others could not or would not even attempt. Would be able to share for days with the boy what made the woman unique, never one thing that made White Dove whole.

"She's our compass," her best friend's son said. "For Cruz and Santiago too. We're lost without her."

Tears slid down Eva's throat as she took in Kai's assessment, confirming her knowledge that the single most important element that was the core of Paloma Arrio's essence—heart and soul—sat next to her.

"Test prep is tomorrow," he said. "No school. Can I hang out with you?"

"Shouldn't you test prep?" she asked, not actually knowing what that even meant.

"Nope. All good." He tapped his temple and winked at her.

"I don't know, Kai."

"Please? I'm going nuts at Santiago's house. He's a hard-ass. Always correcting me. Nothing I do is right."

She couldn't possibly take him on patrol with her, and she would need to work until at least noon. Had to log in miles patrolling in her official vehicle so she wouldn't run out of good favor with the sheriff. And so, she brokered a deal she hoped he would go for. "Maybe in the morning you can take out your new toy and drive around the rez. Try to find that RV. Think you could do that?"

Kai thought for a moment, then nodded. "Yeah. Yeah, I could do that."

Relieved she wouldn't have to worry about him, at least for the first hours of the next day, she said, "Okay, great, so have Santiago drop you off at my house in the morning to pick up your bike, and then we'll get back together in the afternoon. Compare notes. Then we'll figure out whatever's next."

"Sounds like a plan." His next words came out meek and soft. "And maybe you could take me to the place?" Eva frowned, confused, so he elaborated. "Where you found Kishi."

Eva's breath caught in her chest. "Why would you want to do that?" she asked, not wanting to experience whatever feelings would be unearthed for herself and terrified of what Kai might encounter.

"I don't know," he said. "To feel closer to my mom, maybe? See if I feel her hanging around. If I don't sense her, I'll know she's still alive. Do you think that's stupid?"

"No, Kai. Nothing you do, or think, or feel is stupid. I'm going to keep pounding you about that until you get it. Understand?"

"Right. You're right. Turns out you've been pretty much right about everything."

She sat up a little straighter and, in a confident voice she didn't always believe, said, "Yes. I. Am."

Eva clicked the turn indicator, preparing to make the turn toward Santiago's house. Kai reached out and took hold of her arm. She turned to him, confused.

"Can we . . . ?" he asked.

She frowned, confused by his request. He kept his eyes locked on the windshield, and she realized they had just passed the curve to the Gorge Bridge. She slowed and pulled over to stop on the shoulder.

"Do you want to go to the bridge?" He didn't answer, but his grip held on. "You're sure?"

He couldn't seem to speak when he nodded. Unsure whether she should comply, she waited a beat before she confirmed the road was clear and made a U-turn.

Pretty sure this would not be a good idea, she realized the young man needed to face a demon up ahead. She couldn't be more proud as she crept the Beast beyond the first stanchion of the barrier.

As she proceeded, he kept his attention on the gorge, then straight ahead when they reached the midpoint. She considered stopping but didn't want to rush him. Acceptance for one's actions often took time. She slowed down to gauge whether to go slower or faster and turned to him. He sat up straight and pointed to the windshield.

Eva whirled to where he gestured. An RV, at least a decade old, headed their direction. Dark trails of soot where the rain hadn't quite cleaned the dusty vehicle stained its hood.

Pulling her cell phone from the cup holder, she stopped to make sure she got a good look at the driver, then swiped to the camera function. As the motorhome came closer, an elderly couple waved, white hair and smiles turning in their direction as they passed.

"Was that the nurse?"

"No, she wasn't that old."

She wished she hadn't forgotten Kotz's printouts so she could show Kai. All she had was a verbal description to try. "Santiago said she's really tall. Looked fit, like a football player."

"Yeah, that's her." He shuffled in his seat. "Can we get out of here? This place is creeping me out."

Eva didn't doubt that. She accelerated to the end of the bridge and turned around in the rest stop lot. This time she took the bridge faster than she should have. An odd feeling of regret and sadness filled the compartment.

"Too many spirits hanging around," she said. "Did you feel them the other day?"

She glanced over at him. Head lowered, face reddening, he said, "No. I didn't feel anyone."

Although spirits didn't usually visit until the Pueblo who had passed to the other side's cross fell, she had often felt the presence of people still living but nowhere close by. Sometimes so strong she had to pick up the phone to call them, or the feeling would keep hanging around. More than a few times the person receiving the call had been beyond appreciative. Either they were in a grim spot or needed comfort, or were just relieved to know that somebody cared about them.

"They don't always come," she said, an attempt to make him feel he hadn't been abandoned in his time of need. "Letting them know you need them helps. Have you tried that?"

"Maybe I don't really believe in that anyway. My mom showing up and stuff. Anyone in past lives coming to help me."

Eva's heart sank. In her moments of desperation the only thing that had brought her back from the brink of complete misery was the certainty that others watched over her.

"Don't give up on us, Kai. We need you."

"You know, I'm getting pretty damned tired of people telling me how much I'm needed. That I'm the future of the tribe. I'm expected to do good. Be good. All the time. Keep your head down. Don't show your heart."

The boy's tone—conversational, not accusatory, challenging, or angry—as much as the actual words terrified Eva. She realized he had thought about this a long time. Maybe even longer than the number of days his mother had been missing.

"It's exhausting," he continued, sounding much older than his years. "Maybe I don't want to do it anymore. Any of it. Be anything to anyone."

"Like your mom," Eva snapped. A statement, not a question. "That's what you're saying, right? She gave up, so it's okay for you too?" The boy became mute, stone faced beside her.

Again, she pulled to the shoulder of the road. She clicked on the hazard lights and waited until she controlled herself a bit before she said, "Your mother didn't choose what happened. She couldn't heal her heart or body on her own. It's not your fault. It's not my fault. Or your father's, or anybody else's. I'm not giving her an excuse. Not saying her addiction is okay. I've seen a lot of lost ones since taking on this job. Our people too. We don't have a lot, but we do have each other.

Sometimes that's all we have. Family. Blood. Tradition. It's enough, Single Star."

She reached out and placed a tender hand on his arm, grateful he didn't pull away. "Trust me," she whispered.

"I'm trying, Lightning Dance. I really am."

A sob released from the boy. Guttural. Feral. Heartbreaking.

She clicked out of her seat belt, then his, pulled him to her chest, cradled his body to her own. Connection complete. One. As Paloma would have wanted.

Eva squeezed her eyes shut, and cursed herself for having thought of her best friend in the past tense.

CHAPTER
FORTY-FOUR
ALICE

Alice stayed with the jewelry maker every minute, except to freshen the water and towels that she was certain helped comfort the woman. The heroin worked to keep her patient asleep, but there was nothing like the personal touch. She was a seasoned nurse and knew precisely the amount of pressure to use and areas to avoid for wound care. Reverence was paid with every stroke, each dab of antibiotic cream, lip balm applied to avoid the cracked areas.

Dressing the woman had been easier than the drum maker, who was still fit despite the abuse to her body. The jeweler, so delicate, slipped into the oversize covering, her body nearly swallowed up in the deer hide.

"Not much longer now," she lied.

Hours. It would actually be hours. What would come next would require the darkest of nights. Already exhausted, Alice couldn't imagine being able to keep up the focused dedication for eight or more hours.

Her head bobbed, and she realized she had dropped off. She blinked a few times, yawned, stretched her neck. The hand towel had dropped to the floor, the bucket too. She wriggled her toes, wet inside her shoes.

"I'll deal with that later."

She looked at the empty bed across the room, fresh sheets awaiting her. "Just for a few minutes," she told herself.

She patted her patient's hand, eased the woman to her side and tucked pillows along her back so she couldn't turn over, then shuffled to the other bed. The moment she kicked off her second shoe, she drifted off.

Restful sleep didn't last long. Instead, nightmares plagued her. Respirators forcing air in and out, cries from her colleagues when they thought she wasn't listening, too many machines screaming the flat-line squeal, faces hidden behind masks twenty-four seven, identities all but forgotten. Never-ending suffering. Never stopping. Never thinking beyond the next patient. Sometimes thirty a shift. Forgetting to eat. No time to drink. Nobody to look out for those caring for the sick who wouldn't survive no matter how hard she and her colleagues toiled. Every ICU patient discharged to the morgue, never home.

Alice thrashed, kicked out, tried to run away from the memories and pain and stench and filth and misery, guilt for not being good enough to save them. Save them all. Save any of them. Save. Just. One.

Mercifully something wrenched her from the depths of sheer hell. A vision in light-tan leather. Long fringe swayed from the arms, sides, and bottom of the dress, bells on moccasins tinkling, hair swirling to cover the face. But Alice knew the apparition. Not a ghost at all.

She blinked. Breathed. Awake. Alive.

She sat up, her heart still hammering in her ears. "Thank you, White Dove," she said.

During the times of dire lows, the only thing that had kept her going was the thought of her favorite hoop dancer performing only for her. Sun on her face, crisp air stinging her cheeks, clear skies, she imagined herself sitting at the edge of the imaginary ring, heartbeat accompanying the drum that kept perfect time for the light-as-a-feather steps to fall on the sacred ground that had featured legions of other performers. None as talented or renowned as the dancer before her. A low moan broke the spell.

She looked over to see the jeweler, who hadn't shifted her position. She eased over and checked for a pulse. Faint and yet steady. A fighter. Another moan. She smiled and tucked an errant lock of hair behind the woman's ear.

"It's a little early, but I'll give you some more."

Alice inserted the needle beside the vein where she had removed the IV port, administered half the dose from the second syringe. The woman sighed, and every muscle melted to the mattress. Satisfied the patient would be compliant for another few hours, Alice left the room and eased open the door to the other room, beyond the bathroom.

She stood at the doorway to watch her sleeping patients. First the troublemaker. Then she held her gaze on her prize and her joy. Grateful tears blurred her vision.

"Thank you for saving me," she whispered. "Again."

CHAPTER
FORTY-FIVE
EVA

After Eva stopped by her house to pick up the paperwork from Kotz's search, she pulled up in front of Santiago's house. Kai bolted from the truck, didn't look back as he sprinted to the chicken coop and disappeared in the shadows. Santiago again stood on the porch, and Eva wondered if he had a camera mounted somewhere, maybe at the turnoff to his property. The brief rain had settled the dust, so that couldn't have been what alerted him. Unless that's where he stood most of the time. Surveying his kingdom of she didn't know how many hundreds of acres signed over to him by the tribal council over the years.

"What's with the kid?" Santiago asked before she had a chance to shut the Beast's door behind her.

"Nothing. He wants to see his pup. It's still his, right?"

"Yeah, yeah. I let him use a motorbike. Where is it? Did he wreck it already?"

"No. I didn't want him to ride it in the rain. Why do you always go to the dark, Santi?"

"Usually turns out that way. Saves time to get there first."

She raised the printouts and waved them at him. "Could you take a look at some photos? Let me know if one of these women is the nurse you met with?"

"Fresh coffee if you want it."

"That'd be great."

He led her to the front door, eyes on the first nurse's identification. She followed him, then made a quick beeline to give a painting of Paloma a quick look before she caught up. Head on a swivel as she continued through the house, she took in the impressive collection of Native-made sculptures, pottery, baskets and paintings arranged on pedestals and walls around the rooms they passed, each masterpiece lit by recessed lamps set for a low glow. Few windows allowed natural light, assuring the artwork would not fade. Latilla sticks, lined in precise rows in the plaster ceiling, gave each area the feeling of looking up at pine trees in the forest.

The home calmed her each step she took. They reached the kitchen, and she stopped at the threshold. Santiago had remodeled since she'd last visited. The rust-colored cement floor had been polished to enhance the swirl pattern. Pristine white subway tile covered the areas beneath snowy cabinets that must have reached eight feet tall. Stainless-steel appliances, including a double oven topped by eight gas burners and a grill, made her imagine the feasts the master cook could prepare in no time at all.

As if pulled by an invisible cord, she was drawn to the far wall, where floor-to-ceiling windows displayed a view of endless pristine mesa and the Sangre de Cristos. The most jaw-dropping architectural showpiece she had ever encountered.

"Woooow," she said, drawing out the word as she made final steps to the glass.

A mechanical whir made her halt. She glanced over to see Santiago pointing a remote control. One panel of glass after the other revolved and then slid on a track until all four massive pieces fitted side by side at the end of the opening.

"You like it? Redid the kitchen during the shutdown. Had most of the materials in stock. Figured, what was I waiting for? Not like I'm going anywhere."

"Spectacular." If she lived here, no one would be able to move her from this spot.

"All right, let's take a look at what you brought." He sat at a table preset for eight, moved two of the place settings, took out a pair of glasses from his breast pocket, gestured for Eva to sit beside him.

She wrenched her attention from the view and joined him.

"Did you show these to the boy?"

"Not yet. Wanted your opinion first."

"Maybe didn't want to upset him?"

"Maybe."

"Coddling him again."

"No, Santi. It's not coddling to take Kai's feelings into consideration. He's got enough going on. He's already obsessed with wanting to help find his mother. He needs to concentrate on school. That's what Paloma would want."

"You don't know Pueblo men very well."

"What is that supposed to mean?" she asked, finding it difficult not to take offense.

"He's going to do what he's going to do. He may not know what that is. His guides will take him where he needs to go. Even if it's not where you, or his mother, want them to lead."

"So you're saying you Native men have no choice in your paths? No recourse? Does this also mean you don't need to have scruples? That mistakes and victories don't make the man? His course is already set? Journey already taken and he's only going through the motions of living because everything has already been decided?" She took in deep breaths, panting from the rant.

His jaws bulged, clamped so tight she thought his teeth might crumble in his mouth. "That is not at all what I'm saying. Just know that he has guides. He's not alone."

She leaned in close and said through her own clenched teeth, "He was pretty damned alone on that fucking bridge three days ago. Where were his *guides* then?"

Eva regretted her words the moment they left her. Santiago deflated in his chair, shoulders slumped, chin close to his chest. She flashed on her first sighting of Kai on the balustrade. A shudder rattled her body. Fear came next. She may have considered Santiago an older brother growing up, but now he was one of the most respected members of the community. He held power. A respected councilman for the tribe. He had the ear of the entire council and leadership, as well as the chief of police on the rez. If she didn't hold her tongue Paloma could be disenrolled, and so could she. One phone call and *poof*. Disappeared from the registration rolls. As if she had never existed at all.

"That was cruel," she said. "I'm sorry, Santi. Will you forgive me?"

"Don't think I haven't thought the same things, Eva. It's sometimes hard, even for me, to live the life expected from others. Expected to teach the ways. To show no weakness makes a soul tired. And leaves a heart hard."

Hands remarkably still, he took up the first of the information sheets and studied the photo. She realized she would not receive any more justifications or clarification from the man who had opened up to her, perhaps anyone, for the first time.

And probably the last.

CHAPTER FORTY-SIX
KAI

Kai felt foolish for letting himself get so out of control in front of Eva. His cheeks still burned from embarrassment—eyes still stung from crying. No matter what he did, he couldn't seem to hide his feelings from Eva. She saw right through him. Or maybe he was just too tired to care about wearing the mask anymore.

What hurt worse than his shame was the worry that Eva would give up hope on her best friend and stop looking. He couldn't let that happen. He stroked Shadow, and the other pups when they came to explore his sneakers and pants. Comfortable in the company, he didn't need to utter any words he didn't want to. Didn't have to think. He tried to sit there, be in the moment, watch two of the puppies nurse from the momma dog, who thumped her tail every time he told her she was being such a good girl.

He stood up and tossed out the water that always seemed to have something floating in it and refilled the bowl at the spigot by the opening of the coop. At first he had sneered at the structure that looked like an exact model of the main house. Thought it was a stupid idea. A vain attempt to replicate and control what Santiago saw every day. Perfect house, perfect barn, perfect chicken coop, everything inside all of them also perfect.

But maybe he was wrong. Sure beat a house that barely stood up on the rickety walls and wasn't even your own. His mom had been so proud of their little shack when he was a kid. Together they would pick wildflowers or rosemary that would fill the tiny front room with color. Make her own bread in the oven outside, wash the sheets and their clothes by hand, even his dad's jeans that took forever to dry on the laundry line out back.

A wave of homesickness canted his body forward. Not only for the only place he knew as home or for his parents. He wanted, needed, craved structure and a sense of belonging. To anything. Or anyone.

He stared at the big house and tried to imagine what it looked like when it was built generations back, before Santiago had added rooms and changed the outside so everything looked like an original design. His mom had showed him pictures, all faded and sepia toned rather than full color. Simple, plain. A comfortable place you would want to run home to after school. Same amazing view of the open mesa, mountains in the distance.

Kai had never met his grandparents. Whenever he brought them up, his mother would run from the room, tears running down her face. Maybe his uncle would tell him stories about their past. He looked down. Shadow had found him and sat on his foot. "That would be cool, wouldn't it, boy?" he said, and the pup looked up and swished his tail.

He cast his gaze back to the main house. Home. Maybe this could be his, too, for now. He could make it work if he kept his head down and didn't cause any problems.

And if Santi would get out of his ass and let him do what he needed most of all. To find his mother. Because there would never be a home without her.

CHAPTER FORTY-SEVEN
SANTIAGO

Santiago continued to sit at the kitchen table, looking out at the view he had gazed at all of his life, this time seeing nothing. Eva's words still stung, bored into his nerves, bones, soul. She wasn't wrong. He had failed his family. Put the tribe and his reputation at the forefront, rather than doing all he could to care for his nephew and only sibling. Move mountains and earth—blood before tradition—his father would have advised. Words handed down by his grandfather and great-grandfather before him. But had he listened? Even to their spirits, who'd first tapped his shoulder, nudged him, even punched his back? No. Too proud. Drunk on power, the worry of losing his standing in the community blinding him.

No more, he decided. He pulled the cell phone from his pocket and speed dialed a number. "Prep two for me, Tommy. *De inmediato, por favor.*"

Then he stood from the table, hit the remote to close the wall of glass, made his way through the house, to the front door. "Kai," he yelled from the porch. "Come on, we're going for a ride."

The boy emerged, pup in his arms. He looked up at the sky, clouds still gray and ominous. "Now?"

"Bring the pup."

Santiago led Kai around to the side of the house, where a barn almost the size of the main structure sheltered his prized roping horses. A center aisle separated twelve stalls. The enclosure included a tack room and wash area, hay and supply storage. Everything first-rate, top-of-the-line materials. His sanctuary. He inhaled and caught a hint of sweet hay and dried corn. One spotted gelding stood next to a bay tied outside a stall, both saddled and bridled, tails swishing.

Kai looked around as if he had never been there before. Maybe he never had. This, too, he had no idea about. Whether the boy had investigated the property on his own or if his mother had given him the full tour back when he allowed her to step foot on his precious land. Her land, too, actually. He cursed himself again.

The nerve-racking noise of two motorbikes disturbed the horses. The pup whimpered and wriggled in Kai's arms. Santiago turned to the other end of the barn, where two men on the Kawasakis he'd let them borrow a couple of weeks ago came to a halt. He waved his arms, and the motors died. "Idiots," he muttered.

Kai stroked the puppy to calm it. "Who are those guys?"

"New workers. Not from around here. I've got a load of hay and grain being delivered later this morning." The men didn't take off their helmets, and he wasn't sure if they were the same two who showed up every couple of days to help with the grunt work, paid in cash after the end of each shift. He knew nothing about them, preferred it that way. He dealt with enough paperwork for his own three companies, and for the tribe. He had hoped to hire kids from the rez, but these days it seemed no one wanted the dirty, sweaty, backbreaking labor it took to keep a ranch going.

He glanced at the boy, who looked nervous as he turned his attention back to the horses. "Ever been in here?" he asked.

"No. I've seen the horses in the field, but not up close."

"Relax. They're big but gentle."

As if to contradict him, the big bay reared, stood on his back legs, kicked out the front hooves and blew air out of his nose, reins going taut on the rail.

"I've never ridden one. I'll just watch, okay?"

"Tommy, better put the saddle on Sara Sue instead."

His favorite stable hand did as he was told. Of course. Everyone did. And after a brief instruction, puppy settled in a tote bag in front of Kai looking very nervous in the hand-tooled saddle, they started a slow pace out of the barn, then beyond the paddock where one of his three trainers worked out his steed moneymaker—a black-as-night stallion who snorted his displeasure at the regimented conditioning.

Pace relaxed and hypnotizing, the boy started to look more comfortable as they headed for the wide-open mesa that could be seen from the main house's kitchen windows. Then Santiago stopped his horse and showed Kai how to turn his mount around.

"That pup—"

"Shadow," Kai corrected.

"Shadow isn't old enough to leave his mom yet, but he's yours. He'll be a good companion."

"I already love him."

"Just keep in mind he's a working dog. He'll need lots of exercise. And training so he knows who's boss. Everyone needs to have a leader. A dog must respect his owner so it knows what's expected."

"I feel like you're trying to teach me something, Uncle."

"No, you're already smarter than I'll ever be." Santiago chuckled when the boy reared back in surprise. "I'm not sure what I'm supposed to say here."

"Don't try so hard, Uncle Santi. I know you care about me. My mom, too, even though she's pissed you off. I appreciate all you're doing. Place to stay, this little guy. And the bike is awesome!"

The boy smiled, and his mother appeared. Young and fresh. Every opportunity in front of her. The elder had no idea how to respond, so he let out one of his trademark grunts and tapped his horse's side to get him going again. Kai followed the action, and Santiago nodded his approval that the young man caught on without being prompted.

"But I'm not gonna stop looking for my mom," the boy said.

This time Santiago was surprised. He wasn't sure he liked the stubbornness he recognized in himself. "Leave it to the cops. To Eva and Cruz." He couldn't meet his nephew's eyes when he then said, "They'll find her . . ."

"If she's alive, you mean."

Santiago snapped his full attention to Kai. "Why do you keep putting words in my mouth? You couldn't possibly know what I think or feel. Especially what I will say."

"Right. Because you're so much different than me." Kai held the silence, searching Santiago's face. "But you're not. You want her back too. I know it. You just don't want to show it. You keep that painting of her hung up. Not to remind you of who she used to be, but because you want to see her again. Alive. Maybe even so she can share that great big house of yours."

"If she wants." Santiago turned away, unable to meet the boy's eyes he felt burning through him. "I hope she does."

"Again . . . If she's alive," the boy repeated.

He didn't know whether the boy wanted a challenge of words or expected a backhanded slap or to be ignored. Hell, he didn't have a clue what the kid wanted. Normally he didn't give a second thought to anyone's feelings, not even his own. But this situation felt different. His nephew needed something from him. He couldn't tell him everything would be okay, hearts and butterflies would fly out of both of their asses when Paloma was miraculously delivered back to them, all bright and shiny and clean. He could only hope for this.

If she was alive.

Words had not been his friend the entire conversation, and so he said no more. Merely nudged a boot to get his ride going again. Same slow pace. Listening to make sure the other horse followed. Careful not to face the boy, and his demands for honesty. For truth.

CHAPTER
FORTY-EIGHT
EVA

After Eva dropped off Kai, she drove and drove and drove. For three hours, until at last she decided, enough. Time to go home. No more rain had fallen, yet storm clouds remained in the distance, and she kept thinking about the gorge that might be gushing from runoff soon. She considered a drive-by of the bridge, then decided against it. A single time crossing the massive structure that made her nervous even before Kai's incident would be enough for one day.

She parked the Beast, unlocked the front door, stepped inside, and froze at the sound of men's voices at the back of her house. Hand on the butt of her Glock, she eased the door shut and listened closer. After a moment she recognized Cruz and Kai's light banter. She smiled and closed her eyes to concentrate on their words.

"You never learned how to speak Tiwa?"

"No, they didn't offer that in school when I went," Cruz said. "Then the tribal council started to worry about the elders dying off and a whole generation that didn't know the language, because traditionally the words weren't written down. Ours is an oral language. Storytelling, instead of in books. The immersion programs have saved an ancient legacy."

"Can Eva speak it?"

"Yeah, a little bit. She learned mostly from your mother."

"But if you went to school together, how did Mom learn?"

"Don't let the dough get too brown. Turn it . . . yeah, just in time." Without missing a beat Cruz continued where he'd left off. "Part of the regulations for some of the competitions Paloma entered required that the contestants speak their native languages."

One of Eva's regrets. That she'd never become fluent in Tiwa, no matter how hard Paloma had tried to teach her. Either the incorrect dialect or misplacement of words—the language baffled her. But Paloma charmed every judge during competitions, amazed her teachers when she would go back to visit during homecomings or special festivities. Tiwa, spoken in her silky alto voice, lulled everyone around her.

As she moved toward the kitchen, she noticed a pack of playing cards on the cedar chest when she laid down her radio and keys. Eva halted her steps and inhaled. Hot oil and dough sizzling in a skillet, beans simmering, onions fried in butter. Her favorite. Mouth watering, stomach growling, she then relinquished her stuffed holster and badge to the cabinet, went to the kitchen, and stood at the counter, watching.

She had hoped maybe Cruz would take an interest in Kai, and the young man's future, become a mentor so he wouldn't feel so under the thumb of his uncle Santiago. And now here he was, teaching the boy how to make a basic Pueblo meal, discussing the importance of tradition. Pride for Cruz stepping up swelled in her chest.

Cruz must have felt her eyes on his back. He turned around, snapped the tongs together a few times. "About time. Thought we were going to have to eat without you."

"Hey, Eva. Look! Fry bread. Your favorite, right?"

"Yes it is. What are you doing here? I thought Santiago was dropping you off in the morning to pick up your bike."

"Cruz offered."

Eva cocked her head at the cop.

"Thought you'd like a homecooked meal for a change. Nothing fancy."

"I wouldn't know what that is. It does smell good, though."

"Smells excellent," Kai corrected.

"How can you be hungry? You finished off four tamales not that long ago."

"Fry bread. Who can't find room for that?"

Cruz bumped the teenager's fist. "My man."

They both raised their arms, fingers curled into fists that made their biceps bulge. Well, Cruz's bulged. Kai had some bulking up ahead to achieve such an impressive mass.

Smoke began to billow from the skillet. She pointed at the stove. "You've got a situation, Chef Romero."

"Oh, shit!" Cruz snatched a pot holder, shoved the pan to an unlit burner, pinched the golden-brown dough from the sizzling oil with the tongs, and laid the crisp bread on a paper towel next to five other plump discs. "No problem. Caught it in time."

"Dude, that would have been tragic."

"Ow! Dammit," Cruz said, flapping his left hand. "That popping oil hurts like hell."

Without a word, Kai swept up a paring knife, hurried through the kitchen to the front room, and went out the door.

Cruz gave Eva a puzzled look. "What's that about?"

"You'll see," she said.

A few minutes later Kai returned, plant cuttings topped by bright-yellow flowers in one hand and pieces of bark that glistened with pine sap in the other.

"Why'd you bring those weeds in here?" Cruz asked.

"Making you a paste from the añil del muerto for your burns."

"We're gonna be sneezing like crazy in a minute."

The young healer opened and closed cabinets one after another. "Eva, where's your mortar and pestle?"

"Do you really think I'd have those?"

"Right. Probably not. I'll have to improvise."

He reached for the iron skillet, wiped it clean with a dishtowel, poured a little olive oil into the pan, and proceeded to pull bluish-green leaves from the plant and rip them into small pieces. Then he took up a spoon and used the underside of the bowl to smash the leaves in the oil. Intrigued, Eva and Cruz looked over the boy's shoulder as he created a paste. Next, Kai squeezed out a dollop of dish soap in his hand and added the pitch-encrusted bark, then rubbed his hands together until bubbles formed.

"Wash your hands with this first."

He wiped the soapy mixture over Cruz's wounds and instructed him how to clean the area. When Kai was satisfied, he turned on the cold water at the kitchen sink and had Cruz rinse, then handed him a fresh hand towel to dry off.

Kai scooped up the paste on his finger and said, "Okay, give me your hand."

Cruz tucked his arm behind his back. "Nuh-uh."

"Uh-huh."

"I'm allergic to goldweed. What if I have a bad reaction?"

"Let him do it, Cruz," Eva said. "Paloma told me the tea he made from the stuff helped her mom's upset stomach after chemo treatments."

Cruz alternated his suspicious gaze from Eva to Kai and back again, then reluctantly held out his inflamed hand.

"It's good for hemorrhoids too," Kai said as he slathered on the mixture. "Got any of those?"

"Don't push it," Cruz said.

Kai took out three plates from the cabinet, forks and knives from the drawer, and set the table as if he'd done it every night.

She sat at the table, crowded by bowls of refried beans, diced onions, tomatoes, jalapeño peppers, and Valentina hot sauce. "Feeling pretty spoiled."

"Good." Cruz popped the top off a bottle of La Cumbre IPA, handed it to her, clinked the bottle with his own.

Eva wondered when he'd had the chance to shop for the groceries. If he hadn't been able to face his colleagues after the morgue visit, or if he'd had the items on hand at home. She couldn't remember the last time she'd stepped inside his place. Or if he even still had one of the revolving roommates he would offer his couch to if a buddy fell on hard times.

"And the best part." Kai plopped a bear-shaped container of honey in front of Eva.

"I am officially impressed."

Kai and Cruz shared smiles, and they settled at the table to eat. Eva did her best not to moan in ecstasy during each bite.

"How do you think Kishi really died?" Kai asked, his tone conversational.

Cruz choked on his food. Eva dropped her fork to clatter on the plate. "Where did that come from?" she asked.

"She's been on my mind all day."

Eva's too. And by the sadness on Cruz's face, she was pretty sure he felt the same.

"Don't you think it's time to start cracking heads to get answers?" the boy asked.

She couldn't keep her mouth from dropping open. "What makes you think that even works? No, Kai. We can't just go out there and do what we want. Cruz and I are law enforcement officers. We have to follow procedure."

"Yeah, but why not just backtrack and fix stuff you might have done wrong later if you have to. Get warrants or whatever, after you find what you knew you were going to anyway."

"Doesn't work that way," Cruz said. "Everything we discover needs to hold up in court, in case it's determined a crime was committed. It's the only way to catch bad guys these days."

"We don't like this any better than you do," Eva offered. "Paperwork and search warrants and approvals take up way more time than they should. Sometimes the alleged offenders know this."

"They're not all stupid?"

Eva and Cruz shared looks. She tried not to crack a smile. "Many are," Cruz said. "Some stumble into the luck."

"Others know exactly what they're doing," Eva said. "Take pleasure in knowing they have the upper hand. Love to watch us sweat and tread water while they keep on doing whatever they want."

Cruz cleaned his plate with a piece of fry bread. "And don't get me started when more than our own departments need to be involved."

"Like with Kishi, and maybe my mom?"

"Yes. My sheriff's department, Cruz's because Kishi is Pueblo. City cops, too, because . . . who knows what could be discovered within Taos city limits. Jurisdictional factors might turn up."

"And hopefully not the feds," Cruz offered.

Eva scowled, not wanting the prospect given power by being mentioned.

"Is that what it's like?" Kai asked. "Being a cop? Drive around. Look for stuff. Ask a lot of questions and get no answers?"

Cruz stacked the plates and took them to the sink. "A lot of the time, yeah."

"Boring and frustrating." Eva squeezed a dollop of honey from the bear and popped the perfect bite into her mouth. This time she didn't stifle her moan.

"I like this cop work. Maybe I could change my major."

"No," Eva and Cruz snapped in unison. Paloma would be the first to quash the unreasonable shift. Without her there, Eva had to be the adult.

"You're studying biology," Eva clarified. "Plants. Nothing else."

"Okay, okay." Kai raised his hands in surrender. "Jeez. I'm just playin' around. I'll get the cards." He got up from the table, carried the last of the bowls to the counter, then went to the cedar chest.

"How's your hand?" Eva asked Cruz.

He opened and closed his fist. "Better. Huh. *Really* better."

Eva didn't waste any time getting to the question she had wanted to ask Cruz the moment she heard his voice when she arrived home. "Why are you here?"

He stopped filling the sink and slid the dishes in the sudsy water. "I thought you'd be pleased."

"I am. You know I am. But, really, why are you here?"

"Thought we could enjoy some good food, hang out with the kid and play some cards. No big deal."

"You're not answering my question."

It took him so long to answer Eva thought he wouldn't give her an explanation. When he spoke, he kept his attention on the dish he continued to wash over and over. "I didn't want to be alone."

Eva bumped her hip to his. "That's all you had to say, Cruz."

"Words aren't my thing."

"True. But you're getting better at them. I like that you're here. And Kai appreciates it too."

They both turned to the boy, who came back to the room, sat at the table and started to shuffle the cards. "What'll we play?"

Eva's phone caught her attention when the screen flashed an email notification. She snatched it from the counter. "Nine thirty? Is it that late?"

"Uh-oh," Kai said. "I was supposed to be at Santiago's half an hour ago. He's probably standing on his porch, waiting for me."

"Rifle in the crook of his arm to make sure you get the message about missing his curfew," Cruz said, amusement on his face until he turned to Eva's admonishing glower.

Kai stuffed the cards back in the box. "What do you want me to start with, boss?"

Neither adult spoke for a moment. "I know he's not talking to me," Cruz said.

"Up to you," she said. "What does your gut say?"

"I've been thinking. There's an RV park, not far from the bridge. Maybe that nurse is staying there."

"Sounds like a good place to start," Eva said. "How about if you check it out in the morning."

"Sure. I could do that."

"Let me get a copy of the woman's identification," Eva said, pushing away from the table.

"You have a picture of her?" Cruz said from the other room.

"I do now."

She went to her bedroom dresser, peeled off two sheets from a stack of copies she had made, returned to the table, then held one sheet out to Kai.

"Does she look familiar, Kai?"

Cruz snatched it from her hand. "Where did you get this?"

"Kotz. He has clearance to run government searches." She gave the cop his own copy of the nurse's credentials.

"I bet he does," Cruz muttered, staring at the photo and details.

"That's her!" Kai said, thankfully interrupting what Eva feared would become an unwanted confrontation.

"She's a legit nurse?" Cruz asked.

"Yep. Licensed in four states. A travel nurse. Actually a nurse practitioner."

Kai folded the paper and tucked it in his back pocket. "Awesome. I'll be like a real PI now, not just some kid asking questions about a woman. That would be kinda creepy . . . for them and me."

"Just promise me you'll step carefully," Eva said. "Don't push anyone. If they don't want to cooperate, be polite and move on." She opened her junk drawer at the far end of the cabinet and dug out a palm-size notebook and pen. "Write details down for me. Even if you don't think it could be important."

Kai tucked the notepad in the other back pocket of his jeans. "Never know, right?"

"Exactly. And I added more minutes on your phone, so call if you run into trouble, or if something seems off."

"Sneaky. I know you've done that before. I appreciate it."

His voice, so soft she wondered if she had embarrassed him or violated some unspoken teenager's code. Didn't matter—she needed him to be safe and to be able to keep tabs on him. She didn't tell him she had added his device to the Find My app on her own phone years earlier. That had been Paloma's request when she and Ahiga had finally relented and gifted him the phone on his fourteenth birthday. Eva always felt a little guilty keeping that secret. Until now. Right to privacy didn't apply any longer. Not with a teenager who might still be thinking about ending his own life. She shuddered and sent up a silent prayer that the danger about that had passed.

"How's that bike working out for you?" Cruz asked, eyes still on the credentials.

"Ah, man, it's so much fun."

"Maybe Santiago will hire you to do some work around the ranch so you can save up and buy it from him."

"Naw, he's got other workers."

"From the rez?" Eva asked. "Native kids? Do you know them?"

"No, not our people, and not kids. In their twenties, I think. One has light-brown hair. The other one is blond. Santi says they're not from around here. Lets them use his bikes too."

"What the hell," Cruz said. "I can think of ten men who need the work!"

"Don't get pissed off at me. I'm just letting you know what Uncle told me."

"I'm not angry with you, Kai," Cruz said. "Thank you for letting us know."

"I'll try to find out more about them."

"Okay, what else?" Eva said, altering the route of conversation that would only get more contentious.

"And I'll check around the rez too, if the RV isn't at the other place," Kai said. "See if I can remember where it was parked when I found it."

"Good idea," Eva said.

Kai slapped his hands together. "We have a plan. See you tomorrow."

Eva trailed after him, to the front room. "I don't want you riding that trail bike after dark."

"I'll stay off the main road."

"Nope. Cruz, can you help me load the death machine in the pickup?"

"I'll follow him," Cruz said. "Light the way and make sure he's safe."

"Yeah, let's do that. I don't want Santi mad about me leaving it here again."

She thought for a while to make him sweat. "Fine."

"Yes!" Kai put on his hoodie and picked up the helmet from the floor near the couch. "Meet you outside." Then he surprised the hell out of Eva when he walked over and kissed her on the cheek.

So taken aback she couldn't even tell him goodbye, be careful, see him tomorrow, she stood there and stroked where the boy's lips had touched her skin.

Cruz looked as shocked as her. Then he kissed the other cheek and sprinted to his vehicle.

She stood there at the open door, watching the two men now fully in her life drive off, thinking maybe this raising-a-kid thing wasn't so hard after all.

And then her heart sank, knowing Paloma would do absolutely anything to be the one who had received the affection.

CHAPTER FORTY-NINE
CRUZ

Cruz Romero couldn't believe his good fortune. The spirits had been kind the past few days. Relationship with Eva reestablished and comfortable, meaningful conversations with Kai. Could he ask for more?

He considered whether it would be a good idea to return to Eva's after they made it safely to Santiago's. Make sure his uncle didn't lash out at the boy, that he had been with responsible adults the entire time, not off being potentially careless. Or looking for his mother in the dead of night, as he was sure the young man wanted to have been doing. Then he thought he'd better not. Things were going good between them. He didn't want to push his luck. Good fortune didn't smile on him very often, but he smiled now, thinking of Eva's body next to his own. Smooth skin, soft hair, strength of spirit and body. Her scent of lavender and cedar made him light headed whenever he stood close enough to touch her.

Lost in a memory from the night before, he had lost track of his charge. Heart ratcheting up, he squinted through the billow of dust the dirt bike had kicked up, the red taillight now a pinpoint. Then he didn't see the red orb at all. "What the hell?"

Foot lower on the gas until he closed the gap, he rolled past the veil of dust, then slid to a halt and caused his own cloud. No sign of the motorbike or Kai. Panic began to set in as he turned off the motor, got out of the truck, closed his eyes to listen for the high-pitched racket of the Kawasaki. He heard nothing.

An endless minute later a whistle pierced the air. Cruz swung to the direction of the sound. He took the palm-length flashlight from a sheath on his belt, next to one that held a folding knife. The three thousand lumens lit up the scrub and one rabbit that darted to a nearby bush.

"Over here," the voice said. Farther away than Cruz expected, Kai waved his arms above his head to get his attention.

Cruz trotted back to his truck, turned the steering wheel, bumped over the rough mesa, found where Paloma's son stood near the bike held up by the kickstand, helmet in one hand, eyes on the horizon.

"What the fuck, Kai. Thought I lost you."

Kai approached the vehicle and pointed ahead. "I saw a kid run across the road."

"A kid?"

"I swear it. He wasn't very big but really fast. By the time I turned around and came this way, he was gone."

The half moon's light, obstructed by thin cloud cover, didn't allow Cruz to see far ahead. He switched on the spotlight mounted to the driver's-side doorframe, did a sweep to the left, right, back again. "Don't see anything. You sure it wasn't a coyote or wild dog?"

"No. He had long hair. I'm not losing it, Cruz."

"Didn't say you were. Maybe your subconscious is working over-time. You've been looking for your mom for days, can't find her . . . Or it could have been a sign."

"What? That I should be looking for someone else? A kid?"

Cruz's thoughts had not gone that direction at all. "I don't know, Kai," he said. "I don't see anything now. Let's get you to your uncle's house."

"I'm worried about him. What if he's lost? There's not a house around here for miles."

"Kai, there's no one out there."

But that didn't seem to sway the young man. He closed his eyes and put a finger to his lips. Cruz waited, silent as requested, until minutes passed. Finally Kai sighed, put the helmet back on, and got on the bike.

"I saw him." The words came out confident, nonconfrontational, merely a fact.

The visor snapped down, the Kawasaki kicked to life, and Kai did a full doughnut that flung dirt at Cruz's vehicle. The bike dodged vegetation and rocks, then rocketed forward when the smooth road met its tires.

"That went well," Cruz chided himself.

He spun the truck's wheels in the rush to catch up. Good mood snuffed out, along with amorous thoughts of Eva.

CHAPTER FIFTY
NATHAN

Nathan had wanted to see how fast and how far he could go before he ran out of steam . . . or got caught by the big man and his buddies. A test, in case he needed to get away real fast. His grandfather had told him to do it, and he always listened to his grandpa, even after he'd died. He didn't even see the motorcycle coming at him when he sprinted across the road. Shocked, he had turned his face to the headlight and kept running, blinded, no idea where his feet would land.

Flat to the ground, Nathan concealed himself behind a shrub. The leaves tickled his nose when he eased up high enough to see if the men had left. Still there. He could hear their faint voices, see them point in his direction.

He ducked back down. Took the gun from the back of his jeans. Wished he had bullets for it. But they didn't seem any meaner than the guys at his house. The younger one even looked worried when he tugged the sleeve of the guy inside the truck that had the brightest light he'd ever seen.

Then they went away. The motorbike first, then the big truck. Nathan waited until he couldn't see taillights anymore, then he got up real slow from his hiding place and retraced his steps back home.

He went in the back way, off the kitchen, where none of the guys ever went except to get beer out of the fridge. The door creaked closed, and when he turned around the boss stood there, arms crossed, cigarette hanging out of his mouth, his eyes like slits through the smoke. Nathan didn't like that he couldn't read the expression, really didn't like that no words came out of his mouth.

The bad man made a gun out of his thumb and finger, aimed at Nathan, winked, turned around, and walked back to the front room, where the television almost as wide as the wall played video games and movies day and night. Nathan didn't know where the set came from. His parents only had a little TV in their bedroom. They would let him watch for one hour a night if he finished all of his homework, ate his vegetables, took a bath. He hadn't had a bath in as long as he could remember. The tub was in his parents' room, and that door had a padlock on it now. He didn't like showers as much because the shampoo got in his eyes and he couldn't reach up high enough to adjust the nozzle.

The boss let him watch as much TV as he wanted, long as it was what they were already watching. The naked ladies made his eyes pop out and gave him a weird feeling in the bottom of his stomach. And he didn't like the way they screamed. Didn't know if they were being hurt.

He thought back to the days his mother would help him get undressed, careful not to look down there because he was shy. Being clean and smelling good made for a good night's sleep, she would say when he didn't want to get wet. Now he wanted to be wet all over.

Scared, alone, invisible, he locked the bathroom door and stripped off his dusty clothes and shoes. The water spit and spewed until the pressure caught. He ducked under the spray and lathered up everywhere. This time his tears, hot and feeling never ending, were not from the shampoo.

CHAPTER FIFTY-ONE
EVA

After an hour of twisting in the sheets, eyes pinned to the ceiling, thoughts racing, Eva gave up on sleep, dressed in comfortable clothes, and slid behind the Beast's wheel. She drove, aimless, no final destination in mind.

The TAOS PUEBLO 1 MILE sign whizzed past, and she considered taking the turn that would lead to Cruz's house. No, she decided, better not to rush things. They were good at the moment. Better than they had been in years.

Her thoughts turned to Kai. She fully understood the young man's frustration about needing to follow legitimate procedure, rather than let emotions lead. She often wanted to bust some heads while doing her job. Go rogue. Act without thought. To hell with the ramifications that may or may not follow. But that wouldn't do—in life, or as an enforcer of the law—under any circumstances.

To get her mind off the concern for Paloma, Kai, Tonita, and Dora, Eva forced her concentration on what she could control. Next steps for finding out Kishi's last days, hours, moments. To think the woman had suffered wounded Eva. That she, or anyone, had been unable to find any of the missing women seemed unfathomable. The fact that no one but her and Cruz were officially looking, or maybe even concerned, also enraged her. What would it take for Native women's safety to matter, she had wondered more than a thousand times.

All she could do was devote efforts to her own cases, and hope her work as an unofficial Pueblo liaison would matter to the surrounding jurisdictions' higher-ups. She put herself in the victims' position, walked in their shoes, held their hands, comforted the families. And yet the efforts felt meager compared to the dark elements that worked against her. She hoped she brought a little reassurance from time to time.

Although opening her heart to sufferers had taken a toll on Eva, she appreciated the kindness extended to her when sufferers realized she would be a constant in their lives, make sure they felt safe. Most of all, heard. That the worst days of their lives would not be ignored or discarded as the odd occurrence or a mere accident. The "at the wrong place at the wrong time" excuse did not satisfy most casualties of violent crime.

Sadness threatened to take her down an even darker path. "Enough," she said to herself. "Think about something else."

The list of what could be investigated next came to her. Kai had his tasks. Cruz would do his own thing. The sheriff had cleared her to carry on pretty much untethered to unearth whatever clues could be waiting. She would follow up with Dr. Mondragon. Maybe Kishi's tox screen would reveal something—those results should be in by noon. And she wanted to go back to the hunting grounds. Alone, even though Kai wanted to accompany her. Maybe something had been missed there. She would keep looking for the elusive nurse in a Winnebago too.

Movement to her left snapped her full attention back to the road. Eva's foot slipped off the gas pedal. Bathed in the high beams, wings fully expanded as it cruised the current, a creature swiveled its face and stared at her as it crossed her path. She gasped and raised the crook of her arm to her forehead, shielding her vision. Too late. The owl—known to her people as a bringer of no-good news and often, the harbinger of something to come—had made direct eye contact with her.

She pulled to the shoulder and rolled to a stop. Sweat trailed down her lower back. Her heartbeat raced. "Dammit." She strangled the steering wheel and let out a frustrated growl.

"It was only a vision. I didn't really see it, I didn't see it," she chanted over and over. But she knew she had.

And that it had seen her.

She uttered another round of curses, then braced herself for the upcoming storm, warned by the winged premonition.

CHAPTER
FIFTY-TWO
ALICE

Alice sat in the RV, the jewelry maker belted next to her in the passenger seat, body slack, head bowed to her chest, hair covering her face. Key in the ignition, Alice waited for inspiration to guide her. Whether to deliver the younger woman where she would most appreciate or find a more secluded area for the final resting place. A conundrum she couldn't quite work out.

She cursed the cloudless sky, stars as bright as she'd ever seen, half moon low in the sky lighting up everything in view as far as she could see. Which meant anyone could see what she planned to carry out.

She turned to the other woman and said, "I'm not sure what to do now. Any suggestions?" As expected, no answer came, but she felt better consulting her patient. The decision was hers, too, after all.

"Guess not." A sigh escaped her as she flipped on the headlights, then cranked the Winnebago to life. As she always did before leaving the property, Alice looked to the window where White Dove would be in a deep slumber. She smiled as she thought of the dancer's appreciation when Alice had cured the woman.

Disappointment swept over her when she caught sight of her companion in the other seat. This one would never be healed. Or make another pretty bauble, visit with her friends. Then again she wouldn't ever have to live the worthless life of a junkie either.

Alice smiled. "That's right. Much better now, isn't it? No more worrying about how you'll get your next fix, or how to pay for it." She tsked. "That must have been very stressful."

The third and final dose injected right before Alice carried the woman to the RV had brought on a wave of sadness. She couldn't shake off the emptiness that burrowed in her gut. A tremor in her hands concerned her as well. "You just need a good night's sleep," she said as she turned the motorhome to the main road less than half a mile from the house.

She carried on a constant chatter for miles, unaware of what she would say next. Anything to bring comfort to her passenger, and in turn soothe her own nerves.

"I've enjoyed taking care of you and White Dove. I've dealt with a lot of death the past few years. Unimaginable things, impossible to understand for anyone who didn't live it. I hoped that I could save you. I really thought this time would be different."

Four miles from her destination, according to the helpful sign posted at the side of the road, she recalled how she had researched the area on the computer before arriving in Taos for the first time. She discovered that the impressive gorge she was about to approach was actually a tectonic rupture, purported to be thirty-five million years old. That crisp morning, too early to arrive at the reservation before a public festival, she'd decided to take a drive to see if the internet pictures were even close to reality.

She had parked in a lot at the east end of the Gorge Bridge and walked the sidewalk peppered with a dozen others, so awed by the indescribable majesty she hadn't stopped until she reached the middle of the expanse. The breathtaking sight, unlike anything she had ever encountered, amazed her. Directly below, a river cut through the middle of the gorge. From that high up she couldn't gauge how rough the water was, but it looked pretty calm down there. A raft steered under the bridge, eight people on board, oars resting in their laps. Alice yelled down and waved both arms over her head, but the enthusiasts didn't return the excitement.

Exhilaration thrilled her again as she remembered the sight. She sped up, anticipating what would come. Twenty-five minutes from when she'd left, the Winnebago made it across the first section of the remarkable bridge.

She stopped midway. Another decision needed to be made. "Hmm. Should I stay here or go to the lot and carry you? What do you think?" Amused by her game of one-sided conversation, she waited for a reply. "You're not being at all helpful." She laughed at her own joke. A great belly roar that continued until her sides hurt and tears rolled down her cheeks. "Okay, enough of that. Let's get to work."

She gazed out the windshield, then checked each sideview mirror. No headlights approached or came up behind the vehicle. The open windows allowed a crosswind breeze that refreshed Alice. She felt strong and capable.

She drove to the west end of the bridge and turned to the road that led to a rest area. The lane curved, and she reached the bathrooms, recreation area, and parking spots. Relieved to not see a single car, she continued around the bend and wound up where she began. Satisfied no police patrolled the area, she turned the RV back to the bridge, rolled to the middle of the span, then parked close to the curb and extinguished the headlights.

"We need to hurry now," Alice said as she clicked out of her seat belt and then released the jewelry maker's restraint. She opened the Winnebago's side door, unfolded the steps, then hurried back to her passenger.

Surprised again how light the load felt in her arms, Alice carried her from the RV. A gentle breeze swirled the woman's hair and fringe on her dress, reminding her of White Dove spinning in her dance outfit.

She balanced her load as she took the few steps on the sidewalk to where the railing jutted out to offer an unobstructed view of the water directly below, then stopped and leaned the motionless woman against the railing that kept visitors from falling over the edge of the bridge. Not much of a deterrent, or safe, in her honest opinion. The steel bars appeared unsubstantial but held the weight of the lifeless body as she balanced the woman's back to her own front.

The constant hissing roar of the Rio Grande raged below. Whitecaps formed on the ribbon of water when the waves hit large rocks near the beach of stones. The power of the torrent, view, ominous atmosphere stunned Alice as she stood there to catch her breath.

"It is wonderous here." She gazed straight down. "No wonder you loved that place down there. I'm sorry I couldn't heal you. If you had taken better care of yourself, we wouldn't be here right now. Oh well. I'll look for your jewelry at the shops in Taos. Or maybe they're at that place in Santa Fe. Bet they're real pretty."

That moment something the size of a toddler whizzed by, wings fully extended, not more than ten feet beyond the railing. Alice gasped, clutched the woman tighter, swung her head to watch the trajectory of the bird until it disappeared in the darkness.

"Wow. Did you see that owl? Beautiful. I wonder if it was a sign for you. Some Indian thing, maybe. I'll bet something good. Or maybe better news for me! Yeah, that's it. White Dove is going to be all right. I can feel it now." She leaned forward, hoping to get another look at the owl. "Thank you!"

The unobstructed vastness captured her attention again. "It's a nice night. And you don't have anything else to worry about. You won't feel a thing now." She brushed the hair from the right side of the Pueblo woman's face and stroked the egg-size lump on her cheek. "I think you learned enough life lessons, haven't you, missy?"

She scooped up the woman and arranged her to a seated position, balancing atop the handrail. Not quite ready to let her go, worried the wind would kick up and take her over, too, Alice held on as long as she dared.

"Well, I've enjoyed our little chat, but now it's time to say goodbye."

Alice straightened the fringe on a sleeve, then opened her arms.

She visualized how the jewelry maker dropped: back bowed, arms and legs trailing, hair straight up as she fell and fell and fell. Alice listened for some sound to indicate the woman had reached the bottom. It felt like minutes later, and maybe she imagined it, but she swore she heard a faint splash.

A sense of loss captured Alice's heart for a moment. One bedroom would now be completely empty. Two less patients to fuss over, make comfortable, treat to the best of her abilities.

"Oh well. Now I have more time to devote to getting this right." She leaned over the railing one last time to bid a silent farewell. "White Dove still needs me. I'll work on the other one twice as hard now. Tomorrow will be a great day!"

Steps quicker than they had been in days, determination renewed, she sprinted back to the Winnebago.

CHAPTER
FIFTY-THREE
PALOMA

The sound of an engine starting had awakened Paloma. She forced her eyes open and listened as the motor revved, then grew faint. Unsure of where she was, no idea what time it could be. It took a few minutes for her to revive enough to regain her bearings.

Dim light peeked beyond the crack of the plywood that held the window as imprisoned as her and Tonita. She looked around the room as if for the first time. Realization came to her. Bright, hot, at first confusion, quickly followed by the possibility of betrayal.

Memories came flooding back. Her and Eva as little girls, fascinated that they could walk through one bedroom, into the bathroom, then to another bedroom. This bedroom. She sat up in the bed and swung her legs around, dizzy for a moment from the quick movement. Fully awake now, she looked across the room to see the outline of her cousin's body wrapped in the quilt. "Tonita, I know where we are."

After a moment the other woman said, "Where?"

"Eva's grandfather's old place."

Tonita stirred. "You're sure?"

"Yes. There was a bathroom between two bedrooms." She reached above her pillow, ripped off a piece of the curled wallpaper beside her captivity marks and studied it in the inferior light. "And the wallpaper is familiar. This was Eva's room. Can't believe I'm just now remembering."

"The old man's been dead forever. How long has it been since you were here?"

"Years and years. Had to be before Kai was born."

"No wonder you didn't remember."

"You know what this means?"

"Not a clue."

"We can get out of here. We're not too far from the main road. Maybe half a mile? Or less."

"Half mile . . . may as well be twenty. Anyway, how would we get out of here? The bitch has us locked up and nailed in."

"We have to try. Together we can overpower her."

"How? We're both weak as kittens."

Paloma watched a plan evolve in her mind as she spoke. "You distract her, and I'll jump on her back. Then you kick her knee—in front so her leg snaps the wrong direction. When she falls to the ground, we both start hitting her over and over until she's unconscious. Then we can steal her keys and lock her in here. Take the RV and be gone."

"Crazy talk. Have you seen her? She's big and strong as a man."

"We can do it, Tonita," she said, voice raised, an attempt to excite her partner. "We have the will. We're warrior women. Nobody fucks with us."

Paloma thought she had swayed her cousin. Fired her up, until her roommate said, "The wack job could break out and find us. No. I can't risk it, Paloma. What if we don't get away fast enough? Can't find our way to the road, or no one sees us? Withdrawals killing us while we wait for nobody."

"It's better than her doing it."

Tonita gasped and Paloma realized her cousin had never thought about that possibility. "You think she plans to?"

"I haven't heard anyone in the other bedroom for a long time," Paloma said. "Days since Kishi yelled out. Nothing from Dora either."

"Wait. You think they're dead?"

"Do you really think they would just leave without telling us?"

No answer came from Tonita. Paloma didn't push it.

Her mind continued to whirl. Nothing but questions, no hint of a single answer or explanation of any kind. Why would she and her friends be at the Duran family home? Who even would have known about this place after so long but Eva and maybe Cruz? Then her mind spun in a direction that shot a hot arrow that pierced her heart. Thoughts of possible collusion kidnapped her as completely as her own captivity. Could Eva be working with the nurse? Was that the only way her friend could think of to get her clean? Some sort of sick intervention?

Or did Eva want Kai?

Her heart raced, breaths came quick and shallow, oily sweat trickled down her spine. A panic attack threatened, the first in two years, one of the many reasons she had started taking the drugs. Debilitating at times. Baffling because she had never encountered stage fright or nervousness around crowds during her performance days. She had always been in complete control of her body. Could shift her mind, alter her mood the moment her name would be called over the loudspeaker to take her place in the ring surrounded by fans and judges. But this was different. All-encompassing. Terrifying.

She covered her eyes with trembling hands, an attempt to unsee Eva and Kai together. Laughing, riding around in the Rover that could go anywhere on the rez, thinking only of what fun they'd have next.

Friend and mother completely and utterly forgotten by both of them.

CHAPTER
FIFTY-FOUR
KAI

Kai felt a new purpose in his strides as he dressed and got ready for a day out. He jotted a note to his uncle and left it on the kitchen table, stuffed two water bottles and trail mix in his backpack, then checked on Pearl and her pups, paying special attention to Shadow. He refilled the water bowl and fed the momma a piece of leftover steak he had found in the back of the refrigerator. Shadow licked the juice off his fingers until they glistened.

After one last look at the closed screen and front door, satisfied he could slip away unnoticed, he walked the motorbike to the end of the lane, put on the helmet, and started the engine.

He kept thinking about the boy he had seen last night on the mesa. He *had* seen him. Kai was certain. Not a false vision or calling, or a sign like Cruz suggested. A real kid. Pueblo or from some other tribe. Native for sure. No one else could run like that. Legs pumping, arm movements reserved, long hair straight out, head motionless as he sprinted across the road, then disappeared. Literally. But doubt crept in the more he thought about the possibility.

"Maybe he was a vision," Kai muttered to himself.

He needed to let go of what he had or hadn't seen and get his thoughts in the right place. Eva counted on him to follow through. He couldn't risk upsetting her. If he failed his tasks, she might not let him continue working with her to find his mom. She already still thought of him as a little kid. He needed to change that opinion. Today.

No traffic met or passed him for over a mile, so he stayed on paved US-64, grateful the bike had current tags on the license plate so he wouldn't be pulled over. The highway cut loads of time off his ride to the first location, along the same road as the Gorge Bridge. He turned off the main thoroughfare onto a narrower path that led to the Taos Monte Bello RV park, not far from the Taos airport.

As he got closer, he spotted a dozen motorhomes parked in no particular type of order. He stopped and flipped up the helmet's visor so he could get a good look. He killed the bike so the tires wouldn't stir up much dust or make too much annoying noise. Ahead he spotted a separate parking section, where campervans and smaller RVs were parked. Surprised at the number, he counted four Winnebagos. One looked brand new. The other three could have been ten or thirty years old, Kai had no idea. Dust covered all of them.

Pretty sure one of them was the RV he and Eva passed on the bridge the day before, he leaned the bike on the kickstand, took off the helmet, hung it on the handlebars. Walking along the dirt path, he passed a sign that listed instructions about the dump station, a few picnic tables and grills, a building that housed showers and laundry facilities. Even a small convenience store stood on the property.

He smoothed down his hair and brushed the dust off his hoodie as he approached the first motorhome marked by a *W* on the side. Hand raised to knock on the side window, the door flung open. The same older, white-haired man stood there, scowl on his face. Then the woman he also recognized stood behind the man. She beamed a smile at Kai and patted the old guy's shoulder.

"Can we help you, young man?" she asked.

Kai kept a cautious distance and put on his best smile. The one everyone said looked just like his mom's. "Sorry to disturb you," he said. "I'm looking for someone who also drives a Winnebago like yours. My friend and I passed you on the bridge yesterday, so I thought I would try you first."

"Wanna come in?"

The man didn't look like he had yet warmed to Kai, and so he followed Eva's advice to be polite and said, "No, but thank you."

"We've got cold lemonade," the woman offered.

"No thank you, ma'am. I'm all right." He dug the printout of the nurse's identification photo Eva had given him. Shook out the paper, smoothed it on his chest, took a step forward, held out the paper.

The woman shouldered past the man and took the steps one at a time. She stood inches shorter than Kai and had to look up at him when she took the single sheet and held it in front of her face. "No, young man, I don't believe we've encountered her." She tilted the paper for the older dude to see. "Clyde? What do you think?"

He gave it a quicker look than Kai wanted, only a few seconds, then said, "Nope. Why do you want to find her?"

"Clyde! That is none of our business. Don't mind him. He's crotchety before his fifth cup of coffee."

Kai let out a polite chuckle and held out his hand.

She returned the paper and hoisted herself back up the steps. "We've only been here a couple of days. Wonderful visit! We're leaving to go back home to Wichita in about an hour. Are you sure you don't want any lemonade?"

"No, ma'am. But thank you. And thanks for taking a look."

"Good luck," she said, closing the door on the man, who started again to say, "Why do you want to find her?" His last words were muffled, but Kai clearly heard the woman tell him to *hush up*.

"Okay, let's see if the next stop is any less weird." He walked beyond two empty parking spaces and took a good look at the next Winnebago. "No, too new," he muttered and walked to the next one.

He closed his eyes and replayed the vision of the nurse's RV. Almost two weeks since he'd stumbled upon it, but he stilled his mind, relaxed every muscle, concentrated only on the memory. His eyes flew open.

"A sticker," he recalled. "There was a sticker on the window in the side door."

It didn't come to him what the logo was called, but it had dual snakes wrapped around a staff, a pair of wings at the top. A medical symbol . . .

"Caduceus! That's it." He pumped his fist, celebrating the solid lead he had only just recalled.

It had been so long since he'd used his—what most would consider ancient—iPhone that he had almost forgotten to plug it in for an overnight charge. The device felt so strange in his pocket after not having the mobile with him, so he decided to put it in his backpack before heading out that morning. He took off his pack and dug through his snacks, spare hoodie, fresh pair of socks, tumbled out everything, panicked. As he shoved his hand in the very bottom of the bag, his fingers landed on a cool, firm surface. He let out a relieved breath, pulled the phone out, and tapped out a text for Eva.

JUST REMEMBERED—
THERE'S A CADUCEUS STICKER ON THE RV SIDE DOOR WINDOW

Her reply was so immediate he wondered if she had the phone in her hand.

WELL DONE!!!
WILL ADD THAT TO THE DESCRIPTION

He smiled at the compliment. So he could get to the phone fast if she texted again, he tucked it in the front pocket of his hoodie, to join his leather pouch of remembrances that went everywhere with him.

Closer now to the third Winnebago, he didn't see a sticker and hurried to the final motorhome that fit the nurse's rig.

"Nope. Not that one either."

Disappointed but not deterred, he went back to the Kawasaki and rolled it to the end of the lane. The Gorge Bridge taunted Kai, about four miles beyond where he sat on the idling bike.

"Nope. Not yet." He put on the helmet, revved the throttle, and headed in the direction he'd come from.

Right then he felt more aware and relevant than he had in weeks, or months. Maybe three years. Since his family's world took a spin downward and hadn't stopped that trajectory.

Not anymore, he vowed as he hit the US-64 straightaway and raced toward the reservation.

CHAPTER FIFTY-FIVE
ALICE

Alice stared at the RV's ceiling, wondering where the jewelry maker's body could have floated by now. She didn't have a clue if the water would be more rough farther downriver or become a mere trickle. Then again, maybe she landed on the beach from where she dropped, close to where the drum maker had mentioned the woman loved to collect stones for her jewelry.

She hoped for that possibility. For the artist's body to be warmed in the sun later that morning. At peace, no need for the heroin ever again. Maybe no one would find her body at all. That would be best, of course.

Despite the loss of another patient, Alice felt optimistic. Cheery, even. She thought of the owl that had captivated her last night, still believing it was a good sign. One of flight. Renewal. Alice wished she knew what the creature meant to White Dove's people. The curiosity evaporated the moment she flipped off the sheets and began to run in her mind the list of duties that would need to be accomplished for the morning.

As she made the three necessary peanut butter sandwiches, she suddenly wondered if anyone had found the body of the drum maker yet, and if so, would her first patient's death look suspicious? When she left the body, she might not have been as cautious as she should have been. Even the latex gloves weren't foolproof. Epithelial matter could have been scraped off when she'd dragged the body through the brush. She checked her arms but didn't see any scratches, so that was good.

And she had been careful to go back and cover up the tire tracks and her footprints. Sawed off a long limb with plenty of fresh pine needles that acted as a broom. The chore had taken a long time, but she felt pretty certain every trace of her and her vehicle had been eradicated.

Curious now, she turned the key a quarter turn in the ignition, switched on the radio, and spun the dial until she found a local station.

. . . details remain guarded by the Taos County Sheriff's Department, as well as the Taos Pueblo Department of Public Safety, the reporter stated. *Both agencies are believed to be investigating the possibility of foul play. The identity of the female also remains confidential until family members are notified. We will keep you informed as we learn more.*

"Hmm," she said, cutting the first sandwich in half. "Still don't know her name. Oh well."

And now for the weather. Storms are expected later this morning. Look for high winds and possible—

"Enough of that. Time to go over the plan." She leaned beyond the seats and flipped off the ignition.

She took out her legal pad covered in notes and the trusty *Nursing Drug Handbook*, then paged to where she had placed a fluorescent orange sticky note to mark the Schedule II listing of drugs for quick access. As she tapped her lip with a finger, she hummed a pleasant tune and scanned the list of possibilities a few times.

"Nope, that one didn't work." To remind herself, she crossed pantopon off her list. "Oh, that one too. Nope. No good." She drew a line through hydromorphone as well.

She didn't want to eliminate Suboxone because that would be her go-to if she needed to reduce the heroin doses. The mere thought of making another visit to the drug dealer caused her to tremble all over, then fly into a rage she couldn't control.

The few times she had experienced the fits of anger over the past couple of days left her exhausted, head splitting, unaware of her surroundings for she didn't know how long. She would have to lie on the floor of the house or RV until her heartbeat and blood pressure leveled out.

Many times she consulted her published guide to research relief of her own. If she perhaps had a drug on hand that would free her of so many emotions she typically could tamp down without effort, she could regain the control that had been slipping away since she'd arrived on the reservation.

She flicked her hand, erasing the foolish idea. Who would take care of White Dove? Anyway, drugs were the easy way out. Her patients were the perfect example of what went terribly wrong when narcotics were used as a crutch. The escape so intense over time that living even the most basic life no longer held any appeal.

"No. You mustn't even think about that road to ruin."

Instead she decided on a better plan—to work extra hard on a cure, certain that doing so would elevate her mood and solve every problem she felt entangled in.

Two different treatments would need to be prepared for the day. One morning dose for the basket maker, and the revised concoction for later in the night. Twelve full hours for the first dosage to work through her patient's system.

Drive reignited, Alice flipped a fresh page on her notepad and wrote out the medication she would start with, confident that by noon tomorrow she would know which path to take.

White Dove's future depended on her efforts. She would not—could not—fail.

CHAPTER FIFTY-SIX
EVA

Dressed in a fresh uniform, hair pulled back in a tight bun, Eva buckled her loaded duty belt and checked her equipment. Set now for the day, she entered the kitchen, prepared two containers of ice water, scooped a handful of protein bars from a box in the pantry and eyed the stack of full-size Snickers candy bars that taunted her. "What the hell," she said, thinking she might need a little comfort or pleasure in the coming hours. She grabbed two of them as well, dropped the snacks in a cloth tote bag, and went to the front room.

Hand on the doorknob, she hesitated, unsure why. Something kept her feet planted there. A tingle radiated the length of her left arm. A presence joined her. So close she dared to look over her shoulder. The scent of leather and tobacco tickled her nose.

"Duh-thle?" she whispered, imagining her grandpa there with her.

Tender warmth on her shoulder prompted her to pay attention. She usually appreciated her grandfather's visits, thrilled by the feeling only he could bring. This day, however, the presence felt more like a warning.

"What are you telling me?"

She stood there for minutes, torn whether to stay or to go. The wait did nothing to calm her anxiety. The visitation puzzled Eva. His spirit hadn't made itself known for years after his cross had fallen in the ancient graveyard a dozen years ago, then wouldn't leave her alone for months at a time. Sometimes a mere feeling swept over her, other occasions a burst of wind would kick up out of nowhere. One particularly grateful time, after an eighteen-hour shift, she had been driving and had nodded off. Her grandfather's voice had shouted her name, and she snapped awake just in time to correct her trajectory out of the way of an oncoming vehicle.

This time didn't feel like a reassuring drop-in. And then the initial warning, of the owl from the night before, popped into her mind. The energy around her sparked, the air grew heavy, the insistence to be especially vigilant came over her.

"I have to go. I'll be careful, I promise," she told her passed elder, and as a reminder to herself.

An inexplicable sense of dread kept her in place. Always one to face her fears, she patted the badge over her heart, walked out of the warmth of her duh-thle's spectral embrace, twisted the doorknob.

A rumble of thunder met her the moment she walked outside. "I hear you. Don't mess with me today," she shouted to the sky.

Belted behind the wheel of the sheriff's department pickup, tote bag and water on the passenger seat, she held her gaze on the front window of the house. She swore the closed curtain fluttered. Her grandpa had never been so insistent nor stayed so long before. Usually only a fleeting moment, a minute at most.

The urge to go back inside, strip, get back in bed, call Cruz to join her, seemed like a very good idea. Assure her safety. Let the feeling of risk dissipate for hours . . . or days.

The yearning evaporated when her best friend's face abruptly filled her mind. Guilt captured her. She scolded herself for even thinking she could have turned her back on her duties, pushed any possibilities of escape aside, and said, "I'm coming, Paloma. Hold on a little longer. I will find you."

She cranked the ignition. The Ram 4x4 rumbled its readiness. She shifted to cop mode, bared her teeth, and rumbled her own growl.

CHAPTER
FIFTY-SEVEN
KAI

After two full hours of unsuccessfully searching even the most remote areas of the reservation, Kai put the kickstand down under the canopy of a wide tree and pulled out the water and snacks from his backpack.

As he munched, he turned his thoughts back to the day he'd first seen the nurse's Winnebago and imagined retracing his tracks. The motorhome had been parked somewhere close enough to ride his bicycle, but he couldn't recall exactly where. That day he went in search of his mom, he had stumbled upon the RV after wandering rez paths for hours. Much like today. Guilt swept over him at the memory of him pitching his motocross-type bicycle over the railing of the bridge. He loved that bike. A Christmas present from his dad before he died.

Kai kept thinking about the bridge. He had always loved going there before. Looking out at the great expanse of what must have been an even mightier river at one time. The gorge, impressive and mysterious, captivated him every time he and his father visited. Heights terrified his mom, so they would go alone, always a special father-and-son bonding time. The need to be there again swept over Kai. He needed to feel his father's presence. Ask for forgiveness for almost making the biggest mistake of his life.

Urgent to make amends, he stuffed his snacks back in the pack, put on the helmet, fired up the Kawasaki. A few miles later he raced beyond the RV park. Six minutes after that he reached the first section of the bridge.

He coasted to midspan, parked the Kawasaki, took off the helmet and backpack, stood there frozen in place. Now he regretted the decision to return. Curiosity vanished. He only felt nervous, like this was a very bad idea.

His father always encouraged him to face his fears. Look demons in the eye and spit at them. That would make him laugh, but the advice made sense now that he was older. He wondered what his father would tell him to do in this instance. Let it go? Move on? Don't think about what could have happened?

No. He needed to stand up to any demons, ban them from further thought.

First, he faced to the south—the direction of his reservation— raised his eyes to the sky and opened his arms to receive the blessings of any passed souls watching over him.

"Thank you, Universe, for your protection and guidance. Spirits, please be kind. Help me find my mother. Keep her safe until I do."

Satisfied his requests had been conveyed, he turned around to face the opposite side. He crossed the street, then stepped beyond the pedestrian sidewalk, exactly the same place he'd stood three days ago. He put one hand on the guardrail, not as cold as that day. His heart thumped, blood rushed in his ears, hair fluttered in an occasional flurry of wind. He reached in the pocket of his hoodie and clasped the protection keepsakes in his hand, the soft leather and its contents an immediate comfort.

"Sorry, Dad. I promise to be better. Become a good man, like you were. The best person anyone ever met. Mom needs you too. Can you check on her? Let her know you're with her?"

He scanned both sides of the river but didn't see a bicycle on either side of the bank. Calm now, refreshed by his calls to action and forgiveness, he inhaled the clear air, gave another look down. And froze.

Something directly below caught his attention. So small because of the distance, he wasn't certain what it could be at first. He clenched his every muscle and leaned way over, the top rail pinching his stomach muscles, staring until his eyes watered from lack of blinking. The object didn't move on the bank of stones alongside the river.

He fumbled the phone out of his pocket and, hands shaking so hard, nearly dropped it to career a path to the raging water. He managed to hit the camera function, aimed for the area, zoomed in, took burst after burst of photos, then stumbled back to the safety of the sidewalk. Eyes locked on the screen, he sat down next to the bike.

He swiped photo after photo. The first twenty or so were too blurry to see anything relevant.

The last ten came out crystal clear.

"No. No. *Noooo!*" he shouted. To his father, the spirits. The entire universe.

CHAPTER
FIFTY-EIGHT
EVA

Eva sat at her desk, requisite paperwork almost finished enough to take a break. She craved to be outside and on the road, rather than stuck in a bullpen that held the twenty-four-seven funk of scorched coffee, sweaty men, and carryout.

Eva's phone vibrated, and she took it from the pouch on her duty belt. Before she could say her name, a voice said, "Eva . . . Oh god . . . I need you to—to—I need . . . Oh god."

"Kai?" She shot to her feet, which launched her rolling desk chair to hit the wall. "What's happened. Where are you?"

"On the bridge."

Full-on panicked now, she whipped her jacket from the back of the chair, grabbed the handheld radio from her desk, raced to the exit. "Please, don't do anything—" Before she could say *stupid*, she stopped her words and listened. She heard wind and sobbing under Kai's illogical muttering. "Just wait for me," she said. "Don't hang up!"

"Hurry," he whispered, then clicked off the call.

In smooth, quick motions she slid behind the wheel of the pickup, flicked on the flashers and siren, slammed the vehicle in drive, and sped from the lot. Most vehicles pulled over to let her pass, but some needed an encouraging honk, and she almost tapped the bumper of one old-timer who had no business driving a tractor, let alone a car.

It seemed to take hours before she reached the final curve toward the gorge. Eva couldn't remember ever being so nervous, even more than she'd been three days ago, when she'd been summoned to the same location.

The Gorge Bridge loomed ahead and she pushed the Ram faster. She reached one-third of the way across before she switched off the siren and forced herself to take her foot off the accelerator. She spotted Kai's motorbike parked beside the sidewalk. But where was he?

She skidded to a stop, rancid smoke billowing from her tires, mere feet from the Kawasaki, where he apparently had been hiding. He popped up and ran to her door. Tears and snot ran down his face as he pointed. Incoherent words poured out of his mouth. One hand held a phone, the other his leather protection pouch he brought to his lips several times to kiss.

The instant she got out of the vehicle, he gave her the cell. Eva stared at the screen. Found it impossible to breathe. Couldn't remember how to walk. Became mute as her brain shut down.

"Look!" he said.

When she turned, the boy had moved to the railing and was point-ing directly downward. Eva finally took cautious steps to the north-side balustrade. Deep breath in and out. In and out. Then she stood on her toes, leaned over, looked down, down, down.

No doubt, something had been discarded on the county side of the river. A body? Maybe. She hoped not.

But the outline looked like a person, facedown, arms and legs out, dressed in a dark dress and matching-toned moccasins. Black hair bil-lowed in the water on one side, the other half splayed out on the rocks.

Eva pushed back to safety, turned around, and slid down against the rail until her backside hit the sidewalk.

"Is it Mom?"

She stared at him, no clue how to answer the question. Somehow she managed to say, "I need my handheld radio from the truck. Can you get it for me?"

A task seemed to help Kai snap to action, and he returned with the unit in moments.

She found her feet, took the radio and pointed for Kai to stand right there. "Don't do a thing, got it? We're going to figure this out."

When he nodded, she took a good ten paces away. Finger on the radio's button, she hesitated. Should she phone Cruz first? Santiago? "No. It might not be Paloma," she told herself. "Please, don't let it be Paloma. Keep your shit together. Do your job."

She held down the call button. Voice strong, unemotional, she said, "Sierra-Ten-Twelve to Dispatch."

"Go ahead, S-Ten-Twelve."

"Request top priority, Gorge Bridge."

The pause lasted so long Eva thought the transmission had failed, then a somber voice replied over the tiny speaker. "Copy that. Units are on the way."

"Dispatch, request Sheriff Bowen on scene as well."

Another pause. "Message received. Hang tight."

She kept her back to Kai as she took a few steps and looked at his phone. Taking longer to study the images this time, she swiped until she decided on one and zoomed to tighten the image, which convinced her the form was a body, and most likely a female. Many Pueblo males grew their hair long. But she doubted a man would wear a traditional-looking dress. Then again, she wondered, maybe that's why the person had jumped. People, even her own, weren't always accepting of those who didn't choose a conventional life to lead. She found herself hoping this to be the motive— convinced she didn't know this person, and surely they wouldn't be Paloma or one of her two friends.

Guilt and shame followed. No matter who the person was, they deserved her full attention and objectivity. Her mind spun to what they would find when they turned the woman over. The imagined visual overcame her, and she shuddered.

"Are you all right?" Kai asked.

So absorbed in her own thoughts, she had lost track of the young man, forgotten that he needed reassurance, not a weak and indecisive shell of a person who could offer him nothing. She took in a deep breath, let it out, returned to the teen, and said, "Yeah, fine. Thinking. Trying to come up with a plan." He nodded but didn't look convinced by her explanation. "Can you text those last ones to me so I can send them to my boss?"

He took his phone and tapped until her phone buzzed. She took her own cell from the case on her utility belt, selected the clearest three of ten, then texted them to her sheriff and Dr. Mondragon.

"Now what?" Kai asked.

"Now we wait for the cavalry."

"Because that worked out so good for our people in the past," Kai deadpanned.

She almost laughed, then caught his serious tone and spiraled down the path of doubt, right along with the younger member of her community.

CHAPTER
FIFTY-NINE
ALICE

Alice made sure White Dove and the other one were sufficiently incoherent and pliable after their morning meal, sponge bath, and change to fresh nightgowns, followed by stronger than ever before doses of heroin that should last most of the day.

Neither of the younger women offered a single word of conversation, so it was left to Alice to entertain. After half an hour of the one-way conversation, both of her patients issued light snores. And now, Alice felt confident she could proceed with the plan she had worked out in her mind throughout the early-morning hours, before she had finally slept on the RV's foldout, too exhausted to work out any potential further problems she might encounter.

She hefted the one who gave her trouble all the time to her shoulder and went beyond the bathroom to the adjoining bedroom. She dropped the nonresponsive body on the drum maker's bed and arranged her on her side, pillows wedged between the wall and the woman's back so she wouldn't choke on any vomit if she got sick.

Then Alice withdrew a prepared syringe and injected the concoction she felt absolutely certain would be the winning batch. She waited a full ten minutes to make certain of no ill effects, then patted her patient's shoulder and said, "That should do it. Relax now. I'll be back in a little while."

Grateful the woman didn't talk back for a change, or even move, Alice secured the padlock and went to the front room of the house. The need to put everything in order overcame her. She disassembled and re-piled her supplies over and over. The repetitive, identical actions began to calm her.

She stopped, finally satisfied the stacks were perfect. A wave of exhaustion swept over her, and she wished she had waited longer to move the basket maker. All she wanted right then was a comfortable place to rest.

"You're just tired." She studied the peanut butter jars, bread, water, toiletries. She made a mental note to get more gas for the generators, and may as well top off the RV too. "And water! You can never have too much water on hand," she muttered.

But she would need to wait for the cover of night to hit the convenience market at the edge of town. She had been lucky shopping at that place so far. No one questioned her purchases, every clerk had been different, customers didn't even look at her and certainly didn't start a conversation while standing in line at the checkout counter. Most were there to buy cigarettes and beer, their attention set on the upcoming pleasure.

Her eyelids grew heavy, fluttered open and shut, muscles went slack, body swayed. She snapped to, blinked over and over, raised a hand to the wall for balance. The past fourteen days had finally caught up with her, she reasoned.

"Everything is in order. Nothing else to be done for now. A catnap will do you good."

The trek to the RV seemed an impossible feat. Unsure she could even make it across the house, she took small steps, arms out in case she faltered, until she again reached the bedroom door. Keys fumbled in her hand. She chose the wrong one at first, then again. Frustration raised its head, panic thumped her chest, a moan gurgled in her throat. Last key. A twist, and finally the shank popped open. In that instant, relief swept the panic away.

She brushed sweat from her brow and under her neck, swept now-steady hands through her hair, entered the room. No movement came from the bed as she secured the padlock to the hasp on the bedroom side of the door, crossed beyond the bathroom to the other lock, and let out a grateful sigh that she got the correct key on the first try.

Somehow she made it to the basket maker's former bed and dropped atop the mattress. She sighed her pleasure. Muscles and nerves loosened as she turned to her side, settled her cheek on her hands folded in prayer position, kept her eyes on her beloved White Dove until she couldn't keep her eyes open any longer.

"Almost there, White Dove. Today I find the cure. No more suffering. For you, or me."

She believed every word.

CHAPTER SIXTY
EVA

Eva called Cruz right after she requested reinforcements from her own department. Then Santiago, who sounded as freaked as she felt and said he'd be there in fifteen minutes—he got there the same time as Cruz, in eleven.

Santiago barely got his truck in park before he jumped from the cab, ran to Kai, wrapped the boy in his arms, and held him tight. The nephew's eyes went wide, but he didn't ask for Eva to intervene.

Cruz rolled to a stop beside Eva and said, "What do you need?"

"First move your truck to the other side of the bridge. Santiago's too. Then get back here quick."

He nodded and said a few words to Santiago. To Eva's surprise no debate ensued—the elder got in his pickup and waved for Kai to join him.

Relieved to know some help had already arrived, and her own reinforcements would be on the way soon, Eva returned to her pickup, unlocked the utility cabinet in its bed, retrieved her investigation kit and a pair of binoculars. From the front passenger's seat, she fished out the Snickers bars in the tote bag.

Cruz came at Eva in a full run, legs and arms pumping, no head bob whatsoever. He reached her, barely out of wind, reminding her of his days on the high school track team, when he singlehandedly took them to the state championship three years in a row. Kai and Santiago trailed much farther back and looked, to Eva, like they wanted to take their time heading toward the inevitable.

"Tell me," Cruz said, but he looked like he really didn't want to know. "Jumper?"

"No way to tell until we get down there."

She handed him the binoculars, went to the railing, and pointed. Cruz tapped them against his thigh a few times, squinted to the sky, then took slow steps to stand next to Eva. He trained the binoculars, focused the eyepiece, thrust them away from his face.

"I know," she said. "It's bad."

"That's a woman."

"Most likely."

He trained the binoculars to the site again and they bobbed in his hand. When he turned to her again, his face had become ashen gray. "Think it's Paloma?" he whispered.

"No idea. Looks like a woman though. How will we get her out of there? Hike? Rappel off the bridge? And then what?"

"It's a rough hike," he said. "Even harder return trek, especially with the load they'll need to get back to the top."

Eva remembered when an injured hiker had to be rescued a few months ago. "Helicopter, maybe?"

"Better to raft."

Eva clapped Cruz on the shoulder. "Right! Of course."

"Start off at the John Dunn Bridge."

"We'll need two crafts. One for us and the victim, another for the crime scene techs."

"Techs?" Cruz asked. "Think that'll be necessary?"

"Yes. We've got to be absolutely proper. The body's on the county side of the river, so I radioed for my sheriff to come. It'll be his call."

"You think this may relate to what happened to Kishi?"

Kai and Santiago came closer. Neither talked, but they stood close together, as if it took two of them to have the courage to return to where the next painful stage in their journey would play out.

When they reached Eva and Cruz, she folded down the wrapper on one of the Snickers she'd pulled from her pocket, broke off a portion, and handed it to Santiago, then gave Kai the rest. "Eat. You're in shock. The sugar will help."

Eva and Cruz shared the other candy bar. They chewed in silence, although she assumed they each had a dozen questions they didn't dare to ask.

"Is it like Kishi?" Kai asked after he finished his candy. "Could this be the same kinda thing that happened to her?"

Before Eva could give her opinion, she heard engines grow louder, looked beyond her miserable group of men, and spotted her sheriff's official vehicle in the lead, followed by three cruisers, every emergency light flashing.

Sheriff Bowen slid from the passenger seat, pointed, and issued orders to her colleagues. Two of the deputies returned to their cruisers, blocked one entire lane and prepared to deliver instructions to any oncoming vehicles.

Cruz ever so slightly nudged Eva's elbow. "I'll let you deal with the big boss." He held her eyes for a supportive moment, then hitched his head for Kai and Santiago to follow him and wait a few paces away.

As Eva approached her colleagues, she mourned a bit, struck by her superior's grave expression and demeanor as he joined her. "Sir," she said.

"What've we got, Duran?"

"Appears to be a body."

"Damn," Bowen muttered.

She handed him the binoculars, and the sheriff followed her to the railing. He gave her his hat, put the binoculars to his eyes, and leaned over so far Eva resisted the urge to reach for his arm to steady him. "Definitely on the county side of the river."

"Yes, sir."

He stepped back, gave her the binoculars, settled his hat back on. "Almost in the water. The lost souls since I've been in charge didn't make it that far."

"No, sir. The first ledge of the cliff for two of them, second bench for the latest . . . before now."

"Rappel down, like the other recoveries?"

"Actually, Cruz Romero has an idea. He's with the Taos Pueblo PD."

"I'm aware. Why is he here?"

"Well, sir, the person looks to be dressed in Native clothing. Long dark hair as well. High probability she . . . the decedent is Native American. Possibly from the Taos Pueblo."

"I see. What's the general protocol?"

"Well, there's no actual precedent that I'm aware of. You've been real good about allowing me to help Romero's department and Taos PD when necessary. I hope you'll take that into consideration in this case. Romero's an excellent cop, sir. He has tracking skills and is well respected on and off the reservation."

Bowen studied Cruz before he said, "What's his idea?"

"Less dangerous and treacherous for everyone involved."

"I like it already. Call him over."

Eva stuck two fingers against her tongue and issued a single whistle. Everyone turned her way. Cruz reacted first. He said a few words to Kai and Santiago, then hustled over.

"Sheriff Bowen, Officer Romero."

"Happy to have you with us, Officer. Duran said you have an idea. Let's hear it."

"Thank you, sir. I propose a raft recovery. Start at the John Dunn Bridge, then head to the site. Have the ME meet us downriver."

"How long's that gonna take?"

"Two hours on the water from drop-off point to arrival point," Cruz said. "Add whatever we need for recovery. Where we are here is about one-third of the way from the raft launch point."

"Add at least an hour to coordinate," Bowen said.

"Sir, given our first victim, and three other women still missing, I propose we bring in crime scene techs to process the scene," Eva said. "Just in case it turns out the person down there is one of them and we need to catalogue anything."

"Right. Right. All right," Bowen said. "Let's get it done."

"I'd like to accompany the decedent, sir. Be in the lead raft."

"Yes, please do. You too, Romero, if your superior agrees."

"Not a problem there."

"Highest respect."

"Always," Eva said, proud all over again to serve her sympathetic boss.

"I'll reach out to the crime scene team and have Sylvie make the call to the rafting company. Duran, could you see if your ME friend can meet you at . . . ?"

"The Taos Junction Bridge," Cruz offered. "About fifteen miles downriver from where the rafts will take off."

"All right. Be safe. Any pushback, you know how to reach me."

"Copy. Thank you, sir," Eva said as he turned away and headed back to his cruiser.

One of the vehicles that arrived with him remained on the bridge, her colleague at the ready to wave on any gawkers. Clouds hid the midmorning sun, and a downpour loomed larger. Flat, desolate mesa on both sides of the gorge, as far as the eye could see, darkened and muted. The need to act fast lit a fire in Eva. The recovery mission would be dangerous as is. She couldn't even imagine being on the water during a thunderstorm.

She raised her face to a sky that had darkened over the last few minutes. "Universe, if you've ever listened to me before . . . please don't storm."

"I tried that too," Cruz said, startling her. He stepped to the railing and looked down, a burst of wind whipping his ponytail. "Won't take a lot to dislodge her from the rocks."

"Maybe our combined mojo will keep us safe," she said. "And her in place."

A flash of lightning followed by a deafening crack of thunder taunted them. She looked at Cruz, mimicked the shake of his head, and turned to Santiago and Kai, who both saluted the sky with middle fingers.

CHAPTER SIXTY-ONE
PALOMA

Paloma woke from a sleep she wasn't sure had lasted an hour or a day. Mind hazy, body listless, she found the energy to hold only one eye open.

"Tonita?" She tried to pinpoint her vision across the room, to the other bed, saw that the pillows atop the quilt had been smoothed out, nobody on the mattress. "Are you in the bathroom?"

No answer followed. She listened and heard nothing. Whatever the nurse shot her with had zapped every bit of strength and curiosity.

"Probably," she muttered, grateful she didn't need to relieve her bladder. The short walk to check on Tonita seemed an impossible feat.

Head back on the pillow, she thought about her boy. How good and kind and pure he had been as a child. And still to this day, even after all she had put him through. The worry and disappointment and shame. The mere idea that she had killed any bit of the good in him gutted the mother part of Paloma. To think the escape of drugs could interfere with what had once been a cherished relationship would have baffled the old Paloma. The one who danced on the wings of eagles, swayed on the wind, figured the good thoughts and blessed days would last an eternity.

And then the world split apart. Everything lost. All because of a careless driver who chose liquor over the safety of anyone in his path. Even the boy who would take her breath away every time he walked into the room and charmed all in his presence changed. For two years, she had received no more smiles or hugs or attentive company from him.

At first she'd had to push him away, because the crush of his bones against her own felt like broken glass against her injuries. When those wounds had healed, more pain followed, due to his shunning. Either out of blame for the loss of his father, or because she hadn't behaved like she wanted to be his mother any longer, she didn't know for sure.

The alcohol and drugs masked that pain and every other discomfort. But she was ready to be done with all of that. Get help. Quit. Stop lying and stealing. Even avoid Dora and Kishi and her favorite cousin. Forever if necessary. Whatever it took to get her Single Star back.

Tears slid down her face, and she sniffled. Then frowned. Sniffed again. The nurse had been in the room recently. She recognized her scent—not perfume or laundry soap but the harsh, bitter stench of medicine. Not only what had been injected in her own veins, no—the meds that had kept her mother alive weeks too long. Riddled with cancer, veins pumped with toxic poison, smelling of chemicals and fear. Paloma had rarely left her side those last months. Kai, heart breaking, picked and prepared the wild berries and herbs for soups and teas his grandmother had taught him would heal, hoping life from their land and the universe and Mother Nature would help ease the suffering.

"Are you sick?" she asked the ghost of Alice. "Dying like Grandma?"

She used what little strength she had to scoot up in the bed and wondered why she hadn't recognized the odor before. The drugs the nurse had used varied in terms of dosage and day of the week, so she supposed that could alter her sense of smell. Heroin laced with something else, she decided. Something different every time, maybe. A blend of more than one drug, probably to keep her and her friends obedient. But why?

"Why . . . ? Why . . . what?" She frowned, smacked her thigh in frustration. She tried to recall what she had been thinking about but had completely lost her train of thought.

Forgotten as completely as the shadow her life had now become.

CHAPTER
SIXTY-TWO
EVA

An hour after all of the recovery preparations and various assignments had been made, Eva and Cruz took US-64 to Highway 522, Eva behind the wheel. Thanks to emergency lights and sirens, the drive to the Arroyo Hondo location took less than twenty minutes. They blasted by a sign that stated RAFTING, KAYAKING PADDLE BOARDING AHEAD, and she knew they must be getting close.

"An owl crossed my path last night," Eva said, the first words she had spoken since they left the bridge.

"Uh-oh. Last night?"

"Couldn't sleep. Went for a drive. Bastard looked right at me."

It took a while for Cruz to reply. "Now you know why it sought you out, I guess."

He went silent again, and she wondered if he thought—as she had a few times that day—if she hadn't left the house after their nice evening, hadn't taken that drive and therefore couldn't have seen the owl, that the woman wouldn't be dead. Guilt would get her nowhere, so she concentrated on the road ahead and kept her thoughts to herself.

By the time she and Cruz arrived at the launch site, two vivid-yellow-and-red rafts that could easily hold eight people were staged and ready to be released near the John Dunn Bridge. She glanced in the rearview to see a sheriff's department cruiser pull up behind them.

Two burly look-alike men with long beards and wraparound mirror sunglasses loaded gear in the crafts, so involved in their tasks they didn't turn their direction when Eva parked the Ram. She and Cruz watched them work, and she wondered if the Pueblo cop felt as nervous as she did.

"How do you know so much about this rafting nonsense?" she asked. "Have you ever done this before?"

"No. A few buddies told me all about it. You?"

Eva snorted out a breath. "Hell, no. I'm fond of living."

"So we both pretend to be brave."

"Stoic Native Faces. Do we need to practice?"

Cruz whipped off his shades, thinned his eyes and lips, lasered her a look. She did the same. They both cracked up. The light mood didn't last long as they grasped the solemn mission ahead of them.

Movement caught her attention and she adjusted the rearview mirror to see the county crime scene vehicle approach. She recognized the A team getting out of the van, purpose in their steps. Two women and one man, all fit and confident, pulled bags of equipment from the back as if the contents weighed nothing.

"Guess we're doing this," Cruz said, shades and less-daunting face back on.

Her fellow deputy knocked on the window, and Eva whirred it down. "Appreciate you getting my rig to the endpoint, Sam. You know where to go?"

"Yep. Taos Junction Bridge. It'll be waiting for you."

Eva got out, and her colleague took the driver's seat. Cruz took a moment to practice his Stoic Native Face on the newest rookie of the sheriff's force, who proceeded to turn so pale Eva could count every one of the freckles that dotted his nose and cheeks.

She suppressed a laugh as she waited for Cruz to join her, then approached the lead Taos County crime scene technician, Lizbeth Herrero, who handed a golf club–size bag to one of her people, then headed for Eva. Although Lizbeth was only thirty-two, Eva knew the woman to be beyond competent and unflappable in court whenever her findings were challenged.

"Glad to have you with us, Lizbeth."

"Sorry to be here, but we're ready to help in every way you need."

Eva ticked her head upward in welcome to the rest of the team. They returned the gesture and made their way toward the rafts. Cruz took one of the overstuffed duffels, and she wondered if it contained the cadaver bag they would zip their fatality inside.

"What do you know so far?" Eva asked.

"Your people texted the location and photos. Decedent is on the county side of the river, which is why you're here . . ." She hitched a thumb at Cruz, who had remained near the pickup, eyes on the water. "What about the rugged and handsome police officer?"

"Cruz Romero, from the Pueblo PD."

"I'm well aware."

Stunned, Eva frowned. "You are?"

"Don't worry. My wife would not approve of my ogling."

They both chuckled before Eva said, "Victim could be a Native woman."

"Looks that way, from the photos. Sorry to hear that." Lizbeth took a cautious pause before she said, "Do you think this death is related to the other woman you found?"

"Could be. That's why I asked for you. You're familiar with that scene, so if there's anything that relates in the least little bit, I know you'll find it."

"Appreciate the confidence, Eva. Didn't find much in the forest, but we'll do our best." Then Lizbeth clapped her hands together and beamed an excited smile. "Let's do this. *Woo-hoo!*"

Eva followed, not feeling the least bit as eager to get on the water. She crossed to the man issuing orders to his younger look-alike companion.

"Connor Baskins," the outdoorsman said.

Eva returned a viselike handshake. "Deputy Duran."

"This is your show, Deputy, but it's my responsibility to make sure everyone is safe and that we get your girl back to her family as soon as possible."

The man's kindness took Eva by surprise. She blinked back tears that filled her eyes and lowered her head before they spilled. "We all appreciate that."

"All right, everybody, crowd in," his deep voice boomed. The crime scene team stepped closer, and Cruz joined Eva, everyone's full attention on the man. "Little basic info. First, do nothing unless we tell you to. Got it?" He waited until every person had issued a nod of understanding. "Water's gonna be rough in some stretches, so hang on tight to your oar, and keep your butt on the bench."

The other man distributed life vests to everyone and then proceeded to help one after the other lash on the flotation devices properly.

"Topo and I have looked at the pictures, and I'm pretty sure we can get you real close to the body. Not as easy as it looks, so me and my partner will maneuver the final approach, unless I say otherwise."

Connor's second, who had yet to speak a single word, tumbled helmets from a long duffel and proceeded to hand one to each member of the group.

"We'll be traversing what's known as the Taos Box," Connor continued. "Take us about an hour to reach our first location. The pros are here, so I'm guessing you expect a crime scene. We'll beach the rafts upriver for you geniuses to make some magic and get all the shit you'll need, in case a bad muhthuh did our lady wrong."

"*Oorah*," Topo shouted and punched the air above his head. Then he went back to securing evidence bags in one of the rafts.

"*Oorah* is motherfuckin' right," Connor said. "Excuse the bad language to those who may be offended. Nobody makes a fool out of these two marines and sure as shit not on my river. So let's make this count. Anything me and my brother can do to help you along once we reach the spot, you just let us know."

"I don't think we'll need our stoic Native personas anymore," Eva whispered to Cruz as they approached the lead raft that Connor had stepped into.

"Yeah, they've got steely covered."

She reached the craft and tried to imagine how they could secure the body of the woman in the boat. They would need to settle her in the well at their feet, and she already worried there would be a risk of losing their precious cargo. Cruz held out his hand to balance Eva as she stepped into the raft, swaying from the extra weight. She proceeded to thump down on the inflated seat and scooted over as Cruz managed to sit beside her without incident.

Marine number two, along with the three techs, stepped into their boats and checked to make sure the bags were secure. Satisfied, they each held up the "okay" hand gesture to Lizbeth, then Eva. The action prompted Connor to lodge his oar in the stones along the beached raft. He pushed off with a grunt, and they were off, the rocking motion already unsettling Eva's stomach.

She glanced over her shoulder and caught the thrilled smiles of the crew in the other raft. Then she found Cruz's expression and prayed she didn't look nearly as terrified as he did.

CHAPTER
SIXTY-THREE
KAI

Kai knew it would be at least another hour before he would be able to spot the rafts. Maybe two, he had heard Cruz say. He kept his mouth shut around the group of men on the bridge, invisible so he wouldn't be asked to leave. He had decided as soon as Eva and Cruz left that if they tried to take him away, they would experience the wrath of one pissed-off Warrior Pueblo. And it looked like Santiago wasn't going anywhere either. Although a couple of steps away, his uncle hadn't left his side for over an hour now.

"I'm thirsty," he said.

It took a while, but Santiago pulled his attention away from the river and turned to him. "I've got water in the truck. Whiskey too. Let's go."

Kai failed to match his elder's long strides and had to lope to keep up. He glanced at the cops behind him and thought they looked relieved that he and Santiago were walking away. He wondered how many of them had been there last time. Maybe all of them recognized him. A flush of embarrassment burned his cheeks.

They reached the parked truck, nose facing the bridge, both slid in the seats, then his uncle popped open the glove box, pulled out a silver flask, spun the lid, took a swig. After another pull, he handed Kai the container, which felt cold to the touch.

"Are you sure we should be doing this?" He nodded to the white and Hispanic officers on the bridge. "What'll they think if they smell booze on us?"

"What they already think. Why do you care?"

"Not all of 'em are bad." Santiago blew out a breath of disagreement, and Kai felt the need to elaborate. "My biology teacher has been good to me. He's done way more than any of my Indian teachers ever have."

"Probably looking for a kickback once you graduate."

"Why would you say that? I'm worth caring about, not just a statistic," Kai snapped.

"Finally." Santiago gave him a sharp nod of the head. "Finally you see that you're worthwhile. You've been the only one who doesn't think so."

"So what, you just push my buttons until you get me to see what you think I'm supposed to?"

Santiago shrugged. "It's what elders do." He took the flask from Kai, who had yet to take a sip, and tossed it back in the glove box. "There's water behind my seat."

Kai reached in the rear of the cab and released two plastic bottles from an open case, handed over one, and opened the other. They kept quiet as they drank, eyes on the north side of the gorge, where the rafts would come from. He couldn't picture Eva and Cruz navigating the white water, had never attempted what some saw as sport. Never heard of anyone who had taken the trip either.

"Think it's her?" Kai whispered, unsure if he wanted to know what his uncle thought.

"Can't go there right now."

"Yeah, me neither." He pulled out his leather bag of treasures and ran the fringe between his fingers. "What do we do now?"

"Nothing." Santiago pointed to the law enforcers. "They're in charge. We can't do a damned thing but wait."

"Think Eva's okay? And Cruz?"

"They're professionals. Seen a lot of bad stuff. They'll be all right."

Kai swiveled his head to his uncle. "Are you okay?"

Paloma's brother looked at him for the first time since they'd sat down. "You've always had a good heart. Don't let life change that, Single Star."

"Is that what happened to you?"

"What do you mean?"

"Well . . . you can be kinda scary."

"Learned behavior. I have stature in the community. Our people want things from me. I have to be careful who I let in. To my heart, and home. You'll see, when you spend more time with me. Day and night, they show up. Hands out, wanting. Expecting favors or money or forgiveness."

"You sound bitter, Uncle. Is that why you hire guys from the outside?"

Santiago blazed a hardened stare for a while as Kai tried to hold his gaze, attempted not to blink. His elder crushed the empty plastic container in his hand, the item unrecognizable when he finished.

Kai wondered if this was a test too. If he was supposed to stand his ground as before or back down. And so he mimicked the action. The remaining water spewed out and soaked his lap. He wanted his uncle to laugh at the humor of his action, at least smile. Santiago remained stone faced, eyes flat.

To break the discomfort, Kai took out his phone and checked the time. "Shouldn't be much longer, right? They've been gone a while now."

Still nothing from his mother's brother.

"Look, I'm sorry if I ticked you off," Kai said. "I don't know how I'm supposed to be around you. What to say. What not to say. I've gone days without talking to anyone. Did you know that? Days. Entire weekends. Even at school I avoid people. These past four days are the first time, since I can remember, having actual conversations. Eva and Cruz are talkers, and they kinda expect me to have an opinion. Spending time around them is interesting and can be fun and, yeah, sometimes frustrating." He probably shouldn't say what next came to his mind, didn't want to push the man further, risk the shunning his mother had endured. Still, the words needed to be said, so he held his leather medicine pouch tight and completed his thought. "But being around you is like . . . being by myself."

And still no words came from the man, who opened his door, got out of his truck, and started to walk toward the bridge, much slower this time.

"Great talk, Uncle," Kai muttered. "Guess I need to add *don't be honest* to my list of not-to-dos." He tossed the crushed water bottle behind the driver's seat, then followed after his uncle.

"Looks like I'll need to find somewhere else to stay. Sure wish Eva's couch wasn't so uncomfortable."

CHAPTER
SIXTY-FOUR
EVA

Eva's thigh tight to Cruz's in the raft, she thought the experience would be romantic, if not for the dire reason for the expedition. The ride had been smooth so far, and she thought there would be no problems, piece of cake, no danger here. That belief died when the ripples became waves, and those became whitecaps, and they crashed against rocks in their path. The constant up-and-down rocking motion flipped her stomach. She held the oar so tight her knuckles ached.

She concentrated on Cruz, who leaned forward, his oar cutting the water on the left as Connor paddled off the right side of the craft, the repetitive motions hypnotic. Her fear started to dissipate, even though the boat started a much faster course downriver.

"Hang on," Connor said over his shoulder. "First set of rapids is coming up."

"This hasn't been 'rapid' yet?" she asked Cruz.

He laughed for the first time. Eva did not. A loud rush filled her ears. Wind whirled and seemed to propel them even faster. She straightened her back, looked past Connor, and saw nothing but roiling white water and the tips of sharp wet rocks ahead.

"Plant your feet and lean in," Connor instructed.

"Shit!" She wasn't sure if the word came out loud or was trapped in her throat along with her gut.

The raft dipped and rose and crashed back down. She lunged forward and back, neck snapping to and fro, side to side. Her body crashed against Cruz's a dozen times or more. And then the movement stilled and they coasted on the smoothest water yet.

Eva released the oar from her fists and shook out her hands. Shouts of excitement and howls of laughter erupted. She looked behind her to make sure the companion raft still held all of its passengers. The crime scene techs looked thrilled, paddles raised over their heads, faces flushed.

"At least they're having fun," she said to Cruz.

"It was kind of exciting," he replied, eyes wide behind his shades.

Black and dark-gray boulders lined both sides of the river from the cliffs that had slid off the sides of the gorge. Tufts of tall grass and occasional yellow blooms on short bushes were the only vibrant colors. The lack of trees surprised Eva, and she wondered if the volcanic rocks didn't allow for many roots to take hold.

Half an hour later she spotted a bighorn sheep on the ridge, then another and another. They all raised their heads and didn't stop their chewing. A hawk glided on the drifts, high above. During the more still areas, the water so clear she could make out the spots on cutthroat trout, some of the fish a foot long.

More and more rapids followed: again water swirled, spitting droplets into the air. Eva gritted her teeth and held on and cursed herself for not being able to let go of her emotions enough to at least try to have a little fun.

They rounded a bend, and the Gorge Bridge came into view. Closer to their objective, Eva neither saw nor sensed any wildlife. Not even a bird chirped or a butterfly flitted, as if every living creature knew their journey held grave consequences. Eva heard nothing but the water, mostly calm for the moment as she trained her sight ahead and upward.

From the steep angle in the raft she could make out only the tops of vehicles parked in a line on the bridge, emergency lights flashing. Miniature people at the railing looked down at them from the midpoint of the span. No one waved.

The weather began to turn, fast, unsettling. Darker clouds billowed. Wind kicked up and spun Cruz's long ponytail. Lightning flashed. Thunder rumbled.

"Whatever you do . . . ," Connor yelled above the din of the gale. "Don't point your oars to the sky. Rougher ahead, but I'll get us close as possible. Hold on."

She held the oar steady in her lap and held the other hand out to Cruz. He took it and squeezed so hard she stifled a shriek, and yet welcomed the pain. A diversion that took the edge off the bizarre situation. Made their mission more real, and assured her that they were in this together.

No matter who they discovered the victim to be.

CHAPTER
SIXTY-FIVE
SANTIAGO

Santiago felt more nervous than he had in a dozen years. Although he had put on his most unreadable persona, he felt certain Kai knew he had been hiding something. Lying. Half truths. His go-to for most people and instances. After years of the behavior, he wasn't sure he knew how to be completely honest. The curse of being successful, riches his people craved and most envied, had made him detached and unfeeling to others' troubles.

The young man Santiago still saw as a little boy didn't seem to want anything from him, except to be accepted. Maybe forgiven for helping his mother steal the treasured bow and so many other trinkets he had added to a very long list of items gone forever.

From an arm's length away, he felt fear radiate off the boy's body. Still he couldn't find the words of comfort that should spill from his mouth. Eva would know what to say, Cruz too. From against the railing, he studied the half dozen cops who remained. All now watched the rafts drift closer. He bet every one of them had more compassion than he did.

And he should have asked if Kai was all right. Not push to find out why he had almost jumped, maybe from the very spot where they stood right now. He didn't want to know. The idea of taking one's own life sickened him. An unforgivable weakness. Cowardly. Fortunately the boy hadn't gone through with the stupidity. Had come to his senses. Maybe. He hadn't even verified from Eva whether the boy had come off the bridge on his own or if she had talked him down. Word on the rez spread fast as wildfire about Kai's misadventure, but the variations had spun out of control so much that Santiago had no idea what was actual and what had become myth.

Not for the first time Santiago thought about the two men he had hired to do the heavy lifting at his ranch. Nobody, young or old, wanted to muck out stalls or heft and spread hay, help mend fences. Hard work once valued. Good cash pay and short hours. Pueblo youths had become soft, unwilling to look up from their devices, slacking off in their air-conditioned houses or coffee shops in town.

The men had showed up at his door a couple of weeks ago, no vehicle in sight, as if they'd dropped from the sky when most needed. Santiago had yet to find out how the workers found him. He hadn't cared to know why or even asked where they'd come from. Their names might not even match those on their IDs. He hired them on a temporary basis to see if they could follow instructions and put in a good day's labor. After the second day of unceasing ten hours of labor, he tossed them keys to the Kawasakis, and they had returned every couple of days since.

Still, they weren't Natives, didn't belong on the rez. For all he knew, they could be tearing up property and casing remote houses on those Kawasakis. He still waited for the police chief or a council member to mention suspicious activity but had yet to hear of a single complaint related to motorbikes or whites on the rez causing trouble.

Even if he had, would he say something? Do something? Take care of the situation? Fire the young men and look for replacements when the ranch now met the conditions he had always wished for? Most likely not. He couldn't think of a man or woman who could keep up with the two outsiders.

Santiago turned to his nephew and saw the perfect mix of his mother and father. Both were striking. She, the most beautiful Pueblo woman many had ever seen, especially when she danced. And smart! The kid was so smart it made him uneasy—maybe because the teen was destined not to stay on the rez, with so many opportunities away from home once he graduated from college. Abandon Santi as everyone else had.

Now he worried over what he would say if Kai again asked whether the woman down there was his mother. That everything would be all right? No. No more lies, he decided.

He stepped sideways, closed the gap to Kai, and then leaned his shoulder against his nephew's, who stood the same height but inhabited half the powerful bulk and weight. Relieved the boy didn't step away, he sent up a silent prayer for forgiveness. To whom . . . he wasn't quite sure.

CHAPTER
SIXTY-SIX
EVA

Eva couldn't wrench her eyes from the form clad in dark leather about forty yards ahead. The water stirred up again, and she worried they would overshoot where they needed to land. As she prepared to launch herself from the raft, Connor's voice caught her attention.

"Cruz, get on the seat behind Eva," the captain said. "When I say, hold both of your paddles in the water at the left side of the raft, and hold them there."

Cruz did as instructed and they readied their oars. Connor paddled and steered from the right. "Now!" he said, and both oars stabbed the water.

The motions caused the craft to veer toward the rock beach. A jostle, and the raft swept up the right side of the bank. Connor jumped out, pulled on the line tied to the nose of the boat, and heaved—a great roar bursting from deep in his chest. Eva and Cruz continued to hold on until the captain motioned them to jump to the stones.

Cruz helped Connor tie off the raft. The second craft sidled up beside the first, and the crew untied and then tossed their evidence bags to the shore. Lightning flashed. Thunder cracked. Movements became more rushed.

"What can I do?" she asked Lizbeth.

"Nothing. Absolutely nothing until I say. Understand, Duran?"

The use of her last name warned Eva that she meant business. "Copy."

Then the tech lead issued indecipherable instructions to her people, and they got busy. Zippers flew open, equipment was freed from the confines, staging areas of tarps were laid out. Eva and Cruz tossed their vests in the rafts, and Eva watched as white Tyvek full-body suits, booties, and latex gloves were distributed and put on so any potential evidence would not be corrupted.

One of the techs asked Lizbeth a question. The boss looked at Eva, seemed to weigh implications, then nodded and turned back to her duties. The tech reached in one of the bags, took out two more body suits, and handed them to Eva and Cruz. Grateful beyond measure that approval to assist must have been granted, she thanked the specialist and tugged on one of the identical outfits, the elastic-edged hood biting into her cheeks and under her neck.

She and Cruz took cautious steps forward. Lizbeth pointed to a spot and held up a hand for them to stop. The cops followed the instruction. Eva turned to Cruz, who stood at parade rest—face forward, feet ten inches apart, knees slightly bent, hands locked behind his back. He didn't even flinch when another bolt turned everything bright white and thunder deafened her.

Eva, however, slouched. Every muscle slack, legs barely keeping her upright. Unable to look away, she stood there spellbound by the sight, watching as one arm undulated in the shallow water, as if the woman waved to the minnows that kissed the stones near the beach. Drenched by the water, the dark-colored long-sleeved leather dress hid what blood and gore the fall would have caused. Otherwise, Eva knew the find could have been much more gruesome.

Gentle waves soaked her boots as she stood there, riveted to the riverbank. All she could do. The disaster profound. Now two dead women, this one also most likely from her tribe. Feeling a complete failure to her people, Eva felt an intense gloom sweep over her.

"This storm's not gonna wait for us," Lizbeth said. "We need to work double quick."

Lizbeth flicked an open hand, a motion for her and Cruz to move forward a few feet so they could assess more clearly. Arms crossed tight against her chest so she wouldn't be tempted to touch anything, Eva watched their motions. Fine tuned and almost choreographed, the team of three began to catalog the scene. One sketched the body and every detail, starting a few feet from the rafts. Lizbeth raised her digital camera and shot off what seemed to be a thousand photos. The third specialist, bent at the waist, walked in short steps and stuck a few yellow flag markers in the ground to mark potential physical evidence. Not enough in Eva's estimation. She knew the more flags, the greater the possibility of something for the team to process.

She was anxious for the okay to approach closer, and just when she thought she couldn't wait any longer, Lizbeth waved her over. "Not sure if anything is viable," the lead tech said. "I advise a three-foot perimeter."

Eva unzipped her protective covering so she could release the snap from one of the cases on her duty belt, removed the folding knife tucked inside, then secured the suit again. She released the spring-loaded blade, charged forward, and knelt down beside the body.

"What are you doing?" Lizbeth said.

"I need to know if it's Paloma. She's got a tattoo on her right bicep."

The crime scene lead took hold of Eva's wrist so tight the blade dropped from her hand. "No," Lizbeth said. "Absolutely not. You need to wait." She picked up the knife and pocketed it in her protective suit. "Do you think you might know this woman?"

"She's been missing fourteen days."

"Same as Kishi," Lizbeth said. "Eva, you're too close to this. You shouldn't even be here. They'll crucify you in court."

"If it ever gets that far," Cruz said.

"I'm sorry, Eva. I know this is painful and there's nothing you want more than to know who this woman is . . . but you'll have to wait until the ME takes receipt of the body. Proper channels. No mistakes. Nothing that can blow back on any of us. Understand?"

Eva didn't understand anything at the moment. She kept her eyes on the prone form, unable to think of her as a "body" rather than a once-viable person. Maybe the friend she had known her entire life.

"All right, let's see what we've got," Lizbeth said. "Ready to roll her?"

"Wait," Eva said. "Can you give it a second?"

She looked up to see Kai, who remained in the same place, binoculars now trained in her direction. She took her phone from its case and dialed a number. "Santi, we're going to turn her over. Please take the binoculars from Kai. And try to get him to leave, okay? You too," she said, not wanting the two of them to suffer any more than they already had.

She clicked off the connection, eyes still on the two above. "Go, Santi, please," she whispered. After an endless minute Santiago wrapped his arm around Kai's waist and turned the younger man, and they started a slow, reluctant walk toward the other side of the bridge.

"Ready," she told Lizbeth, actually not ready at all.

Two of the crime scene techs turned over the body.

"Advanced rigor mortis is present," Lizbeth said as she crouched low and carefully swept the hair away from the woman's face. "Muscles beginning to slacken."

Eva gaped at the face. Not a face at all. A grotesque bluish-purple mask. Nose flat, lips split, dimples in the cheeks and forehead from resting atop the stones for hours. Tongue swollen, front teeth missing.

Cruz broke off, his tactical boots crashing a few steps into the water. Bent over at the waist, he vomited in the river and then retched until Eva worried he would pass out. His intent was solid—so as not to potentially taint the crime scene area near the body—but Eva felt certain that being careful was a moot point. There would be no viable evidence around the body. Nobody had brought this woman to her final resting spot, as they had Kishi. Someone dropped her from the bridge. Or pushed her. And yet, maybe she jumped. As usual for this case, only questions took the lead.

Hands on his knees, back to her, Cruz said, "Is it Paloma? Please don't be Paloma."

She didn't know. Couldn't possibly be sure. Eva wanted not to look but found herself unable to turn away, entranced by the gruesome sight that could never be unseen. And actually didn't know for certain whether the corpse was male or female, except for the dress. The only thing that resembled any of the three missing women was the long dark hair. She had learned early in her career not to assume a single thing.

To guard her heart, Eva took a moment to shut off the switch to her emotions, then scanned the area directly around the body. She took in the knee-high moccasin boots, uneven hem of the dress, double row of crushed antler tips that were barely held on by the leather stitching.

"Cruz, check the stitches. Pretty sure this dress is a knockoff too."

He nodded but didn't approach, kept his back to the scene. She decided not to push him. The photographs would be enough in the unlikely case he wanted to ever study the aftermath.

"Intentional harm, or suicide?" Eva asked.

Lizbeth shrugged. "The damage is so extensive it's doubtful we'll ever know for sure."

A bolt of lightning, followed immediately by a crack of thunder resonating throughout the canyon, so loud Eva swore nearby boulders the size of cars trembled. In the distance gray streaks of rain slashed from the clouds at a thirty-degree angle. Her heartbeat raced—the urgency unmistakable.

"We gotta go," Connor shouted. *"Now!"*

Lizbeth and her second exhibited extreme care settling the body in a full-length bag and then zipped the confinement shut. Along with Cruz, they hustled their burden to the lead raft and settled her in the well of the boat, then the investigators jumped in their boat. The moment they hit their seats, Topo pushed and they were off. As they passed, Lizbeth tossed a rope to Eva. The cord caught a gale and veered off course, inches from Eva's hand.

Cruz hurried, face ashen. He looked up and all around, as if waiting for the entire cliff face to come down on them. Eva grabbed his arm, ushered him to the raft, pushed on his taut shoulder for him to sit. She dropped to the seat opposite, facing Cruz, the body in the well between them.

"Clear!" she said, and Connor pushed off as well.

Moments later, another round of lightning and thunder that clapped so loud Eva covered her ears. Rain crashed down, massive drops at first, then in sheets. She glanced back to see the flag markers, which flapped in the wind and then were swallowed by water in moments. Eyes forward again, she gasped when the second craft bobbled and Eva thought for sure it would tip over and toss everybody overboard. Shouts cut through the storm, all oars slashed the water, and soon the raft righted.

Their own boat started to rock, and she realized the movement came from beside her. Cruz clawed at his protective covering, designed to withstand tearing and cuts. He only frustrated himself. The motions became frantic, and the raft shifted in the already-rough water.

"Be still back there, or this raft is going over," Connor shouted from the front.

Eva imagined them flipping, neither of them in life vests, the body gone forever. She reached back, grateful to see the life vests and helmets still in the well behind her, and handed Cruz one of each, then clasped hers on. She mourned the lost rope and could only hope the body would stay in place.

Another round of flash and crash, even closer this time.

Eyes shut, she prayed to her grandfather to keep them safe. Then to the parents she hadn't visited in fifteen years.

CHAPTER SIXTY-SEVEN
ALICE

Alice had awakened from her nap more refreshed after an hour than from a full night's slumber. Best rest she could recall in years. While she'd been in the presence of White Dove, all of her cares and worries had evaporated. And now she felt the need to complete the next task.

Rain had continued to pelt the RV, and she worried about being able to move the massive vehicle without getting stuck in the mud and decided the run to the convenience store would have to wait. She tapped her fingers on her knees as she sat on the bench and worried that the generators' tanks might not have enough gas to power on much longer.

Bored and anxious to find out if the concoction of buprenorphine she had decided on would be successful, she decided to prepare a second dose for the basket maker. Her hands trembled, and she overfilled the chamber beyond what she'd intended. "Shoot, shoot, shoot," she scolded. "Now you've done it."

She considered tossing the nearly full hypodermic and starting over, then reminded herself of the need to ration the heroin.

"Oh well. It'll be all right."

She snapped the protective cap over the needle, tucked the syringe in her pocket, opened the side door, and looked out at the deluge, which had been constant for nearly an hour. Dressed in fresh scrubs, but hair still wet from the house-to-Winnebago dash, she wished she had a hat or raincoat. Even an umbrella would be nice. She looked down at the puddles below the steps and longed for galoshes too.

Keys in hand, she launched off the steps and sank ankle deep in mud. "Shoot, shoot, shoot," she yelled and sprinted to the front door of the little house, which seemed to lean even more than before. Where her patient awaited delivery from the shackles that would no longer contain her.

The now two-week-long routine evaporated. Overjoyed as on day one, when Alice had first discovered White Dove and the three others, she flew through the house, hit the lock on the first try, flung open the door, and crossed the four long strides to the basket maker's bedside. She clamped the needle cap between her teeth, yanked, didn't bother to cleanse the site before she hit the vein.

Drugs administered, she blew out a breath, took up the edge of the quilt, wiped the rain from her face. "Whew! That was exciting."

After a full minute she checked the woman's pulse. "Slightly elevated, strong beat. Nothing to be concerned about."

The moment the last word left her lips, the patient clutched the fabric of her nightgown over her heart, rasped in gasps of breath, thrashed on the mattress, back bowed, legs jerking.

"Don't you dare!" Alice shouted at the woman. "Why are you doing this to me?"

She patted her pockets. "Narcan, Narcan, Narcan." She reached into her scrubs pocket, hands fumbling, she dropped one package, pulled out another, anxiety ramping, panicked. Inserted the nozzle in the distressed woman's nostril, pressed the plunger halfway, repeated the process in the other nostril. No reaction. She took out another dose and repeated the administrations. Again, nothing.

Too late, she realized. The basket maker's open, pinpoint-pupil eyes stared unseeing, and her mouth began to turn dusky blue. Body unresponsive when Alice twisted her fist on the woman's breastbone.

"No you don't, little lady."

Alice took hold of both arms, dragged the pliant body to the floor. Administered thirty chest compressions, then two mouth-to-mouth breaths, repeated the method. Again and again. After seven rounds, unable to pump a single time more, Alice pushed away from her clearly dead patient, sat there staring until her breaths evened out.

Words failed her. Anger seemed a moot point. Instead, she went to the bathroom, opened the cabinet door under the sink, withdrew two jugs of bleach, and proceeded to pour the caustic liquid over her now-useless guinea pig. Rain continued to pelt the roof. An incessant drip in the corner of the room caught her attention, and she raised her head to the water-stained ceiling.

She looked at the closed door beyond the bathroom, where only one remained. Her jewel. The one she must not fail.

But did she dare risk another botched experiment? Did she have any other options? "What do you do now? Huh, Alice? What now?"

Queasy, eyes watering, nose stinging from the bleach, she closed the door behind her, went to the front room, glanced at her precisely sorted provisions.

She sat down in front of the beehive fireplace, imagined warm flames dancing, and emptied her mind. Another drip sounded nearby. Normally she would find the noise annoying, but this time she altered her thinking and became lulled by the sound of each *plunk* that hit the tile floor.

A blank slate appeared behind her closed eyes. Then a boy entered her thoughts.

And she had her answer.

CHAPTER
SIXTY-EIGHT
EVA

After battling three more rounds of rapids, Eva wasn't sure she could maintain a firm hold on the bag under her palm next to Cruz's for much longer. Back screaming from keeping the same position for over an hour, soaked, exhausted, spent. The journey seemed never ending.

Now and then she glanced at Cruz, who had yet to raise his eyes to her own. Concern for him grew the farther they glided from the recovery site. She recognized the signs of shock: flat affect, detachment from surroundings, disinterest in engaging.

With neither of them of physical use since they had pushed off, Connor had taken on the responsibility of guiding and paddling, without complaint. And so now, the captain's voice took her by surprise when he said, "Sorry to tell you this, but I'm gonna need some help steering and paddling up ahead. Gets rough after this bend."

Cruz didn't look as upset about the request as she felt. Reluctant, she released the bag, sat back down next to Cruz, and took up the oar she had trapped under her foot. Cruz followed her lead but tucked one leg over the prone form. Eva did the same, resigned that their limbed cage would have to be sufficient.

As Connor swayed, working the paddle double time, she caught glimpses of what lay ahead. Waves reminded her of swells that crashed to a beach, but these did not subside or flow back outward. The water churned and somersaulted and spit in the air. The deluge continued to slash down. Occasional streams rushed down the sides of the gorge to become one with the river. The raft footwell had filled to midcalf level, and that troubled Eva the most. She envisioned the body floating right out of the boat. Her stomach lurched. She clenched her teeth and the oar in her hands, prepared to react the moment she received the signal from Connor.

The boat inclined and smacked down so hard her neck snapped and a bright light filled her vision—lightning or from the force, Eva wasn't sure. The single good thing was that the motion had emptied the water, and she could now see the tops of her boots.

"Now!" Connor ordered. In tandem, Eva and Cruz stabbed the river, dragged their paddles, lifted, stroked again. Unable to wipe her eyes, she squeezed them shut to ease the needle stings of river and rain. "Go. Go. *Keep going!*" They did, until she felt certain she would pass out from the exertion. "Almost there."

The "almost there" took another few minutes that felt like as many hours, when Connor repeated the instruction to aim for the shore. Legs shaking, she managed to step out of the inflatable and help Connor tug the raft farther on the bank. Bent over, hands on her knees, panting, hoping she wouldn't puke, she felt a hand on her back and looked up.

"Good work, Deputy," Connor said as he squeezed the end of his soaked beard. "I'll be thinking about you and your people."

"Thank you," she mouthed. All she could manage.

When she recovered enough to straighten up and take a step, she spotted a man dressed in a wide-brimmed hat and a clear full-length slicker over a dark suit. Rain streamed off of him and she wondered how long he had been waiting in the downpour. Dr. Mondragon. She had never been so relieved to see the man who, since her university graduation ceremony, she encountered only on the worst of occasions.

The seasoned medical examiner approached, squeezed her arm, a sympathetic gesture she hoped she could return someday. For now she could only prepare him as best she could. "It's bad, Tavis. Really, really bad," she told him, her voice low to convey the importance.

Mondragon matched her tone and said, "Thank you for the warning, Eva. I will take great care."

A much younger man carried a flat transport board to the edge of the water, and he spoke a few words to Connor, who then helped Mondragon's assistant ease the body from the well of the raft to the board. Cruz hovered—Eva figured, in case of a botched handoff—and continued to hold his hand on the form as they walked up the incline. Pride and sorrow for him battled for Eva's attention.

Tears choked her and threatened to flow while she managed to follow Cruz, who had yet to shift his attention from the body bag until it disappeared inside an unmarked white van.

The moment the door closed, she breathed easier. The assistant hustled to the driver's seat and slammed his door. Mondragon remained beside Eva and Cruz, who looked even more distraught than before.

"Consistent findings?" the ME asked.

"Who could know?" Cruz snapped. "She's destroyed. Nothing recognizable there at all."

Eva started to apologize for the cop's callous remarks, but Mondragon held up a hand, signaling no need to do so. "Long hair like a Native," she said. "Clothing resembles Kishi's. Traditional ceremonial dress, but I'm sure it's not crafted by our people. Other than that . . ." She shrugged.

"I'll do my best, Eva."

"I know you will, Tavis. We appreciate all you can offer. Right, Cruz?"

Cruz issued the slightest nod. After a moment he stepped forward and held out his hand. "Help us figure out how to catch whoever's doing this."

Mondragon met the handshake. "I'll begin right away."

"When will you release Kishi's body?" Cruz asked. "The family needs to know when they can make the traditional funeral preparations."

"Given we now have two victims who could be connected, I can't answer that. Initial steps are to determine if there are any potential replicated findings."

"So, when?" Cruz pushed again.

"Please extend my apologies to Ms. Reyna's people."

"Not good enough, Doc."

"Cruz," Eva said. "Knock it off."

"I understand your disappointment, Officer Romero. Believe me, I do. However I absolutely will not rush the work. I will prioritize the toxicology to begin with and have cleared my entire schedule in order to work exclusively on your young ladies. That's all the consolation I can offer right now."

"There's one thing you can check right away," Eva said. "Paloma Arrio has a tattoo on her right bicep."

"Very helpful."

"Thank you," Eva said as she continued to glare at her colleague. "We do appreciate your efforts. You're the smartest person I've ever met." She let out an embarrassed chuckle. "Not sure if I've ever told you that."

"You have not, but please know the respect is mutual."

"Can we cut this little lovefest and get to it?" Cruz said.

"Of course. I'm off. Eva, I'll let you know the moment I have anything solid to contribute to your investigation."

"I appreciate that."

The moment Mondragon got in the passenger seat and the van pulled away, Eva whirled on Cruz and stepped a foot from him. "I really need you *not* to be a dick to that man. He's an ally. And a good friend. So knock it off. Copy, Officer?"

She spun on her heel, charged for her official pickup, swept the key fob from the top of the driver's-side front tire, slid in, slammed the door harder than necessary, fired up the engine. Cruz stood there, undeterred by the rain, staring at her, as if deciding whether to join her.

Unsure if she should leave him there, drive off, let him figure out how to get back to his house, she waited another minute. He looked so sad. Reminded her of a drenched little boy who'd lost his favorite toy. Her heart softened as she felt his pain from twenty feet away. She leaned across the console and opened the passenger door.

He considered so long she revved the engine to prompt him, wipers going double time yet barely able to clear the windshield. It felt to Eva like a very long time before he took measured steps in her direction. When he reached the vehicle, he placed one foot on the running board, one hand on the doorframe, eyes averted. Waited again as the rain splattered the seat.

"I apologize for my behavior. This is killing me," he confided.

"Get in, Cruz. I need you near me."

He complied. Their body heat fogged the windshield. She wanted only one thing at that moment. Not food or drink or any other creature comfort. Only her naked body cradled by his in her bed, the door closed to the world. The terrifying, puzzling, infuriating circumstances forbidden to intrude any further.

She sighed. No way that would happen in the near future. Maybe ever again if he didn't look at her soon. Finally he lifted his head, emotion so raw she wanted to cradle him.

"I don't think I can do this," he said.

Dread took hold of her, not sure if he meant their relationship or the investigation. "We're going to get through it. Together. We'll know if it's Paloma soon."

"Drive," he said, no clarification offered.

She shifted the truck to reverse, still uncertain whether their relationship had taken an irrevocable turn.

CHAPTER SIXTY-NINE
PALOMA

Paloma lifted her head and managed to fully open one eye. "Ahiga?" she asked, thinking her dead husband had come to claim her. Hazy and unsure, it took a few minutes for her to regain her bearings, realize nothing had changed. Same room, mattress that had surely formed to her body by now, fresh peanut butter sandwich and chocolate drink waiting on the table next to her.

Everything the same as the past fourteen days. Except that Tonita still wasn't in her bed, which confused her more than before.

"Tonita? Are you still in the bathroom?"

When no reply came, Paloma attempted to sit up. Too weak and high to manage, she dropped back to the bed. A strong smell made her wince, and her eyes began to water. She wrinkled her nose. Bleach, she realized, and figured the nurse must be cleaning up in there.

Her mind wandered, no particular thought fixed for more than a moment. Snippets of treasured memories. Kai's smile, Ahiga clapping as she finished a dance, the two massive ancient houses on the rez, playing cards with Eva, racing ponies alongside Santiago on the open mesa.

Although the ache of loss twisted her heart, she smiled, grateful for being able to remember. For years she had shoved away anything pleasant from her life. Everything prior to the shift in her universe. But now she felt a new possibility shine. Faint. Way in the distance. Led by Kai and Eva, hands out, waiting to usher her from this hell and back into their arms.

"I'm still here," she told the vision she hoped would soon be a reality. "Find me."

She took smooth breaths in and out, relaxed every muscle, released her location out to the universe. Waited for her saviors to find her.

And hoped, beyond all hope, they wouldn't be too late.

CHAPTER SEVENTY
EVA

Eva stayed under the hot needles of her showerhead until the water tank spit nothing but a cold spray that reminded her of being in the raft again. She shoved that experience out of her mind and changed into fresh jeans, a long-sleeved T-shirt covered by a thick flannel, two pairs of insulated socks, and cowboy boots.

Brain working seven steps ahead of her actions, she clipped her off-duty badge and holstered Glock on her belt, secured her still-wet hair in a tight ponytail, and went to the kitchen to prepare a pot of strong coffee.

Stainless-steel to-go container ready, she munched on a protein bar and wished it was Cruz's fry bread slathered in honey as she looked out the window over the kitchen sink and waited for the fresh brew that gurgled from the coffee maker to finish.

She glanced at the sky. Although the storm had moved on shortly after they'd bid farewell to Connor and his brother, dark clouds now loomed and threatened another downpour.

"Keep it together or you'll get sloppy. One step at a time, Deputy," she reminded herself. "Nothing you can do about the rain. Stay on point. Focus only on what you have control over." She chuckled at her own comment, knowing full well she had *control* of so very little, if anything at all.

Coffee container, pair of galoshes and slicker in hand, she slid in the Beast, fired up the engine, and twenty minutes later arrived at Santiago's. The house and chicken coop looked freshly painted from the deluge.

As always, Paloma's brother stood on his porch. She opened her door and angled her body to put on the galoshes, then slid from the Rover. She didn't want Santiago or the boy to think of her as anything but a friend and ally, not a cop, not right now, so she stripped off the gun and badge and secured them in the console between the seats.

Kai stepped from the chicken house, Shadow in his arms, scowl on his face, lips tight, nostrils flaring. The look screamed *pissed off*. She lifted a cautious wave. And he charged her way. Puddles exploded in his wake under already-filthy sneakers. Shadow wriggled in his arms, but Kai didn't set the pup down.

"Some cop! It's your fault," he accused. "If you found Kishi and Dora, they'd still be alive. Mom's dead for sure. Tonita, too, probably, 'cause you're so shitty at your job."

His words wounded her, but she knew he needed to vent. Still, this defeat would take him lower if she didn't at least try to pivot his thinking. "Don't give up, Kai. On me or your mom."

As if he hadn't heard her, his rant continued. "They just wanted to be her friend. Helped out after the accident. Tonita too. And then she goes and gets *them* addicted. No wonder everyone hates me. Probably think I'm just like her, able to bend minds and the will of others. A conjurer of bad shit."

"That's not true," she snapped. "Your mother's or anyone else's addiction isn't your fault. Nobody hates you. They may not know what to say because maybe they're scared about how you'll react or worry that your pride will be hurt if they push too hard to help. You don't know what's going on in other people's lives or hearts. Sometimes *they* don't even know."

"Stop talking," he said, soft and low. The tone hit her harder than if he'd shouted the words. Head bowed to the puppy's, he spun on his heel and returned to the shelter.

Eva sighed, shook her head, baffled and near defeat. She turned to Santiago and said, "I need your counsel, brother."

She waited for him to invite her inside or at least to join him on the porch. He remained in place, expressionless, until he finally said, "Walk with me."

She did her best to match his steps to the barn. Horses whinnied and bobbed their heads as their leader walked past their stalls, to the far opening of the building.

When he turned to her, arms crossed, she thought he might throw hurtful words and insults too. Risking reprisal, she said, "I don't know what to do. Kai hates me."

"No. He's frustrated and scared."

"So am I."

"Yes, but you can't show him that. You need to be strong."

"That's all I ever am, Santi. When is it *my* time to be a little weak and vulnerable?"

"Never, Lightning Dance."

As always, whenever someone called her by her Native name, she thought of her mother, who had gifted her the name because she'd come out wriggling, spinning, tiny hands already graceful as they reached out. Ironic, because Paloma had been the dancer ever since she could walk. They'd wanted to swap their gifted names and even threatened to go to the tribal council for permission when they were seven years old. But as Eva was never meek or shy, the Native name "White Dove" didn't describe her either. "Covert Suspicion" suited her better, but that one surely would never fly.

She let his comment go and asked, "You're going to let him keep that puppy, right?"

"Dog's a champion in the making. Best lines and temperament in five litters. Could get three thousand dollars for it, easy."

"To Kai it's not an 'it' or a thing or a moneymaking prospect. Shadow will be a companion. Your nephew needs that. Now, more than ever." She used the dog's name as an effort to make the sanctimonious killjoy realize a connection between boy and canine had been made.

The high pitch of engines approached, drawing her attention to the other end of the barn. A couple of motorbikes, identical to the one Santiago had offered to Kai, parked, and two men dismounted, took off their helmets, and hung them on the handlebars. Eva noted that one had light-brown hair, the other blond. Same description Kai had given her for Santiago's new workers.

"Start spreading fresh straw, all right?" Santiago instructed.

Both men nodded, stripped off their black gloves and silver-zippered leather jackets, took up rakes, and got to work. Eva did her best to ignore the men and said, "You say you know Paloma, but you don't. You don't have any idea what she went through after Ahiga died. She always put on a brave face, but the walls came up even before she left the hospital. Please, brother, don't risk losing Kai too."

"I was supposed to be in the van. Did you know that? Was all set to be one of the judges at the competition. Then one of my horses got sick with colic the night before, and I decided to stay."

Stunned, she wondered how long he had been waiting to say those words. Guilt had bothered many people on the rez because of the death of Paloma's husband and the women riding in the vehicle, who had traveled to Texas to represent their tribe. But she had no idea Santiago had also carried the burden. "No, I . . . No," she said.

"It's my fault she became a junkie."

Eva flinched. The horrible word—so defining and careless—would never, in her mind, represent her best friend. "Where did she get the heroin?"

"No idea."

"Come on, Santi. You know everything that goes on around here. Every person on the rez. Know what they're going to ask for before they find the courage to seek you out."

"Don't know a thing about drugs. Sure as hell not heroin. Everyone knows that shit is restricted on the rez. Nothing stronger than pot, and the incoming police chief is gonna be firm on that, too, soon as she's sworn in. Like you said, I know things. Believe me when I say the only Pueblo addicts I know of are Paloma and her friends . . ." He dropped his head, remembering. "And Tonita. No one else has come to the council's attention or the chief of police's."

Eva noticed the men had stopped their labor, arms resting on the handles of their rakes, looking their way, scowls on their faces. Santiago turned to where she stared. He issued his own glower, and they went back to work, double time.

Eva stepped fully outside the barn and waved to Santiago to join her so they couldn't be overheard. "Since when do you let non-Natives work for you? Who are they? How did you find them? How long have they been here? Since COVID closed down the rez? Did they rebuild your kitchen? Give *them* full access inside your precious house? Unlike your own sister."

"What's this about?"

"Answer me, dammit."

"Watch your tone, young lady."

"I'm not young, or a lady. Answer my fucking questions."

He blew out an appalled puff of air. "They're from out of town. Came here looking for part-time work a couple weeks ago. Come by every other day to see if there's anything they can do. Hard workers. I'm grateful for the help."

"What do you have them doing?"

"Unload hay, take sacks of grain off the delivery trucks, muck stalls. Grunt work."

She took out the palm-size notebook from her back pocket and clicked her pen. "Names? Addresses?"

"Don't know. Idiot One and Idiot Two."

"Santi, what the hell? You've got unknowns working on your property, access to everything you have. So, who exactly is the idiot?"

"Enough!"

"It's my job to ask, Santi. And as your friend, I'm trying to look out for you. So quit being all tough." She tapped him with a closed fist, a playful jab, although she wanted to hit him full force to get him to realize her concern.

His demeanor eased a bit, and she risked pushing again when she said, "Are you sure those men aren't taking advantage of you? Ever since I can remember, you said you wanted to help our people. That's why you ran for tribal council membership so many years ago. Everyone respects you and follows your advice. Paloma was the same growing up, remember? She looked up to you. Wanted to be like you—an honorable Pueblo for our people to be proud of."

"Same goes for you," he said. "It's your path to be strong for others. Decided long before you were born."

"A conspiracy, you mean."

He chuckled, although no humor rang through. "No, Lightning Dance. The spirits are never malicious."

"I hope you're right, Santi," she said. "I really do."

CHAPTER SEVENTY-ONE
EVA

Eva decided to let Kai sit in his anger a while longer. No need to push him. She had other things to worry about, and so, hoping for inspiration, she decided to revisit the hunting grounds. The Beast's tires spun and spewed muck the entire way up the incline, and again she had to shift to four-wheel drive before she reached the clearing.

When she jumped from her seat, she sank in mud to the ankles of her galoshes. She wondered if she would ever get the floorboards clean again. Thunder boomed, and she raised her head. A fat drop of rain smacked her nose. "Great. That's what I need."

She shrugged on the long slicker, eyes on the console. Always best to be safe, she cautioned herself as she raised the padded lid and then attached the holstered Glock back to her belt. The firepower usually added a boost of confidence, but this time the weight felt heavy on her hip. Although an excellent markswoman on the range, she had yet to actually fire the weapon on duty. But she had taken the oath to protect citizens, her fellow LEOs, or herself, so she always kept her gun clean and oiled . . . just in case.

The scent of freshly washed pine and greenery put her in a better frame of mind as she stepped farther into the trees to where she had discovered Kishi. She attuned her senses and sent up a plea for Mother Nature to guide her. She supposed she wanted to feel Paloma hanging around, or maybe even the remnants of Kishi's essence. After five full minutes, nothing otherworldly had honored her.

She walked on and found only a few of Lizbeth's flags still in the ground. And then, much to her surprise, she spotted cuttings of flowers indigenous to the area. Strange, but she figured the offerings must have been left by her own people, those who knew this part of the rez. Then she wondered again if someone from her community had killed Kishi. Or helped to dump the body. If the cuttings were an act of remorse or a request for forgiveness.

"Don't assume anything," she reminded herself. "You don't know if Kishi was murdered." But in her heart, she did.

A steady, light rain picked up as she pulled her phone from her pocket and snapped photos of the curious assemblage. The sound of a motor began to grow louder as the moments passed. She assumed from a chainsaw, probably a local after free firewood. Not sanctioned but a good way to clear detritus, which helped keep down the threat of a forest fire spreading.

She frowned when the jarring noise became louder, now two distinct motors. A *ree-ree-ree* split the quiet. Birds rocketed to the sky. A motorbike, she realized, and looked for Kai atop an annoying Kawasaki. She figured he must have followed her, otherwise how could he know where to go? Then another racket rattled her nerves. And another. Four in all, identical dirt bikes, riders wearing matching helmets and leathers. They wove between tree trunks, then broke off and circled Eva, around and around and around, until she thought she would drop from the dance of vertigo.

Eva put her hand on the butt of her Glock, unsnapped the trigger guard on the holster, ready to take action if necessary. One of the bikers held up a hand, and they all stopped. The leader raised the shield on his helmet, and Eva recognized the blond man from Santiago's barn.

She charged toward him and commanded, "Sheriff's deputy! Get off the bike."

"Quit askin' about drugs!" the man yelled over the idling engines. "You hear? It's none of your business. Back off or the old man and the boy die. Then you."

The man belted out an ominous laugh, lowered the shield, revved the motor, spun out three doughnuts. Eva squinted through the stones and dead leaves that flung from the tires. A crack discharged from her right, so close she flinched. Two more followed. Gunshots, Eva realized.

She pulled out her Glock, alternated her aim from the biker, who continued to spin, and where she believed the shots had come from. More rapid pops, one kicking up forest detritus three inches from her foot.

The Kawasakis dodged trees. Rain impeded a clear view. She wasn't sure which direction to aim. She fired a double shot. Waited two seconds. Let loose another round of doubles. Noises grew faint, and she could see no more flashes of the bikes.

Realizing it was pointless to call for backup, she raced to the Beast, fired it up, slammed the gearshift into drive. And had no idea which direction to go.

CHAPTER SEVENTY-TWO
EVA

Still rattled by the encounter in the forest, Eva pulled into the sheriff's department lot, locked up the Rover, charged for the entrance. She avoided everyone she encountered and beelined for her desk. The phone rang the moment she sat down.

"Duran," she barked into the handset.

"Hello, Officer Duran," the voice said.

"Oh . . . Dr. Mondragon," she said, embarrassed by her initial tone. "Excuse me, I wasn't expecting to hear from you so quickly."

"I don't have much to offer yet, but thought you would want to know that toxicology testing for both women detected high levels of heroin. Other substances as well, but we're still running panels to pinpoint those."

Eva pulled the notepad and pen from her pocket and jotted down the info as he spoke.

"Also," he continued, "both women appear to have the same injection site on the top of their hands." She heard the clack of keys and assumed the doctor was at his computer. "Curious, because Ms. Reyna's injection site is on the left hand, and our new victim exhibits an injection administered between the right metacarpal bones."

"Why the top of the hand?" she asked.

"In many cases, veins are more pronounced there. Better chance of hitting a viable delivery source for the drugs."

She couldn't avoid the one question that had burned in her mind from the moment she'd spotted the woman on the bank of the Rio Grande. "Does she have a tattoo?"

"No tattoo on either bicep. There's a great deal of damage to the body, but I am certain about that."

"Thank you, Creator," she whispered. "Anything else you can share?"

"As with Kishi, this woman is a bit malnourished, but I found undigested wheat bread and peanut butter and a creamy chocolate substance in her stomach. Also curious that neither woman is dehydrated. They both either started taking care of themselves lately, or someone has been looking after them. That's all I'm comfortable providing until I've completed my findings. I'll keep you informed as we progress."

"I appreciate that, Doctor."

"Oh, my friend, you can always call me Tavis. Please take care out there."

"Yes, sir. Absolutely."

As soon as she ended the call, Sheriff Bowen waved her to his office. So much had gone wrong on her watch, and now she expected the worst-possible outcome for her future as a cop. She told herself not to cry like a little girl when he demanded her badge and sidearm.

He sat at his desk and said, "Have a seat, Duran. Catch me up, please."

Deciding not to mention being shot at for now, she said, "I just spoke to the medical examiner, sir. Both victims had heroin in their system at the time of death. Dr. Mondragon also found undigested food that matched the stomach contents of the first victim. She hasn't been officially identified yet, but I'm certain the woman isn't Paloma Arrio."

"Your friend."

"Right. She has a distinctive tattoo on her bicep. The woman in question doesn't have any ink there."

"Well, that's somewhat of a relief."

"Yes, sir, I suppose so, sir."

"Right. Still a passed soul we need to put a name to." He leaned forward and pinned her with his eyes. "We've got two dead women, Duran. One for certain Taos Pueblo, the other a good possibility. I've got no choice but to contact the FBI. Minimum, I'll need to alert the feds about Ms. Reyna's fatality. That it could possibly involve foul play committed on reservation land."

The mere mention of feds caused Eva's heartbeat to thud in her chest. "But we're not sure about that. Officer Romero is only certain the boundaries of county and reservation lands are very close to the location."

"Yes, I realize this, but the Taos Pueblo Police Department isn't exactly being forthcoming to me. They've yet to return a single call."

"I understand, but could you give me more time? These are my people. I know how to deal with them," she pretty much lied. She had no idea how much time it would take for anyone in the TPPD to figure out a mapping system that probably didn't even exist for that part of the reservation.

He reclined in his office chair, hands locked behind his head, studying her. She took the action and silence as a sign that he wanted to be swayed and said, "Please, sir, could you hold off a little longer? If we can't get answers from the tribal police, I'll contact the tribal leadership. Nearly one hundred men will need to confer and advise accordingly. Nothing moves very fast when so many people need to agree on matters that affect the entire tribe. It's a big deal to allow the FBI on our sovereign land."

"How much time are you thinkin'?"

"A week," she tried.

"Too long. If this shitstorm gets worse, and the feds find out we've been holdin' out, that won't look good for us the next time we need their assistance. And there's always a next time. I'd say more like three days. It'll take that long for the request to process."

"Thank you, sir."

"Get crackin'. The clock has started, as of now."

Eva rushed back to her desk but halted three steps away. Cruz stood there, chatting with three of her colleagues, smiles all around. "Hello, Duran," he said.

"Officer Romero." She waited until the others had dispersed before she said, "What are you doing here?"

"Anxious to know if you heard from the ME."

"I was about to text you, then the sheriff called me in."

"You in trouble?"

"Naw, but he gave me the heads-up he's about ready to invite the feds to our miserable party."

"No way. When?"

"Bought us some time. Asked for a week. He gave me three days."

"What about our latest . . . ?" He seemed to struggle about how to refer to the as-of-yet-unidentified woman now under Mondragon's care. "Tattoo?"

She shook her head, and they both let out a relieved sigh.

"Who do you think it is?" he asked.

"Tonita or Dora."

"Yeah, me too."

"This is so bad." She hitched her head and he followed her to where she'd parked the Beast. "I need to tell you something. Someone shot at me, and I discharged my weapon."

"What? Who? *When?*"

"Just now. At the hunting grounds, where I found Kishi. Like they were waiting for me. But actually I think they followed me. Four guys on motorbikes, like Kai's. I recognized two of them working at Santiago's earlier today. Must have heard me talking to Santi about drugs on the rez. They warned me to back off, or they would kill the old man and the kid and then me."

"You're shitting me."

"Wish I was. Haven't filed the paperwork yet."

Both strict adherents to procedure, she felt the need to validate her statement. She pulled the Glock from its holster, stripped the magazine, handed it to Cruz, then partially pulled back the barrel to expose one brass round in the chamber.

He studied the magazine and said, "Four rounds missing."

"Right. A pair of double shots."

"Adhered to your training. Didn't freak out at the possible attempt on your life. That'll look good on your reports."

"Don't really care about that."

"You should." He handed back the magazine, and she slapped it home.

"I'm sure my rounds didn't hit anyone," she said. "And they may not have been trying to actually hit me."

"Still, you gotta follow through, or the sheriff will be pissed. And the altercation took place on the rez. I'll need a formal statement for our records."

"I know. Later today, I promise. I'm still trying to find that nurse, or at least the RV. I thought maybe Taos PD can help with that. They control access to the security cameras around town."

"Keep in touch," Cruz said. "Stay safe."

"Yep, you too. Head on a swivel."

"Copy that."

As she took the remaining steps to her Rover and slid behind the wheel, every muscle screamed, and although the dashboard clock read only 4:10 p.m., she felt like this day had to be the longest of her life.

Sitting there, the Rover's comfortable seat cradling her, she became sleepy, eyes nearly closed, as if a force worked against instead of for her. She slapped her cheek. Hard. The solid smack rang in her ears. "Nope. No rest. No stopping. Not now."

The remainder of her day did not bode well when rain started to pour down. She pulled out of the lot and continued her private pep talk. "Three days, Deputy. Get to work."

CHAPTER
SEVENTY-THREE
ALICE

Alice cursed the rain. So much of it. Flat, mud-soaked plains left and right of the highway, black clouds the entire view through the Winnebago's windshield, wipers barely able to keep up. But she had to continue moving onward. Her to-do list required much attention, and she needed to stay busy. Especially to turn her mind away from the patient on the mattress of the first bedroom, cleaned up and dressed in the ceremonial attire, awaiting her final destination.

She had felt a shift since the basket maker's final moments. *Stay or go* played in her mind, a constant loop. No final decision came, so she decided to fulfill the most essential duty first: to refuel the generators so water and basic power would continue to flow in the house. She glanced at the gas gauge. Less than a quarter tank. She stroked the top of the dashboard. "Let's top you off too."

Now adept at maneuvering the big rig, she avoided the few vehicles in front of the convenience store and parked at the farthest island's gas pump, where the covering was tall enough to accommodate the height of the Winnebago. She hurried from behind the steering wheel to the back of the RV, took up two now-empty five-gallon gas containers, stepped down from the side door, and proceeded to fill them up.

Fueling the motorhome came next. Then she loaded the filled gas cans back inside, took up a nearly empty propane cylinder for the RV's needs, and approached the entrance. Excitement caused a flutter in her chest. The old man who had been so helpful before sat in the same folding chair under the awning near the double doors. He surely knew White Dove, and again she ached to talk to him about her.

She shopped faster than the three times before. Two cases of water, jar of peanut butter, two loaves of bread—then put one back when she remembered there were now only two mouths to feed.

As the clerk rang up the purchases, she plucked an umbrella from a display at the counter. The young man never even looked up when he asked, "Anything else?"

"Propane tank refill. I left the other container in the cage out front."

He added that to the total, and she peeled off twenties from a fold of cash from her pocket, then held out her hand to receive the change.

It took three trips to carry her purchases to the RV. She waved at the old Indian each time, and he smiled at her, as if each encounter had been the first. Exhausted and winded, she wanted nothing more than to enjoy a restful visit with the elderly man, who greeted her as if they had been friends for years. The first person who had seemed happy to see her in longer than she could remember. Even before the mask mandates.

She wiped the rain from her face and thought over what she would say as she approached the man. "Hello, sir. You were very helpful to me last time. May I ask you another question?"

As a reply, he reached out a gnarled nicotine-stained finger and tapped the pack of cigarettes on the table, then beamed his smile even bigger.

She nodded, no words of clarification needed, and reentered the store.

CHAPTER
SEVENTY-FOUR
EVA

For no particular reason, except that Eva missed her grandfather and his constant wise advice, she found herself on autopilot as she bumped on the muddy ruts along the path to the house where she had spent the most cherished years of her life. She needed . . . What did she need, she wondered. Clarity.

Rain filled already-overfilled puddles as far as she could see when she came to a halt in front of the property. Water continued to slide down her windshield when she looked through intermittent swipes of the wipers. Chatter emitted from her handheld radio, and she turned her attention to the unit on the passenger seat. Noise complaint, abandoned car off the highway. Nothing related to her investigation.

She turned her interest back to the place that looked even more dilapidated than the last time she had ventured there. Then she remembered that had been years ago. She wasn't sure who laid claim to the property now but assumed the tribal council held the right to decide who would live there again, if anyone wanted to. It would take a lot of work to make the place comfortable again.

She puzzled over the new hasp and padlock that secured the front door, then noted plywood mounted on the inside of the front windows. "Strange. Why wouldn't they put the wood outside?"

Curious now, she worked up the oomph to go out in the rain and take a closer look. Her cell phone buzzed from the cup holder. The letters KAI lit up the display.

Before she could say hello, he said, "Please don't be mad at me, Eva. I don't know what'll happen if I lose you too."

"You're not going to lose me, Kai. But you need to quit pushing me away." Silence on his end followed. "Where are you?"

"Your house. Can you come home?"

"Now?"

"Yeah, right now. We—I have a surprise for you."

The clock on the dash flashed to 4:34. Close enough for a meal break, she decided. Her stomach rumbled, and she remembered she'd only eaten one protein bar all day. She needed real food and figured Kai probably did too. Also a good excuse not to venture out in the rain again. She'd had enough of the wet stuff on her body for this day.

She didn't want to take the time to order and pick up takeout, but maybe she could scrounge something up for them both. "Okay," she said. "I'll be there in twenty-three."

Exactly that many minutes later, she pulled up in front of her house. Kai and Cruz waited for her on the porch. They hadn't entered uninvited this time. Both looked miserable and contrite when she joined them. Kai held a stuffed brown paper bag in his hand.

Cruz nudged the boy's elbow with his own, then Kai said, "I'm really sorry. I didn't mean what I said. Will you forgive me?"

More disappointed than angry, she released any ill feelings and headed to them. "Depends. What've you got there?"

"Orlando's!" Kai squealed. "Steak burritos and chiles rellenos."

A food apology. She'd take it. They all entered the house and stripped off their wet jackets and muddy shoes. Cruz started right away to stack firewood in the beehive while Kai set the table.

"I need to get out of these wet things," she said. Kai and Cruz shared glares. "I'll hurry."

After the fastest shower ever, hair wrapped in a towel, dressed in warm comfortable clothes, Eva joined them at the table. She opened the containers and the luscious aromas of her favorite Mexican food in all of Taos hit her full force. She inhaled so deeply her head spun. Steak and cheese, beans, Hatch green chiles. Nothing better, in Eva's opinion—except maybe Cruz's loaded fry bread.

Now deep into their meal, they had yet to speak since their first bites, the only sound piñon wood popping in the fireplace and utensils scooping food to their mouths. Eva appreciated the company and time together, but she couldn't risk much more downtime.

The food helped her feel sharper than before the discovery on the riverbank earlier that day. She took a deep breath and hoped Cruz would understand the need for his opinions on the case. "Both of the ceremonial dresses are knockoffs," she said. "The craftsmanship sucks. Not created by anyone on the Pueblo. Most likely reproductions sold at a gift shop. Probably not in Taos, most likely Santa Fe or Albuquerque, so that's a clue for sure. The heroin links them too. Cruz, who do you think could be dealing on the rez?"

"Nobody," he snapped. He cut his eyes to Kai and back to her. "Really think we should be talking about this now?"

Kai ripped off a piece of tortilla and scooped up sauce from his plate. "I want to know too. Don't hold back because I'm here. Not much you need to keep from me now." His expression darkened, and Eva figured he must be reliving his discovery from the bridge.

"No," Cruz said. "We're not doing this now."

"Actually, we are," Eva said. "Please don't take offense, Cruz. I need to brainstorm. With people I trust. No risk of moccasin telegraph or cop gossip."

Cruz wiped his mouth, pushed his empty plate aside, and to her relief waved her to continue.

"There was heroin in Kishi's and Dora's systems," she said. "They've been hiding out somewhere, maybe even on the rez. They had to have gotten it from someone. I know you don't want to believe anyone could be dealing on the rez, but I really think we need to consider it."

"Not from our people," Cruz snapped.

"How could you know for sure?" Eva said.

"I would know."

"Fine. Then help me understand."

Cruz remained stone faced, nothing to offer. Eva wanted to shout at Cruz to quit snubbing what could be the first break in their case. She felt certain that heroin was what linked everything they had discovered so far, and so she tried again. "Where do *you* think Paloma was getting the heroin? She didn't have a car—hell, none of them did. Come on, Cruz, think about it. I really need to know what you can offer."

"They probably got a ride," Cruz said. "Lots of drugs in Santa Fe. Huge problem in Albuquerque too. Or someone from town sold it to them."

"Maybe nobody *sold* it to them," Kai said. "Maybe someone's *doing* it to them. Making them take the dope."

The boy's first interaction in the conversation intrigued her. "Why do you say that, Kai?"

"Because my mom's been gone for so long. She's never left for more than a week before. She always checks on me, no matter what condition she's in. She would find a way."

Eva waited as Kai shoveled a huge bite of burrito in his mouth, then chewed as he thought. "Maybe those guys on the motorbikes have something to do with it," he finally said. "Something doesn't feel right about them. They avoid me when we're in the barn together. Never talk to me."

"I agree. Something's off. Kai, I haven't told Santiago yet, but they shot at me earlier today."

Kai stopped chewing. Set down his fork. Looked like he might lose his meal. "You're sure it was them?"

"Pretty damned sure. There were four of them."

"Why would they do that?"

"Just spitballing here, but what if they dealt heroin to Paloma?" Eva said. "Maybe she told them about her rich and powerful brother. And now they figure Santiago will protect them. Probably think they're invincible because your uncle holds big power on the rez. That he wouldn't want to risk his standing. They probably know everything about him. That he's on the tribal council. Everything."

"Santiago said he doesn't know anything about *them*, though," Kai said.

"Unless he's lying," Cruz said.

She turned to him. "You don't believe that."

"No, he's right," Kai said. "What if they're actually really bad guys and they're hiding behind Santiago because he's so important. Everybody respects him. No one would ever think he'd do anything wrong."

"Exactly," Eva said. "Cruz, I think we should look into this."

"Maybe," Cruz said. "Are we going to flip a coin to see who lays this out with Santiago? Because I sure as hell don't want to be the one—"

Kai raised his hand. "I'll do it."

"Uh, no, you won't," Eva replied the moment the teenager finished the offer. "Needs to be more formal than a clandestine operation. I'll talk to him."

Task claimed, Kai prompted the next thought for Eva to ponder when he said, "What else bothers you?"

Eva looked to Cruz and he raised one eyebrow. She paused, unsure whether she should provide further information with a nonprofessional in the room. The details risked more nightmares for the boy. But the bright young man had offered useful insights so far. And she figured anything that kept the teenager engaged and interested would be a good thing. She hoped.

"The body placements. We found Kishi where she would hunt deer and elk for her drums." She took Kai's hand and gave it a squeeze. "And

I really think the other woman is Dora Pando. The bank of the river is where she would gather stones for her jewelry."

"What does Tonita use to make her baskets?" Kai asked.

"Strips from willow trees," Eva said. "Some of them are along the water on the rez."

"Yeah, but the biggest one is where Tonita's grandpa used to live," Cruz said.

Lost in their own thoughts, they all stayed quiet, no one looking at each other, until Kai asked, "Where would you find my mom?"

"Not sure. The rez's open field between the main houses, where she would dance at celebrations, maybe?" Distracted, deep in thought, she hadn't intended to be so matter-of-fact.

"Do you think Dora jumped—if it is Dora?"

Eva often worried that Kai kept returning his thoughts to the bridge. The mere thought of him thinking about, and possibly completing his attempt, terrified her. She waited. Considered lying but knew honesty had been kept from him for so long, and that doing so again risked alienating him, so she finally said, "There was no blood where she landed. Most likely, she was gone . . . before—"

"You mean somebody did this?" Kai interrupted, a horrified look twisting his features.

Still struggling with the reality of the situation, she hesitated before she replied. "Yes."

"Dropped off the south side . . . or the north side? Like, where I was sitting, or facing the Pueblo?"

"Probably no actual way to know that," she said. "Does it matter?"

"If the person who did this was Pueblo, they probably wouldn't face our land when they . . . did that to Dora," Kai said. "Right?"

Eva thought about this for a while. Clearly that would be true. "Good point."

Cruz tossed his napkin to the table, scooted his chair back, and stood up. "All right, enough creepy talk. Kai, let's go. I'll get you to Santiago's."

Eva kept a watchful eye on Kai as he helped clear the table and put the dishes in the sink. He seemed reserved but not freaked out, and she wondered if he put on a brave face for her. If the conversation would keep him awake when night fell. If nightmares would invade his sleep, visions of his mother's lifeless body laid out on the open area in front of the ancient houses.

She shook the troubling thoughts off as she crossed to the front room, looked out the window, and waited until Cruz's truck disappeared around the bend, knowing he would not be pleased about her next steps for the day. Then she clipped on her badge and sidearm, swept up the keys and radio.

The rain had stopped, and crisp air met her cheeks as she locked her house. She took the single good thing to happen all day as a positive sign as she fired up the Rover, her mind already at her next destination.

Clouds remained, now white billows high in the sky. Sun bright. Birds flitted and dipped their beaks in puddles as others darted from tree to tree in Eva's front yard. Although the sights seemed calm, many hours in this seemingly endless day remained. So much tragedy and heartbreak had happened already. And so, as she urged the Beast toward town, she conjured her grandfather's face. The one that warned her not to get too cocky.

"Right, Duh-thle. Stoic Native Face."

She put that face on and wore it proud.

CHAPTER
SEVENTY-FIVE
KAI

Kai entered his uncle's house and caught the aroma of garlic and spaghetti sauce. Specialty of the house, Santiago had told him earlier that day. *Don't be late.* His last words before Cruz had picked Kai up. Then the two made their own plans for dinner. They needed to make up with Eva, and that seemed way more important than sharing noodles with someone who probably didn't want to anyway.

He walked through the house to the kitchen and the windows that showed everything out back. A wild view. They could see anything coming. Except for what had already hit them.

"Dinner's cold," Santiago said. "Where have you been?"

"At Eva's. I already ate."

His uncle didn't look up from the stack of papers he worked on. "Could have called."

Kai felt bad for not doing so. He could feel his elder's disappointment from ten feet away. "Is there any ice cream left?" he said, voice cheerful to lighten the mood.

"Chocolate chip or rocky road?"

"Both?"

Santiago didn't chuckle as Kai hoped but at least didn't dismiss him. Instead, he crossed to the huge freezer, pulled out two containers of ice cream, and dipped massive scoops into two clear glass bowls.

"What did you talk about with Eva and Cruz?" Santiago asked after his first bite.

"Lots of stuff." He shrugged, hoping the vague answer would suffice.

"Like what?"

"Okay . . . like those guys who work for you. Eva said they shot at her. Tried to scare her, where she found Kishi."

"Shot at her?" Santiago dropped his spoon to clatter on the table. "What guys?"

"I told you—your guys. On the same bikes you let me ride. They had helmets on, but she was sure she saw two of them here earlier today." Kai pushed his bowl forward, the treat no longer appealing to him. "She doesn't know them. But you do. And I do. You don't want to admit it. If you did, you'd be wrong about deciding to let them on your property. And you're never wrong about anything, right, Uncle?"

Santiago leaned back in his chair, crossed his arms tight to his chest, defiance in his pose and manner. "Tell me what's really pissing you off."

Kai hesitated to say what had been a pain in his heart ever since he'd reestablished ties with his uncle. He weighed the consequences, knowing it could mean banishment, like his mother had been faced with. His defiance could also mean losing the only male in his direct bloodline. Forever this time. And still, he wanted—needed—to know. And so he took a big breath and said, "I think you know where my mother is. That you've always known. Are you hiding her from me? Please, Uncle Santiago, tell me."

His elder looked too stunned to speak before he said, "No, Kai. I don't know where your mother is. I haven't seen her for months."

"I don't believe you."

"Why would I lie?"

"Because you don't want her to come back unless she's clean."

"Is that what you think? That I've taken her somewhere. To a rehab facility or something like that?"

Kai broke down, a heavy sob so raw that Santiago's shoulders slumped. "It's what I hope," Kai said. "Please say it's true."

Santiago went to his nephew, tugged him from the chair, wrapped his arms around his trembling body, held him tight. "I wish I could. That I came up with the idea and am protecting her—making sure she follows through with the treatment. But it's just not true, son. I'm sorry."

Kai pushed away. "Fine. You're no help at all. Never have been. You just wanted her gone. And now she's probably dead. Does that solve your problem? Bring you peace? Know that you'll never have to face the people who whisper behind your back? Makes you a failure though. You'll hate that. Weak. Uncaring. Unable to fix your own sister, so how could you possibly help the people of the tribe?"

"Stop," Santiago hissed through clenched teeth. "I won't have you disrespecting me in my own home. You're working yourself up over nothing. I want Paloma back too."

"Bullshit. You just want to control her, just like you want to control me. No wonder she got hooked on drugs. Ran off. You held on too tight."

His uncle spewed out a puff of air and waved a dismissive hand, which upset Kai even more. "Just like your mother," Santiago said. "You're going to do exactly what *you* want and nothing else."

"I'll take being like her over you. Anytime."

Kai ran from the room before his uncle could try any more words to sway him. He'd had enough manipulation. His first instinct was to get on the Kawasaki, race on the mesa, no destination in mind. Stay away overnight, and maybe forever. He slammed the front door shut and took the porch steps two at a time. Straight to the chicken coop.

Pearl emerged from the dark opening, followed by Shadow. They trotted toward him, tails and tongues wagging, wanting nothing from him but pure affection. He dodged mud puddles, and they followed him back to the protection of the coop, where he dropped to the ground and stroked their furry faces and muddy legs, already embarrassed by his outburst.

He envisioned his mother, the headshake and tsk of her tongue, knowing that if she were here, she would say, *The spirits will not be happy.*

Tears blurred his vision of the pack of pups gathered all around as he said, "But hopefully they'll be kind."

CHAPTER
SEVENTY-SIX
EVA

Eva wasn't sure if her request would fly, but thankfully, even though off duty, Kotz was more than happy to meet her at the station and help her out. Dressed in street clothes, he waited for her at the entrance, and she followed him inside. A different roster of cops sat at desks, every eye on her.

He booted up his computer and wriggled his fingers above the keyboard as they waited for the terminal to fire up. "Okay, what are we looking for?"

"A late-model Winnebago."

"Tall task. Lots of those in and out of this region. Can you be more specific? Start with a location? Date and time would be helpful too."

"Don't know any of that. Thirteen days, for sure."

"We've got quite a few traffic and CCTV cameras set up in and around town. But if it's an RV you're looking for, Allsup's has a covering tall enough for one of those to gas up."

"Good thinking. Yeah, let's start there."

"Copy. Lots of shoplifting at that location, so TPD has two cameras stationed outside the property. Won't need approval from the business owner. Starting point?"

Eva shrugged, wondering what their best use of time would be. "Right now?"

"Okay. Here we go."

Kotz signed in to the security site and proceeded to run the footage backward. The jittery images made Eva queasy and she had to look away every couple of minutes. "That one, maybe?"

Eva raised her head and leaned in to study the paused image of an RV. "Maybe. Can you rewind to when it drives up and then slow it down?"

She pulled her chair closer as he cued up the playback. The images ran in slow-motion, showing a Winnebago that pulled in at the farthest island and stopped at a pump. A moment later, the side door opened, and a woman stepped out, carrying two five-gallon gas cans.

"That's her!" She pulled out the printout of Alice Jones's details to be certain. "Gotcha." Eva raised her hand to high-five her companion.

The nurse proceeded to pump gas in the containers, then returned them inside the cabin. Eva took note that the canisters seemed to weigh nothing as the woman hefted them. When the woman reemerged, she held a propane canister, strode toward the entrance, replaced one container with another, took that inside the RV, came back out a short time later, locked up, and reapproached the store. She waved to someone, then entered the shop.

"Fast-forward until we see her again."

Kotz did as she requested, and they watched in fast motion as their subject exited and entered. For two trips, she carried a case of bottled water to the motorhome. The third time, she held a plastic bag and an unfurled umbrella and put them inside too. Then she turned back to the store and halted her steps. Less than a minute later she entered the store again.

"When was this?"

Kotz pointed to the lower-left side of the screen. "Four thirty-nine."

She checked her phone for the time. "Less than ninety minutes ago?"

"Uh-huh," he said, eyes glued to the screen. "Gas, propane, two cases of water. Some stuff in a bag. Looks like she's topping off to move on."

"Or replenishing her reserves," Eva said.

"Good point."

Something felt off. She replayed the visuals in her head. "Kotz, go back again to where she enters the store for the last time." He did so, and she pointed to the monitor. "She goes back inside. Why?"

"Maybe she forgot something?" He let the video play on. "She comes back out with a carton of cigarettes."

"A nurse who smokes?"

"Seen it. Stress, you know."

"No, wait." She pointed to the screen. "She talks to someone. Who is that?"

"I see him there all the time. Manager says it's okay. Never any complaints about him." Kotz glanced her direction. "Do you know him?"

She watched as a car rolled in, blocking the camera's view. She fluttered her hand, prompting it to move. By the time the sedan pulled forward, the woman had walked away, but the man looked unmistakable to Eva—rounded hunchback, ancient even by Native standards, big smile for the woman who approached. "That's Torrie Lujan. I'm sure of it."

In her mind, puzzle pieces clicked in place. "What direction does she go?" she asked.

Kotz tapped keys, worked the mouse. "North."

"Toward the rez," she muttered.

Before Kotz could say anything more, Eva thanked him and then raced from the department to the Beast. She cursed when she splashed directly in a puddle, her fresh socks now soaked, and launched herself behind the wheel.

It took only six minutes to reach Allsup's, where always-friendly Torrie Lujan held court nearly every time she drove by, usually a can of Blue Sky black cherry soda in one hand, always a lit cigarette in the other. The manager had even set up a chair and small table for him, convinced the elder brought good luck and customers. A "real Indian" for the tourists to talk to. For years now the greetings had worked.

"Please be coherent, old man," she said to herself, remembering the last time she'd tried to carry on a conversation with the elder. Tangents often captured their visits. This time she needed only one answer.

She backed into one of the front parking places, slid out of the Rover, approached the old man. "Hee-yah-ho, Torrie."

He lit up his trademark smile. "Beautiful, beautiful, girl. Best law enforcer in our universe. Is your duh-thle with you?"

A question asked every time. As always, so as not to upset her grandfather's old friend, she replied, "Not today."

"Blessings to him."

"And to you." She pulled a sheet of paper from her back pocket, shook out the folds, and held it close to Torrie's face. "This woman. You spoke to her earlier today. What did you talk about?"

He leaned close, nose an inch from the paper, squinted. "Nope. Don't think so."

Eva tamped down her frustration. Waited a moment to calm her breathing. Reminded herself to remain respectful. Be patient, don't pepper him with questions. "I think you did, Torrie. She drove a motorhome. Had a big *W* on the side?"

He took a swig from his drink, screwed up his lips, looked up sideways, deep in thought. "Hmm . . . meebee. Big tall lady?"

Her excitement fuse lit. "Yes."

"I do, I do, I do remember." He tapped the carton of Camel unfiltered smokes on the table. "Gave me the good stuff this time."

"This time?" she asked.

"Last time she gave me two packs of cheap smokes."

She wondered why a health worker would gift someone coffin nails. "Did she talk to you?"

"Sure. Nice lady. Seen her a few times. Wanted to know things about the rez. Asked about stuff tourists don't care about. Big rig didn't have New Mexico plates. Not sure where she was from."

"What did she ask you about?" she said, doing her best to keep him on point.

"First time, where the hunting grounds are. Hard to find. Gave her real good directions so she wouldn't get lost."

Two more puzzle pieces snapped into place. "What did you talk about today? When she gave you the carton of smokes."

"Wanted to know where to find the biggest willow tree in all of Taos."

"And where is that?" she asked.

"The Conchas' old place. Where the basket weavers used to live."

The blood ran cold in Eva's veins. She didn't breathe. Uncertain if she remembered how.

"Know where that is?" the elder asked.

She did, and the knowing chilled her. Tonita Concha's original family home. Paloma's cousin. Also one of the missing women.

Eva wasn't sure if she'd even thanked the old man for the information as she spun the Beast's tires out of the convenience store's lot. The willow tree they mentioned earlier during their meal couldn't be a coincidence. Could that have been only a couple of hours ago? Time seemed to slow down and rush forward in tandem.

First she sent up a prayer to the Creator, then took up her phone, tapped a number on the Recents list. His voice answered on the first ring.

"Wolf Song. I need you."

CHAPTER SEVENTY-SEVEN
EVA

Lost. Completely turned around. Eva considered calling Cruz back for better directions. She had only visited the place a couple of times, so many years ago she couldn't remember the actual date. But he had told her he wasn't sure of the location and would text her when he figured it out. No ping of assistance had come in yet. She looked closer at the cell's screen, slapped the steering wheel in frustration. No bars. No service. A dead spot, not uncommon in certain areas on the rez. She took up the handheld radio and turned up the volume. Chatter emitted, confirming reception via that route if she needed immediate assistance, so that gave her a bit of comfort.

She drove a few minutes more, and then, as if the universe intuited her frustration, the biggest tree she had ever encountered in all of New Mexico filled the view of her windshield. Massive, its canopy wider than the circumference of her house. She drew closer and parked near the home that hadn't weathered any better than her grandfather's, and got out of her vehicle.

Something about the tree seemed off. Taking a better angle, she noticed that someone sat cross-legged, back against the tree, hands clasped in their lap, head down. Long dark hair obstructed the face. At first Eva thought it was a woman sleeping. Then she noticed the dress and moccasins. Different shade of leather, but style much like what Kishi and the woman from the river had been wearing when discovered.

"Hello?" Eva called out from where she stood, unsure at first why she felt hesitant to step closer. "Taos County Sheriff's Deputy. Are you all right, ma'am?"

A moment later Eva knew the woman would not respond. Could never be all right, ever again.

She raised a trembling hand to her mouth to trap the scream that threatened to escape. "Go to your training," she reminded herself, returned to her vehicle, took up her handheld radio, plunged the call button. "Dispatch, Sierra-Ten-Twelve."

"Copy, S-Ten-Twelve. Go ahead."

"Request assistance to . . ." She trailed off, still unsure of the actual address. Cruz hadn't been sure there was even a street name when she called him. Santiago might, but she didn't want to take the time to answer a thousand questions before he offered her anything at all. She would need to walk or drive until cell phone reception could be acquired. "I'll have to text an approximate location."

"Copy that. What do you need?"

"Everyone. Lizbeth and her team, deputies to cordon off the scene. The sheriff too. And alert Taos PD. We need an urgent BOLO for a late-model Winnebago. Driver is a white woman, late forties." She took the Alice Jones printout from her pocket and rattled off the other descriptors.

"Copy, S-Ten-Twelve."

Already feeling slightly more at ease now that reinforcements would be arriving as soon as she could provide a location, she considered driving to find cell coverage but didn't want to contaminate any possible evidence. Instead, she decided to walk to the end of the lane, eyes to the ground to make sure she didn't step on anything crucial.

Grateful she didn't need to trek too far, she dropped a pin on her map feature, then texted the GPS coordinates to the dispatcher's private cell phone. Then she returned to the Rover, opened the rear door, reached for a smaller version of her official evidence kit, tugged out two pairs of latex gloves and booties, put one pair of each on.

"Where are you, Cruz?" she muttered.

Unwilling to wait any longer to know if she recognized the woman, she took cautious steps and used her phone to click photos, praying with each footfall that she wouldn't find her best friend in the final resting place. She knew she shouldn't venture closer, that she could already be compromising the scene, but she couldn't stop. She had to know. Now.

Lizbeth's imagined voice screaming *Stop* in her ear, Eva crouched down, reached out one finger, carefully tilted up the woman's chin, which rested against her chest.

Not Paloma.

"Tonita," she whispered.

She used the index finger of her other hand to ease up a closed eyelid. Pupil fixed and dilated. No possibility of life returning. No matter what Eva attempted to right this horrible wrong.

The rumble of a powerful engine caused Eva to rise, hand on the butt of her Glock, until she recognized Cruz behind the wheel of an official tribal police vehicle. The tires slid in the mud to halt beside the Rover, then he got out, dressed in his uniform. Eva wondered if he had taken the time to change clothes in case this very result would need his professional attention.

He stood there, waited, hopeful look on his face. She shook her head and he lowered his own. He turned and placed his hands on the pickup's hood, as if he needed the support to remain standing. Then he balled his fists and slammed them on the hood, forceful enough to leave side-by-side dents.

Patience waning, Eva gave him only a few minutes. She needed an ally. A one-on-one assessment of her discovery. If nothing else than not to feel so angry and scared and all alone. "Officer Romero!" she snapped. He whirled his head to her, a good sign that she hadn't lost him to overwhelming emotions. "I need you over here."

She tossed the gloves and booties his direction. Careful where he stepped, he reached for the coverings, put them on, followed her footprints to where she stood. They shared the heartbreaking discovery in silence.

"I don't think she's been here long," Eva finally said.

"Looks so peaceful. A soft passing."

"You don't believe that. Nothing is soft about this."

To get him back on track, mind on the case, she said, "I know who did this. Who killed them all."

"Who?"

"The nurse. I'm sure of it." She stood up, walked a few paces, gestured to the ground. "Wide-body tire tracks. Most likely a heavy vehicle. One person's footprints, not as big as a man's. Kotz checked CCTV. Spotted her RV at Allsup's, no more than a few hours ago. She spoke to Torrie—"

"Lujan? You believe him? He's old as this tree."

"He told Alice Jones about this place. It's her."

"You think she's the heroin dealer, not the guys who shot at you," he said, not a question.

Frustrated and exhausted, she barked, "Maybe they're working with her. Or she's in cahoots with them. Look, I don't have all the answers. Hell, I don't even know the questions to ask to get them yet."

Cruz stood there, considering, eyes everywhere but on their latest victim. "What do you need?" he asked.

"Time," she said.

Sirens wailed in the distance, growing louder with Eva's every heartbeat.

"Time's up," Cruz said. "This is rez land. The investigation won't be yours by the time they get here."

"Then get your people here," she tried. "Do all you can to stay involved."

He smirked. "Be your mole, you mean."

"Be my friend." She hitched her thumb to the woman against the tree. "And Tonita's, and Kishi's. And Dora's, because we both know the woman from the river is her. Be a Taos Pueblo Native protector, Wolf Song. Make the call . . . for Paloma."

Whether he needed the prompting or not, she risked twisting the knife further into his broken heart when she said, "Because she's next."

CHAPTER SEVENTY-EIGHT
PALOMA

Paloma woke to darkness and silence so profound she felt like she was underground. Groggy, mind fuzzy. Her bladder urged her from the bed. She reached for the pole that held a constant bag of clear liquid and didn't find it next to her. Then she noticed that the IV needle had been removed from the top of her hand.

At first grateful the uncomfortable and sometimes painful medicine delivery device no longer pinched her, she then wondered, "Is this a good thing, or a bad thing, Tonita?"

Again, her cousin didn't reply, and a sense of impending misfortune draped a heavy cloak of doom over her. She limped to the other bed and laid a trembling hand atop the still-empty mattress. She frowned, confused by the different quilt, smelling of fresh laundry soap.

A hint of bleach stung her nostrils, not as strong now as she took cautious steps toward the bathroom. "Tonita?" she called out, to no reply.

Hand skimming the wall to help her balance, she grasped the cold ceramic sink. Grateful as always not to see a mirror, she splashed cold water on her sweat-covered face, then relieved her bladder. Feeling much better, she turned to the closed door that led to the other bedroom. Locked when she tried to turn the knob.

She remembered the nurse had said earlier that day, *"If you need anything, just knock."*

And so Paloma knocked. Again and again and again, until completely spent of energy. She managed to get back to the bed and flop down, too tired to lift one foot from the floor to join the other.

She ached for paper and a pencil so she could write Kai a note. In her head she practiced what she wanted him to know. Only good things. That he was the best baby. Curious and kind. The perfect little angel she never wanted to put down. That he had grown up to be an honorable young man his father would be proud of.

Sleep called to her. Before she gave in, Paloma scratched another captivity line in the wall.

Fourteen scores now.

Her hand quivered as she did so, unable to shake the premonition that this would be her last night. Maybe ever.

CHAPTER
SEVENTY-NINE
EVA

Newspaper covered Eva's kitchen table under her disassembled Glock—a jumbled mess of unrecognizable pieces. Much like her investigation, she thought as she wiped down one piece, set it aside, reached for the next. The scent of the lubricant and cleaner familiar as the childhood T-shirt she used to polish the steel barrel and slide. Silicone cloth in hand, she spent extra time on the polymer frame—the need to clean her on-duty firearm deemed necessary after she'd discharged the rounds earlier that day. The mindless and meticulous actions usually soothed her. But not this night, when all she could think about were the three Pueblo women. Dead. Probably murdered. On her watch. She scrubbed harder.

Eva had stayed as long as possible at the discovery spot while Lizbeth and her crew processed the scene. Would still be there if the lead forensics technician hadn't warned the deputy she would be banned from future crime scenes if she didn't leave. And so as soon as the sheriff arrived, Eva was dismissed, ordered to report to his office at 9:00 a.m. sharp.

To her relief, as a representative of the Taos Pueblo Police Department and its tribal sovereignty, Cruz had been cleared to remain on site. He hadn't said goodbye or offered companionship or a drink to commiserate later. Now nearing midnight, she had yet to hear from him, and she hadn't reached out either. What would she say anyway? she wondered. Hang in there. Take care. It'll be all right? No. Mere words would never be sufficient.

Two hours ago Santiago had texted her to watch the nine o'clock local news. She rarely turned her TV set on and had to search for the remote, and by that time a press conference was well underway. Sheriff Bowen stood at a podium, reading from a sheet of paper. Standard prepared statement, this time featuring news that would alter so many lives, on and off the reservation. Verification that three women's bodies had been found, and that potential foul play could be involved.

Why her superior did this she had no idea. Probably never would. At first she felt slighted, figuring she should at least have been contacted to give her opinion. Although he mentioned no names, he did state that at least two of the women had been identified as being from the Taos Pueblo community.

And then, as if her boss had known he was on her mind, he'd called. She ran the phone call from her sheriff in her mind for the tenth time.

We've officially got ourselves a shitshow. Media vultures are already swoopin' down. Had no choice but to do the press conference. I hate to do this to you, Duran, but I'm making the call to the FBI first thing in the morning. Got no choice since this last lady's body was found on the reservation. Already spoke to the TPPD chief. He agrees with me. He had sounded regretful but also relieved not to have the burden exclusively on his shoulders.

A whirlwind of accusations would hurl at first light. Switchboards at the Taos Pueblo PD were probably overwhelmed with inquiries and eyewitness accounts of elements that most likely would be disproved yet nevertheless would need to be checked out. Impossible tasks for the small reservation force.

As she began to reassemble her handgun, one of the newspaper articles caught her attention. She had yet to read the days-old edition she had purchased primarily to ball up under kindling to help start fires in the beehive. Drops of oil marred the photo, but even in profile Eva would recognize Paloma "White Dove" Arrio from across the room. The piece featured an action capture of the hoop dancer, dressed in full regalia, five hoops in each hand. Eva ran a tender finger along the oil-splatted face. The article touted Paloma's legendary performances and awards as she danced across four states, representing the Taos Pueblo and its people with her grace and talent, and explained that she had been missing for at least three days.

Eva held her breath the entire time she read the article. Thankfully no mention of drugs had been reported. But probably not for long.

Oil and water melded as her tears dropped to bloom on Paloma's photograph.

CHAPTER EIGHTY
ALICE

As Alice stepped out of the RV she inhaled the fresh scent of rain and raised her head to the dark clouds that prevented dawn's light. She had slept well after coming up with her final plan, woke refreshed and ready to roll. "Time to get busy!"

It took a dozen trips to deliver to and stow all of the items from the house in the Winnebago, and now she looked forward to accomplishing the last few tasks.

She took up a battery-powered lantern, and back to the house she went, six fully loaded fentanyl- and heroin-laced syringes and two doses of Narcan in her smock pocket, heart aflutter. Careful not to wake her patient, she crept into the room and set the lantern on the bedside table.

At the closet, she took out the single remaining dress and matching pair of moccasin boots. The most elaborate outfit. Fitting for the Jewel of the Pueblo. She held the dress up against her body and swayed, fringe slapping with each movement. "Beautiful, isn't it, White Dove?" she whispered. "Saved the most perfect one for you."

Dressing her patient proved difficult for Alice. Limp limbs and head lolling on her neck, her patient wasn't helpful at all. She feared ripping one of the sleeves when a hand finally peeked from the opening.

"It's just the two of us now," she said. "I'm going to take you home with me." She brushed the dark hair, long strokes, trying not to pull when she reached a tangle. "I think you'll like Texas. I have a sweet little house. You can even have your own bedroom."

Alice withdrew one of the syringes, readied one-quarter of the full dosage, administered the shot in the vein beside the inflamed one, where the IV port had been positioned.

"Just a little more so you're comfortable. Not too much, though. I want you to be awake soon. It's a long drive, and we have so much to talk about!" She clapped her hands, already giddy for the adventure. "We'll have so much fun."

She scooped up the woman and carried her like at the end of her favorite movie, *An Officer and a Gentleman*, when the sailor swept the woman off her feet and carried her out of the factory. So romantic. Richard Gere saved Debra Winger's life. Just like she was doing now for her White Dove.

After belting her friend in the passenger seat of the Winnebago, she ran through the list of what she had already accomplished to make sure she hadn't missed a step somewhere. She had decided to keep one of the generators but left the other behind the house, where she doused it with bleach to obliterate any fingerprints. She figured she wouldn't need to do that to anything inside the house.

She took both of the full five-gallon gas containers from the porch, opened the caps, left one in the front room, and carried the other to the farthest bedroom. Fumes burned her nostrils as she poured gasoline over the two beds and tables, splashed the walls, then dispensed the remaining contents over items in the other bedroom.

Second gas can in hand, she returned to the hall and walked backward as she poured a trail to the kitchen, all the way to the fireplace.

"Thank you for your shelter," she said from the open front door. Then she struck a match, waited a moment for the flame to hold, tossed the wooden stick.

A wild *whoosh* sounded. A snake of fire caught, speed dizzying as it raced ahead, then split right and left. Mesmerized by the dazzling sight, she stood there as long as she dared.

Safely back in the RV, hoping she didn't smell too much like gas and smoke that would upset her patient's stomach, Alice reached across the aisle and patted her companion's shoulder. "I need to make one stop before we leave your beautiful land."

Foot on the accelerator, eyes on the sideview mirror, she watched black smoke billow and meld with the dark clouds. A moment later the reflection evolved into a fireball.

Alice smiled at the flames that danced as furious and magnificent as White Dove's finest performance.

CHAPTER EIGHTY-ONE
EVA

Eva took extra time getting ready for what she hoped would not be her last day as a deputy. Although she wasn't sure why she had the feeling, had no evidence she had actually done anything wrong, she remained on edge. She put on a sharply ironed uniform, polished her badge and ID tag and pinned them on, pulled her hair back in a tight ponytail, secured her duty belt to her waist—peacekeeping items lined in precise order. Checked her Glock. Fully loaded. One in the chamber.

Coffee, keys, radio in hand, she intended to sign in early at the department so she could catch up on any paperwork that couldn't easily be handed off . . . in case her hunch became fact after her meeting with the sheriff in a few hours. As she locked the front door and headed for her official vehicle, her cell phone rang.

"I can't stay here anymore, Eva."

"Kai?"

"Please. When can you come for me?"

Gripping the door handle of the official pickup, she said, "Let's talk about this later, okay? I really need—"

"No. Now. You said I could help you find Mom, but all you do is blow me off."

His insistence halted her. "What's this—?"

"I'm at Santiago's. Come and get me, or I'll . . ."

His voice trailed off, and Eva alerted to the vague threat. "You'll what, Kai?" she asked, but he had ended the call without clarifying. Dreadful possibilities of yet another crime scene to deal with filled her mind if she didn't get to him fast. She belted herself in and headed for the reservation.

By the time Eva pulled up to Santiago's property, the older man on the porch pointed toward the teenager at the mouth of the chicken coop, Shadow in his arms. To show she didn't have time for this nonsense, instead of getting out of the truck, she rolled down the window and told Santiago, "Kai called me. What's going on?"

"He wants to leave. Wants to be yours now."

"Mine?"

Kai set the pup down, took up his stuffed duffel bag and backpack, headed for Eva's truck. "That's right. I'm outa here."

The boy slid in the passenger's seat, crammed his bags on the floor between his feet, slammed the door shut, lowered his head. "Can we go now?"

She remained parked. Studied Santiago. He wiped his face, and she wondered if Paloma's brother had begun to soften. That all he needed was time with someone who needed him. That he wanted another shot to make the relationship work. She knew only time would move the two men closer, hopefully lessen the pain they had dealt each other. And she knew how fast Kai could pivot his volatile moods, change his mind in an instant, hissing snake one moment, cuddly kitten the next. All she could think of was to separate them for now.

"Please, drive away," Kai whispered.

She did. Santiago remained in the same position until the vision of him in her rearview mirror disappeared when she rounded the bend in the road.

"Kai, I know you're in pain, but you're gonna stop this bullshit when your mother gets home. She'll have enough on her mind to constantly worry that you're always thinking of hurting yourself."

"Not *always*."

She slammed on the brakes and the truck screeched to a halt on the asphalt. Smoke from the tires billowed, the stench of burnt rubber harsh in her nose. She turned her full attention to Kai. "Enough. You keep saying you're a man. Fine. Act like one. You'll have your own family sooner than you can wrap your head around. But for now, your number one responsibility is to your mother. She'll need your help for a while. I don't think you get that."

"I get it. Who do you think has been taking care of her the past three years. Never got to hang out with other kids. Never went off the rez except to shop and for school. Missed vacations. Couldn't even go hunt because I couldn't leave her for a single night. All I ever do—"

"I don't want to hear it. This isn't about you. Or what you had to do. That life is over. Things are about to get hairy. I'm pretty sure about that."

"Yeah, yeah, if we find her," he said, seeming resigned to stay in his funk.

"We *will* find her. But first I need to know you've got your shit together. Or I'll leave you here and get her on my own. Don't think I won't," she warned.

He crossed his arms tight to his chest, pissed off. No agreement came, but also no further opposition.

CHAPTER
EIGHTY-TWO
ALICE

Alice had parked down the street from the heroin house and kept watch for half an hour. From her vantage point she could see four of the green dirt bikes parked in front and a new Mercedes two-door at the side of the property. No other vehicles had come or gone since she'd arrived, and she detected no movement behind the front room's open curtains.

Her patience waned, boredom set in, and she became anxious to get the next phase of her life started. She crept the Winnebago forward and stopped in the wide yard, then got out of her seat and pushed the button to recline the other one all the way back.

"That's comfy, isn't it?" she asked her passenger slumped in the seat, head slack, hair covering her face. She closed the curtains at the windshield to shield the rising sun.

Certain of her patient's comfort, Alice pulled the cushions off the bench, released the hatch. She patted the pocket of her smock, satisfied by the feel of the cylindrical syringes as she studied the contents of the hidey-hole. "Shotgun or handgun," she said, running the floorplan of what she had seen of the house in her mind.

Surely the men would still be sleeping. She hadn't ventured to any of the bedrooms so had no idea if there could be one or four down the hallway beyond the front room. Stealth would be out the door the moment she walked inside. But she might need the shotgun to breach the entrance, because surely they would lock the front door.

And so, decision made, she took up the Remington stuffed with three shotgun shells and dropped the fully loaded Ruger in her empty smock pocket.

"Sit still, now," she told her best friend. "I'll be right back."

Then she stepped out to the crisp clean air and approached the house, careful not to step in puddles. On the porch she put on her *Don't mess with me bear* pose, pushed the pump forward to load a shell. Steadied the shotgun at waist level, blasted the doorknob, shoved back the forestock. The spent cartridge ejected as she kicked the door, stepped inside.

Three men sat on the couch. Main man in the recliner. Eight eyes open wide, palms open and raised to their shoulders. Alice flicked her sight from the men to the row of three handguns lined up on the coffee table in front of the couch, just like last time she had been there. She remembered Nathan's "gun" and wondered if these, too, were replicas of the real thing.

"Whoa, whoa, whoa," the leader said. "We can work out whatever you want. Put the gun down and let's talk." He tried a smile that didn't convince Alice of his sincerity.

She laid the shotgun against the wall, pulled the Ruger free from her pocket.

The leader lowered his hands to the arms of the chair and rocked back and forth. The men laughed. Roils of hilarity spewing forth.

Nerves or arrogance, she wondered. She tilted her head at their curious behavior. Alice turned to movement next to her. The boy had appeared from somewhere and now stood next to her. She had read about Indian shapeshifters and that moment wondered if he could be one.

The boy matched her stance, gun up, pointed forward. The dealer and his minions laughed even harder. Roars so loud Alice winced.

She turned to the kid. He looked at her, then they turned back to scowl at the sorry excuses for humanity. Both pulled their triggers, again and again and again.

Brass shells arched up, out, spun, dropped to dance and *ting* on the tile floor.

Alice swept the Ruger's barrel left to right until the clip emptied.

Gun smoke thick in the air, she waved a hand in front of her face to clear her vision and make sure no threat remained. She took up the Remington and pointed it in their direction. None of the men moved.

Voice rushed, she asked the boy, "Is there anyone else in the house?"

Eyes locked on the dead men, he nodded, tucked his gun behind the waistband at the small of his back, pointed a finger at the hallway.

Shotgun up and forward, Alice took cautious steps, inched around the corner to find four doors—three open, one closed—and a bathroom at the end of the corridor. She checked one room after the other. No threats. At the closed door, she frowned at a padlock secured to a hasp high on the jamb that reminded her of how she had kept her patients safe. She wondered what she would encounter behind this door.

She rushed back to the front room. "Do you know where the keys are to the locked door?"

The boy remained in the same spot. He ticked his head to the leader of the pack. She didn't want to get any closer, in case her aim hadn't been true and he was playing possum. "Could you get them for me?"

The boy turned to her, head on a slow swivel. She thought of the owl she had seen on the bridge two nights ago. He continued to stand there, and she thought he might not help her; then he took a couple of steps closer to the recliner, stopped, looked at her again.

She lifted the shotgun's barrel. "Don't worry. I won't let anything happen to you."

Her words seemed to work. He took more steps, reached out, closed his eyes tight, dug into the dealer's front jeans pocket, and pulled out a phone. He patted the other side and tugged free a ring of keys, tossed them to her.

"You're being very helpful. Thank you," she said over her shoulder as she pounded down the hallway and then tried the smallest key.

The shank clicked, and she swept the lock and hasp free. Gun ready, she placed her right foot on the bottom of the door, pushed until it thudded against the back wall. She wrinkled her nose at the stench of urine, feces, putrid body odor. Another step and she took in the room. Five-gallon bucket she was pretty sure acted as a toilet, clothes scattered on the floor, fast-food wrappers and containers on the bedside tables and dresser. Two outlines of bodies on the bed.

Alice remained vigilant as she went to one person, a woman, took up a wrist so tiny it resembled the jewelry maker's. When she detected a pulse, she went to the other side of the bed. A man this time. Pulse strong and steady. Neither adult moved.

She couldn't possibly be more thrilled!

CHAPTER EIGHTY-THREE
NATHAN

Nathan stared at the big guy's flip phone in his hand. He wanted so much to go to the bedroom where the nice lady went. He hadn't seen his parents in so long. Couldn't remember how many days it had been. He missed them so much. Every day, since the big guy broke in their house and pointed his gun and took over the place like he owned it. But he didn't own it. None of them did. His daddy and momma worked hard on the place. She had a garden out back and was so proud of her tomatoes and green peas. Dad had a workshop out back and had promised to show him how to make bowls on the lathe when he got tall enough. And then these guys showed up.

He spit on the nearest bad dude. Then felt bad because his mom wouldn't have wanted him to be mean, no matter what the jerk had done.

He should be brave. Run down the hall. Help the lady. But he was too scared, because what if his mom and dad were dead too? Instead, he went to the porch, flipped open the cheap phone, dialed digits he had been taught and reminded of since he was a little kid.

"Taos Police Department, what's your emergency?" a voice said.

He ignored the direct question and said, "My name is Nathan." The police would need to know where he lived, so he thought real hard and told what he remembered to the voice. Then said, "I wanna talk to the lady police officer."

"Could you repeat that, young man?"

"The Pueblo lady cop. I only wanna talk to her."

"Do you have an emergency?"

"They're all dead."

"Excuse me? Could you repeat that?"

"The bad guys at my house. They're all dead. We killed 'em. Tell the police lady to come here. I don't wanna get in trouble."

He snapped the phone shut before the voice could say another word.

CHAPTER EIGHTY-FOUR
EVA

Eva's cell phone buzzed, its interruption the only thing that kept her from continuing the discussion with Kai, attempting to get him to realize he needed to change his attitude and alter his thought process. The entire conversation so far seemed like a hostage negotiation. For her or him, she wasn't quite sure.

She released the phone from its sheath on her duty belt and frowned. The screen announced KOTZ. Not interested in chitchat, she considered ignoring the call, reprimanding Kai some more. Instead, she accepted the request. "Hey, Andrew. What's up?"

"Hey, our 911 dispatch picked up a strange one. Kid calling from the reservation. We're not authorized to respond, so thought I should give you a try."

"A kid?"

"Yeah. Said he wanted to talk to the Pueblo lady police officer. We don't have any of your people. And I remember you saying the reservation cops only had men on their roster. And you're the only female Pueblo on your force, right? Anyway, the boy said his house is full of dead guys. To come quick."

Eva pressed the phone closer to her ear, unsure if she'd heard the city cop right. "Dead guys? What the . . . ?"

"Yeah. Kid said his name is Nathan. Got an address . . . well, not exactly an address. A location. Hang on, I'll text it to you. Maybe you know the place?"

A moment later Eva's phone chimed and she opened the map pinned with a destination. She didn't recall who lived at the house. "Maybe. Did he give a family name?"

"Nope, hung up before dispatch caught anything helpful."

"Okay. I'll reach out to TPPD if the tip turns out to be solid."

"Want me to assist you?" he said, concern in his voice. "I could take a ride out in my personal vehicle."

Eva rolled her eyes. Last thing she needed or wanted was to be thought of as unable to execute every aspect of her job on her own. "Not necessary. I'm on it. I'll let you know if I find anything."

"Well, let me know even if you don't hit a situation, all right?"

"Copy that. Thanks for the heads-up." She ended the call before he had a chance to baby her some more.

"What's up?" Kai asked.

"Hopefully nothing."

"Where are we going?"

"The rez. Need to check something out."

"No. We're going to—"

"After, Kai. I need to handle this call."

"On the rez? If it's cop stuff, you shouldn't go. Call Cruz."

"I don't need Cruz," she said, louder than she intended but tired of people assuming she needed constant help.

"Fine. Jeez. Just don't want you to get in any trouble."

"No, you want me to do what *you* want."

"Does that make me an awful person? Isn't that what everyone wants?"

A *ping* sounded, and Eva glanced at the screen. She opened her map app and zoomed in on the reservation boundary, found the location, then put the Beast in drive and pushed as hard as she dared toward the rez.

CHAPTER EIGHTY-FIVE
EVA

Eva took the final turn so fast that Kai grabbed the strap above the door and seat belt secured across his body and held on tight. "Eva, what's going on? Why are you going so fast?"

Mind already spinning about what she could face in less than a minute, she didn't take the time to answer as she halted the pickup as soon as she could see the house.

"That's the kid from the other night!" Kai pointed to a young boy, long hair to his waist, standing near the front door. "Ran right in front of me. I'm sure that's him."

She barely registered who Kai had keyed on. Her own attention locked on an RV parked nearby. "I need you to stay in the vehicle. I mean it, Kai. Stay put."

Eva reached for the door handle, and Kai reached for her sleeve. "Shouldn't you wait for backup?"

"Just gonna check it out. Stay here. Got it?"

She blazed a stare at Kai so he would know she meant business. She took his non-answer as agreement that he would follow her order and left the keys in the ignition, just in case, she told herself. A quick getaway might be necessary, and the need for Kai to be safe surpassed anything else that awaited. No matter what happened to her.

Taking deep breaths as she got out, intent on the boy ahead, she hardly noticed when her boots hit a puddle directly below the running board. The kid faced her but stayed in place, attention at his feet.

First she decided to check out the RV. She found all three doors to be locked. No answer when she knocked. The motorhome, being so high off the ground, didn't allow her to look in the windows. Deal with that later, the cop in her commanded.

She took slow steps. Assessed the exterior surroundings. Four motorbikes, one Mercedes sedan, front door wide open. She detected the unmistakable scent of gun smoke when she drew closer.

Hand on the butt of her Glock, she raised the other hand and pointed to the badge on her chest. "My name is Eva Duran. I'm a deputy for the sheriff's department," she told the boy, voice even, non-confrontational. "Are you Nathan? Did you call for help?"

"Yes," he said. Nothing else.

"Nathan, do you know who owns that RV?"

"A lady drives it. She's my friend. Made me a peanut butter sandwich."

She keyed on the sandwich comment, remembering the significance Dr. Mondragon had mentioned about undigested peanut butter in Kishi's stomach.

"I helped her kill those guys inside." He stood up taller, stuck his chest out, a proud stance.

A shiver ran the length of Eva's body. She let the comment pass but went on high alert. "The woman. She's in the RV now?"

Nathan shook his head, raised a filthy hand, pointed to the house.

The boy swayed a bit on his feet, affect flat, no emotion on his face. In shock, Eva realized. "How about if you go to my truck?" He shook his head, held his position, reached behind him. A movement Eva did not appreciate.

"What've you got there?" She unsnapped the trigger guard on the holster, prepared to pull out her weapon. "I need you to show me both hands, all right? Nice and slow, okay?"

The kid complied. One hand open and raised at his shoulder. The other came from behind him, one inch at a time, until he revealed a gun in his grasp.

Eva cleared her Glock from the leather, two-handed grip, aimed at body mass. "Drop it!"

The boy flinched, eyes wide. Eva took a step forward. "I don't want to hurt you, please believe me. I'm here to help, nothing else."

"You're a good guy . . . I mean, lady?"

"I try to be."

"Me too." He lowered his arm, bent his knees, laid the gun on the ground.

Eva pointed her weapon downward and rushed to the porch. She swept up the handgun and frowned at the light weight. "It's not real," she said.

"Looks it though, don't it?"

"Real enough to get you killed."

"You can keep it. I never liked it."

"Are there more guns inside?"

The boy turned to the doorway, then back to her. "Lots."

The single word put Eva on high alert. "Get to the truck. Now!"

Her commanding tone rang in her ears. The boy sprinted to the vehicle.

The moment she heard the door to the pickup slam shut, she took one step. And another. Unsure if she would meet her fate, or destiny . . . or her grandfather.

CHAPTER EIGHTY-SIX
ALICE

Thrilled to have two new patients to work with, Alice took one of the syringes from her smock and administered a dose, first to the woman. Then she went to the other side of the bed and plunged another hypodermic into the crook of the man's arm.

Decision made the moment she spotted the couple, Alice couldn't believe her luck. She needed to work quick. Get everyone out of there in case anyone had heard the gunshots.

Nathan could help her. Everyone would fit in the RV, if the boy sat on the floor.

She had a four-bedroom house waiting to be filled. A high so profound she thought drugs must be in the air swept over her, and she imagined what her life would soon be. Laughter, meals to share, chores to be assigned. They would play board games, take walks together. White Dove would teach her how to dance . . .

The sound of talking snapped her back to the room.

One voice sounded like the little boy's, but she thought for sure she'd heard someone else. She took a few cautious steps toward the door, picked up the Remington from against the wall.

Behind her someone stirred, thrashed at the sheets, moaned, called out. "Nathan?"

Alice hurried to the man. Slapped her hand over his mouth. Put the gun's barrel to her lips, and hissed, "Shhh."

CHAPTER EIGHTY-SEVEN
KAI

Kai angled in his seat and opened the back door for the much smaller kid, who monkeyed his way up and inside the pickup, then slammed his door shut.

"Hey," Kai said. "I'm Kai Arrio. Single Star. You good?"

The boy offered nothing, kept his gaze trained on the front of the house.

"My mom is Paloma. I've been looking for her. Has anyone told you about her? Maybe the nurse who drives that RV." He took out his phone, tapped the Gallery icon, scrolled the images until he found a favorite picture of his mother, showed it to him.

The kid turned to Kai, as if seeing him for the first time, then looked at the photo. "I've seen her. Lots of times. She comes here to . . ."

"Does she come alone?"

The boy shook his head. "Three other ladies come with her. Your mom's real pretty." His cheeks turned red and Kai wondered if the kid had seen anything unpleasant happen to his mother or her friends. "I'm hungry. There's peanut butter in there," the boy said, pointing to the Winnebago. "Can we get some?"

Kai considered defying Eva's order to stay put. He kept his eyes on the RV and wondered if the nurse could be in there. Maybe even his mother. The perfect reason to check out the motorhome. "Let me see if I can find some. Stay here, okay?"

The kid looked relieved to be told to stay put.

Kai made sure Eva wasn't watching, then slid out and eased the door closed. The muddy Winnebago looked abandoned, curtains drawn to cover the inside of the windshield. He went to the side door and raised a triumphant fist to the air. "Gotcha," he said as he slapped his palm against the caduceus sticker on the window. He returned to the front of the RV and tried to stand on the front tire to see in the passenger's window, but his footing slipped and he nearly fell in the mud.

He needed something to stand on and went to a neat pile of wood and fencing materials, took up a cinder block, hurried back to the RV. Kai set the brick on edge and stood on one foot, a precarious balance, but he could see that someone sat way back in the passenger seat.

Nose pressed to the glass, he reeled as recognition slammed him in the chest. "Mom?" He pounded on the window, tugged on the locked door, pounded again. "*Mom!* Open the door," he shouted.

He raced to the side door and found that one locked, too, went back, grabbed the cinder block, ran to the same door, raised the cement block above his head, slammed it to the window. The thick plastic popped inside and clattered on the floor of the RV. He leaped to the top step, reached inside the gap, turned the handle.

Lump in his throat, he hesitated, unsure if he wanted to approach the person up front. His mind battled, but his heart won. The moment he reached the seat reclined way back, he knew for certain.

"Mom!" He released the seat belt, knelt down, took her in his arms. "Wake up, wake up, wake up," he said, sobbing in her hair.

"Ahiga?" she asked.

"No, Mom. It's me. Kai."

She let out a light chuckle. "That's a relief. Thought I was dead for a minute."

Her arms lifted, circled his body.

He held her tighter.

CHAPTER
EIGHTY-EIGHT
EVA

Eva froze inside the house that reeked of nothing good. Unsure at first, she stared dumbfounded by what she'd encountered. Four men. Skin and clothing torn. Gunshot holes in their chests, faces, limbs.

"They deserved it."

Eva whirled, Glock up, arms out, double-handed aim trained toward a voice. A woman emerged from the dark hallway. Slow steps, shotgun tucked against her body, barrel pointed to the ground.

"Didn't belong here." She looked from the man in the recliner to Eva. "I did you a favor."

"You killed four men."

Alice stood tall, chest out, defiant. "Yes, I did. Every one of them scum. You're welcome."

"And three women. Are you proud of that too?"

The woman's prideful smirk dropped off her face. Eyes lowered to the floor, she said, "That was unfortunate. A true loss." The woman took a few strides toward Eva. "To your community and to you. I did all I could to find a cure. I'm so close. Will you let me try again?"

The statement, so unexpected, surprised Eva. The gun, suddenly heavy in her grip, wavered. "Where is Paloma Arrio?" she shouted.

The woman let out a crazed cackle and charged. So fast and surprising Eva didn't have time to reposition her firearm. She squeezed off a shot the instant the butt of her offender's gun slammed on her forearm. The pain was so intense Eva dropped her weapon and curled her arm to her chest.

The crook of an arm wrapped around her neck, a hand raised a syringe high enough for her to see in her peripheral vision. Eva whipped her body side to side, kicked out, tried to break the chokehold. Stars dotted her vision. Strength faltered.

A scream split the air. The syringe flew across the room. Viselike hold released, Eva bent at the waist, hands on her knees, gulped air. She turned her head to see a commotion. Fringe whirled, long hair whipped, moccasins jumped up and down.

Paloma. Eva barely recognized the woman, who released a feral wrath on Alice, punching, scratching, kicking the other woman, now flat on her back. Open hands raised, she didn't fight back. Kai burst into the room and pulled Paloma away from Alice.

On autopilot, grateful for her training because her thought process still hadn't fully returned, Eva released the handcuffs from their sheath, flipped the assailant over, ratcheted the cold steel on one wrist, then the other. She wrenched the woman to stand and led her a safe distance from Paloma in case her friend decided to attack again.

"I only wanted to help you, White Dove," the nurse said, blood dripping from a fingernail gash along her temple and down her chin from the split lower lip.

"Help me?" Paloma shouted.

"Yes. Please tell her to let me go," she pleaded. "I'm so close to figuring it all out."

"Where are my friends?" Paloma asked, teeth clenched.

The woman fell silent, as if gauging the proper response. She looked down at her blood-spattered scrubs, then said in a soft voice, "You can be proud of them. They were perfect patients, to the very end."

It took a moment. Then another. But then Paloma released a growl, and only Kai's tight hold kept her from launching at the prisoner.

Nathan ran in the house, didn't look left or right as he flashed by, turned down the hall. Confident her detainee, who never took her loving gaze off Paloma, would stay in place, Eva retrieved her Glock and went in search of the little boy.

She detected voices and kept walking. Gun at the ready, she swung her head around the corner and back out. After she processed for a moment, she believed no threat would meet her as she approached the bed. Two adults hugged Nathan. All sobbed and cooed and apologized over each other.

Eva left them to their reunion and returned to the front room, where she thought Kai might never let go of the woman he thought had abandoned him. Then she brushed off his embrace, full attention on something across the room. She knelt down and picked up the item. The syringe, Eva realized. Paloma raised the full hypodermic to the light that streamed from the open doorway and studied it, as if entranced.

"Please, Mommy. Don't," Kai pleaded, his voice childlike, fragile, broken. "I want you to come home. I need you. Eva does, too, right, Eva?"

Eva couldn't find her voice. Knew her words didn't matter. This was between mother and son. Then Paloma looked at Eva. Really looked. The pain and suffering and worry evaporated. She felt returned to their childhood. Best friends full of joy and anticipation for the future.

Paloma dropped the syringe to the floor and raised her foot.

"No!" Eva said, realizing what Paloma was about to do could compromise crucial evidence.

Before Eva could take a step, Paloma crushed the hypodermic under the heel of her beaded moccasin boot.

Eva watched Kai rush to Paloma and wrap her in his arms as sirens wailed, growing closer.

CHAPTER EIGHTY-NINE

Four months later

The Taos Pueblo Community Center hummed with conversation as members of the community chatted in the open room filled with Eva's people, eager to celebrate, anticipating the feast of handmade delicacies on a dozen tables. She inhaled the comforting aromas of Hatch green chiles and pork stew, fry bread, beans. Imagined the potato salad and plum pies hidden under foil and round loaves of bread, pulled fresh from many *hornos*, keeping warm under white cloths.

She took her time to admire the art pieces that hung on one of the walls, reverently exhibited under cubes of plexiglass. One ceremonial drum, two pieces of unique jewelry, and three intricately woven baskets. All treasured creations crafted by the three fallen Taos Pueblo artists, gone too soon.

She wiped away a tear that trailed down her face as she thought of what they must have gone through. How they would all be missed. Turning from the memorial in their honor, she spotted Kai and his constant companion, Shadow, who seemed to wear his IN TRAINING harness with pride. She took note of the University of New Mexico–Taos hoodie and looked forward to talking to him about his classes.

Paloma stood nearby and looked stunning in traditional garb and jewelry, her brother's arm looped in the crook of her arm. Santiago had been an attentive brother and uncle. Had opened his home and his heart fully, and he and Kai had settled in together while they waited for Paloma to complete a ninety-day stay at the finest rehab facility in all of New Mexico.

The woman who had wrought so much pain and carnage remained in the women's ward of Santa Fe's Adult Correctional Facility, awaiting trial. Most thought she would claim to be too insane to face a jury, but Eva believed the narcissistic nurse, intent on curing a nation of Indian women, would want to explain herself. To the world, if possible.

The bodies of the dealer and his minions had been identified and claimed by their families, to be buried in hometowns around the state.

The only unsolved element tied to the case was related to the 3D printed guns that kept popping up around Taos over the past few months.

Eva pushed thoughts of Alice, drug issues, and illicit firearms from her mind and found Cruz, who stood back to the wall near the entrance, at parade rest stance, scanning the room. Always on duty, even when not. She smiled at him, and he winked—she knew the most affection he would exhibit while in uniform.

The high-pitched cackle of a laugh captured her attention. Andrew Kotz, huge smile on his face, shushed his flirty companion. Officer Tallow, she recalled, relieved she would no longer need to rebuff the young cop's advances.

Motion caused her to turn and spot Nathan "Little Bear" Trujillo, who waved at her, then his parents lifted their hands and did the same. All smiles, they remained in their own little cocoon, and Eva figured they were too shy to approach. The boy pointed to his chest, where a gold medal on a ribbon swung due to his exuberance. A token from the tribal leadership for his bravery helping to capture the woman who had caused so much pain to their people.

The Trujillos' house had been completely fixed up, painted, and cleaned spotless, until no trace of the chaos that had taken place there for over three weeks remained. All of the furniture in every room had been purged and replaced with new items most envied when they took the tour Nathan's mother loved to lead. No one laid claim to all of the repairs and new items, but Eva and Cruz, even Paloma, felt certain the balance had been paid anonymously by Santiago. And thankfully the little boy's parents had recovered from their drug-induced stupors inflicted so the dealers could invade and inhabit their once-peaceful home.

As often happened when she came upon the little family, Eva thought about her grandfather's place. Nothing but a shell of ashes now, completely destroyed, no possible way to restore the structure back to the treasured home she hoped to one day claim as her own.

She sighed her regret about that broken dream as she watched Santiago. He took the three steps to the raised stage, where New Mexico, POW, Taos Pueblo, and American flags hung from poles that lined the back of the stage. Santiago raised his arms for the crowd to settle. "Thank you for joining us this evening," he said, voice booming so loud he needed no microphone. "It's my honor to present our newly sworn-in police chief, June 'Bobcat Leaps' Lefthand."

Attendees clapped, whistled, stomped their feet as a woman a few inches shorter than Eva stepped on the stage, an elaborate box in her hand. "Thank you, Santiago. And thank you all. We're gathered to remember the lives of our magnificent Pueblo women who no longer physically walk with us, but will never be forgotten." The people remained quiet in their reverence as they nodded.

"As well, I would like to introduce you to our newest member of the Taos Pueblo Police Department. This is my first hire as your chief, and I know you will be welcoming to the law enforcer who has represented and spoken for our people across all jurisdictions of our area, and was instrumental in bringing the offender of our fallen women we celebrate today to justice. This brave soul is one of us. One of you." The chief's lips swept upward before she said, "And is one helluva shot."

The crowd rumbled a collective chuckle, and Eva's heart beat faster, knowing what would come next. She never appreciated being in the spotlight. Had to resist the urge to bolt out the nearest exit. Cruz Romero appeared at her side. His shoulder to her own, as if he sensed he might need to restrain her. She leaned against him and let out a nervous breath.

"I present, Taos Pueblo Police Officer Eva 'Lightning Dance' Duran."

The uniform had yet to feel comfortable, even after a dozen cycles in the wash, and she felt a little naked without a gun or the equipment that usually lined her duty belt. No need for that today. This ceremony was for show only. But that didn't calm her racing heart as she straightened her back, tried to exhibit the confidence she didn't quite feel, and took the first official steps to her new job.

Cheers and claps erupted as the two female law enforcers for the tribe shook hands. For the first time, she realized she didn't need the praise or admiration. She only wanted to be there for her people. Do her best to keep the Pueblo and its residents safe. Earn their respect by being respectful of the traditions and ceremonies established hundreds of years ago. To always remember she belonged. They were all one— now more than ever.

Then Eva raised her hand and took the oath, vowing to keep her community safe. She beamed at the police chief, who removed a silver Taos Pueblo Police Department badge from the box. Three male voices resonated as they sang the traditional flag song in the Tiwa language of their people, as her new boss pinned the shield to Eva's chest.

ACKNOWLEDGMENTS

Writing crime fiction takes loads of professionals to help create real-world situations, and I have a cherished go-to team on speed dial.

The crime scene and forensics were a bit of a bear for this one, and I am beyond appreciative of Tracie Paolillo, forensic operations manager for the Scottsdale Police Department. Thank you, Tracie, for always having my back.

Drugs are tricky, so I turned to Associate Dean Jennifer R. Hartmark-Hill, MD, of the University of Arizona College of Medicine—a.k.a. the Tragic Concoctions Maven—who guided me through the medical, overdose, and medication elements and came up with a truly harrowing answer that had me baffled.

Guns! C. W. Miller, assistant police chief (ret.) for the Phoenix Police Department, is my pro for the care and feeding of the firepower.

Law enforcement elements have been gleaned over years and years of research and spending time with former officers, detectives, and commanders. You know who you are—I won't embarrass you here. Thank you for having my back.

While each location and its elements are based on reality, this is a work of fiction, and liberties have been taken to keep the momentum flowing.

The Taos Pueblo reservation is a wild and wonderous location. The people of the tribe share cherished traditions that go back over one thousand years. It has been an honor and a privilege to have Floyd

"Mountain Walking Cane" Gomez lead the way to representing how members of the community would deal with the situations I have thrown at my characters here on the page. Floyd's fact-checking, and his own jaw-dropping stories, also gave me ideas to advance the story. You're the best, brother. Let's do this again!

Isabella Maldonado. *Wow.* Cherished friend, former patrol officer / captain / commander, now awesomely talented bestselling author. Your introduction to my firecracker of an agent, Liza Fleissig at the Liza Royce Agency, lit the flame to securing a two-book deal with the most brilliant Liz Pearsons, and her team of sharp eyes at Amazon Publishing's Thomas & Mercer. You three made this happen, and you will never know how much you have touched my heart in granting the "Go!" for me to tell this story.

Jon Reyes! Your spot-on insights and sharp developmental editing skills caught a multitude of elements for me to flesh out. Also to Patricia Callahan, copyeditor extraordinaire, and the rest of the editing team— massive thank you for catching the blunders!

I have done my best to convey the wise guidance of my advisers to the best of my ability. Any and all mistakes are my own. Truly.

My family and friends were often put on the back burner as I wrote and revised at rocket-speed pace for months. Apologies for my failings. I haven't forgotten you and know you understand. Also, many thanks to Paige Johann and Dr. Kathleen Fry for keeping me clear and focused—not an easy task.

First, last, always at the top of my appreciation list is my husband, John. Best friend, travel companion, confidant in all things. You keep me grounded. You make me whole. And sane!

It is an honor to present these words to you, kind reader. I do hope you've enjoyed this journey. Blessings to you and yours.

ABOUT THE AUTHOR

Photo © 2022 Ted Stratton

Deborah J Ledford is an Agatha Award winner, three-time nominee for the Pushcart Prize, two-time finalist for the Anthony Award, and the Hillerman Sky Award nominee for best mystery writer who captures the landscape of the Southwest. *Redemption* is her fifth crime fiction novel. Part Eastern Band Cherokee, she lives in Phoenix with her husband and their awesome Ausky. To find out more, visit DeborahJLedford.com.